# Also by Anna Schmidt

WHERE THE TRAIL ENDS
*Last Chance Cowboys: The Drifter*
*Last Chance Cowboys: The Lawman*
*Last Chance Cowboys: The Outlaw*
*Last Chance Cowboys: The Rancher*

COWBOYS & HARVEY GIRLS
*Trailblazer*

*Christmas in a Cowboy's Arms* anthology

★ COWBOYS & HARVEY GIRLS ★

# RENEGADE

# ANNA SCHMIDT

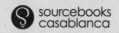
sourcebooks
casablanca

Published by Sourcebooks Casablanca, an imprint of Sourcebooks
P. O. Box 4410, Naperville, Illinois 60567-4410
(630) 961-3900
sourcebooks.com

Printed and bound in Canada.
MBP 10 9 8 7 6 5 4 3 2 1

# WANTED:

Young women, 18–30 years of age, of good moral character, attractive and intelligent, as waitresses in

## HARVEY EATING HOUSES ON THE SANTA FE RAILROAD.

Wages $17.50 a month with room and board. Liberal tips customary. Experience not necessary.

**Write Fred Harvey, Union Depot, Kansas City, Missouri**

# Prologue

LILY TRAVIS STOOD WITH THE REST OF THE HARVEY Girls, eyes brimming with happy tears at the sweet scene before them. Grace Rogers, former Harvey Girl, was repeating her vows with Nick Hopkins, the handsome ranch foreman they'd all met on the train from Kansas City just five months before. The lump in Lily's throat was as much about her own sadness, however, as her happiness for Grace. A few years earlier, Lily had made a huge mistake—one that promised to prevent her from ever finding the true love Grace and Nick shared. She forced a smile when her friend Emma nudged her. This was Grace's day, after all.

At the reception that followed, Lily helped pass slices of the wedding cake as Grace and Nick cut them. She nodded in agreement at guests bubbling with joy for the couple, until, cake in hand, she found herself face-to-face with Sheriff Cody Daniels. He was his usual serious self, a blessing considering Lily's mood that day. On the rare occasions when he did smile, the man had dimples, and Lily was a sucker for a man with dimples. Emma and Grace used to tease her about that, and Lily couldn't deny that the lawman was definitely good-looking. But he also played life by the rules—something Lily had trouble doing. Something that had been the source of her problems from the time she was sixteen. No, it was best to keep her distance from Cody Daniels.

She handed him a large slice of lemon cake. "Bon appetit," she said as she prepared to move on.

"Nice fandango," he replied, unintentionally blocking her way as he looked around the large hotel dining room. "You're not having cake?"

"I…" He was being nice to her. That made her suspicious. In her experience, most men wanted something, especially when they took the trouble to be nice. "I'm helping serve…"

He surveyed the room. "Looks to me like everybody has cake." He turned his gaze back to her. "How about sharing this piece with me?" Dimples weren't his only appeal; he had deep-set eyes that were brown with flecks of gold.

To avoid getting lost in those eyes, Lily deliberately focused her attention on his forehead, where a cowlick of dark-blond hair was in need of taming. Her breath quickened while her cheeks grew hot, and she forced herself to concentrate on the dusty tips of his boots. *Finally*, she thought, *a detail that is just ordinary*.

Sheriff Daniels didn't seem to notice her discomfort. Instead, he retrieved a clean fork from a nearby table and placed it next to the one already resting on the glass plate. "Could we sit a minute, Miss Travis?" He nodded to a table for two near the windows. "The truth is I owe you an apology, and I'd like to get that covered."

*Get that covered?* She imagined him seated at his desk and making a list: arrest drunks at Sagebrush Saloon, attend Hopkins's wedding, apologize to Miss Travis. She straightened to her full height, just a few inches shorter than his, looked him in those deep-set gold-flecked eyes, and smiled. "Consider it *covered*," she said sweetly, deliberately placing emphasis on the last word.

She edged past him and went to join Emma Elliott and Jake Collier, the hotel's kitchen manager. Everyone who worked in the hotel was well aware that Jake had a huge crush on Lily. But employees of the Harvey Company were not allowed to pursue romantic relationships with each other—friendships, yes, but nothing more. Lily liked Jake but really could not see any chance for romance between them. Even if it were possible. And kind as he was, he had accepted that. Still, for the remainder of the afternoon, she flirted shamelessly, laughing at his jokes and later even taking his arm as everyone headed outside to watch the happy couple leave for their new home.

All the while, she was aware of Cody's whereabouts—the ease with which he chatted with guests, which made him seem so much a part of the community, even though he was relatively new to Juniper and his position there as sheriff. Clearly, he was well-liked, and more than one of the town's unmarried women were making blatant efforts to draw his attention. Well, good luck to them. As far as she was concerned, she and the good-looking sheriff were like oil and water—they simply didn't mix.

Once the guests had seen Grace and Nick on their way and drifted back to their homes, everyone on the hotel staff pitched in to make sure the dining room was back to normal and ready for receiving customers the following day. After bidding good night to Jake and the rest of the kitchen staff, Lily followed Emma and the other girls up the three flights of stairs to their quarters. The room she and Emma had shared with Grace suddenly seemed too large for just the two of them.

Bonnie Kaufmann, head waitress and housemother for the girls, had seen to it that the third bed in the room—Grace's former bed—was removed. "The new girls can share a triple," she'd told them at the party. "You and Emma have earned the right to spread out a bit. After all, you have seniority."

It was true that she and Emma were among the waitresses employed the longest by Fred Harvey's Company—five years for Emma, and Lily was beginning her fourth. Was this her entire future? Waiting on train travelers who stopped for a meal or stayed for a few days in the hotel? Serving them with a smile, all the while wondering what adventures awaited them once they moved on?

She stood in the doorway of the room she now shared with only Emma and wondered, *Where is my adventure?*

# Chapter 1

*June 1899*

SUMMER CAME WITH A BLAST OF HEAT AND DROUGHT. No matter how much Lily and the other girls cleaned, there always seemed to be a fine coat of grit on everything. The dust made for longer hours, making sure everything met the strict standards of the Harvey Company. Lily felt like she was smothering by the time she and Emma climbed the stairs to their room in the evenings.

"Are you having a bath?" Emma asked Lily as she untied her apron and lifted the bibbed front of the white pinafore over her head. The two of them had worked a double shift, and even as they climbed the stairs, Lily had plucked at the fabric of her uniform to separate it from her sweat-soaked skin. The high-necked, long-sleeved black dress, apron, and heavy black stockings looked smart, but the summer heat was not kind.

"You go ahead," Lily replied. She lay back on her narrow bed and covered her eyes with her forearm. "I'm exhausted."

"Well, at least take off your uniform and hang it," Emma advised.

Lily knew Emma was right, but she heard the caring suggestion as an order and bristled. "I'll get to it," she muttered.

Emma hesitated before gathering her toiletries. "I won't be long," she said softly before stepping into the hall and closing the door behind her.

Lily sighed and sat up. The months since Grace and Nick's wedding had been especially busy. It seemed they barely had a chance to catch their breath after one train before a new one was arriving with a flood of passengers, all eager for one of Fred Harvey's renowned meals and the welcoming smiles of the crew of waitresses known as Harvey Girls. And yet the time had dragged. Lily was at loose ends, the future stretching out before her as a great unknown.

Still frowning, she undressed, hung her uniform, and put on her robe. It had been some time since the hotel staff had done anything that could be remotely called fun. They were short-handed, and business was booming. On top of that, she missed Grace. The fact that her friend was now married and expecting a baby made Lily consider her own future—and her past. Perhaps Emma had the remedy. A nice soothing bath would wash away some of her melancholy.

Lily stood at the open window that overlooked the yard at the back of the hotel while she waited for her turn in the bathroom shared by all the girls. Part of their compensation was room and board, not to mention free travel.

*Maybe I should take a trip.*

Below, she saw the hotel's kitchen manager, Jake Collier, pacing in the courtyard. He was smoking a cigarette and kept looking around as if expecting someone. Maybe at long last he'd given up pining for her and found a girl worthy of his attention. She treasured Jake's friendship, and thankfully, Jake had agreed that if friendship was all she could offer, he would accept that.

She was about to step away from the window when two men approached Jake. He tossed his cigarette on the dirt yard and crushed it with the toe of his shoe. He shoved his hands in his pockets and stared at the ground. One of the men—neither of whom she recognized—was talking to him and making threatening gestures, although she could not make out the words. The man gave Jake a shove. He stumbled but regained his balance and said something, glancing nervously from one man to the other.

*What's going on?*

Lily watched until the strangers finally left and Jake returned through the hotel's kitchen entrance below. "Something's up with Jake," she said as soon as Emma opened the door. Lily reported what she'd seen.

"Did you recognize either of them?" Emma peered out the window, but there was nothing there now for her to see.

"No. But trust me, Jake was afraid of them. Do you think I should talk to him?"

"He'll just laugh it off the way he does everything," Emma replied. "Why don't you mention what you saw to Sheriff Daniels? At least then he'd be aware something might be amiss."

Lily glanced at the clock on the table between their beds. Nine o'clock—an hour until curfew. Plenty of time to walk to the sheriff's office and back. She took off her robe and grabbed a skirt and shirtwaist from the wardrobe.

"Well, no need to go tonight," Emma said. "I mean surely—"

"You didn't see the way Jake was acting. What if those men come back?" Lily tugged on her shoes, checked her reflection in the mirror, and pushed back an errant strand of hair. "I'll be back before curfew," she said as she left the room.

Another girl was just going into the bathroom. "Going out at this hour?" she asked, her eyes filled with curiosity.

"Just a quick errand," Lily replied as she ran down the back stairs. On her way, she decided that if Jake was in the kitchen, she would speak to him first about what she'd seen. If not, she would go to the sheriff.

The kitchen was dark and deserted, so she slipped out the back door, making sure to leave it unlocked so she could return. She hurried across the plaza to the building that held the jail as well as the sheriff's office and living quarters. Music and raucous laughter spilled from the Sagebrush Saloon, the rowdiest of three lining the main street of Juniper. She was also aware of the blackness of the night and the fact that the two men she'd seen in the hotel yard could be lurking about. She quickened her step and was out of breath by the time she reached her destination.

She hadn't seen much of the sheriff since Grace's wedding. He rarely ate in the hotel dining room. She'd seen him a couple of times passing through the lobby, and he'd tipped his hat to her as he continued on his way. Now, once she reached the office door, she hesitated. The window that faced the street was dark, but a dim light was coming from a window at the side of the building. She rapped sharply on the door and after two seconds repeated the action, doubling the force.

"I'm coming," a male voice grumbled, and light flooded the window that overlooked the street. Lily stepped back, and when the door opened, she rushed inside, brushing past the sheriff, who was hooking his suspenders over his broad shoulders.

"Miss Travis?" He ran his hand through his tousled hair. "What on…" He stepped outside and glanced around before returning and shutting the door. "Are you all right?" He looked her over.

"I'm perfectly fine." She touched her fingers to her hair. "I would like to report a possible…situation that requires your attention, Sheriff Daniels."

The man had the audacity to smile just enough to expose those dang dimples.

"This is serious," she informed him.

He cleared his throat and indicated she should take a seat while he took his place behind the scarred table that served as his desk. "No doubt. Why don't you tell me what's got you so riled up?"

"I am not *riled up*. I am seriously concerned about a friend."

He leaned forward, his eyes studying her face. "I can see that, Miss Travis. Tell me what I can do to help." Both his tone and demeanor had shifted to something more professional and distant.

All of which made her aware that the three small cells at the rear of the room were unoccupied and she was alone with this man at an hour that would surely raise both eyebrows and questions were she to be discovered.

She stood and started for the door. "This was a mistake," she murmured.

Despite knowing he should just let her go, Cody was at the door ahead of her. "If you have information about someone in danger," he said softly, "at least give me the details while I see you back to the hotel."

His words were straightforward, but he couldn't seem to drag his gaze away from a tendril of her white-blond hair that fluttered around her cheek, moved by his breath. He swallowed and stepped away.

Although he'd accepted her lack of interest and kept his distance ever since the Hopkins' party, his fascination with Miss Lily Travis had not abated in the least. Sure, he'd thought about finding a woman he could spend time with, but Lily Travis? She was impulsive and headstrong—hardly a suitable match for a law-and-order, by-the-book man like him.

"Let me get my hat," he managed in a voice that was suddenly hoarse. He stepped just inside his living quarters and returned with his Stetson and jacket. She stood in the open doorway where he'd left her, but she'd crossed her arms and was hugging herself, rubbing her upper arms. The June days might be unusually hot, but the nights could still be chilly. He realized she'd come in such a hurry, she hadn't worn a coat or shawl.

"Here," he said, draping his coat over her shoulders, and for once, she didn't argue. It occurred to him that in every encounter he'd had with Lily, she had taken offense at something he'd done. When he'd had to arrest her friend Grace for a crime he was sure she hadn't committed, Lily had challenged him. And during the lead-up to the trial, although he had done his best to protect Grace, Lily Travis had made it clear she did not trust him. Then there'd been the Hopkins party, and she'd taken offense again when all he'd wanted to do was share a slice of wedding cake and apologize for any misunderstandings still lingering over her friend's arrest.

"It's Jake Collier," she said as soon as they started across the plaza to the hotel. She told him what she had observed from her window earlier that evening, whispering as if someone might overhear.

"Did you speak with Jake about this?"

"No. He would just laugh it off. That's what he does, but I am telling you, he was frightened by these men. Trust me, I know frightened when I see it," she added defensively.

He wondered just what in her life had made her an expert in fear. "And you didn't recognize the two men?"

"No. It was dark, and they wore hats with wide brims. They didn't look to be the sort of men who might patronize the dining room."

"Cowhands?"

She shrugged. "Maybe one of them. The other

seemed like more of someone in charge." They had reached the far side of the plaza. Across the street, the lights of the hotel glowed bright. "I'll be fine from here," she said, handing him his coat. "You'll talk to Jake?"

She was looking up at him with such earnest concern—Jake Collier was one lucky guy to have Lily watching out for him. "If he won't talk to you, Miss Travis, what makes you think he'll talk to me? Best I can offer is to keep my eyes and ears open, and if anything seems out of place…"

"Something is already out of place," she said in the tone of a teacher instructing a none-too-bright pupil. "Jake was afraid of these men, and they were threatening him. I'm sure of it."

"I don't know what it is you think I can do," Cody said.

"Your job," she replied as she hurried away.

He watched until she disappeared around the corner of the hotel toward the back entrance reserved for the staff. It was in that yard she had observed Jake and the two men. Couldn't hurt to have a look around.

Fortunately, there was enough light spilling out from occupied guest rooms to let him explore the area. From what Lily had told him, Jake had met the men next to the sprawling pine tree. He picked up a cigarette butt, then knelt to study the tracks in the soft dirt, striking matches to give himself more light as he examined the prints. Male employees of the hotel did not wear boots like most men in town, so it was easy to pick out Jake's tracks forming a pattern in the loose dirt where he'd paced back and forth. At one point,

Jake's shoe prints faced a pair of boots with a unique heel pattern. In the years Cody had worked as a guide and tracker for the army, he'd learned a lot about noticing differences in the prints left by particular horses. He saw no reason that experience shouldn't apply to humans.

The man's right boot had made an imprint of a half-moon in the dirt. Cody traced the outline with his finger, studied the left print that went with it. Normal, as were the tracks left by the second man. Boots that could belong to pretty much anybody—except for that single unusual heel print. The match went out. Cody stood, dusted off his hands, and glanced around. He walked away from the hotel toward the darkness. No sign of horses. The men had come on foot, maybe from the main street. He'd check with Sally at the Sagebrush, the most popular saloon in town. She'd have noticed any strangers.

He felt eyes on him as he crossed the yard. Looking up, he saw a figure watching him from an open third-floor window. Lily Travis was checking up on him.

He chuckled, then did something so out of character that, as he walked back to his office afterward, he was awfully glad nobody but Lily had seen. Cody Daniels swept off his hat and gave her a deep bow.

He wondered if his action had made her smile. Lily didn't seem to smile nearly enough. Oh, she was very professional in her role as the cheerful Harvey Girl, but on those rare occasions when he encountered her off duty? If she did smile, it never seemed to go far enough to light a fire in those pale-green eyes.

"All right, Daniels," he muttered. "Lily Travis is

not the point. Strangers in town who might be threatening Jake—that's the point. *Trouble* is the point."

But now, just when he'd pretty much decided he and Lily had no connection, there was something about her that made him think she might be trouble of a whole different sort. And that he might be about to get to know her a whole lot better.

As Lily watched Cody Daniels leave, it occurred to her there was always the possibility she had imagined the sense of danger. Maybe the two men had simply been ruffians from the saloon who had accosted Jake on their way out of town. That would give anyone pause, but other than the shove, there had been no real harm. And if she had jumped to conclusions, did that mean she now owed the sheriff an apology for rousing him?

She'd observed him exploring the yard, watched as he knelt and studied the ground. And then he had spotted her and offered that ridiculous bow that made her stifle a giggle, hoping Emma wouldn't notice.

But Emma noticed. When Lily turned from the window and offered her report on the sheriff's investigation, Emma grinned at her.

"What?" Lily demanded.

"Nothing. Just on the rare occasions when you speak of our handsome sheriff, your cheeks blossom into this becoming shade of pink and your voice quickens. Sort of like you might be having trouble breathing."

"You are being absurd. I barely know the man."

Emma lifted her eyebrows and picked up her book. "If you say so."

"I do, and it's been another long day. Before we know it, we'll be running downstairs to start another shift." Lily got into bed and kicked the covers away as she turned on her side to avoid Emma's prying eyes.

Emma sighed, closed her book, and trimmed the wick on the oil lamp. The two of them lay in the darkness for some time, neither sleeping and each aware of the other's wakefulness.

"Lily?"

Lily grunted.

"That man from your past…"

Emma and Grace were the only two people who knew Lily's secret. That before she'd become a Harvey Girl, she'd met a man who had tricked her into marriage. The morning after the wedding, he'd left her high and dry and with no way to contact him. As far as Lily knew, they were still married, something that would cost her her job if her employers ever found out.

"What about him?"

"You say you were married, but was it real?"

Lily turned over to face Emma. "Well, I didn't dream it," she said irritably.

"I don't mean that. I mean I've been thinking about it. Was the union performed by a judge or priest? I mean, from what you told us, it all happened so fast. Did you choose the officiant, or did he?"

"He set everything up," she whispered. Lily had never considered the possibility that the marriage she'd embarked on, thinking she'd finally found someone who would love her, might not have been legal. All she had ever thought about was what a fool she had been. After a night spent lying next to him, when he'd drunk enough that he passed out before anything could happen between them, she had wakened to find her new husband gone. In his place was a note saying he had business back east and would "be in touch." She had not seen or heard from him since.

Lily sat up. What if Emma was on to something? What if she was actually free to love anyone she chose?

She felt a tug of hope as she brushed away the tears that teetered on her lashes. "It's been three years," she said.

"Still, there's a trail. I mean maybe not to him, but certainly to the person who performed the ceremony, certainly to whatever papers would have been filed." Emma sat up and wrapped her arms around her knees. "I want you to be happy, Lily, and how can you be with this mess hanging over you?"

"And what if I find out it was real—that I am indeed married?"

"Then we deal with that."

"We?"

Emma stretched her hand out to Lily. "You don't think I'd bring this up and not be right there with you every step of the way, do you?"

Lily grasped her friend's hand and squeezed it. "What would I do without you, dear Emma?"

Emma sighed. "The way I figure things, once we get your situation sorted out, you can help me with mine. Wouldn't it be wonderful if you and I could find true love as Grace has?"

Emma'd had her heart broken once, same as Lily.

Only the young man she thought loved her had taken off to join Roosevelt's Rough Riders in Cuba without so much as a by-your-leave. To Lily's way of thinking, that young man had made the wrong choice, and he certainly wasn't worthy of someone like Emma. "Grace isn't the only Harvey Girl who deserves it," she said. "There's somebody out there for you—and maybe even for me. And with us working together, they don't stand a chance."

Emma laughed and gave Lily's hand a final squeeze before settling back under the covers. "Good night, Lily."

Lily realized all the ire and angst she'd felt earlier had disappeared. There was something to be said for having really good friends like Emma and Grace. It made getting through the tough times a lot less challenging.

Instead of heading back to his office from the hotel, Cody decided to stop by the saloon. Sally Barnett looked up from her regular station near the stairway that led to the rooms provided for her girls and smiled at him. She wore a red velvet gown, cut low enough to leave not much to the imagination, and too much rouge and powder. Cody suspected she used the cosmetics to try and hide the fact that she was not a young woman—she had to be forty at least.

"Sheriff," she called out, acknowledging his presence for the other customers. "What are you drinkin'?"

Cody stepped to the bar and rested one foot on

the brass railing. "Shot of rye, Billy," he ordered. He waited for Sally to saunter over, taking her time. She sashayed through the room, running her fingers along the shoulders of a man playing cards and nudging another who sat slouched in his chair, staring at one of the girls.

Leaving the shot glass untouched, Cody surveyed the room through the large gilt-framed mirror behind the bar. Regulars, as far as he could see. He was new to the job in Juniper and might not know every man by name, but he recognized them. Several boys who worked for the railroad. Frank Tucker, the town's mayor and owner of the mercantile, was one of the card players. And there in a corner, Jake Collier sat alone.

"Quiet night," Sally observed.

He knew she was trying to figure out what had brought him in. Most people in town had come to understand the new sheriff rarely did anything for simple pleasure.

"Yep. Looks like the usual gang," he replied, downing his whiskey in a single gulp. He placed a coin on the bar and turned to go. "But don't you worry. Summer's here, so there's bound to be new cowboys coming to town for the branding and calving."

*Jackpot*, he thought when Sally took the bait.

"Already started. Had two fellas in here earlier sniffing around trying to find out where to find work. I suggested the Lombard place, but they seemed more curious about the hotel. Didn't have the heart to tell them they were far too common for Aidan Campbell to give them a chance. He wouldn't even take men like that for the kitchen."

"They decided to move on, did they?"

Sally shrugged. "Guess so." She laid her hand on his. She wore a ring on every finger. "Don't be such a stranger, Sheriff," she murmured.

Cody tipped two fingers to his hat. "Miss Sally, you have yourself a nice evening."

On his way out, he made sure to pass close to Jake, saw the way the usually affable young man avoided meeting his gaze and the way Jake's hand trembled as he raised a pint of beer to his lips.

There were plenty of men who frequented the Sagebrush whose shaking hands would be the sign of a need for their next drink. Not Jake. In fact, this was one of the only times Cody had ever seen him in the saloon. So instead of leaving, he pulled out a chair and sat across the table from the stocky, red-haired kitchen manager.

"Mind if I join you?" He signaled the bartender, pointed to Jake's empty glass, and held up two fingers.

Jake eyed him suspiciously and nodded. One of Sally's girls set the beers down, and Cody paid her. Jake sipped some of the foam and swiped it away from his upper lip with his sleeve.

"What brings you in tonight, Sheriff Daniels?" he asked.

Cody smiled. He respected Jake for cutting through the chitchat. "It's about Lily Travis," he said.

That got Jake's attention. "What about her? I mean, is she all right?"

"She's fine, far as I can tell. A little high-strung, but then that seems to be her natural state."

"She's just really passionate about things she cares about," Jake defended.

"Then she must care quite a bit about you."

"I don't get your meaning. Me and Lily are just friends. That's all she wants, and I'll take what I can have when it comes to Lily."

"She saw you earlier in the yard behind the hotel." Cody paused and took a long swallow of his beer as he watched Jake's reaction. He probably could have fished around for information without invoking Lily's name, but Cody had always believed in the direct approach. "Came all the way to my office to tell me about it—about two men she'd never seen before having a serious conversation with you."

With every word Cody spoke, Jake's eyes grew wider with panic. He glanced around the saloon like he wanted to make sure nobody was listening and then leaned across the table. "She can't get mixed up in this," he said. "Tell her we talked and that meeting was nothing she needs to be worried about, okay?"

Cody leaned back in his chair. "How about you tell me what's really going on, Jake, so I can keep Lily out of things and help you?"

Jake hesitated, then downed his beer, and stood. "I can handle this, Sheriff. It's nothing. A misunderstanding is all. Just make sure Lily doesn't have cause to ask any more questions." He adjusted his hat, adding, "Thanks for the beer," as he headed through the double swinging half doors.

Cody watched him go. Jake had lied. Whatever he was caught up in was more than a simple misunderstanding. Jake was in danger and afraid Lily would also be in danger if she didn't let this go. And Cody was still no closer to learning who the two strangers had been. With all that in mind, he had no intention of dropping the matter. But he would do his level best to make sure Lily wasn't involved.

# Chapter 2

THE DINING ROOM CONTINUED TO BE UNUSUALLY busy the following week, making Lily's intent to pull Jake aside and ask him more about the two men impossible. Sheriff Daniels had not seen fit to get back to her with any information. Typical male. Heaven forbid a mere woman might have some ideas—or might actually have something to contribute!

*Speak of the devil.*

Cody Daniels stood at the entrance to the dining room, surveying the room. When he chose a table in her section, she thought perhaps she had misjudged him. Perhaps his presence here might be his way of giving her information without raising suspicions. She pasted on her Harvey Girl smile and crossed the dining room. "Good afternoon, Sheriff."

"Miss Travis," he replied as he studied the lunch selections listed on the menu. "I'll have the rabbit stew and coffee."

Following the Harvey protocol, she set his cup upright for the beverage girl to fill and went to place his order, practically colliding with Jake as she entered the kitchen.

"What's Sheriff Daniels doing here?" Jake asked in a tone that was both demanding and panicked.

"He came in for lunch," Lily replied. "Are you all right?"

Recovering his usual lighthearted demeanor, Jake grinned. "Right as rain, Lily—just surprised to see the sheriff. Usually where he goes, trouble follows."

"I think he just wants to eat, Jake." She recited Cody's food order to the chef and returned to the dining room to check on her other tables, more certain than ever that Jake was wrapped up in something that was keeping him on edge.

When she set Cody's lunch in front of him, he thanked her and started to eat. She remained standing next to him. Glancing up at her, he set down his fork and asked, "Was there something else?"

Of course, she should be asking *him* that. "Sorry, I…" She lowered her voice while maintaining her professional smile. "Did you find out about those two men?"

Just then, head waitress Bonnie Kaufmann passed them. She gave Lily a questioning look. "Hello, Sheriff Daniels. How nice to have you join us," she said. "Is everything to your satisfaction?"

"Absolutely," he replied, grinning up at her.

"In that case, Lily, your table over there has requested their bill."

Lily had no choice but to attend to her other customers, and by the time she had finished, Cody was already on his way out the door. He'd left money to cover his meal plus a ten-cent tip for her. As she

cleared and reset the table, she watched him cross
the lobby and stop at the front desk where Aidan
Campbell, the hotel manager, greeted him warmly.

"Lily!"

She whirled around and found Emma standing next
to her. "What?" she grumbled as she turned her attention back to resetting the table.

"You're a thousand miles away today, and Miss K
is taking note," Emma whispered.

"It's just that I thought he might have news."

"And did he?"

Lily shook her head.

"Then let it go. Jake seems to be just fine."

Emma was right—Lily was sticking her nose in
where it didn't belong. But she couldn't entirely dis-
miss the way Jake had asked about the sheriff's arrival
at the hotel. Something was wrong. She'd bet her
month's tips on that.

On the other hand, if she didn't get back to work,
she'd have no tips to wager.

It was after six before the last customer left and Lily,
Emma, and the other girls sat down to supper with Jake,
the head chef, George Keller, and the rest of the kitchen
staff. Emma returned from checking their mail slots and
handed Lily two envelopes, one stamped and one from
the hotel with just her name on it. Her hand shook as
she opened the first, avoiding the second. She was pretty
sure the message on hotel stationery was a summons to
Aidan Campbell's office to be reminded of her duties.

Emma had already opened an envelope identical to Lily's. "It's a note of thanks from Grace," she said, and there was general excitement as the other girls around the table opened their letters from Grace. They had all chipped in for a layette in celebration of Nick and Grace and their coming baby.

While everyone shared memories of the day they had all celebrated Grace and Nick's union, Lily pulled a single sheet of hotel stationery from the envelope. She did not recognize the handwriting. It certainly was not Aidan Campbell's flowing script.

Dear Miss Travis,

Would you be free for a carriage ride in the country on Sunday?

If so, I will call for you at one o'clock. Please wear sensible shoes, as we may decide to walk a bit.

If you are otherwise engaged, we can perhaps find another time. Please reply at your earliest convenience by sending the bellboy, Tommy, with your answer.

Sincerely,
Cody Daniels

Lily blushed, then she bristled. Just who did he think he was? And what was the meaning of this sudden invitation? She could take it any one of several ways. And how dare he order her about! Wear sensible shoes indeed. She spent her days in sensible shoes waiting on people like him. If she chose to indulge herself by wearing impractical, beautiful shoes on her days off, that was no business of his. She crumpled the note in her hand, stuffed it in her pocket, and sat down to finish her supper.

But later that evening after she and Emma had changed and come down to the room off the lobby reserved for writing letters or quiet reading, she smoothed out the paper, scrawled a one-word reply on the bottom, tucked it back into the envelope, and stood. "I'm going to stretch my legs a bit before bedtime," she said. "See you upstairs."

Emma was engrossed in her novel, so she simply waved her hand, acknowledging she had heard, before turning the page of her book.

Lily crossed the plaza and approached the jail. Once again, there was no light in the window, but this time, she had no need of a direct encounter with the sheriff. She glanced around, making sure she was not being observed, and slid the envelope under the door before hurrying back to the hotel.

Cody spotted the envelope as soon as he returned from making his evening rounds. It still showed his writing, and the flap was tucked in as he'd done before sending it. *Did she open it or reject it out of hand?* Of course, how would she know it was from him unless Tommy had told her? He'd instructed the bellboy to simply place it in her mail slot. He was about to toss the envelope in the trash, certain she had told Tommy to return to sender, when he noticed the crumpled condition of the note as if it had been returned to the envelope in haste. He frowned. So she had opened it—and read it. He ripped open the envelope, saw his message in his large scrawl and, just below his name, a single word.

*Yes*.

No signature.

Cody smiled. He had convinced her to step out with him, although he was pretty sure she understood this was purely business—a cover to allow them to talk more about Jake and the two men. He'd thought there would be a chance for them to talk at lunch, but he'd quickly understood that would never work. Still, he had to find a way to convince her to stay out of the situation. If Jake was in some kind of trouble—and everything so far indicated he was—Lily Travis was the last person anyone needed meddling in the matter.

He slipped the note in his desk drawer and headed to the livery to reserve a buggy for Sunday afternoon. Then he walked to the back entrance of the hotel and asked one of the cooks to send Jake out so they could talk but without letting on who was waiting. He wanted to watch Jake's actions when—or if—he decided to show. The kitchen manager's encounter with the two strangers had occurred about this same time of night.

Several minutes later, Jake stepped to the doorway and looked around, wiping his hands on a towel. After a minute, he edged out the door. Cody had taken a seat on a bench where he would be half hidden from Jake's view. He could see the kitchen manager, though, and he knew the exact moment Jake spotted him. That's when he stood and revealed himself. Cody had the information he'd sought. Jake Collier was as nervous as a horse facing a rattlesnake.

"Jake, I won't take much of your time," Cody said when they were close enough to speak in low tones and not be overheard.

"If this is about those two…" Jake blustered.

"This is about Lily," Cody replied quietly.

That got Jake's full attention. "What about her? Has she…did those men…?"

"I came to let you know I'm taking Lily out for a buggy ride Sunday afternoon. I didn't want you thinking what most will think—that me and her are stepping out in a…that I'm courting her."

"Why would that matter to me? You know well as I do there's nothing but friendship between Lily and me."

Cody wondered if whatever Jake was mixed up in had something to do with trying to make enough money to leave his job at the hotel—to maybe get away from such close contact with Lily. "Look, Jake, everybody knows you've got feelings for her. I just didn't want you thinkin' I was ignoring that."

"Then what's your reason for taking her for a Sunday ride?"

"I hope to talk some sense into her. You and I both know she has a leaning toward being pigheaded, and whatever you may think, she has feelings for you. Maybe not the kind of feelings you have for her, but she cares, Jake. My guess is that means she's not going to stay out of whatever business you've gotten mixed up in."

"She won't listen," Jake said miserably. "You shoulda heard her that day you hauled Grace off to jail."

Cody nodded. "I've had one or two run-ins with her myself. The thing is, Jake, we need to come up with a story that will make her think she's got nothing to worry about."

"What kind of story?"

Cody met the smaller man's gaze. "First, I have to know what's really going on. I can't help you or protect Lily if you don't trust me."

"Mr. Collier!"

Both men looked back toward the kitchen door, where hotel manager Aidan Campbell stood. The fact that he had addressed Jake so formally told them this was hotel business.

"I have to get back," Jake said, already edging away.

"Come see me after you finish for the night," Cody said.

Jake hesitated, then nodded as he trotted back to the hotel.

Cody watched him go. Chances were fifty-fifty the man would come to his office later, so Cody figured he'd best come up with something on his own that would dampen Lily's suspicions. Or he could distract her. He wasn't bad-looking, and it was pretty clear she wasn't seeing anyone. Pretending to seriously court her, keeping her so busy she didn't have time to worry about Jake...

*That's a lousy idea, Daniels*, he thought as he strode back across the plaza to his office. If he understood anything about Lily, it was that she was not a woman to be trifled with. Once Jake told him what was going on, he'd be able to honestly tell Lily that he and Jake were handling things and she needn't give the matter another thought. Yep. Honesty was always the best policy.

The Harvey Girls had a free day on Sunday—at least a day free of donning their uniforms and serving travelers and other customers. But they were expected to attend church services, and Bonnie Kaufmann waited for her "girls" to gather in the lobby before leading them out of the hotel to the church that anchored one side of the plaza.

Lily relied on Emma to see that she was up and dressed on time. She relied on Jake to greet her at the foot of the back stairs with a cup of hot black coffee that she downed like a man would toss off a jigger of whiskey. She relied on years of routine to keep up with the ritual of the service—stand, take part in reciting a prayer or singing of a hymn, sit, and repeat. All the while, she focused her attention on the back of Cody Daniels's head.

The sheriff had taken a seat on the aisle three rows in front of where Lily sat with the other hotel employees. This Sunday, he wore a blue shirt under a dark-brown leather vest with the badge of his office pinned to it. The man was always on duty. She wondered if he'd be wearing his badge when he called for her later that afternoon.

*Stop worrying about what he's wearing. What will you wear?*

Once word had spread that Lily was stepping

out with the sheriff, all the girls had suggestions. The debate over who the handsome lawman might choose—should he decide to court any of them— had raged from the day he took the job. "You could borrow my shawl," Emma had suggested as everyone gathered to offer ideas the night before.

"You'll need a hat with a brim," Miss K warned. Even she had taken part in the discussion of just which of the girls Cody might choose. "The sun can be damaging to one so fair."

"You'll need a blouse to match that skirt," another girl advised, pointing to the brown serge skirt on the bed. "Here, take mine." She held out a cream-colored, high-necked, long-sleeved blouse that fit Lily as if it had been made for her.

All these contributions to her wardrobe for the outing were spread across her bed, including a wide-brimmed felt hat in chocolate brown provided by Miss K, ready for her to change into once services ended. Lily was touched by the excitement of her fellow Harvey Girls, but at the same time, she was determined they not make more of this "outing" than it warranted.

"We're going for a simple drive in the country," she protested.

"Nothing about that man is simple," one of the girls had muttered, and the others had nodded in agreement.

Later when they had returned from church and were alone in their room again, Emma helped arrange Lily's hair. "I know everyone is hoping for romance, but there may be another reason he wants to see you," she said. "Whatever made the sheriff invite you out, it seems likely it has to do with Jake and those men."

"Well, thank you so much," Lily huffed. "Heaven forbid the man might actually be attracted to me."

"Oh, Lily, I never meant to imply…"

"I know." Lily looked in the mirror as she pinched her cheeks and bit her lips. She didn't dare apply the rouge she felt she needed. If Miss K noticed, Lily would have a second warning—for the same offense—and likely be forbidden to go. She sat on her bed and tugged on the fancy-stitched boots she'd purchased months earlier. They certainly were not nearly as comfortable—or serviceable—as her work shoes and had cost her a small fortune, but she was not about to allow *Cody Daniels* to dictate how she should dress.

"Well, that's the best I can do," she announced, taking one last look in the mirror.

"You look lovely, Lily," Emma said. "Have fun."

*Unlikely*, Lily thought. Cody did not strike her as the fun-loving sort. Besides, Emma was probably right about Cody's true reason behind this outing. It would be business—nothing more.

Business was one thing, she thought later as the sheriff helped her into the buggy, but did he have to be so danged good-looking while he did it? Well, at least he wasn't flashing those dimples. No, he had taken one look at her boots and set his mouth in a straight, stern line of disapproval.

Undaunted, Lily waited until he had climbed aboard and picked up the reins before lifting her skirt just enough to show off the fancy stitching. "Aren't they something?" she said, admiring the handiwork. "They cost me half a month's wages, but worth every penny."

Cody snapped the reins, and they headed out of town. "They don't seem very…practical," he said.

Lily laughed. "And that is the point. I spend every day wearing sensible shoes and a uniform. There are even rules for how I am to wear my hair and trim my nails. I hardly think you can blame me for wanting a bit of fun on those rare occasions when I have the freedom to do so."

Cody frowned as he kept his eyes on the narrow dirt road. Lily nudged him lightly. "Fun," she repeated, drawing out the word. "Are you familiar with the concept, Sheriff Daniels?"

"Yes, Miss Travis, I am. I just suspect you and I have different definitions."

"Meaning?"

He glanced at her. "Meaning everything requires certain boundaries. Even fun. You seem to me to be something of a rebel when it comes to rules and boundaries."

She swallowed a bubble of incredulous laughter, because it was evident the man was serious. "And who sets those boundaries—the ones for having fun? I know for my position at the hotel, Mr. Fred Harvey sets the boundaries for all his employees, but when it comes to free time…"

"Each person is responsible for his—or her—conduct," he replied.

*Oh my stars*, Lily thought as she rolled her eyes and decided to change the subject. "Did you speak with Jake?"

"I did."

"Good. What are we going to do to make sure he—"

"Nothing."

Lily bristled. "Jake is my friend, Sheriff Daniels, and I will not sit by and do nothing while he might be in danger."

He drew in a deep breath and let it out with maddening slowness. "Couple of things," he said. "Since it's just you and me and the horse, maybe you could call me Cody?"

"Very well, Cody. What else?"

"And if it's all right, I'll call you Lily."

She sighed. "That's my name."

He pointed to the horse. "And this is Paint."

Lily rolled her eyes. "Pleased to make your acquaintance, Paint. Now what about Jake?"

"Jake will be just fine. He doesn't need your help. In fact, the way you worry about him draws attention, and he's concerned for his job."

"That's ridiculous. And you cannot tell me those two ruffians who accosted him in the yard that night are nothing. Jake was afraid of them."

"You saw all that from a third-floor window, at night, a good hundred feet or more from where he was standing?"

Lily tried to recall the specifics of what she had seen. It annoyed her that he was right about her inability to clearly make out exactly what was happening. It irritated her more that he was questioning her as if she were a witness on the stand. "I know what I saw," she muttered.

They rode in silence for several minutes. She felt

him glance at her a couple of times and, by the way he worked his lips without speaking, knew he wanted to say more.

"Oh, for heaven's sake," she grumbled when the silence grew as uncomfortable as the sun beating down on them. She let the shawl fall to the crooks of her elbows. "I am not a child in need of protection from difficult things, Cody. I am seriously worried about a man who—"

"—is in love with you," he said softly. "You know that, don't you?"

There was no use protesting the truth. Lily nodded.

"And because he loves you, Lily, he's more likely to place himself in further danger if he thinks he needs to keep you safe. The more you try to involve yourself, the more you add to his jeopardy."

"Do you know what it is—this business he's involved in?"

Cody didn't answer her question. "Let me help him, Lily. Stay out of it. Just be his friend."

"*Can* you help him?"

"I think I can."

*That's not good enough*, she wanted to say, but instead, she murmured, "Very well then. I'll try." *Big mistake*, she thought, because he looked directly at her and gave her a big smile. And when she saw the dimples deepen, she smiled back at him.

"I brought a picnic," he said. "I mean, if you're hungry."

"What on earth made you think of that? After all, it's after lunch and too early for supper and surely…"

"Well now, my thinking was we'd need to stay out

at least a couple of hours so folks wouldn't wonder why we came back so quick. On top of that, I got to thinking you might take offense at my suggestion you wear sensible shoes, so hiking wasn't likely to be part of the schedule. There's a grove of trees up the way a piece where the creek bends. What do you say, Lily? It might be *fun*."

The way he said "fun"—with a twinkle in those gold-flecked eyes—told her he was mocking her.

She scowled at him. "Fun? You do understand there will need to be certain boundaries?"

"Yes, ma'am." His expression had changed from teasing to serious to questioning, all of which told her that when it came to Cody Daniels, she might just have met her match. "I look forward to hearing just what your rules might be."

He was calling her bluff. Lily pressed her lips together and stared straight ahead as he navigated the buggy over the rougher terrain. When they came to a stop near the large cottonwood, she did not wait for his help but climbed down and started walking toward the creek, pretending an interest in the scenery.

Following her, he set down the picnic basket and spread his jacket over the thick branch of the tree that jutted out over the water. "Is this okay?" he asked.

She nodded and settled herself on the tree branch, waiting for him to join her. They shared an apple Cody sliced with his pocketknife, crusty bread that coated her skirt and his trousers with crumbs, and a covered tin pail of lemonade. He rolled back his sleeves, exposing tanned, muscular forearms. They talked about the weather—already unseasonably warm even for June. He asked how long she and Emma had known each other and worked for the Harvey Company. She asked if being a sheriff was something he'd always wanted to do. And all the time, she was far too aware of his hands—long fingers that she found herself imagining stroking her face.

*Good heavens, Lily, get a grip.*

Damn, she was beautiful. Why hadn't he noticed the lusciousness of her creamy complexion? Why hadn't he recognized the danger that lurked around the edges of those lips when they curved into a teasing smile? His original idea had been to distract her by pretending to court her, but he'd rejected that thought as unworthy of him—and insulting to her. Now as he sat next to her, watching her nibble an apple slice and seeing a crumb of the bread cling to the corner of her mouth before she captured it with her tongue, he felt he was the one being seduced.

Not that anything she did seemed intentional. Lily Travis was as guileless as a kitten, from what Cody could tell. There was no duplicity in the way she laughed or spoke or moved. He had always been a very good judge of people. He knew who was lying and who was trying to con him. He was pretty sure Lily wore her true feelings on a face that was currently staring up at him with a slight frown.

"I'm sorry, what did you say?" he asked, realizing she was waiting for his response to something.

"I asked if you've always lived in the area."

"I grew up in Arizona Territory," he replied. "You?"

"Chicago."

"City girl?" He studied her. "Yeah, it fits."

"I'm not sure if that's an insult or not," she said, a smile tugging at the corners of her lips.

"Not at all. You just have that way of being with people. Like you're used to having lots of them around. Folks out here are more spread out, and that makes us more cautious, less comfortable with strangers."

"I never thought of it that way." She stared out at the horizon. "Sometimes Emma chides me for coming on too strong—that's how she sees it. I'll admit I don't quite understand what that means. Maybe it is being used to people. Lots of people unafraid to state their opinions."

"I like the way you speak your mind," Cody said. "In my line of work, I have a lot of conversations where people are trying to figure out what I want to hear from them or how best to hide the truth."

"Oh, so you think because I don't hold back, you know everything about me?"

He could hear in her tone that she was teasing him. He grinned. "Well, maybe not everything. I'm hoping to change that though."

She looked away, evading his smile. "Everyone has secrets, Cody," she said softly, then brightened. "Why, I'll bet even you have things you'd rather no one discovered."

"Not me, Miss Travis. I'm an open book. Ask me anything."

"All right. Here's the question on every single girl in Juniper's mind: why aren't you married?"

He shrugged. "I might ask the same of you."

In a split second, the lighthearted mood between them shifted, like a sudden thunderstorm rolling over the mountains. Her body tensed, and she made a show of brushing her skirt free of crumbs and gathering up the remains of their picnic. "We should get back," she said, replacing the lid on the tin pail without looking at him. Then she glanced his way with the smile he'd seen her use while on duty in the hotel—the smile that never reached her eyes. "Shall we?" she said.

He hopped down from the log onto solid land, turned, and held out his hand to her. She hesitated before accepting his help. As she landed, the heel on one of those ridiculous boots snapped, and she faltered. He caught her before she could fall. They stood for a second—a kiss apart.

"Are you hurt?" he asked, stepping away without releasing her.

"Only my pride," she replied as she made a show of examining the broken boot. Her cheeks had turned a rosy pink, and her breathing was uneven, same as his.

"Let me see," he said, bending to have a look at the damage. "Pretty sure Mick over at the livery can fix that. Couple of nails…"

She made a sound that at first he thought was one of derision but then realized was laughter. "What's so funny?"

"Couple of nails—like shoeing a horse?" She was laughing hard now.

He ducked his head and chuckled. "I am not comparing you—or your boot—to a horse, Lily."

"Still, if the shoe fits…" And that set her off on a

fresh round of giggles. She was laughing so hard that when he stood, she rested her hand on his arm to balance herself.

Without hesitating to consider the right or wrong of it, Cody scooped her up into his arms and carried her back to the buggy. It was only steps away, but by the time he set her down, neither of them was laughing.

She stroked his cheek. "It seems I may have misjudged you, Cody Daniels," she murmured. "You are a kind and caring man."

It would have taken little for them to kiss, but something in her eyes held him back. He couldn't put his finger on what he saw there, but it was enough to know kissing her would be a mistake—not for him but for her. "We'd best be getting back," he said.

Neither of them said much on the ride back to town. He pointed out a hawk soaring toward the sunset. She told him about the party planned for Nick and Grace, and he told her he'd also received an invitation. And all the while, he tried to put a name to what he'd seen in her eyes. It wasn't until he had left her at the kitchen entrance to the hotel and returned the buggy to the livery that he found his answer.

*Regret.*

Lily Travis had wanted that kiss as much as he had, but something important had stopped her.

Lily hurried through the kitchen and on into the reading room just off the lobby. Thankfully, it was deserted. She stood at a window that gave her full view of the plaza and Cody's office. She wasn't ready for their time together to end—not yet. Even if being with him for real was impossible, she'd cling to the memory of the afternoon they'd shared.

*Fun*, she thought and smiled at the memory of their banter. Maybe she had misjudged him. Maybe...

"Hello, Lily."

That voice! She wheeled around, searching the shadows for the source of the intruder on her reverie. The room was large and illuminated by only one lamp positioned near the window, leaving the rest of the space in shadow. Lily felt her breathing quicken as she saw a large man wearing a black sack coat and a hat that covered his features step into the weak light. "Good to see you, sweetheart. It's been a while."

Victor Johnson grinned at her. He reached out to touch her cheek.

She backed away.

"What are you doing here, Victor?" Her voice was drowned out by the pounding of blood in her head. Surely, this was a nightmare.

He chuckled. "Now, is that any way to greet your long-lost husband, Lily?"

There was no way out. Victor stood between the open door and her. Beyond him, she could see guests passing on their way out of the hotel or up to their rooms. Aidan Campbell stood at the main desk. She considered calling for help, but she could hardly afford for the hotel manager to find out she'd lied—that she was not the single, pure young woman the Harvey Company thought she was. She needed this job. It was her only ticket to independence. To freedom.

Victor apparently guessed her thoughts. "Now, Lily, let's just you and me have a nice visit without involving other people. You've got secrets and so do I, but together—"

"There is no 'together' for us, Victor. I don't know what game you're playing at, but you gave up the right to have anything to say about how I live my life when you decided to walk out in the middle of our wedding night."

She saw her mistake in challenging him the minute he covered the distance between them and grabbed her jaw. "You're my wife, Lily, so let's have no more talk about 'rights,' shall we? Don't tell me you've turned into one of those women trying to change the natural way of things."

She jerked free of his hold and turned away. Through the window, she saw Cody on his way back to his quarters. *Please come in*, she thought, but he kept walking. "Why are you here, Victor?"

Victor struck a match and lit a cheroot. "I'm in town on business. Honestly, Lily, I had no idea you were here. Last I heard, you were working up in Kansas City. But then the other night, I happened to be sitting near the bandstand when I saw you crossing the plaza. Couldn't believe it was really you, but there's no mistaking the way you move. The sway of your hips, that brought back memories that have kept me awake more nights than I care to count. Those long legs of yours wrapped—"

"Stop it," she whispered. She clenched her fists and tried to think what to do. Her mind was a tangle of fear and impotence. Through the door, she saw

Emma and several other girls returning from evening vespers at the church. They laughed and chattered as they made their way through the lobby. Jake was with them, along with other members of the kitchen staff. They headed around the closed lunch counter and on into the kitchen where they would share glasses of lemonade and continue talking until curfew.

"I have to go," Lily said.

"No, you don't. You're off duty until noon tomorrow, and curfew isn't until ten, so we've plenty of time."

"Time?"

"For catching up." He put on his hat. "What say we take a walk—somewhere we might not be interrupted?"

She started to step back and realized Cody had taken her boot with him to the livery, promising to have it repaired and returned. "I broke my shoe, so I've only got one on. I'll just go change," she said, hobbling toward the door.

Victor stepped in front of her. "Nice try, sweetie." He glanced at her feet, saw she was telling the truth, and sighed. "I'll be in touch, Lily."

"I have to work," she reminded him.

"So do I," he said, turning to leave.

"And what if I have no interest in seeing you ever again?" It was a bluff, and he saw right through it.

Pivoting and taking a long draw on his cigar, he blew the smoke in her direction. "Then I'll have to start asking questions of your boss out there, and maybe get your friends in some trouble. I can do that, Lily. You of all people ought to understand that I always get my way." He stepped closer and kissed her temple, then left. As he crossed the lobby, she heard Aidan Campbell say, "Good evening, Mister Johnson. Is everything to your satisfaction?"

"Getting there," Victor replied.

And that was the moment Lily realized he was staying in the hotel.

# Chapter 3

Juniper was a railroad town, so it wasn't unusual for Cody to see new faces. Some stayed around, while others were only there for a few days before moving on. Either way, he paid attention. Life in the West was a lot less rough than it had been even five years earlier. Towns had grown up from the squalid mining camps and trading posts, there were schools and churches and civic organizations now, and supposedly there was law and order. That was where he came in.

Still, outlaw gangs continued to roam the territory, robbing banks and holding up trains. Cody had recently received word of just such a gang operating across the border in Arizona. Odds were they'd head south to Mexico once they'd gotten what they wanted, but they might also move on, seeking a new, closer target. Juniper was small but prosperous—the perfect prey. So on Monday when Cody observed the stranger in the black sack coat headed for the mercantile, he decided to follow him. The man had come to town a few days earlier. Word was he'd taken a room at the hotel and not given a date for departure.

"Said he liked to get to know a place before deciding to stay or move along," Aidan Campbell had told Cody while the two of them were waiting their turn for a shave and haircut at the barber shop.

"What's his line of work?" Cody had asked.

"He didn't say, but he flashed a roll of bills and a gold pocket watch when he checked in. Paid in advance for a week's stay."

"Name?"

"Victor Johnson. He said he was from out east— didn't offer specifics." Aidan had frowned. "Funny thing is he takes all his meals at the cantina at the edge of town. He hasn't once patronized either the lunch counter or the dining room."

After leaving the barber shop, Cody had stopped by the Sagebrush. Sally had no information to add. "He's been here twice," she had said. "Sat alone at that table in the corner—nursed two shots for the next hour and left. Big tipper."

Cody had seen the type before. He would bet his badge Victor Johnson was either a professional gambler looking for an easy mark or he was casing the town. Maybe deciding whether to rob the bank or pull a heist at the saloon. Some nights, the poker tables saw a significant amount of cash changing hands.

So when he saw Johnson enter the mercantile, Cody waited a minute, then followed him inside.

"Be right with you," Frank Tucker called out from his position behind the counter in the rear of the store.

Cody picked up a fresh notebook and new pencil, some beef jerky, and a calico bandana before approaching the counter. "Frank," he said by way of acknowledging the shopkeeper. He nodded to the stranger, all the while taking stock of the man now that he was near enough to notice details. Victor Johnson was a big man, tall and out of shape. He had the look of a man who did not do his own dirty work. His clothes were expensive and well-tailored, but Cody saw the bulge of a shoulder holster and knew he was armed.

When Johnson glanced at him, his eyes widened in surprise and just as quickly narrowed with suspicion. "Sheriff," he said, nodding toward Cody's badge.

"You two have met, then?" Frank wrapped a dress shirt in brown paper.

"Not exactly," Cody replied.

"Victor Johnson," the stranger said, thrusting out his hand.

Cody accepted the handshake, taking note of the smooth palm, the garish gold ring on the man's little finger. "Welcome to Juniper," he said. "What brings you to town?"

Johnson broke the handshake and laughed too loud and long. "Gets right to it, does he?" he said to the store owner.

Cody smiled. "Just doing my job, Mr. Johnson."

The man turned his attention to Frank. "What do I owe you, sir?"

Frank named a price, and the man pulled out a roll of bills and peeled one off. He laid it on the counter and waited for Frank to punch in the amount of the sale on the cash register and retrieve the change. Then, still not talking, he prepared to leave.

"You didn't answer my question," Cody said quietly.

"I have some business here," Johnson replied.
"Personal business." He picked up his package,
nodded to both men, and walked down the aisle to
the door.

"Mr. Johnson," Cody called. "The food at the
hotel is top-notch. You might want to give it a try
before you move on."

The stranger had not turned around, and he didn't
make any response other than a slight tensing of his
shoulders, but Cody had made his point. Johnson now
knew the sheriff had been making inquiries.

Once Johnson left, Cody waited while Frank tallied
his bill. The two men didn't speak. There was no need.
The storekeeper knew what had just happened, and
Cody knew Frank Tucker would tell Cody about any-
thing he observed should Johnson return. He handed
Cody his purchases. "I'll put it on your tab," he said.

Cody nodded and left. The truth was he didn't have
time to worry about what Victor Johnson might be
up to. His conversation with Jake a few nights earlier
had been less than satisfactory. Although he'd led Lily
to believe he knew everything, the truth was Jake had
refused to say exactly what he was mixed up in, assur-
ing Cody that he could handle himself. He'd implied
the problem had to do with money he owed, but that
didn't ring true. Jake rarely frequented the saloon, and
he never joined a card game. And when Cody pressed
him, Jake insisted all he needed Cody to do was make
sure Lily kept her distance.

*Lily.*

Ever since they'd returned from their ride in
the country, she'd had this way of popping into his

thoughts at odd moments of the day and night. And the worst of it was the way he ended up watching for her as he went around town attending to his job. It didn't help that he often heard members of the hotel staff as they sat together at one end of the hotel's long veranda after work. And it didn't help that he'd learned to pick out Lily's laughter from the general chatter. Mostly, it didn't help that one night after checking shops up and down the street on his evening rounds, he'd seen her sitting alone in one of the rocking chairs on the veranda, wrapped in a shawl to ward off the cool night air. It had taken every ounce of willpower he possessed to go on about his business instead of stopping to speak to her, sit with her.

So when later that day he found himself thinking seriously about having supper in the hotel dining room just to be near her, he decided it was past time to put a stop to such foolishness. Instead, he chewed on a piece of the jerky he'd bought earlier at Tucker's, finished some reports he needed to send off to territorial head-quarters, and then headed to the Sagebrush.

As he had hoped, Jake was there.

And so was Victor Johnson.

Cody ignored the stranger and joined Jake at the bar. "We need to talk," he said, gesturing toward a table. Cody didn't miss the way Jake's gaze skittered in Johnson's direction before he pulled out a chair and sat.

"I just wanted to let you know I can't be watching out for Miss Travis. I've got other things needing my attention." Cody glanced at the man in the far corner.

"But if Lily—"

"Admit it, Jake. You're in love with her, so figure

out what you need to do to win her. I'd say giving her a life where she didn't have to work double shifts and such might be a good start. Your position at the hotel is secure, and surely you can support a wife on what you make there. Lily doesn't need to work if you two—"

"I love her," Jake interrupted. "She doesn't love me."

"She told you that straight out?"

Jake nodded miserably. "And Emma confirmed it. She said Lily worried she would end up hurting me without meaning to, and she said that would break Lily's heart. I can't be responsible for anything that gives her pain, Cody, so I've accepted that we're going to be really good friends—and nothing more." He let out a laugh that sounded more like a snort. "Truth is, one of the reasons I asked you to look out for her is I think the two of you... I just want her to be happy."

Although he'd known his share of matchmakers, they'd all been women—his mother and his sister, mostly. "I don't need you arranging my life," Cody grumbled.

"You could do a lot worse than Lily—and certainly not any better. Think about it. She's far too good for waiting tables the rest of her days. She'd be a wonderful mother—and wife. Not sure she can cook, figured I could handle that, but I know Lily would keep a man guessing and laughing the rest of his life."

"Maybe I'm not the marrying kind. Thanks for thinking of me, but..."

"Your loss." Jake stood and downed the last of his beer. "Truth is those two guys seem to have moved on, so you're off the hook when it comes to me. Thanks for the beer, Cody."

Cody didn't miss the way Jake spoke this last in a voice loud enough for others to overhear before setting his empty glass on the table. Jake grinned, offered Sally a tip of his hat, and left. Cody dug in his pocket for change to cover his drink and Jake's and noticed Johnson leaving once he'd settled his tab. Was he following Jake? Cody handed Sally the money on his way out.

Pausing on the boardwalk, he glanced up and down the street. Jake was crossing the plaza, headed for the rear of the hotel.

There was no sign of Victor Johnson.

The clock in the plaza was tolling ten when Lily returned to the room she and Emma shared.

"I was worried," Emma said.

Lily shrugged. "Just needed to do some thinking. I was right downstairs on the veranda."

"You've been in a mood since you stepped out with the sheriff. What's going on?"

"Nothing." Lily knew her tone was sharp, so she softened it with a smile. "Seriously, Emma, it wasn't what you think. He wanted to talk about Jake."

"So you said."

Lily changed into her nightgown and sat on the side of her bed to brush her hair. "I know what you're thinking, and stop matchmaking. You know it's out of the question."

"You should have talked to him about that. I mean, he has resources for gathering information, and what if—"

Lily's grip on the hairbrush tightened. "Can we please just drop it," she said, the words catching in her throat.

"Of course. I just want you to be happy, Lily."

Lily turned to face her friend and pasted on a bright smile. "You do know I worry about your happiness as well."

Emma's lips tightened. "I'm pretty much a lost cause. But you…and Cody Daniels?"

Lily laughed and tossed her pillow at her friend. "You are impossible."

Once they had said their good nights and put out the light, Lily lay awake thinking about the sheriff. If she told him about Victor and their past, would he think less of her? Or maybe as Emma suggested, he could help her. She hadn't told Emma that Victor was no longer off to parts unknown but was in Juniper—in the Palace Hotel, possibly one floor beneath where she slept…or rather couldn't sleep.

Just as dawn broke and light filled the room, Lily heard a soft knock at their door. Emma's bed was empty. Lily had slept after all, and Emma was already across the hall in the common bathroom, getting ready for the day. Trembling with fear that the person on the other side of the door might be Victor, Lily pulled on her robe and waited, trying to decide what to do.

"Lily? Emma?"

That was Miss Kaufmann's voice, not Victor's. Releasing a breath she hadn't realized she was holding, Lily opened the door.

"Good morning, Miss K," she said brightly. "Emma is across the hall, and I was just—"

Miss K waved away her explanations. "I need your help. Nancy's ill, and there's no one to serve at the counter. I can adjust assignments by the time the dining room opens, but I need someone down there now."

Just then, Emma opened the bathroom door. Her freshly washed hair was wrapped in a towel. Since neither of them was on duty until later in the morning, Emma had washed her hair, expecting to have the time to sit outside and let it dry in the sun. Miss K glanced from Emma to Lily and chewed her lower lip. Then she let out a long breath and gave Lily her full attention.

"Get dressed, Lily. I need you at the counter in twenty minutes." And with that, she hurried away.

Lily picked up her toiletries and crossed to the bathroom. "Twenty minutes," she mimicked the head waitress as she and Emma passed in the hall.

Fortunately, by the time Lily got downstairs, everything was ready for serving the stream of railroad workers, cowhands, and others who would fill the swivel stools surrounding the black marble U-shaped counter. No doubt Jake had heard Lily would be working there so had made sure everything was in its place, ready for her. As expected, the stools filled with customers as soon as the doors opened. For the first hour, Lily was kept busy serving coffee, squeezing fresh orange juice, taking orders for eggs and steak and potatoes, and serving everything up with a bright Harvey Girl smile.

With every cup refilled and every dirty dish whisked away and the place reset, ready for the next customer, Lily relaxed into the rhythm of the job—a job she knew she did well. It was a job she enjoyed more than she was usually willing to admit. The change of pace from working at the counter instead of the more formal dining room was invigorating. She moved from the counter to the kitchen and back again, exchanging banter with Jake and the cooks and dishwashers. She felt her moodiness of the last several days lifting like the low-hanging clouds outside, gray that the sun had finally conquered.

"You're looking mighty spunky today, Lily," George, the head chef, said as she hurried into the kitchen to pick up an order. "Ain't she lookin' spunky, Jake?"

Jake glanced at her and grinned. "Never saw Lily looking anything but beautiful," he replied. The chorus of teasing from the kitchen staff made him duck his head and shout with mock gruffness, "Hey, how about filling those orders?"

Everyone knew Jake's feelings for Lily. Most understood it was a lost cause, but that didn't keep them from giving Jake a hard time. He handed Lily two plates filled with steaming food—fried eggs, a strip of steak, cubed potatoes browned to a golden crisp. "Sure like working with you, Lily. Nancy's such a nervous little thing, she hardly ever gives us a smile."

"She's new," Lily reminded him. "And speaking of hard times, how are things with you and…?"

"All taken care of," Jake assured her as he turned away to bark out an order to a dishwasher who was trying to balance a stack of freshly washed plates.

Lily hurried out to deliver the orders and nearly dropped her tray when she saw Cody seated at the counter next to Victor Johnson. Both men glanced her way. Victor smiled. Cody studied the menu.

She served the breakfast plates to two railway workers and then refilled their cups before heading to the far end of the counter to wait on Cody and Victor. *It's your job*, she reminded herself. *So smile and get to it.*

"Good morning, gentlemen. Coffee?"

"Black," Cody said, setting his cup upright.

"Lots of sugar," Victor said, his eyes sending a double message.

What had she ever seen in that man?

*Escape.*

Lily took their cups and filled the orders at the large silver urns behind her, all the while listening to hear if the two men were talking—were *together*. "We have a fresh batch of our griddle muffins this morning," she said.

"Just coffee, thanks," Cody said.

"Sir?" Lily refused to acknowledge that she and Victor were acquainted.

He smirked. "Griddle muffins, you say. Not sure I've ever tried those."

Lily waited. He was flirting with her, trying to draw her into conversation. From the corner of her eye, she saw the railway workers leave. She needed to clear their places and reset them for the next customer, but Victor was deliberately stalling as he pretended to study the menu. Miss K was crossing the lobby and glanced at the counter, her eagle eye ever on alert for some infraction of the Harvey Company's strict standards.

"I can vouch for the griddle muffins," Cody said. "You can't go wrong with those and a couple of fried eggs."

Victor scowled at the menu, then handed it to Lily. "You heard the man," he said. "Bring me the muffins with lots of butter—and honey."

"Yes, sir," Lily managed and hurried off to clear the dirty dishes and place the order. By the time Victor's food was ready, she had served two new customers coffee and orange juice and cleared another place at the counter, all the while keeping an eye out for any interaction between Cody and Victor. It could have been coincidence that the two of them sat at the counter next to each other. On the other hand, what if they knew each other—or worse, had known each other before? What if Cody knew her secret? What if…?

"Lily? Order's up." Jake was holding a tray loaded with Victor's griddle muffins, a dish filled with butter, and a small pitcher of honey.

"Thanks." She took the tray and hesitated. "Jake, do you know that man sitting next to the sheriff?"

Jake shrugged. "He's staying here. Saw him in the saloon last night. This is the first time I've seen him take a meal here." He frowned. "Is he bothering you, Lily?"

"No. Just wondered." She hurried away to serve Victor. The last thing she needed was for him to cause a scene, complaining about cold food. Setting the meal before him, she kept her eyes lowered, refusing to meet his gaze—or Cody's curious glance.

"More coffee, sir?"

Victor grinned. "Sure, sugar." Lily shot him a look. "Lots of sugar," Victor added with a smirk.

Cody cleared his throat. "You're new in town, Mr. Johnson, but I would wager you've dined at other

Harvey establishments," he said in a low tone meant only for Victor's and Lily's ears.

Victor bristled. "Of course. I travel a good deal. What's your point?"

Cody took his time draining the last of his coffee, placing a coin on the counter, and standing. "Then I'm surprised at your manner with Miss Travis, sir. The women who work for Fred Harvey are ladies, and they deserve respect." He fitted his hat low on his brow and nodded to Lily before leaving.

"Well, well, well. That lawman seems mighty interested in you, Lil. Have you been stepping out on me?" Victor was the only person ever to call her "Lil" and now she hated the sound of it.

"Juniper is a small town," she replied as she cleared Cody's cup and saucer. "Folks here tend to watch out for each other."

"The sheriff's watching, all right." He lowered his voice to a whisper. "Does he know you and me are married? Does your boss? Seems to me I recall you Harvey Girls are bound by—"

Lily's hand shook so badly that Cody's empty cup rattled on its saucer. "What do you want, Victor? Why are you here?" she hissed and then pasted on a smile when she saw other customers glance their way.

"I've got business," Victor replied as he slathered a muffin with butter and honey and stuffed half of it into his mouth. "And the bonus is you're here. Never thought we might—"

A cowhand down the way raised his cup, signaling the need for more coffee. "I'm working," Lily said as she hurried away.

On his way back to his office, Cody thought about the interaction between Victor and Lily.

Instinct told him they had known each other before this morning. It was something about Lily's manner. Usually, she was friendly with customers, especially strangers, making them feel welcome and special. She always had a smile at the ready. But with Johnson, she'd been nervous, anxious. And even when she was serving other customers, she'd kept glancing back at Johnson—and at him. Maybe he should talk to her.

He turned back toward the hotel, but the train whistled in the distance. Once it pulled into the station, Lily would be busy with customers for the rest of the morning. Maybe later. Meanwhile, he intended to see if he could find out anything more about Victor Johnson. He headed for the telegraph office instead.

Ellie Swift was sorting mail. "Sheriff," she said by way of acknowledging him. "Be right with you."

"No rush, Ellie. Just want to send out a couple of telegrams." Ellie kept a pad of paper on the counter, and he pulled it closer, perching on a stool while he composed messages to his counterparts in Santa Fe and Tucson.

```
VICTOR JOHNSON STOP ANY INFOR-
MATION STOP SIX FEET EASTERNER
STOP WEARS GOLD RING ON LEFT
LITTLE FINGER STOP
```

He signed it and slid the pad to Ellie. She read the message and glanced up at him. "Needless to say, Ellie, we need to keep this between you and me," he said. If there was one person he could trust in this town, it was the gray-haired postmistress and telegraph operator.

She nodded and sat down to send out the wires. "I'll let you know as soon as anything comes back," she said.

"Thanks." Cody left and stood for a long moment on the boardwalk outside, trying to figure out his next move. Normally, he would go on about the business of keeping law and order in Juniper, but his mind kept going back to Lily and her interaction with Johnson. If Johnson was somebody from Lily's past, maybe that was why he'd come to town. Maybe Cody's instinct that the guy was trouble was right, but he'd been looking in the wrong direction. Maybe Johnson wasn't casing the town for a robbery. Maybe he was stalking Lily.

But if that was the case, why wouldn't she come to him? Ask for his help?

*Because she's stubborn*, he thought.

Well, Cody knew from experience that stubborn could get a person in a lot of trouble. How many times had he seen a rancher or cowhand determined to handle trouble alone? And how many times had that turned out to be a disaster? Lily Travis struck him as the kind of woman who was sure she could handle herself. Victor Johnson struck Cody as the kind of man who might just prove her wrong.

He made his morning rounds, stopping to hear a

complaint from Abigail Chambers who owned the hat shop about damage to her alley-side rear door. "I'm sure it's those Howard boys," she ranted. "They're nothing more than a trio of hooligans, and you need to arrest them and teach them a lesson."

"Well now, the problem with that, Miss Chambers, is a lack of proof."

She rattled the doorknob. "Here's your proof."

"How many times have I stopped by in the last couple of months to remind you that knob needed tightening?" he asked.

"I'm alone here," she whined.

It was always her plea. Cody was well aware that the woman saw him as her protector.

"Tell you what," he said. "Soon as I finish my rounds and take care of some business over at the hotel, I'll come by and fix that knob for you."

She lowered her eyelids and gave him a half smile. "Will you stay for cake and tea?"

"That's a mighty tempting offer, Miss Chambers, but in my position, it wouldn't do to—"

Her mouth tightened into a hard, straight line that erased most evidence of her thin lips and made her look every one of her thirty-plus years. "And yet you rode out with that Harvey Girl the other afternoon."

"That was personal. You wouldn't deny me a little pleasure, now would you?" He gave his best version of a boyish smile.

Abigail released a huff of breath. "I suppose not. She's certainly pretty—they all are. A girl like me hasn't stood a chance since that lot came to town."

Cody fought a smile at her use of the term "girl"

and tried to look sympathetic. "The thing about the West is there are plenty of single men around, Miss Chambers. And if you ask me, there are plenty who'd be lucky to catch your eye." He tipped his hat and moved on down the street.

Since he'd started this job a year earlier, Cody had been surprised at the number of women who seemed to see him as the cure for their loneliness or the answer to their prayers for an unattached daughter. Early on, he'd sat at more Sunday dinner tables then he cared to recall. Frank Tucker had been the one to counsel him against it.

"Unless you're in the market for a wife, I'd advise you to find ways to avoid accepting any more of those invites," the owner of the mercantile had said. "You've no doubt had some experience with range wars, but trust me, that's nothing compared to a bunch of women thinking they've got their brand on you."

It wasn't long after that when a sensational case involving Lily's friend Grace had legitimately taken most of Cody's time and made it impossible to accept invitations, even if he'd wanted to do so.

*Grace.*

She'd been a Harvey Girl. She'd also been accused—and cleared—of murdering Jasper Perkins, the town banker. She was married now, to Nick Hopkins, the foreman at the Lombard Ranch. Maybe Cody could take a ride out there, have a visit with Grace, see if she knew anything about this Victor Johnson. After all, when Cody'd attended the celebration of Grace and Nick's marriage, hadn't Grace hugged him and whispered, "Thank you so much for everything you did to help me. If ever I can be of help to you…"

Cody finished his rounds and then collected his horse from the livery, making sure the blacksmith knew where he'd gone in the unlikely case there was trouble.

When he reached the ranch, Grace Hopkins was hanging wash on a line stretched between a porch pillar and a branch of the ponderosa pine that shaded the small cabin. The house sat some distance from the main house, near a creek formed by a waterfall that cascaded down from the mountains. It was the kind of place a man could find some peace and quiet. Grace shielded her eyes with one hand at the sound of his approach, then broke into a smile and waved.

"Cody!" She started toward him.

"Hello, Mrs. Hopkins," he called back as he dismounted and wrapped the reins around a hitching post. "How are you?"

"Now don't you go getting all formal with me, Cody. We're friends, so unless this is official business, call me Grace."

"It's good to see you looking so well, Grace," he replied.

"Come on inside out of this hot sun. How about a glass of cool water?"

"That would be real nice," Cody replied as he followed her to the small cabin. Things were neat and tidy inside, and the place had a homey feel without being all frilly, not like some of the homes he'd visited in Juniper. Nick Hopkins was a lucky man.

"Nick's down at the ranch," she said as she filled two glasses, handing one to him. "He'll be back later this afternoon, but…"

"I came to see you, Grace."

Her eyes widened with concern. "What's happened? Is it Emma or Lily?"

"Everyone is fine," he assured her and took a long swallow of the refreshing beverage, letting it relieve his parched throat. "The thing is there's a stranger in town—Victor Johnson." He watched carefully and saw the name meant nothing to her. "He seems to know Lily, and I wondered if maybe you'd ever heard her mention him."

The way Grace chewed her lower lip and busied herself refilling his glass told him she'd indeed thought of something. "Is this man dangerous?"

Cody shrugged. "Hard to say. He's well-dressed. Talks with an Eastern accent. Clearly not used to manual labor."

"Why is he in town?"

"Well now, that's a mystery. He's been staying at the hotel for close to a week now."

Grace drummed her fingers on the table. "And why would you think he has anything to do with Lily?"

"Just a hunch. He was at the lunch counter this morning, and Lily was filling in for the new girl, so she waited on us."

Grace's eyes sharpened as she peered at him. "You and this man were having breakfast together?"

"Coincidence. I was there, and he took the next stool. I think we were both surprised when Lily stepped out of the kitchen to wait on us."

"That doesn't explain why you think Lily might…"

"She was nervous, Grace. Have you ever seen Lily be anything but professional on the job?"

"Maybe it was seeing you and had nothing to do with this stranger."

"It wasn't me making her jumpy as a jackrabbit. The fella was flirting—sort of—but more like baiting her, watching to see what she would do."

Grace smiled. "That's hardly unusual, Cody. Lots of men come to the lunch counter, or even the dining room, thinking they can trifle with a Harvey Girl the way they might with one of the girls at the saloon."

*Maybe she's right*, Cody thought. "But have you ever seen Lily not be able to handle that kind of disrespect? I mean, I still have memories of a couple of standoffs with her while I had you in custody, and I was on my best behavior."

Grace laughed and drank her water. "I've been meaning to have Emma and Lily visit," she said, patting her rounded stomach. "I mean these days, it's not proper for me to be seen out in town, and I know Rita and John Lombard are planning a party for July—just close friends. Still, I miss Emma and Lily."

Cody grinned. "Nick sure is excited about that baby. If you like, I could carry a note back to Lily and Emma," he offered.

"What a good idea." She went to the small desk near the window and penned a quick message. "I suggested Sunday, and maybe have Jake and Aidan Campbell come along as escorts—and you, if you'd like."

Cody folded the note and stuffed it in the pocket of his vest. "I expect Lily would be more comfortable with Jake."

"Ah, you see, I was right," Grace said. "You do make her nervous, Cody Daniels, and that's a good thing."

Cody felt the heat of embarrassment creep up his neck. "I should get back to town," he said. "It was good to see you, Grace."

"And you."

She walked out with him, and it wasn't until he was well on his way back that he realized Grace had deftly deflected his concern about Johnson and Lily, and he was no wiser on the subject than he'd been before coming. He thought about the note she'd given him to deliver, and it occurred to him that the sudden decision to invite her friends for a visit was not entirely innocent. Grace was being cautious. She wouldn't betray a friend's confidence until she'd had a chance to check with that friend. He just hoped the stalling wouldn't cause more problems for Lily.

# Chapter 4

LILY FINISHED HER SHIFT AT THE LUNCH COUNTER before going straight to the dining room to make sure everything was ready for the afternoon train. Emma was already checking each table to be sure the place settings followed the strict rules.

"Honestly, Emma, you get more like Miss K every day, the way you're always straightening a fork or moving a glass a fraction of an inch." Lily had meant to tease her friend, but when Emma looked at her and frowned, she knew her tone had been snappish and annoyed. "Sorry," she murmured.

"You must be exhausted," Emma said sympathetically. "Aidan told me the counter was unusually busy."

"*Aidan*, is it?" Lily grinned at her friend.

Emma blushed. "He told us to call him by his given name when we weren't around guests. You were there when he said it."

"Yep, I was. Well, Aidan was definitely right about the counter. As soon as one customer left, another was right there to fill the spot."

"Hopefully we won't be nearly so busy for supper.

Once the four o'clock comes and goes, I expect it will be a quiet night. Aidan said the hotel is fairly empty."

"Good. I could use a quiet night." Lily inspected her tables to make sure they were ready to quickly serve the train passengers and get them back on their way on schedule.

"Lily? Is something bothering you?" Emma's voice was filled with genuine concern.

"I'm fine. Just a little tired is all. I sure hope Nancy has a quick recovery." She was aware that her voice shook slightly. The mere thought of Victor being so close by made her throat tighten and her insides clench.

Voices from the lobby made both girls look toward the door.

"Got a message," they heard Cody tell Aidan.

"It's Sheriff Daniels," Emma whispered and scurried off to the kitchen just as Cody stepped into the dining room and shut the door.

Lily started straightening flatware that was already perfectly aligned on a table.

"Hello, Lily."

She turned to face him. *Golly darn, but he is so appealing!* She cleared her throat. "Why, Sheriff Daniels, what brings you here? I mean we're not exactly open for business yet, and come to think of it, you've already taken one meal at the Palace today. Highly unusual for you to grace us with your presence twice in one day." She was babbling, and he was doing nothing to stop her. He just stood there, hat in hand, and waited, like he had nothing better to do.

Lily clamped her mouth shut.

"I brought you—and Emma—a message from

Grace Hopkins," he said, fishing a folded note from his vest pocket and holding it out to her.

Lily took the note. "You saw Grace? How is she? She isn't ill, is she? Or is it the baby?"

The dimples in his cheeks deepened. "Read the note, Lily. She's fine."

Partly for the light and more to escape the effect those dimples had on her, Lily moved to one of the large windows and read Grace's message. "Oh, how lovely," she murmured. "You saw her?"

"I stopped by."

Lily had a niggling feeling his visit to see Grace hadn't been entirely social. "Why?"

"Why?" he repeated.

She moved closer so she could read his expression. "Middle of a weekday when I assume you've got sheriff stuff to do, why ride all the way out to see Grace?"

Her heart hammered. Grace had been badly injured in a fire that had killed a prominent Juniper citizen— the banker, Jasper Perkins. The man had stalked her and attacked her. Grace had gone to jail and only been declared innocent after Miss K and another waitress had stepped forward to reveal the same man had assaulted them. But if Cody had gone to see her, maybe Jasper's widow had brought new charges. "Is Grace in some kind of trouble?"

"Grace isn't the one I'm worried about, Lily."

She started to assure him that she was just fine, but he stopped her from speaking by gently touching her lip with his forefinger—and then pulling it away as if he'd been scalded. "Sorry," he muttered. "The thing is that man at the counter this morning. You know him. He knows you, and he scares you."

"That's ridiculous, and what on earth has any of that got to do with Grace?"

"I wanted to see if the name Victor Johnson rang a bell with her."

Lily fought and lost the battle not to have her shoulders tense, and she knew Cody noticed.

"So you do know him." He studied her closely. "Look, Lily, if this man is harassing you in any way, maybe—"

"My personal life is hardly your business, Sheriff Daniels, and I do not appreciate you going behind my back and questioning my friends. Unless you have some kind of official matter that involves me, please do not do that again." She put the invitation from Grace in her apron pocket and started folding a stack of freshly laundered napkins. "If there's nothing more, I have work to do."

He hesitated, then tugged on his hat and turned to go. "A word of advice, Lily," he said as he reached the door. "Whatever's going on, Grace sent this invitation for more than one reason."

"She wants to see her best friends," Lily said.

"That and she's worried about you. She knows why Victor Johnson is a problem for you, doesn't she?"

Lily released a laugh she knew was as phony as the smile she'd greeted him with when he first arrived. "Is that the man's name?"

Cody turned to her so quickly, she gasped. He covered the distance between them until they were standing far too close for comfort. "Stop playing games. You know his name, Lily. You know him. The thing you don't seem to understand is he might be trouble. People get hurt when someone like that is around. *You* could be hurt."

Lily reacted the way she always did when threatened or scared—she pretended she wasn't. "And what's that to you?"

He allowed his eyes to roam over the features of her face, settling on her lips. He let out a long breath. "To me?" he murmured. "More than maybe it should be." And with that, he turned and left, closing the double dining room doors behind him with a soft click.

Lily hardly realized how hard she was clutching the stack of unfolded napkins until she heard Emma approach. "Are you all right?"

"Of course. Look at this." She smoothed out Grace's note and passed it to Emma. "Grace has invited us for a visit on Sunday. She says maybe Jake and Aidan could come as well."

Emma studied the note and smiled. "And Cody—she mentions Cody."

"Cody will not be coming," Lily said firmly. "Let's just let it be the four of us with Nick and Grace, like old times." She did not miss the curious look Emma gave her. "Please?" she added.

"All right," Emma agreed.

Just then, they heard the whistle announcing the arrival of the four o'clock train. Miss K entered the dining room, opened the double doors leading to the lobby, and began her inspection while other Harvey Girls hurried to their stations. Outside the window, Lily caught a glimpse of Victor crossing the street.

*Please don't let him come in for supper.*

To her relief, he headed for the Sagebrush Saloon, but she knew Cody was right about one thing. Sooner or later, she would have to deal with Victor.

Cody strode out of the dining room, barely acknowledging Aidan, who looked up from the hotel register and appeared about to say something. But Cody was in no mood to talk. He'd made a mistake with Lily. He'd let her know he cared. When he first started work as a lawman, he'd told himself romance could not be part of the picture. He dealt with dangerous men and situations. It would be unfair to put a woman in a position to get caught up in that.

More than that, he was twenty-four years old, and he was ambitious. Taking the position in Juniper was a stepping stone. He had a dream of doing his part to shape the future of New Mexico as it moved from territory to statehood. Running for political office—that was the time to have a strong woman by his side. But was that woman Lily, especially with her tendency toward saying whatever fool thing popped into her head?

He slammed open the door to his office, forgetting he'd arrested Sam Jones the night before on a drunk and disorderly charge and had left the man to sleep it off in one of the small cells.

"What the…" Sam leapt to his feet and ran his hand over his shaggy beard.

Cody grabbed the keys and opened the door to

the cell. "Behave yourself," he muttered as he walked back to his desk, leaving the cell open.

"You letting me go?"

"Looks that way," Cody replied, and Sam was out the door before he could change his mind. A message he recognized as coming from Ellie Swift lay on his desk.

*Heard back from Santa Fe.*

He wadded the paper and tossed it in the wastebasket on his way out the door and around the corner to the Western Union office.

"Ellie," he said, tipping two fingers to his hat.

She handed him a telegram. "Didn't want to trust it with a delivery boy," she said. "Seemed like it might be something you'd rather keep to yourself."

"For now," Cody said as he scanned the message.

```
HERE AND GONE STOP HOTEL HIT
STOP NO PROOF STOP
```

The hotel in Santa Fe was La Casita, a Harvey establishment. Was it possible Johnson had orchestrated a robbery there and was now casing the Palace? If that was true, then a lot of people Cody considered friends could get hurt. His mind turned to Jake and the two men Lily had seen with him in the hotel yard. Were they part of this? Was Jake? And where did Lily fit into the picture?

"Thanks, Ellie."

The older woman nodded, already focused on

something else. Cody knew he could count on her not to gossip.

He returned to his office and drummed his fingers on his desk while he tried to figure out his next move. He couldn't outright accuse Johnson without some kind of evidence. On the other hand, if the hotel was in danger of a burglary, he owed it to Aidan to warn him. Cody needed more information. He studied the brief message from Tyson Drake, his counterpart in Santa Fe. Maybe he should just go out there and talk to Ty about what had happened.

A new thought occurred to him. If Lily went with him—if she heard from Ty how dangerous Johnson might be—surely that would scare some sense into her. He'd seen enough of her to know that Lily was the kind of independent and willful woman who thought she could handle whatever came her way. That made her vulnerable. There was no way she'd ever come out unscathed in a battle with a man like Victor Johnson.

Sunday was two days away, when Lily and the others would go to visit Nick and Grace. And Cody had an invitation as well. The Hopkins place was more than halfway to Santa Fe. If he remembered right, the Harvey Girls had a ten o'clock curfew on Sundays. What if, later in the afternoon when the others were ready to return to Juniper, he asked Lily to ride on with him and have supper at La Casita—without telling her Ty would also join them? La Casita was the crown jewel of Harvey's empire, at least in this part of the country. Cody was willing to bet Lily would have trouble turning down the opportunity to see the place for herself.

He grinned, feeling better than he had for days. He would let Aidan know that La Casita had been robbed without giving away any details, keep tabs on Johnson, keep his distance from Lily—at least until Sunday—and hopefully by Monday morning, he'd have a lot more cause to suggest Victor Johnson move on.

The one thing Cody had learned on the job was things did not always go as planned. Late that night, he was wakened by a banging on his office door. He stumbled from bed, pulled on his trousers, and opened it to find Lily on his porch—again.

"You've got to come now," Lily demanded. "It's Jake."

She gave him no further information as she raced back across the plaza and around to the back of the hotel.

Cody pulled on his boots, strapped on his gun belt, and followed.

Once in the yard behind the hotel's kitchen, he spotted Jake Collier on the ground, propped up against the wall, his face a bloody mess. Pretty much everyone who worked in the hotel had formed a circle around him. Emma sat on the ground next to him, gently dabbing at his cuts with a wet cloth.

"Where's the doctor?" Lily demanded.

"Right here, young lady," Doc Waters said as he made his way through the throng gathered around Jake. "Can we get the patient inside?"

Two men from the kitchen staff picked up Jake and carried him into the hotel. He moaned with pain.

Lily followed close behind, admonishing them to be careful.

"What happened?" Cody asked Aidan.

"Not sure. Jake didn't show up for work this afternoon. I went to check his room, but he wasn't there. Jake's been here five years and never missed a day of work. The dining room was about half full of customers at the time, so we got them served and were just about to organize a search party when one of the girls saw him stumble into the yard and collapse."

"Did he say anything?"

Aidan shook his head. "Though I'll tell you, I've never seen any man more frightened than Jake was."

"Let's see what Doc has to say." Cody waved Aidan forward to precede him through the open kitchen door.

Lily had directed the men to Jake's small room off the kitchen. By the time Cody and Aidan got there, Jake was lying on the bed, his eyes closed, his head in Lily's lap. She stared up at the doctor, her eyes brimming with tears.

Cody and Aidan stood in the doorway, waiting for Doc to finish his examination. Emma squeezed between them, bringing a pan of water.

"Finish cleaning those cuts, Emma, and then apply some of this salve. His jaw's broken and his nose. Nothing but time for the nose. I'll wire his jaw and bandage his chest—I suspect a couple of broken ribs—and I'm most worried about that lump at the base of his skull. We'll see how he fares through the night." He looked up and focused on Aidan. "He shouldn't be left alone. We need to watch for any sign of fever, and with a beating this bad, there could be some internal bleeding."

"I'll stay with him," Lily announced, and the fierce determination in her expression dared anyone to debate that statement.

"I'll need to ask him some questions," Cody told the doctor.

"Can it wait until morning?" Doc asked. "I'll give him something for the pain, and once I do, he'll likely sleep most of the night. Besides, once I wire that jaw, talking's not going to be easy."

Cody was torn. On the one hand, Jake was clearly not up to telling anyone what had happened. On the other, anything he might say could help in the hunt for the culprits who'd done this. And whoever had done this was long gone by now. "If it's okay, I'll stay awhile." He pulled a wooden side chair close to the bed and sat, setting his hat on the floor.

Doc hesitated, then nodded and stepped aside to allow Emma to wash Jake's battered face. Once she finished, he took her place next to Jake, expertly lifting and moving him while wrapping bandages tightly around his chest and wiring the jaw. Doc mixed a powder in water and fed it to Jake with an eye dropper, holding his mouth closed and forcing him to swallow the concoction. And through it all, Cody felt Lily glaring at him as if somehow this was all his fault.

Once Emma had left with the pan of now-bloody water, Doc packed his bag and snapped it shut. "Nothing by mouth until morning," he instructed, focusing on Lily. "Wet his lips if needed. Send for me at once if his fever spikes or you see blood coming from anywhere. Understood?"

Lily nodded.

Satisfied, Doc squeezed his way past the hotel workers crowded outside the small room. "Mr. Campbell, I would suggest these folks get to bed." A moment later, Cody was alone with Jake—and Lily, who seemed intent on pretending he wasn't there.

"Are you going to hold him all night?" Cody asked.

"No," she replied, her voice dripping with sarcasm. "I thought in an hour or so, Jake and I would dance a jig."

"I just meant it could get mighty uncomfortable for you both. My guess is eventually he'll need to move around some, and well, with the headlock you've…"

Lily loosened her hold and stroked Jake's hair from his forehead. She was sitting with her back against the bare wall, which had to be uncomfortable. Cody reached for the pillow that had been pushed aside and stood. "At least put this behind your back," he said.

She leaned forward slightly, and he stuffed the pillow behind her.

"Thank you," she murmured.

"Did he say anything?" Cody asked. "Even just ranting?"

"Just moans because of the pain. You think those two men did this, don't you? I thought Jake said they were gone."

"Maybe they came back. The thing is, Lily, the only one who can help me catch whoever did this is Jake. So if he says anything—a word, a name—you've got to tell me."

"You're right here," she pointed out.

"It's likely to be a long night. My suggestion is we take shifts keeping watch over him, and that way, we both get some sleep."

"But if we need Doc, you'll go right away?"

"We'll send somebody. If you've never seen a man out of his head with pain, Lily, then it's hard to understand how difficult he would be for you to handle on your own. He might accidentally…"

"Jake would never hurt me."

"Not intentionally, but trust me."

She studied him through narrowed eyes. "And just how do you know so much about this?"

He looked toward the small, high window above the cot. "Before I got into the law and order business, I was a government scout. I knew the Arizona and New Mexico country well, so troops dealing with border skirmishes and raids on isolated settlers came to rely on me when they were ordered out on expeditions."

"I don't see what that has to do with—"

"I saw terrible things, Lily—things I wouldn't want to ever see again. There were times when I was as much a medic as a scout. Sometimes, in spite of everything we could find out before setting off, we were ambushed. Sometimes, the camp was raided at night." He shook off the memory and looked at her. "Just trust me. Jake might not be in his right head if the pain gets too bad."

From the kitchen, they could both hear dishes and flatware clinking together. A minute later, Emma brought them each a bowl of elk stew. She left again and returned with a stack of pillows she'd collected, placing one behind Cody's back, insisting he sit on another, and giving two more to Lily.

"I couldn't eat," Lily protested.

"You can and you will," Emma replied. "Do it

for Jake, and try to get some sleep. I'll be back in the morning to check on you."

As Emma left, Lily rolled her eyes and allowed Jake's head to rest on her lap, freeing her hands to accept the bowl and spoon.

"I could feed you," Cody offered.

"I'll manage." She set the spoon aside and held the bowl just under her chin so she could simply drink the stew, pausing between sips to chew the meat and potatoes it contained. Cody couldn't help but admire her resourcefulness.

Later, Miss Kaufmann came to the door of the room, carrying a lamp that she set on an upended crate by the bed. "If you insist on staying here through the night, please understand this door must remain open at all times. Sheriff Daniels, I would be far more comfortable if you would agree to place your chair as far as possible from Lily. This arrangement is most unseemly, but Mr. Campbell has persuaded me to allow it. Still, there must be rules."

"Yes, ma'am," Cody said. He stood and placed his chair at the far end of the bed. "Does this suit?"

Miss K pursed her lips. "It is better. Hardly suitable, but better." She turned her attention to Lily. "I will make sure your shift is covered tomorrow. However, the day after…"

"I know," Lily said softly. "Thank you for understanding."

"Very well. I shall bid you both a good night and pray for Jake's speedy recovery." She adjusted the wick on the lamp to strengthen its output, touched her fingers to Jake's forehead, and left.

Cody waited until he heard the head waitress climb the stairs to the staff's quarters, then got up and lowered the wick. "For Jake," he said when Lily shot him a look of alarm.

"I think the medicine is working. He seems to be resting," she said.

"Let's hope that lasts. Why don't you try to get some sleep? I'll take first watch." He took her bowl and set it with his next to the lamp.

Lily arranged the pillows Emma had brought against the iron foot railing of the bed and rested her head on them. "Good night, Cody," she said softly.

"Good night, Lily." He took out the small notebook and pencil he carried everywhere. While he had the time and the memory was fresh, he began to write down the details as he knew them—as well as his thoughts about why Jake Collier might have been attacked and beaten half to death.

Lily fell asleep almost at once. The lack of sleep from the night before and the stress of the day had exhausted her. Unfortunately, after only an hour, Jake began to move restlessly, flinging his arm up and nearly striking her in the eye. He moaned and bucked, and when she tried to stroke his face to settle him, he lashed out, the force of his blow knocking her sideways.

Cody was on his feet at once. "Get up," he ordered as he pressed Jake's arms down against the bed. "Now."

It looked like it was taking all of Cody's strength

to subdue Jake as she scrambled free of him. But even once she was standing, Jake continued to fight Cody.

"Go wake the kid in the lobby and have him get Doc over here," Cody managed between dodging blows and tightening his grip on Jake's thrashing body.

Lily ran through the kitchen and into the lobby. "Tommy," she shouted, and the boy bolted awake. "Get Doc," she said. "Hurry."

The bellboy pulled on his shoes and ran out the front door.

Lily made sure the hotel entrance was closed and returned to the kitchen where she could hear Jake's incoherent shouts. When she reached the room, his eyes were open, and he focused them on her, which seemed to calm him some. He mumbled something that sounded like "Lily."

Cody continued to restrain him, and finally, Jake's body went limp, tears rolling down his battered face. With no concern for her own safety, Lily moved between Cody and Jake. She knelt and cradled his head between her palms. "Shh," she whispered. "You're safe, Jake. I'm right here." She looked up at Cody who stood over them, his breathing rough from the energy it had taken to contain Jake.

Jake gagged, blood pooling in the corners of his mouth, some of it leaking down his chin.

"Do something," she pleaded as Doc came through the door.

With Cody's help, they got Jake stretched out on the bed. Tommy brought the lamp closer.

"As I feared," Doc muttered. "He's bleeding internally. We need to get him to my office. I don't have…"

Lily saw that before Doc could finish his sentence, Cody had already lifted the now-docile Jake and headed for the door. "You stay here," he instructed Lily as he and Doc started across the yard.

"Not on your life," Lily replied and ran to catch up.

Dressed in her nightclothes and clutching her robe, Doc's wife, Sarah, met them at the door. She led the way to the rear of the house where Doc had a small operating room. Once Cody laid Jake on the table, Sarah ushered him and Lily back to the front office. "Wait here," she said.

"But…" Lily protested.

Sarah Waters ignored her as she hurried back to assist her husband, shutting the door to the operating room firmly behind her.

"Jake," Lily whispered, her hand outstretched toward the door as the tears came. She felt Cody wrap his arms around her, holding her as he stroked her hair, making no attempt to soothe her with words. There were no words. Jake might die. They both knew that. And if he did, would it be her fault? He'd called her name. Was he trying to tell them his beating had something to do with her?

Cody tightened his hold on her. She could feel the strong pulse of his heart against her cheek, her ear pressed to his chest. It had been so long since she'd allowed herself to rely on anyone. *Not since Father died.*

From the time she was twelve and her mother had remarried, there had been no one she could trust. No one to make her feel safe and protected. Foolishly, she'd thought that Victor Johnson was that person, but she understood now that she'd connected with him out of sheer desperation. Victor had come along at a time when she was struggling to simply survive from one day to the next. Her wages as a shop girl hadn't been nearly enough to cover even the minimum costs of room and board. When she met Victor, she'd been so desperate, she'd even thought of taking the job the madam at a seedy saloon had repeatedly offered her.

It was the Harvey Company that had saved her. Once Victor left and she'd gone through the money he'd left behind, all the while not knowing where he was or how to contact him, it had been the Harvey Company that had come to her rescue. She'd been passing the headquarters, had seen two girls leave all excited about their new positions, and had decided to go in.

"Lily?" Cody's voice was soft and close enough to her ear that she could feel his breath.

She gathered herself and gently stepped away from him. "I'm all right," she said.

He frowned. "Forgive me if I doubt that. You've been through a lot today, and now with Jake taking a turn for the worse—"

"He can't die," she said fiercely. "Why couldn't I love him the way he deserves? What's wrong with me? Jake has been the kindest, most…" She burst into fresh tears.

Cody led her to a pair of chairs near the window, easing her into one and taking the other for himself. He clasped her hands between his. "Now you listen to me, Lily," he said, his voice sounding like he'd swallowed sand. "Whatever happens, Jake has always known you care for him. Caring the way you do is, in a way, a kind of love, isn't it? A man would be lucky to know that kind of caring."

She stared at the way his thumb traced patterns on her palm. The streetlamp glinted on his badge. He was a good man, and he was the law in this town. Maybe it was time to start trusting again.

"You know that man sitting next to you at the counter the other day?"

His thumb stilled. "What about him?"

"I do know him, and maybe he…maybe Jake…" Her voice shook, and she couldn't find the words.

Cody cupped her chin, forcing her to meet his gaze. "Lily, are you in trouble?"

A completely inappropriate laugh worked its way past the lump blocking her throat. "You might say that," she admitted.

Just then, the door to the operating room opened, and Doc emerged, wiping his hands on a hand towel.

Cody and Lily stood, and Lily grasped Cody's hand. Doc shook his head. Jake was gone.

# Chapter 5

THEY WAITED A WEEK TO BURY HIM. WITH AIDAN'S help, Lily and Emma did everything they could to contact the only family they'd ever heard Jake speak of—a sister in Ohio. Finally, after several days passed with no word, Ellie Swift delivered a telegram to the hotel.

CANNOT COME STOP SENDING MONEY
FOR THE FUNERAL STOP MAY OUR
JACOB REST IN PEACE STOP

"She wired five dollars," Ellie had reported as she handed the money to Aidan.

Lily was astounded—not that the sister had not tried to come but that she had said nothing about possibly shipping the body to Ohio for burial. "Surely, he has family buried there," she raged. "Parents, siblings, grandparents. He should be brought home."

"I think this was home for Jake," Emma said. "I think he thought of his friends here at the Palace as his family."

Lily bit her lower lip. It seemed ever since Jake died, she was never far from tears. "I wish..." She shook off the thought and drew in a breath to steady herself. "Well. I may have disappointed Jake in life, but I will see to it that he has a proper funeral—and that whoever is responsible for this is caught and brought to justice."

"Cody is working on that, but he has little to go on. We don't even know where Jake was attacked," Emma reminded her.

"Then it's high time we found out," Lily muttered. She and Emma were spent after another chaotic meal where orders got mixed up in the kitchen and apologies had to be made. The cooks and other kitchen staff did their best without Jake to keep things humming along, but it wasn't enough. Once Aidan closed the doors for the night, Lily and Emma found chairs on the veranda, drawing in the cool night air as they sat for the first time in hours.

"Aidan has made all the arrangements for the funeral," Emma said. "Miss K wants us to wear our uniforms without the aprons."

Lily nodded, but her mind was elsewhere. What *had* happened that night? Jake hadn't shown up for work, and the four o'clock train had come and gone with no sign of him. Most of the men who worked at the hotel had taken rooms at Myrtle Davison's boardinghouse, but Jake had always insisted on being in that small room near the kitchen. When he didn't show up, George had checked, figuring he was ill or had overslept, and that was the first anyone knew of him being gone. Then the train had come, and they were simply too busy to do more. Aidan was upset, and the dining room was jammed with customers from the time the train arrived and on until closing.

They had all been standing outside the kitchen, trying to decide their next move, when a waitress saw Jake stagger into the yard and collapse.

Why hadn't they thought to have one of the cooks or other hotel employees search the area to find the culprits who'd done this to him?

She stood. "I think I'll walk over to the sheriff's office."

"At this hour?" Emma's disapproval needed no further definition.

"It's just after seven, hardly fully dark. I just want to see if there's been any news."

"And what if Cody isn't there? Maybe he's out on his rounds or following a lead."

Lily shrugged. "Then I'll come back."

Emma tightened her shawl and stood. "I'm going with you."

"That's hardly necessary."

"Lily, someone attacked Jake and murdered him. Judging by the shape he was in when he stumbled into the yard, this all happened close by. Perhaps in the plaza. You are not walking anywhere alone after dark."

Lily felt a twitch of a smile. "Very well. Come on, Mother Hen. I'm sure Sheriff Daniels will be delighted to see the two of us."

They linked arms and started across the plaza, tightening their grip as they realized how deserted the expanse of land was and how quickly the shadows deepened. They focused on the light burning in the front window of the jail and the silhouette of Cody pacing back and forth inside.

When they reached the boardwalk in front of the office, Emma breathed a sigh of relief and knocked on the door. "Sheriff Daniels?" she called. "It's Emma Elliott and Lily."

The door swung open, and Cody stood there, studying them. "Has something happened? Something else?"

Lily brushed past him. "Not at all. We just wanted to make you aware of the plans for Jake's funeral and see what progress you might have made in finding his killer—or killers."

Cody stepped aside to allow Emma to enter before pulling two chairs together. "Have a seat," he offered as he returned to his side of the desk, sending a strong message about who exactly would be in charge of this meeting.

Lily was undaunted. "The funeral is scheduled for this Sunday. Both the service and Jake's burial will take place in the town cemetery on the hill behind the hotel at sunrise. It was Jake's favorite time of day. He always said a new day meant a new chance to get things right. He was such a decent man." She folded her hands in her lap and looked at Cody expectantly.

"That sounds real nice," he said. He met her gaze, clearly determined to wait her out.

Emma coughed and cleared her throat. "Well, we should get back—"

"Not before we hear what the sheriff has to report," Lily said sweetly, never once wavering as she continued to stare straight at Cody. She felt a twinge of victory when he blinked but then noticed how thick and long his lashes were, which distracted her from her mission. She felt warmth rise in her cheeks.

Cody leaned back in his chair, folding his hands behind his head. "This is an investigation, ladies. The details aren't something I can share with others. You can rest assured that I am doing everything I can to—"

Lily thought about the way he'd been pacing his office as they approached. "You have no idea who did this to Jake, do you?"

He bristled. "I have some thoughts," he muttered defensively.

"Will you be able to attend the services for Jake, Sheriff?" Emma asked, clearly anxious to break the tension that filled the room.

"I'll be there." He stood, dismissing them. "Now, if you ladies don't mind, I'd like to see you back to the hotel and then get back to work."

"Thank you," Emma said at the same time as Lily announced, "We hardly need an escort."

Cody removed his hat from a hook and put it on. Then he opened the door and waited for them to exit, closing it before offering each his arm. "Lovely evening," he said. "Nothing like spring and early summer in the desert."

To Lily's relief, Emma kept up a running monologue about that year's spring with the desert in full bloom. "It was quite spectacular."

"It was indeed," Cody agreed, his upper arm touching Lily's shoulder as they walked. She supposed his other arm was also touching Emma but doubted Emma was having the same reaction—the desire for more contact.

Jake's murder was important to Cody on several levels. In the first place, he took a good deal of pride in Juniper being a place where people felt safe to go about their business. In the second, he'd never had a situation with fewer clues. And in the third, he had to admit, he wanted to impress Lily. For reasons he was not about to take time to analyze, he hoped to change her skeptical scowl into an admiring smile.

Only all he was getting was frustration. The truth was he'd questioned people in town, asking if they had noticed any strangers hanging around the day Jake was attacked. No one had. His only real lead was that half-moon boot print in the dirt outside the hotel the first night Lily had come to him. Meanwhile, Victor Johnson stayed on at the hotel, spent his evenings in the saloon, and gave no clue as to why he was in Juniper. Thanks to Jake's death, Cody hadn't gotten to Santa Fe.

Maybe after the funeral.

Maybe Lily would agree to go with him.

*Maybe elephants would fly.*

Cody thought about the walk back to the hotel the previous evening. Emma had willingly tucked her hand in the crook of his elbow, but Lily had hesitated and then rested only the tips of her fingers on his arm, as if anything more might soil her. But as they walked, he caught the fragrance of the soap she used. It had taken him most of the night to identify that scent, and finally, he'd realized—lilies of the valley.

*Lily*. The connection made him smile every time he thought of it.

His mother used soap like that. His had been a happy childhood on the whole, happy times with his parents and siblings. There had been hard times as well—dark days they'd had to weather when his father's store burned and through the rebuilding. Thinking about those hard times brought his thoughts back around to Lily. She struck him as someone who had suffered her fair share of sadness and hardship. What part had Victor Johnson played in that history? She'd admitted knowing him but said nothing more.

On Saturday, he got his hair trimmed, as much for the barber shop gossip and the chance of a new lead as needing to show respect when he attended Jake's funeral. As dawn broke on Sunday, he dressed in black pants, a cream-colored collarless shirt, and his brown leather vest with the badge pinned to its front. Folks in town were nervous, and it would ease their minds to see their sheriff at the service. That, and he hoped to see something out of the ordinary. Maybe someone unexpected.

He was fairly sure that whoever had beaten Jake that day had not meant to kill him. They might have started out trying to send him a message and gone beyond what they'd intended. Jake had something they wanted, that much was clear. Information, perhaps.

And since he was dead, they hadn't gotten what they'd come for. They might think he'd passed it on to someone in the town. Or maybe they imagined they were being tricked—that Jake wasn't really dead but had been spirited away for his own safety.

Either way, it was entirely possible the killers might mix in with other mourners at the funeral.

Cody climbed the hill behind the hotel to the small cemetery. The space was surrounded by a low wrought iron fence and already half filled with markers of citizens of Juniper who had passed on. The Harvey Girls formed a circle around the open grave, solemn in their black uniform dresses, while the men from Jake's kitchen staff, led by Aidan Campbell, slowly carried the pine coffin from the hotel to its final resting place. The priest took his place at the head of the grave and began the service, intoning the prayers and scriptures.

Scanning the group, Cody saw Nick Hopkins among the other mourners, alongside Nick's employers, Rita and John Lombard. There were Doc Waters and his wife standing next to Frank Tucker and Abigail Chambers. Other business owners and townspeople who had counted Jake a friend, including Ellie Swift, formed a half circle behind the priest. A little apart from the others stood Sally Barnett, along with her bartender and her girls, all dressed as sedately as their wardrobes might allow. Their faces were devoid of rouge and powder, and Cody realized with a start how young some of them were.

But it was the presence of Victor Johnson that gave Cody pause. Why would he come to the funeral of a man he'd never met? Jake worked in the kitchen, so even with Johnson staying at the hotel, it was unlikely the two men had had any reason to interact. Of course, they had both been in the Sagebrush that night. Jake had been nervous, more nervous than Cody had ever seen him before, but all he'd seemed to care about was making sure that Lily stayed away. The gears of Cody's mind clicked into place. Maybe Johnson had come to the service because of Lily.

Cody watched as the coffin was lowered into the ground and the men began filling the grave. Every head bowed while the priest prayed aloud—except Victor Johnson's. Following the man's gaze, Cody saw that Johnson was not staring at Lily but at the grave.

When the mourners began slowly filing back down the hill to town, Johnson approached Abigail Chambers. They exchanged a few words before he took hold of her elbow to guide her over the rough ground. He leaned in to hear whatever she might be saying, and once he had seen her to the well-worn path that led back to town, he tipped his hat and watched her continue on her way in the company of other townspeople.

The man's gallantry surprised Cody—and raised his suspicions. What possible interest could Victor Johnson have in Miss Chambers? Certainly not enough to single her out from the throng of those gathered to bid Jake a final farewell. Cody watched as Johnson turned his attention back to the grave—and Lily—ready to intercede should he try and approach her. But after a moment's pause, Johnson left, following the others back to town.

Cody walked over to where the man had stood. He glanced at the loose soil and saw what he'd been looking for—a heel print with a clear half-moon. He followed the prints for a short distance until they blended with prints left by others. They fit the path Johnson was taking back to the hotel. He had nothing more than this to go on—the boot print could have been someone else's—but his gut told him otherwise. Johnson was definitely mixed up in recent events, possibly including Jake's death.

*Past time I get to Santa Fe and talk to Sheriff Drake,* he thought. *Past time I find out exactly what Lily knows about Victor Johnson.*

He turned back to Jake's coworkers, still gathered around the grave. The Harvey Girls were covering the mounded dirt with branches of juniper as Aidan hammered a wooden cross into the ground at the head. Cody positioned himself on the path he was sure Lily and the other girls would take back to the hotel, but as they passed, he realized Lily was not with them.

He glanced back and saw her kneeling next to Jake's grave, carefully rearranging the evergreen branches to be sure they fully covered his final resting place. Cody waited, respecting her need to have this final private goodbye. By the time she turned to go, everyone else was well away. A westerly wind stirred the remains of the fine sandy dirt the men had used to fill the grave and pressed the skirt of Lily's uniform against her legs. She pushed back a tendril of hair that had escaped its bonds, gathered her skirt, and started down the hill, glancing briefly at Cody and nodding as she continued on her way.

As he fell into step beside her, Cody was surprised to see that she was dry-eyed. In place of the grief and distress he had expected, he saw resolution and determination in the way her jaw jutted forward. Her full lips were pressed into a thin line, and her eyes glinted with something he recognized—the need for revenge.

"Lily, I..."

She stopped so suddenly, Cody had moved two steps ahead of her by the time he realized she wasn't still beside him. He turned and squinted back at her, the rising sun temporarily blinding him.

"The next time you speak to me, Sheriff Daniels, it had best be to tell me you have an idea who did this." Her fists were clenched, but her lower lip quivered.

"Okay," he said. "I have an idea who did this." He waited for expressions of first disbelief and then doubt to play out over her face. "What I need is proof. Come with me to Santa Fe, and maybe we can find out more."

She blinked. "Santa Fe? What could that possibly have to do with any of this?"

Cody took hold of her hand. The action was instinctive, but the truth was he felt he needed to touch her in order to convince her. Although he wanted badly to cup her face in his palms, taking her hand seemed wiser. "I can't say yet, Lily, but the sheriff there may have some information. If I'm right, it may be enough to catch Jake's killer. That's what you want, isn't it?"

She nodded. "That's what everyone wants," she murmured. "Why me? What can I do in Santa Fe? I mean, surely I would be better off here, going through Jake's room and belongings."

"I've done all that. Come with me. I'll explain along the way. But first, I want you to look at something." Without releasing her hand, he led the way over to the tracks—Victor's tracks. "Do you recognize this unusual heel print?"

Lily looked at him as if he'd lost his mind. "Of

course not. Why would I know one boot print from the next?"

"Look closer." He tugged on her hand until she reluctantly bent for a closer examination. "See that?" He traced the half-moon with his forefinger. "It's on the left boot but not the right."

"So some local cowboy decided to brand his boots. What of it?"

"That night you saw Jake in the yard with the two men?"

She waited.

"One of those men left this exact print."

Her fist went to her mouth, possibly to stop herself from crying out. "You're telling me the killer was here today?"

Cody got to his feet, dusted off his hands, and then helped her stand as well. "Come to Santa Fe, Lily. You've got the rest of the day free, and I promise to have you back before your curfew."

"Tell me who this print belongs to first," she bargained.

Afraid of what she would do if he told her, Cody shook his head. "On the way to Santa Fe," he countered.

She scowled at him. "I have to change," she grumbled and started down the hill.

The church bell chimed, calling worshipers to service. "We can go as soon as you get back from church," he said. There was no crossing Bonnie Kaufmann, and she required church attendance for all the girls.

"We'll go now—as soon as I get changed," she shouted over her shoulder as she picked up her pace.

"You get the buggy and meet me behind the hotel in twenty minutes. I'll bring food from the kitchen."

Cody couldn't help himself. He chuckled as he watched her go.

To Lily's relief, Emma had left with the others for church by the time she reached their room. She scribbled a note telling her friend she was going to Santa Fe with Cody. *Possible break in the case,* she added before signing her name. Emma would cover for her, and everyone else would simply think she was too grief-stricken after the funeral to join the others for church or lunch or any other activity the day might bring.

She took off her uniform and laid it on her bed. She would brush the dust from it later while she told Emma what she and Cody had learned. She dressed in the navy wool skirt and matching blue plaid jacket she'd bought from Tucker's Mercantile with the tips she'd been saving. She unfurled her hair from the Harvey Girl chignon, brushed out the tangles, and used a clip to hold it in place at the nape of her neck. There was something so powerful about feeling the weight of her unleashed locks cascading down her back. Grabbing a shawl and a wide-brimmed felt hat, she hurried down the back stairs.

Cody was already waiting.

"Let me just pack us a lunch," she said.

"No need. We'll eat at the hotel there while we talk to my friend."

*La Casita*. She'd always wanted to see that place. "It's Sunday," she reminded him.

Cody shrugged. "Not every Harvey establishment shuts down on Sundays. And even if it's closed, there's bound to be some place we can eat."

Ignoring his logic—his typical *male* logic—Lily grabbed half a dozen poppy seed muffins, four oranges, and four cooked lamb chops from the refrigerator and stuffed them into one of the canvas sacks the staff kept by the kitchen door for leftovers. She added two cloth napkins and hurried outside. She had to admit it felt good to be doing something that might lead to justice for Jake.

Cody relieved her of the bag, hefting it to test the weight. "I said we'd eat," he said.

"Snacks," Lily replied as she hurried around to her side of the buggy and climbed aboard without waiting for his assistance. For some reason, she was determined to avoid having Cody Daniels touch her, even to be a gentleman and help her climb onto the seat. Under the circumstances, it felt as if she was somehow being disloyal to Jake. "Let's go."

He climbed up to take the reins, setting the sack under the seat before releasing the brake and clucking his tongue to the team. He was still wearing the clothes he'd worn to the funeral, but Lily had noticed the addition of a blanket and the heavier jacket he sometimes wore at night in the back of the wagon.

She waited for him to negotiate the relatively deserted main street that took them out of town, up into the foothills, and on across the prairie. Once they reached open country, she exhaled a long breath and said, "So, who killed Jake?"

She was not going to allow him to evade her questions for one more minute. She faced him. "Well?"

He stared straight ahead, his jaw set, his fingers tightening on the reins. "I don't have proof, so—"

"But you have your suspicions, so who is it?" She fully expected him to say it was some stranger Jake had somehow gotten mixed up with, perhaps someone he owed money to.

He glanced at her. "Victor Johnson."

"No. I mean…Victor?" She thought of Victor's obsession with cleanliness, his manicured nails, his perfectly tailored clothes. The idea of Victor engaging in fisticuffs was ludicrous.

"Victor and Jake didn't know each other," she pointed out.

"That boot print I showed you earlier? Victor was the man who left the prints we saw at the cemetery, and I'd bet my job he was one of the two men you saw in the yard that night."

Lily felt a chill spreading through her chest. Her mind raced. The night she'd seen Jake with the two men, she hadn't yet known Victor was in town. But now that she thought about it, yes, one of the two could have been Victor. Had Victor known she was there in Juniper all along? Had his claim that it was all just coincidence been a ruse? Had he been trying to use Jake to get to her? Victor was clever and observant— he'd have noticed Jake's affection for Lily right away.

"Well?" Cody kept his eyes on the trail, but his tone told her it was his turn to be impatient for information. "I need to know everything you know about Victor Johnson, Lily."

"Why would you think I know anything?"

"Don't go back to pretending the two of you don't know each other. A man is dead," he snapped.

"And that's my fault?" Lily was afraid she already knew the answer to that question. If Victor was involved and he'd tried to use Jake to get to her, then she had blood on her hands.

"I never said that." His tone softened, and his shoulders and hands relaxed. "Look, Lily, if this guy is causing you trouble, don't you want that to end?"

His obvious concern was her undoing. She stared straight ahead. "We're married," she finally whispered, picking at a loose thread on her sleeve.

If she had expected an explosive reaction, Cody surprised her. He continued to stare ahead, nodded, and said, "I see."

"I doubt you do," she replied. "I doubt anyone could understand why." She wrapped her arms around her body as if in need of a place to hide. "I'm not sure I understand it myself."

Without a word, Cody turned the buggy off the trail and headed cross-country toward a cluster of trees. Lily recognized it as a place she, Jake, and some friends had picnicked once. "Why are you stopping?"

He shrugged. "Thought we might enjoy that food you brought. I missed lunch. So did you." After setting the brake and jumping down, he came around to her side. He held out his arms to her, offering to help her down. "Coming?"

Lily placed her hands on his broad, sturdy shoulders, his hands practically circling her waist. When they were both standing steady on the ground, he immediately stepped away to retrieve the sack of food before offering her his arm. He led her over the uneven ground to the rocks near the creek. There, he unpacked the food and spread it out on a flat rock. Not once did he look directly at her.

"I suppose you have questions," she ventured, breaking a small piece off a muffin.

"It's your story to tell or not, Lily. All I ask is that you tell me anything you know about…your husband that might either clear him or help me." He sounded tired or—dare she hope—disappointed?

She continued to pick at the muffin while he consumed two cold lamb chops plus a muffin. He peeled an orange into six pieces, leaving the fruit on a napkin between them.

"I left home just after I turned sixteen," she said. It seemed the place to start.

"Why'd you leave?"

"My stepfather liked rules, and I didn't. We didn't get along." She decided not to mention that her stepfather had also liked *her*—and not in a fatherly way.

"So he put you out?"

"I ran away. I had a little money put aside, money he'd given me thinking it was for a new outfit for church. He was very religious."

Cody handed her a tin cup of water he poured from a canteen. Her hand shook as she accepted it. "Where did you go?"

"I bought a train ticket—one way—and ended up in Kansas City. With the money I'd saved and earned working at a department store in Chicago before I left, I had enough to rent a room in a boardinghouse for a week, but I needed a job. Fortunately, I'm pretty good at meeting people and talking my way into things."

Cody smiled. "Yeah, I know." He sucked the juice from a section of orange. "Go on. You got to Kansas City, then what?"

"I got hired on cleaning rooms at a hotel—not a Harvey establishment. That's where I met Victor. He was so sophisticated and charming. He dressed so nice, and at first, he seemed to genuinely care about me. I could talk to him. Or I thought I could."

"At first?" He continued to eat the orange. A drop of juice lingered on his lower lip, and Lily fought the temptation to touch her finger to it. "How did that change?" he asked.

Lily forced her mind back to the past. Reliving the memories let her see things she'd been too desperate—or perhaps too young—to notice then. "He kept pushing me. A kiss on the cheek became a kiss on the mouth. Holding hands became touching me in places I'd never been touched. And he wanted more—always more."

"So you married him."

"I told him I could not do what he was asking of me. I was saving myself for marriage. I never thought he would take that so literally. Actually, once I said that, I thought I would never see him again."

"But instead, he asked you to marry him." Cody rinsed his hands in the creek and dried them on his trousers.

"No. He never asked." It was the first time Lily had recognized this. Oh, how stupid she had been! "One night, he called for me, and instead of taking me to dinner as was usual for us, he took me to an office. There was a man there he called 'Judge,' although we weren't introduced. Before I knew what was happening, the man was having us repeat the wedding vows, Victor slid a gold ring onto my finger, and the judge pronounced us man and wife."

She stopped, unable to go on, embarrassed to tell him what happened next. To her relief, Cody did not press her.

"When did he leave you?" he asked.

"The next day," she said softly. "Actually, it was some time during the night. I was asleep."

Cody sucked in his breath, and she noticed how his fingers curled into fists. "He left no word?"

"Only a note saying he had business back east—where he was from—and he would be in touch." How little she knew of Victor even now.

"Where in the east?"

Lily shrugged. She felt stupid. She, who had always been so confident and sure of herself, felt embarrassed by what she had failed to ask. She'd married Victor knowing nothing about him. The first tear hit the back of her hand. The second followed and then a third and then a steady rainfall.

Cody wrapped his arm around her and guided her head to rest on his shoulder. "Okay," he said. "No more questions." He smoothed her hair away from her face, caught her tears, and brushed them away with his thumb.

She relaxed against him, soaking up his strength. They stayed like that for a long moment.

"Lily?"

She sat up. "I'm fine." Her admission that she and

Victor were married had destroyed any chance there might ever be more than friendship between Cody and her. "We should get going. Your friend will wonder what happened to us." She busied herself packing up the leftover food, her back to him so he could not see how humiliated she was.

He placed his hands on her shoulders and turned her so they were face-to-face, only inches apart. "Want to know what I think?" he asked. "What I hope?"

She nodded.

"I think Johnson tricked you. I think that so-called judge was just a friend of his playing the part. I think Victor is a man very accustomed to having what he wants, when he wants it. He wanted you, and he did what was necessary in order to have you."

It all sounded reasonable. "And what do you hope?"

He ran his finger along her cheek. "I hope I'm right, because I've never met a woman like you, Lily. And I want to know I'm free to get to know you a whole lot better."

"Me too," she admitted, lost in his gold-flecked eyes. He looked at her as if trying to make a choice, and she realized her hope was that he would decide in favor of kissing her.

He let out an audible breath and stepped away. "Let's go," he said, his voice husky. He took the sack of leftovers from her, then cupped her elbow as they walked back to the wagon.

# Chapter 6

CODY FILLED THE TIME IT TOOK TO COVER THE REST
of the distance to Santa Fe pointing out the beauties
of the desert, a soaring eagle, and plants in full bloom.
He wasn't usually so talkative, but standing so near to
Lily at the creek, wanting more than anything to kiss
her, had unnerved him. He had a murder to solve, and
he couldn't ignore the possibility that a gang might be
looking to rob the hotel. What he didn't know yet was
whether the two events were connected.

Beside him, Lily sat quietly. He'd never known her
to be so passive. As they reached the outskirts of town,
he placed his hand on hers. "We're going to find out
who did this to Jake."

She nodded.

"And if you'll allow it, I'd like to look into the
circumstances of your marriage to Victor." To his
surprise, she smiled. "What?" he asked.

"Emma suggested I confide in you. Of course I
refused. I was just thinking how she'll react when she
learns I did exactly that."

"And how will she react?"

"Oh, she'll try real hard not to smile and say 'I told you so.' Of course, she'll fail miserably, but we'll both have a good laugh about it." She turned toward him. "Do you think you can learn anything? I mean, it's been three years."

The way she was looking at him, Cody would have walked through fire if she'd asked him to do so. No wonder Jake had been willing to do whatever she wanted—even give her up. Lily Travis was a woman no man in his right mind could ever refuse—unless, of course, that man had political ambitions. "I'll do my best," he murmured and turned his attention to navigating the narrow side streets on the way to the impressive La Casita Hotel.

Sheriff Ty Drake stood at the entrance, tipped his fingers to his hat when he saw Cody, and crossed the street to meet them with his eyes on Lily. Cody jumped down and shook hands with his fellow lawman, noting the way Drake kept glancing over her way. "Sheriff Ty Drake, this is Miss Lily Travis. She may have a connection to what we need to discuss."

"Howdy, miss," Drake said, helping her down from the buggy. "Ever been to Santa Fe before?"

"No, sir." Cody saw her eyes widen at the sight of the hotel. "I've heard about La Casita, of course. Everyone who works for Mr. Harvey in this part of the country has. It's quite…" Words failed her.

"Let me show you the inside." Drake offered his arm, and Lily grinned up at him as she took hold, gathering her skirt with her other hand.

Pure, unadulterated jealousy rushed through Cody's veins as he followed them inside. Drake had a reputation among his fellow lawmen as something of a ladies' man, and the way he paraded Lily through the doors and into the impressive lobby made Cody's blood boil. He hurried forward.

"We've had a long trip. Maybe Miss Travis would like to freshen up a bit," Cody suggested.

Drake's attention remained on Lily. "Now where are my manners? Ladies' room is right there." He pointed to a hallway off the main lobby.

"I won't be long," Lily promised and hurried away.

When Drake tore his gaze away from her, he was grinning. "You devil," he said, punching Cody on the arm. "How did you manage to land that?"

"*That* is a lady, a respectable one at that."

"Oh, don't go all self-righteous on me, Daniels. None of my business what you've got going on the side. Have to admit I never used the excuse of being part of a case to keep a woman around."

Explanation and debate were obviously useless. "Is there somewhere quiet the three of us can talk? Miss Travis is a Harvey Girl and has a curfew we need to respect."

"Sure." Drake led the way to a small table near a window, well away from the hustle and bustle of guests coming and going. He indicated a seat for Cody, then pulled over a third chair for Lily. "Ah, here she is," he said, a broad grin spreading across his face as he went to meet her.

Cody stood. Lily had washed the dust of the trip from her face and done something to repair the damage the wind had done to her hair. And once again, she had taken Drake's arm and was laughing at something he said. Cody pulled her chair out and waited for her to be seated. As soon as the three of them were settled, a Harvey Girl appeared to take their order, but Cody noted Lily made no effort to share the fact that she, too, worked for Fred Harvey. Instead, she studied the menu offered for afternoon tea, and it dawned on him that for once, she was playing the role of the one to be served rather than the server.

"My treat," Drake boomed. "Whatever strikes your fancy, Miss Travis."

She smiled at him, but Cody realized this was that Harvey Girl smile—the one that didn't quite reach her eyes. It dawned on him that she didn't especially care for Drake. His heart filled with joy, and for the first time since arriving, he relaxed.

"How about a pot of tea and a plate of assorted sandwiches and cakes?" he suggested.

"That would be lovely," Lily said, and the smile she gave Cody made her eyes sparkle.

"Coffee for me—black," Cody said and then looked at Drake, one eyebrow cocked.

"Yeah, coffee," the other man said. "Cream and sugar."

They talked of mundane things until they were served, and then Cody got straight to business. "Tell me what you know about Victor Johnson."

Drake took his time adding three sugars and an ample amount of cream to his coffee. "He was in town about a week and caught my attention right away. I guess it was the fancy clothes and no sign of having spent any time doing regular work."

Cody understood by "regular work" Drake meant

manual labor. "You said the hotel here was robbed. Do you suspect Johnson of being party to that?"

"Just a hunch. Haven't been able to prove anything. But there was something about him. He looked like he never sees the sun."

"How did he spend his time here?"

"That's just it. Days, he would be out and about in town, stopping in at the shops, flashing a wad of money. Nights, he was either in the saloon across the plaza or stepping out with one of the girls here. He made no attempt to keep a low profile."

Lily gasped. "A Harvey Girl?"

"That's right. Seemed partial to one in particular. Word has it she got so tangled up with him, she quit her job."

"And when he left town?"

"He left alone. Not sure what happened to the girl. I tried to find her after the robbery, to see what she knew about Johnson. The Native couple that runs the trading post just outside town said a girl matching her description stopped there one day looking for work. They didn't have anything for her, and last anybody saw of her was at the train station."

"Did she have a roommate?" Lily asked.

Drake rubbed his hand over his chin. "Not sure what difference that would make, Miss. I mean…"

"We girls confide in each other," Lily continued. "She might have told her roommate—or one of the other girls—something that could help."

Cody could see Drake was impressed. For his part, he was bursting with admiration. Lily was not just beautiful, she was smart.

Their waitress returned with fresh pots of tea and coffee, and Lily wasted no time introducing herself. "I'm Lily Travis," she announced. "I work for the Palace Hotel in Juniper."

"Connie Evans," the waitress replied with a grin. "Welcome to La Casita."

"I've got a little bit of time in town today. I don't suppose you could arrange for me to maybe tour the kitchen and meet some of the other girls?" Lily ventured.

Both Cody and Drake sat slack-jawed at her brazenness.

"Sure. Things are slow today. Let me just check with our head waitress, but I'm sure there will be no problem." She hurried away.

Lily popped a tiny cake into her mouth. "And that, gentlemen," she said as she licked a dab of frosting from her lips, "is the Harvey Way." She was clearly quite pleased with herself.

Drake scowled at her. "Young lady, I don't think you should insert yourself into matters that don't really concern you." Suddenly, all hint of charm was gone. It was evident Ty Drake didn't like someone else being in charge, even for a minute.

"Actually," Cody said slowly, "I'd like to talk to you some more about the robbery, Ty. I suspect there are things you've learned that might best not be shared with…civilians just now." He nodded toward Lily.

Across the room, their waitress stood chatting with an older woman. After a moment, she beckoned Lily to join them. "I won't be long, gentlemen," Lily said as she touched her napkin to the corners of her mouth and then hurried away.

Cody turned his attention back to Drake. "What are the chances the gang that hit the hotel here are casing the Palace Hotel for another hit?"

Drake drained his coffee and reached for the pot. "Pretty good, I'd say. Trouble is I don't know how you might stop them."

"Assuming Victor Johnson is involved, any chance he tried to use people from the hotel staff to set things up?" Cody was thinking of Jake and the meeting in the yard. Had Victor been trying to use Jake for the same thing?

"Maybe. Are you thinking this was an inside job? That girl he was courting?"

Cody shrugged. "I've spoken to the manager of the Palace. From what he told me, it looks like anyone trying to get to the payroll and valuables would have to have inside information—schedules of money coming in and going out, location of the safe, that sort of thing."

Drake nodded. "Makes sense."

"And there's one more piece to this," Cody said, lowering his voice as he leaned in closer. "Things might have gone from robbery to murder."

Once she'd been introduced, Lily followed Connie and the head waitress, Miss Spencer, into the kitchen. It was larger than the one at the Palace, but any difference ended there. The place ran like a perfectly timed Swiss clock—cooks and chefs turning out orders and Harvey Girls delivering them exactly as the process worked in Juniper.

Miss Spencer continued the tour of the common spaces after Connie went back to work. "How is Bonnie Kaufmann?" she asked.

"You know Miss K?"

Miss Spencer laughed. "We went through training together. It seems a long time ago now. Please give her my best."

"I will." Lily was trying to think how to broach the subject of the unnamed waitress who had gotten involved with Victor when Miss Spencer gave her the opening she needed.

"We have an opening for an experienced waitress, Lily, if you know of anyone interested in making a change," she said.

"You're shorthanded?"

Miss Spencer sighed and indicated for Lily to join her sitting on a settee at the base of the hotel's stairway. "Yes, quite suddenly," she admitted. "Molly was one of our best. While the other girls are good, Molly is exceptional. At least she was until she started stepping out with that man." This last was said almost as an aside, and when she realized she'd spoken aloud, she looked slightly alarmed. "Of course, that's not information you need to share."

"Of course not." Lily searched her mind for a roundabout way to lead in to her question and then decided there was no time for beating about the bush. "Was that man named Victor Johnson by any chance?"

Miss Spencer bristled. "How would you know of Mr. Johnson?"

As briefly as possible, Lily told Miss Spencer what she knew of Victor, skipping the whole marriage part but including the fact that he had appeared in Juniper and was harassing her there. She also did not include Cody's suspicions that Victor was somehow connected to the hotel robbery. "So you see, he tricked me the same way he did Molly. He uses false promises to have his way with girls and then leaves. He really must be stopped before someone gets hurt."

"How can I be of help?"

"Let's start with Molly's last name and anything you can tell me about where she might have gone."

"Stone—Molly Stone. The day Mr. Johnson left, she saw him off at the station, then returned and quit on the spot. She told me he was travelling on business but would return within the week, and they were to be married and move back east. She packed up her things and moved out of the dormitory that very day, taking a room with Mrs. Harris—a widow who runs a boardinghouse in town."

"But he never returned."

"No. She waited for days. The other girls would see her on the plaza or in the shops. Connie was her roommate in the dormitory and told me Molly spent a good deal of money those first couple of days, buying her trousseau. But as time passed with no word from him, it became pretty clear what had happened. Her savings were gone, and so was he. I offered her the chance to come back here, but she was too mortified. I know Connie gave her money from her tips, but one day, Molly just packed up and left."

Lily's heart broke for Molly, and her rage caught fire. How many other girls had Victor done this to? "Do you know where her family is?"

Miss Spencer shook her head. "Molly grew up in an orphanage in St. Louis. As far as I know, she has no family."

"Men like that should be shot," Lily muttered.

"I couldn't agree more, my dear. Now, back to business. What are the chances I might steal you away from the Palace?"

For a brief moment, Lily was tempted to consider the offer. If she worked in Santa Fe, she wouldn't have to deal with Victor. On the other hand, she would also be leaving Emma and her other friends—and Cody. She smiled and shook her head. "Thank you. I'm flattered you would consider me, but I'm happy where I am."

"That doesn't surprise me, knowing Bonnie Kaufmann. She's strict but fair, and she does take good care of her girls." Miss Spencer extended her hand. "It's been a pleasure, Lily. Please give Bonnie my best."

"I'll do that. Thanks for the tour."

The two women parted company, Miss Spencer on her way to the kitchen and Lily back to the table where she'd left Cody and Sheriff Drake. As soon as they noticed her approach, both men stood.

"We should be getting back," Cody said.

"Of course." Lily turned to Sheriff Drake. "It was a pleasure meeting you."

"Pleasure was all mine, Miss Travis." He walked with them to their buggy, where the two men shook hands. "I'll wire you if I get any information," Drake said. "In the meantime, as long as Johnson's around, I'd watch my back." He stood on the boardwalk outside the hotel, watching them as Cody drove down the street and out of town.

"Well?" Lily had held her tongue as long as possible, expecting Cody to start filling her in on what he'd learned from the other lawman.

He glanced her way, then back at the road ahead. "Nothing that will help solve Jake's murder."

She felt deflated, like a balloon someone had punctured. She'd had such hopes.

"How was your tour?"

"Fine…nice. Miss Spencer offered me a job."

He was quiet for a moment. "Might be a good step up," he ventured. "Bigger hotel in a larger town?"

It was the last thing she wanted to hear from him. She wanted him to say he'd miss her if she left. She wanted him to say anything that might indicate he cared.

"I have a job," she said through tight lips.

"Is it enough?"

She shot him a look. "Is being sheriff in Juniper enough for you?" She meant it to come out as sarcastic, but when he didn't laugh, she wondered. Could he be the one to leave?

"It's not forever," he said.

"A stepping stone?"

His mouth twitched. "Yeah, something like that. I'm trying to build toward something different for the future. The work I do right now can be dangerous, and one day, I hope to have a family, so…" He shrugged.

"A future doing what?"

"Don't laugh, but I've been thinking of going into politics. The territory is headed for statehood one of these days. I'd like to be part of shaping that."

Lily was speechless. She'd never met a man with such big dreams. It spoke well of his confidence, his conviction he was up to the challenge. Once upon a time, she'd had big dreams for her life as well: a shop of her own, where she designed clothes and dressed the society women of Chicago for the many charity events she'd read about as a kid.

*Whatever happened to that girl?*

"Uh-oh," Cody muttered.

"What is it?"

He jerked his head toward the mountains. "Storm coming. We need to find shelter." He spurred the horse to greater speed with a snap of the reins.

"The sky is blue except for that—" Lily turned toward the mountains and saw that the sky had darkened to a deep charcoal gray. A distant rumble of thunder confirmed Cody's suspicions.

"Hang on," Cody shouted. He turned the buggy off the road and started overland toward the base of an arroyo, where large boulders pocked the land. When they reached it, he leapt from the buggy and unhitched the horse. "Grab my jacket and that blanket from the back there and come on," he called as he led the horse away.

The wind clawed at Lily's hair and skirt as she climbed down, grabbed the blanket and his jacket, and ran to catch up.

"In there." He pointed to an opening in the hillside just as the first flash of lightning split the dark sky. A torrent of water followed immediately, pouring down on them.

Lily scampered into the shelter, a shallow hollow that didn't entirely protect her from the rain as it gushed down over the rocks above the opening.

Clutching the blanket, she tried to see Cody but only heard the panicked cries of the horse. "Cody!" she shouted, getting no reply. She was about to go in search of him when suddenly, he was there.

He filled the opening, water dripping off the brim of his hat, his soaked shirt outlining the muscles of his arms and chest, and a huge grin lighting his handsome face. "Wow!" he declared with pure joy, ducking inside and crowding next to her. He put his arm around her shoulders. "Did you ever see such a storm?"

His boyish excitement was contagious, and Lily laughed. "You love this," she shouted above the noise of the pounding rain.

"Yes, ma'am. Nature at her best—nothing like it." He grinned down at her, and then his expression sobered. He fingered a lank wet curl that had plastered itself to her skin, then spread his fingers to cup her cheek.

*Kiss me*, she thought and closed her eyes as she leaned into the cool wetness of his hand caressing her face.

Never in his life had Cody wanted a woman more than he wanted Lily Travis. If he gave in to that desire, he was pretty sure there would be no going back—not for him. *One kiss*, he thought, at the same time knowing it would never be enough.

*Besides, she's married—or might be.*

Everything he knew about men like Victor Johnson told him the marriage had been a sham, a trick to get Lily in bed. But he had no real proof. And until he did, a married woman was off-limits.

He cleared his throat, tucked the curl of her hair behind her ear, and took half a step away. Her eyes flew open, and she looked up at him with confusion and disappointment, and he took the blanket from her and wrapped it around her shoulders. "Can't have you getting a chill," he murmured.

True to form, she jerked away from him. If he'd learned one thing about Lily, it was that she was a proud woman. She'd enjoyed that kiss as much as he had, and now she was embarrassed. He gently but firmly took hold of her by the shoulders and forced her to look at him.

"Look, Lily, I wanted that kiss. I still want it. I'll go to sleep tonight and wake up tomorrow wanting it."

Her gaze collided with his, green eyes flashing like the lightning outside. She placed her hands on his face and stood on tiptoe as she drew him closer. Just before their lips met, she whispered, "Then let me put us both out of our misery."

Her mouth was soft, pliable, and so damned inviting. It was all Cody could do not to wrap his arms around her and deepen the connection, probe her lips with his tongue, test her willingness to take the next step. But as soon as it started, the kiss was over. Her hands dropped to retrieve the fallen blanket, and she turned away, brushing sand and grit from a flat rock and sitting on it.

Cody leaned an arm against the wall of the opening, his back to her as he watched the storm pass. Once the downpour softened to a drizzle, he cast about for what he might say or do next. "There's probably a rainbow," he muttered.

No answer.

He let out a long, frustrated breath. "I'll go corral the horse and get him hitched up," he said, resisting the urge to tell her to stay put. It was Lily, and she was stubborn enough not to do it just because he'd told her to.

He stalked off, rounded up the horse, and led the still skittish animal back to where he'd left the buggy. Once he'd finished calming and hitching the horse, he took off his sodden vest and laid it over the side of the wagon, then pulled his shirt over his head and wrung out the excess water. As he was about to put it on, he glanced toward the rocks and saw Lily watching him, and when their eyes met, she looked down. He pulled his shirt on and walked back to where she stood.

"You can look at me now," he said.

She glanced at him from beneath lowered lashes. "We should go," she said and marched past him toward the buggy.

He chuckled. Given the high color in her cheeks, the tight set of her lips, and the way she held the folded blanket protectively over her chest, he was pretty sure Lily had seen something she liked.

# Chapter 7

"How was it?"

Lily had barely reached her room when Emma asked the question.

"La Casita? It's gorgeous, but so much larger than the Palace, I'm not sure—"

"You know I'm not asking about La Casita," Emma interrupted. "How was your day with Cody?"

Lily shrugged. "Disappointing. We didn't learn anything that will lead to Jake's killer." She started changing out of her still-damp clothes.

Emma sniffed the air. "Did you get wet?"

"We got caught by a sudden storm."

"How romantic?" Emma lifted an eyebrow, questioning her guess.

Lily took a deep breath. She had to talk to someone or she would surely burst with the feelings she seemed incapable of sorting out on her own. She flopped onto her bed. "It might have been," she grumbled. "He's so…" She searched for the right words and failed.

"Did he kiss you?"

"I kissed him."

"Lily!"

"Oh, it wasn't like that—nothing romantic about it at all." She told her friend the details of the hour she and Cody had spent caught in the storm. "I'm nothing to him, Emma. He has political ambitions, and I certainly don't fit into that picture."

"Why on earth not?"

"Did you forget the part about me being married?"

"And what if you aren't? What if that man tricked you?"

"It doesn't matter. I'm still not what he wants." She felt the breath in her chest congeal like the grease of a steak left on the plate too long.

"And you don't think Cody understands? Lily, he's a good man. A man who knows people make mistakes." Emma sat beside Lily on her bed, stroking her back.

"He might as well take up with one of the girls over at the saloon," she whispered. "A soiled dove—like me."

"Stop that kind of talk. There's no comparison." Emma stood to hang up Lily's damp clothing. "How about a nice bath? That always relaxes me. Then a good night's sleep and things will look much better in the morning."

"A bath is your remedy for all ailments," Lily said with a smile.

"And it works," Emma replied.

Lily went through the motions, as much to pacify Emma as anything. But the bath did help, as did the sweet smell of a freshly laundered nightgown. It was the sleep part that didn't materialize. What was it Cody had said? *I'll go to sleep and wake up thinking about kissing you.*

Had he? Would he?

She shook off the thought. It was time she faced facts. The idea that she could ever have anything serious with Cody was laughable. Why torture herself by continuing to seek his attention? She would keep her distance, and in time, he would get the message. And in time, maybe they could be friends—like she had been with Jake. But then what? She'd be back facing a future waiting tables in the small town of Juniper. Even if she moved on to Santa Fe, she would sleep the rest of her nights alone in a single bed on the top floor of the hotel. It was all too ghastly.

Things did not get any better the following morning. With Nancy still sick, Lily once again reported for duty at the counter. Victor Johnson was already seated when Lily arrived for her shift.

"Well, good morning, Miss Lily," he said with a mocking smile.

She squeezed oranges for his juice and, once the glass was filled, set it on a bed of shaved ice and presented it to him. "Coffee, sir?"

He downed the juice and nodded, squinting at her as if trying to interpret her mood. "Heard you and the sheriff took a ride up to Santa Fe yesterday."

She tightened her grip on the cup she held beneath the spigot of the large silver coffee urn. Thank goodness her back was to him, but he must have noticed the tensing of her shoulders. She forced herself to relax before turning to serve him. "Why, yes. Sheriff

Daniels had business up there, and he was kind enough to invite me to come along. I've always wanted to see La Casita. Did you want to order breakfast?" She was smiling so hard that her mouth actually hurt.

"Just coffee," he said. "You know, I—"

"Excuse me, Mr. Johnson," Lily interrupted. "Customers waiting," she called cheerfully, hurrying away to serve some railroad workers just arriving. As the stools lining the counter filled, Lily kept busy taking and delivering orders, squeezing oranges for juice and refilling coffee cups—including Victor's. He seemed intent on lingering until she could no longer avoid him. She ducked into the kitchen to allow herself a moment to regain her composure.

Even without Jake to keep things in the kitchen running smoothly, George had taken charge, and the cooks were back to turning out orders with remarkable efficiency. The only difference Lily noticed as she returned to her customers and scurried back and forth, placing one order and picking up another, was how quiet it was back there. The usual banter was missing.

Jake was missing, and everyone felt it.

There was a bit of a lull after the railroad men headed off to their jobs and before the late morning train arrived. It was during that pause that Victor held up his cup to signal for his third refill. Lily forced a smile and did her duty.

"I heard there was some trouble at La Casita a week or so ago," he said.

"Really?" He was fishing for information, no doubt. He had to be dying to know what had made Cody go there. She would not be the one to take his bait.

"Everything seemed to be running smoothly when I was there. I had the chance to speak with Miss Spencer, the head waitress—lovely woman. And Connie Evans, one of the girls." She saw Victor's grip tighten on the cup. "It was especially kind of them to take time to show me around," she continued. "Considering they were shorthanded. Apparently, one of their best girls—Millie or Molly—" She pretended to search her memory for the name. She watched Victor's expression shift from mild disinterest to undeniable alarm.

Right on time, the train whistle sounded.

"Well, that's my call to duty," Lily said with an exaggerated sigh. "You have a good day, Mr. Johnson." She laid his bill next to his saucer and began wiping the counter and resetting the places, moving away from him as she did. By the time she reached the far end and looked back, he was gone.

On his way to meet with Aidan Campbell at the hotel, Cody saw Victor Johnson leave and head for the livery. He couldn't help wondering what the man was up to and just how deep his involvement in the La Casita robbery and Jake's murder went. Right now, the best he could do was work with Aidan to make sure the hotel's money and safes were secure—and keep an eye on Lily. He figured the first would be a lot simpler than the second.

His attraction to her complicated matters. His work required concentration and focus. Distractions could be disastrous, and Lily Travis was most definitely a distraction. So much so that he had sent a telegram to Kansas City to see if there was any evidence that Victor Johnson had been married there. He wasn't about to mention Lily by name. If there had been a wedding, Victor's name would be on the license. All he had to go on was the year, and a liar was involved, so to be on the safe side, he'd asked for any record in that name for the last seven. He was going to cover all his bases.

*And if she was free, what then?*

Cody considered the possibilities. With Lily by his side, he was sure they could build a good life, one filled with adventure and laughter as Jake had said. He'd probably have to reconsider his political ambitions, but the more time he spent with Lily, the less important those ambitions seemed.

*And if she's really and truly married to that louse?*

He really didn't want to think about that possibility.

"Good morning, Sheriff Daniels." Aidan Campbell was at his post, his demeanor courtly and proper whenever he stood at the front desk of the hotel. "If you'd like to wait in the reading room, I'll be with you momentarily." He turned to his assistant to finish their discussion, pointing to a list and gesturing toward the dining room.

Cody wandered into the small room off the main lobby. Books filled the shelves along one wall, two small tables near the windows were set for games of chess or checkers, and a desk stocked with hotel stationery, pen, and ink waited for any guest wanting to write a letter or record an entry in a travel journal. A settee and two upholstered chairs completed the furnishings. Cody sat at one of the gaming tables. He wanted a view of the street. He wanted to see where Victor went after the livery. Would he return to the hotel, or was the man leaving town?

"My apologies for keeping you waiting," Aidan said as he pulled out the chair opposite Cody. It always took Cody back a bit to realize that, in spite of his prissy, formal attire, Aidan Campbell was solidly built. His formal clothing was filled out by a well-muscled upper body. Cody wondered if others misjudged the man's physical power as well.

Cody took out his notebook, turning to the notes he'd made during his meeting with Ty Drake. "La Casita was able to keep news of the robbery fairly contained," he said. "Fred Harvey's son came down to check things out and threw his weight around with Sheriff Drake and the city fathers."

Aidan nodded. "I can imagine. Mr. Harvey is most protective of the reputation of his holdings, and his son has learned his ways. They've made enough of a success of things that he can indeed influence others."

"Have you sent word to the Harveys that there might be trouble coming here at the Palace?"

Aidan glanced out the window. "I'd rather keep that between us for the time being." He nodded toward Cody's notebook. "Anything substantial we could use?"

"Not really. Drake thinks it was at least partly an inside job."

"One of the employees?" It was evident from his shock that Aidan could not imagine such betrayal from anyone on his staff.

"There was a waitress. She got hooked up with Victor Johnson, apparently told the other girls he had proposed. He left town, but she was so sure he'd come back for her that she quit her job, spent all her money on things for the wedding. Once she realized he'd abandoned her, she left town."

"And went where?"

Cody shook his head. "Nobody seems to know. She's got no family—she was raised in an orphanage back in St. Louis."

"Did you ask Mr. Johnson about her?"

"Not yet. Until I can figure out how Jake was tied to all this, I'd rather lie low."

Aidan bristled. "Jake Collier was one of the finest, most honest men it has ever been my privilege to know. If you are thinking that there is a plan in motion that involves the assistance of someone on staff to make it work, I can assure you that Jake is—*was*— not that person."

"I agree. But the night he was attacked, he was scared, Aidan. Somebody had threatened him. Or maybe threatened to harm someone he cared about."

"Lily?"

"Look, Aidan, I don't want to think either Jake or Lily is somehow connected with this business, but they are the only two people in Juniper who I can say with certainty knew Johnson and have had dealings with him."

Aidan's eyes widened as he repeated, "Lily? Our Lily is acquainted with this man?"

Cody had gone too far. He'd forgotten Aidan was Lily's boss and her previous association with Johnson could get her fired if Aidan knew the extent of it. "He's been sniffing around her, coming to the counter since she's been filling in for the new girl. He makes her nervous."

The explanation appeared to satisfy Aidan. "He does have a way of flirting, even with one or two of our female guests. Perhaps I should have a word with him."

"Just keep an eye out. Might make things worse for Lily if he thinks she's complained to you."

Aidan nodded. "You're right, of course. Nancy should be back to her duties in a couple of days, if not sooner. Once Lily's back to her regular shift in the dining room, that should solve the matter. Mr. Johnson does not dine with us in the evenings."

"Yeah, I noticed that as well. Wonder why that is." Cody hadn't given Victor's eating habits much thought, but now it occurred to him that taking meals in the rundown cantina at the far end of town instead of the hotel might have something to do with the second, still-unidentified man Lily had seen with Jake that night. He made a mental note to look into that. "In the meantime, you'll need extra security for any cash or valuables the hotel may be holding."

"The payroll arrives at the end of the week," Aidan said. "That's also when I withdraw the money I've deposited in the bank and send it back to headquarters."

"Why don't you pay your people out of those funds first before sending the rest on to headquarters?"

Aidan shrugged. "That would seem sensible, but the receipts determine staffing. If business slows or gets more demanding, staffing is adjusted to react to those numbers, while payroll is based on the information headquarters received two weeks ago. It's a way of keeping control of profits and expenses."

Cody tapped his pencil on the table as he tried to think of some way they might throw a wrench into a theoretical robber's plans. "No doubt whoever is in charge of the gang that hit La Casita knows the schedule. So what if, instead of delivering the payroll here, it was stored in the safe at the bank instead? Your employees could pick up their wages there, at least until the coast is clear."

"Of course. That makes a good deal of sense, especially since it removes any danger of guests getting caught up in a robbery." Aidan stood and offered Cody a handshake. "I'll see to it at once. We may not be able to prevent the scoundrels from striking, but we can limit the amount of damage they might do."

Cody accepted the man's firm handshake. At least they had come up with a plan that might keep the hotel guests—and the girls who served them—safe.

Through the window, he saw Johnson outside the livery, holding a horse's bridle while the blacksmith saddled it up. Cody watched until Johnson mounted and rode out of town, noting the direction he went. There was nothing that way but canyons and mountains and desert for miles. Unless he was doubling back somewhere, the only possibility Cody could think of was that Johnson was on his way to meet someone.

Cody sprinted across the plaza to where his horse was tied to a hitching post. Since learning of the robbery in Santa Fe, he'd developed the habit of being ready at a moment's notice in case of trouble. He loosened the reins, mounted, and took off in the opposite direction. He wasn't about to follow Johnson directly. He knew these back trails better than anyone, and he knew how to circle up and around so he could observe Johnson's movements without being seen. With any luck, Victor Johnson was finally about to make a mistake and expose himself for the outlaw Cody suspected him to be.

Every seat in the dining room was filled, and the girls hustled to get the passengers from the four o'clock train served and on their way. When the doors to the kitchen swung open on cue and the scent of sizzling steak wafted across the room, Lily turned. She half expected to see Jake with the large meat tray poised on the flat of one hand high above his head, his grin testament to how much he enjoyed this moment of being center stage. But of course, it wasn't him carrying the tray. Tears filled Lily's eyes as they did every time she watched George Keller set the tray on a counter and carve the meat into portions. The girls hurried to plate the meat and deliver the meals to their assigned tables.

"Steady there," George said in a low bass voice as he plopped thick slices of beef onto the plates Lily offered. He glanced at her, and she saw his eyes were also glistening. "Jake would want us to do this right."

She nodded and forced a smile as she delivered the plates to her tables. But her chest filled with loneliness. It surprised her to realize how much Jake's friendship had meant to her. Losing him was like losing a brother. He'd been family. She thought of happier days when she, Jake, Emma, and Grace would sit together on the veranda long after the hotel guests had gone inside for the night. Jake would keep them entertained with wild tales of his adventures working for the Harvey Company. Emma and Lily suspected he exaggerated the details for Grace's sake, teasing the naïve girl.

Now Grace had moved on to married life and was soon to be a mother as well. Lily and Emma hadn't seen Grace since Jake's funeral thanks to her confinement, and they both missed her terribly. Later, as they sat together catching a bit of night air before climbing the stairs to their room, Lily reached over and took hold of Emma's hand. "We never had our visit with Grace. Let's go Sunday after church."

"What a good idea," Emma readily agreed. "I'll ask Aidan…"

"No. Just us girls this time, okay?"

Emma pursed her lips. "And how will we get there? I've seen you on a horse, Lily, and…well, it wasn't exactly…"

"We'll rent a buggy. You can drive." Like Grace, Emma had grown up on a farm. Surely, she was familiar with things like horses and wagons and such. "How hard can it be?"

Emma burst into laughter. "Oh, Lily, if only every woman had your confidence, we could rule the world."

"You'll do it then?"

"On one condition."

Lily narrowed her eyes. Emma's "conditions" could sometimes ruin the best of plans. "And that is?"

"We have a man accompany us at least as far as the Lombard ranch. Nick can meet us there and see us safely to their cabin."

"That's ridiculous!"

"Need I remind you that there are unsavory sorts around, Lily? Two women alone in the countryside? Not a sensible idea."

She had a point. "All right, but not Aidan, okay? I don't want to watch every word that comes out of my mouth, and the way Victor has been dogging me these last few days, I could easily slip."

"I'll take care of it. You talk to George about preparing a lunch for us to take. I don't want Grace fussing over us in her condition."

Lily smothered a yawn. "Deal," she agreed. "One more day at the counter and then I can finally sleep another hour in the mornings." She stood and stretched. "Coming?"

"Right behind you."

In spite of her double shifts, Lily was in an especially good mood when she hurried through the kitchen the following morning. "George, could you put up a picnic for a few people for Sunday? Emma and I are going to see Grace after church."

George nodded. "Give her and Nick our best. Looking forward to seeing that baby. It's got to be pretty soon, right?"

"Won't be long now." She tied the sash of her apron, smoothed her hair, and stepped around the corner to the counter.

Victor sat in what had become his usual place. He glanced her way, and Lily's high spirits plummeted.

She prepared his juice and served him. "Will you be having breakfast with us today, Mr. Johnson?"

"Did you talk to your boss about me, Lily?" He was scowling at her as he drained the juice and set the glass down with more force than necessary.

"I don't…I didn't…"

"I could ruin you, you know. In more ways than one. I suggest you keep that in mind." He picked up his hat and left without paying for the juice.

Lily stood for a moment, speechless with shock. She'd never seen Victor so angry, and his threat frightened her. She watched him stride across the lobby, ignoring Aidan's greeting as he pushed through the front door. Aidan glanced her way, one eyebrow cocked in a question Lily didn't know how to answer. She smiled and went to greet another customer. As for the juice, she could either report that to Aidan or pay out of pocket. She decided the latter was the wiser choice.

The morning dragged on. Lily went through the routine of serving and clearing, always smiling, but her mind was frozen in that moment. It was the second part of the threat that ate at her. "In more ways than one," he'd said. What could he mean by that? Of course, if he told Aidan they were married—or even that she was not as innocent as everyone thought—Aidan would have no choice but to let her go. She was not the stuff of Harvey Girls.

*But what else?*

She didn't tell Emma about the encounter. Instead, she focused on getting to Sunday and the visit with Grace. It had been too long since the three friends had been able to enjoy an entire afternoon together.

During church, she tapped her foot impatiently until Miss Kaufmann rested her hand on Lily's knee the way she might have quieted a child. Finally, everyone rose for the benediction, the organ music swelled, and the congregation broke into greetings and chatter as everyone moved up the aisle to the exit.

Outside, Emma linked arms with Lily as they waved goodbye to Miss K and the other girls and headed across the plaza.

"We have to get the picnic basket," Lily reminded her friend.

"Already done." Emma tightened her hold on Lily's arm as she smiled and waved to the man seated in the driver's seat of the wagon.

"You didn't," Lily blurted when Cody Daniels grinned and tipped two fingers to his hat before climbing down to wait for them.

Emma pulled her forward, relentless. "Everyone I asked was already engaged for the afternoon. And then Cody overheard me asking Frank Tucker at the mercantile and offered. Well, what was I to say?"

"A simple 'No thank you' would have worked nicely," Lily grumbled. She had worked out that Cody must have said something to Aidan about Victor bothering her. Then Aidan had spoken to Victor—which made Cody the reason Victor had threatened her. She was sure of it. All the more reason to keep her distance. He meant well, no doubt, but he wasn't aware of Victor's threat. "I thought the idea was for someone to take us to the ranch and then go away."

Emma pointed to Cody's horse tied to the rear of the wagon. "Cody knows the plan. He'll take us to the ranch and leave us there. Nick or one of the ranch hands will see us to the cabin and then home again."

"I'll ride in back," Lily announced.

"You'll do no such thing. If you insist, I'll sit between you and Cody."

"I insist," Lily whispered as they reached the wagon.

"Ladies," Cody greeted them. "Ready to go?"

"This is so kind of you," Emma said as she accepted his help climbing aboard and settled herself in the middle of the seat.

Cody turned to Lily and offered her his hand. "My pleasure," he said, his gaze fixed on her.

She ignored him and climbed up to the seat without help. While Cody checked his horse, Emma whispered, "I thought you'd be pleased."

"You thought wrong," Lily muttered and immediately regretted her sharp tone. She wasn't angry at *Emma*. "I'm sorry. It's all right," she assured her. "Don't let it spoil our day."

Cody climbed to his seat next to Emma and took the reins. "Ready, ladies?"

"Yes," Emma agreed with a sideways glance at Lily.

"Lombard Ranch, here we come," Lily replied. After all, all she needed to do was make it to the ranch without snapping at anyone. Then Cody would leave, and the day could proceed the way she'd imagined— just Grace, Emma, and her. Like old times.

But even before they reached the ranch, they saw a wagon headed toward them. Nick was driving, accompanied by Grace's parents. Nick had brought Jim and Mary Rogers to New Mexico to live with him and Grace after finding Grace's father in poor health. Their doctor had agreed the dry air and warmer temperatures might help. They'd always intended to return to their own farm once Mr. Rogers's health improved, but this seemed pretty sudden.

"What's up, Nick?" Cody asked.

"I'm taking them to the train," Nick explained when the two wagons came abreast of each other.

"We just received word late yesterday one of our older boys was thrown by his horse," Grace's mother explained. "He's in a bad way and…" She pressed a wadded handkerchief against her lips as if trying to stifle the tears filling her eyes.

Lily turned her attention to Grace's father. He had improved a good deal—she'd even seen him about in town once—but she had to wonder if the trip was wise. "Are you sure you're well enough to travel, Mr. Rogers?"

He smiled. "Have to be. My boy needs me—he needs us both."

"We should get going," Nick said. "Train won't wait."

"We'll be back," Mr. Rogers promised as Nick snapped the reins. "Soon as we're sure everything's all right back home." He wrapped his arm around his wife and pulled her close. "We'll be back to see that baby, right?"

Mrs. Rogers sniffled and nodded as she leaned her head on her husband's shoulder.

"Don't worry about Grace," Lily shouted after them. "Emma and I will take good care of her." She waved until the dust stirred up by the wagon blotted out the sight of them. "Grace must be so worried," she murmured as she settled herself again on the seat. And then it struck her. With Nick off to take Mr. and Mrs. Rogers to the train, who would get them from the ranch to the cabin?

As if he'd read her mind, Cody said, "Well now, I don't see any reason to stop by the ranch, considering. Might as well head straight for the falls, don't you think, ladies?" He winked at them.

"You mean the cabin," Lily corrected him primly.

"Okay, the cabin by the falls." He chuckled.

The man was laughing at her, and Lily had had quite enough of him. "Just take us to the head of the trail. It's a lovely day, and Emma and I can walk the rest of the way."

He had the audacity to look down at her shoes, expecting no doubt to see the fancy boots she'd worn before. She thrust her foot out at him, exposing not only her sturdy work shoes but a bit of ankle as well.

"Lily!" Emma turned bright red as she tugged at the hem of Lily's skirt.

"I'm taking you all the way there," Cody grumbled, all sign of humor gone. He stared straight ahead and snapped the reins to urge the team to a faster pace, the wagon jostling over the bumpy road.

Emma bit her lip as she looked first at Cody and then at Lily and then down at her hands clutching the edge of the seat. Lily fought to maintain her balance and sent a look of pure fury in Cody's direction.

Beneath the brim of his hat, the man had the audacity to smile.

# Chapter 8

CODY DIDN'T KNOW WHAT IT WAS ABOUT LILY THAT made him want to needle her. Maybe it was the way her expression shifted when she didn't get her way. Instead of pouting, her jaw tightened, and she practically announced her determination not to be bested again. He might think he had won this skirmish, but he was pretty sure over the long term, Lily Travis would always come out triumphant. He kind of liked that idea, and the thought made him smile.

But when he heard Lily suck in her breath and saw her grip the edge of the seat with both hands, he suspected she'd misinterpreted that smile. "Look," he said, "I'm going to take you to Grace and let you off there. I've got some thinking I need to do, and I'll just take a ride while you visit. And if you'd prefer, I'll ride over to the Lombard place and ask if one of the ranch hands can see you back to Juniper, and I won't bother you anymore."

He saw Lily start to say something—probably to grudgingly agree to the plan—but before she could speak, Emma placed her gloved hand on his forearm.

"Please, don't think we aren't grateful, Cody. Isn't that right, Lily?" She didn't wait for a response but hurried to add, "George packed us enough food for a small army. At least join us for a late lunch before you go on to the ranch."

Looking past Emma to Lily, he said, "If you're sure…"

"Of course we're sure. Aren't we, Lily?"

"I'm sure Grace will be pleased to see you," she replied. Cody noticed she had refused to address the question directly. "Besides, you have to eat."

"Well now, that would be real kind of you ladies," he drawled. "I have to admit I've been thinking about that basket full of food for the last little while."

When they reached the cabin, Grace was on the porch, no doubt eager to welcome their arrival. Her pregnancy appeared to have advanced quite a bit just in the short time since Cody had seen her with Nick at Jake's funeral. Truth was, he didn't quite know where to look. He wasn't used to being around expectant mothers, and worse, when he glanced at Grace, what he was really thinking was how Lily might look carrying a child—his child. He felt a blush bloom as he approached the cabin, hanging back to allow Emma and Lily to go ahead of him. Grace welcomed them with hugs and then turned to him.

"Well, come on up here, Cody. I assure you nothing is going to jump out and bite you."

He ducked his head, set the picnic basket on the porch, and took hold of her hands. "Sorry about your brother's fall," he said.

"He'll be fine," she assured him, although clearly, she was operating purely on hope. She eyed the basket. "I do hope there's a huge piece of George's applesauce cake in that basket. I've been thinking about it all morning."

Lily set the basket on a warped wooden table and started unloading it. "Surely, George packed something healthier," she said, smiling as she burrowed through the contents. She removed a package. "Well, look at this…" She opened the wrapping, and all three women squealed.

Cody reached over Lily's shoulder and took the cake. "Pretty sure that's for me," he teased.

"Not on your life, mister," Grace exclaimed as she reached for the cake Cody held just above her head. "Gimme."

Emma laughed. "Best do as she says, Cody. You never want to mess with a woman like Grace. She may look fragile, but we all know she's as tough as they come." She looked at her friend with unabashed admiration.

Cody sighed in mock defeat and presented the cake to Grace, then pulled a chair closer so she could sit.

"Thank you, kind sir." She unwrapped the cake, broke off a corner, and took a bite. She closed her eyes and moaned. "Heaven," she whispered, and they all laughed.

Cody took a sandwich from the basket. "Well, ladies, I'll leave you to your visit."

"At least sit a minute to eat your sandwich," Emma protested.

"I can ride and eat," he said, not allowing himself to look at Lily.

But then he heard her say, "That's not necessary, Cody. You should stay and eat with us."

He looked at her, their eyes locking. "If you're sure."

She licked her lips and then turned away, busying herself with filling tin cups with orangeade from a covered tin pail. "We're sure," she said. "Aren't we, girls?"

"Absolutely," Emma agreed as she sat on the only other single chair available, leaving a bench as the only choice for Lily and Cody.

"There are plates and utensils on the table inside," Grace said.

"I'll get them," Lily volunteered.

Cody finished unpacking the basket. "This is quite a feast," he said, and when Lily brought the plates, it seemed only natural for the two of them to work side by side doling out the food. They served Emma and Grace before taking their own plates and sitting next to each other on the bench.

Lily was left-handed. He hadn't noticed they had that in common until now. He wondered what else he had yet to discover about Lily Travis. He ate in silence while Emma and Lily filled Grace in on the latest gossip from the hotel. He noticed neither of them mentioned the presence of Victor Johnson. And because he wanted Lily to confide in her friends—and had the faint hope that they'd be motivated to share some of those confidences with him later—he finished his lunch and stood.

"I'd best get on my way." He took out his pocket watch and checked the time. "Emma, Lily, you should be ready to start back around four. I'll either be here or one of John Lombard's hands will come for you, if that suits."

"Maybe Nick will be back by then," Grace volunteered.

"Wouldn't want him having to make the trip twice. Besides, I expect he's reluctant to be too far away from you these days." He blushed again, realizing his comment had been far too personal for a single man.

Lily cleared her throat. "Seems silly to bother one of the Lombard cow hands. We're all returning to Juniper. If you don't mind, why don't you just plan on calling for us at four, Cody?"

Something had shifted for her, and for the life of him, Cody could not figure out what that might be. But he wasn't about to question it. Feeling uncommonly happy, he grinned and tipped his fingers to his hat. "Yes, ma'am."

This time, Lily was the one to blush.

The three women were silent as they watched Cody ride away. Then Grace let out a long, audible sigh. "Lily Travis, if you don't find some way to say yes to that man, I may never forgive you."

"You seem to forget I may not be in a position to say yes or no to Cody. Besides, he hasn't asked me anything," Lily protested, feeling her cheeks warm.

Grace snorted. "He's asking every time he looks your way. Take my word for it, Sheriff Daniels is falling hard for you. He may not yet realize it, and you may try to deny it all you please, but I know true love when I see it." She cradled her stomach and waggled her eyebrows at them.

Emma giggled. Lily tried to remain adamant, but Grace's antics were so ridiculous that all she could do was grin. And then she was laughing—they were all laughing—and it was like old times.

When they recovered, Emma and Lily insisted Grace enjoy her cake while they cleared away the remains of the meal. Emma carried the dishes inside while Lily packed the hamper and wiped crumbs from the table.

"I understand Victor Johnson is staying at the hotel," Grace said softly.

Lily nodded. "He's been there nearly two weeks now. No one seems to know why he's in town. I think Cody suspects he might be part of some plan to stage a robbery—La Casita in Santa Fe was robbed just before Victor showed up in Juniper."

"So you don't think he came to find you?"

Lily told Grace about her first encounter with Victor. "He seemed genuinely surprised to have discovered I worked at the hotel, but…"

"But you know better than to trust a single word that comes out of that man's mouth," Grace concluded.

Emma rejoined them on the porch. She wiped her hands on a flour sack-turned-dish towel. "He's stalking Lily, Grace. Lily's been covering the counter because the usual girl is ill, and he's there every morning."

Grace frowned. "Anything more? I mean, does he try to see you when you aren't working?"

"Not so far, but he seems to know everything about me. Where I go and who I spend time with. It's unnerving. I find myself looking over my shoulder all the time."

Grace nodded. "Yeah. It was like that when Jasper Perkins made his threats."

"Victor hasn't threatened you, has he, Lily?" Emma asked. "I mean you've never said anything about that."

Lily thought about how angry Victor had been earlier that week when he'd accused her of complaining to Aidan. "Not until recently." She told them about the incident and did not miss the look of alarm Grace exchanged with Emma. "But surely, he would never... I mean whatever his business in Juniper, that's bound to take precedence over anything to do with me."

"What if you are his business?" Emma asked, and Lily felt her throat tighten.

What if Emma was right?

"All I can say is I am mighty glad you have Cody watching out for you," Grace said as she gripped Lily's hand.

When her grasp tightened and she didn't let go, Lily looked at her. Her friend's face was contorted in pain. Emma was already on her feet. "Grace? What is it?"

"Probably shouldn't have eaten all that cake," Grace managed to gasp out, forcing a smile probably meant to reassure them and failing in the attempt.

Lily exchanged a look with Emma. "We need to do something."

Emma nodded. "Let's get you inside so you can lie down."

Between them, they half carried Grace into the cabin and helped her stretch out on the bed. Emma removed Grace's shoes and massaged her feet while Lily collected water from the creek. It was obvious that the pain had not abated by the time she got back. While she filled a glass with the water, Lily motioned for Emma to come closer so they could talk without alarming Grace.

"You stay here, and I'll go for help," Lily whispered.

Emma shook her head. "I'll go. I can take the horse from the wagon and ride to the Lombard ranch. The Lombards can send someone to town to bring Doc Waters."

Lily shot a look in Grace's direction. Her friend was now writhing on the bed, and her face was streaked with sweat. "All right. Go." She gave Emma a gentle push toward the door and went to sit with Grace, grabbing a dish towel and the water.

"Grace, Emma is going for help. I'll be right here with you until she can return, okay?" She heard Emma outside speaking softly to the horse and then the hoofbeats of her riding away. When she dabbed at the sweat dotting Grace's cheeks and forehead, Lily realized part of the moisture came from tears. "Do you want to try a sip of water?" she asked, not knowing how else she might comfort her friend.

Grace shook her head. "Doc was just out here to see me, and he said it would be at least three weeks yet. I can't lose this baby," she whispered hoarsely. "It would break Nick's heart."

"Now you listen to me. You and the baby will be fine. It's just…let's just try to stay calm until Doc can get here. Would you be better sitting up?" She was grimacing less—maybe her pain had ebbed a bit.

"All right." With Lily's help, Grace pushed herself higher against several thin pillows Lily stacked behind her, her dress bunching up around her.

And that's when Lily saw the three spots of blood on the bed.

Not wanting to further alarm her friend, she

tugged at the dress to straighten it and cover the spots. "Better?" she asked.

Grace nodded and gave Lily a wan smile. "I don't mean to be such a bother." Then her eyes widened. "How is Emma getting to the ranch?"

"She took off on the horse from the wagon— bareback, if I know her." Lily smiled. "Can't you just see her galloping across the land?"

Grace laughed. "Let's just say I can see Emma in that situation a lot easier than I could ever imagine you. Remember the day Aidan planned that ride and picnic for all of us?"

Lily ducked her head but couldn't hide her smile. "Nick had me singing, remember?"

"He was singing as well. That's when I learned my husband-to-be had many talents, but he was definitely not musically inclined."

The two of them giggled at the memory.

"You should try and rest, maybe even nap," Lily suggested and with a grin added, "Want me to sing you a lullaby?"

Grace smiled and tried unsuccessfully to hide another grimace.

Lily took her hand. "Is the pain worse?"

"No. It comes and goes. It's a little better. Maybe if I close my eyes…"

Lily continued to sit with Grace, lightly stroking her hand. After a short time, she realized Grace's breathing was steady and regular with the ease of sleep. She freed her hand from Grace's and stood.

Outside, the silence was broken only by the distant spill of the falls and the occasional call of a bird. Lily prayed for the sound of hoofbeats. Surely, blood wasn't normal. Grace needed help. Lily scanned the horizon, one hand shielding her eyes against the sun's glare. She prayed help would come soon. She longed for the sight of Cody galloping toward the cabin—and her.

Cody had hoped to spend some time at the cabin talking to Nick, feeling him out on any gossip he might have heard about the robbery in Santa Fe or Victor Johnson. But with Nick on his way to Juniper, Cody had nothing but time. The truth was it had been too long since he'd had an afternoon to himself or really any time when he wasn't working or trying to figure out some case or finish a report. Realizing that, he'd stopped shortly after leaving Grace, Emma, and Lily, dismounted, and started walking, letting his horse nibble at patches of grass while he looked for arrowheads to add to his collection. He had plenty of time before he needed to meet Lily and Emma for the trip back to town.

He chuckled as he recalled how the day had started. Lily Travis had looked like she might be capable of chewing nails when she saw he was their driver for the trip. He still hadn't figured out why she was so all-fired upset with him, but he was glad her ire seemed to have passed. After all, it had been her suggestion, not Emma's, that he come back for them. One thing was certain—she was a woman capable of driving a fellow crazy. And she was also a woman any man would come back to again and again, no matter how frustrated he might be.

Was that the story with Victor Johnson? Had he changed his mind and regretted leaving her? The thought of that man putting his soft, manicured hands on Lily made Cody want to punch something—or somebody. He hadn't heard anything from his inquiries to Kansas City about Johnson getting hitched up there. First thing tomorrow, he'd have Ellie Swift send another bunch of messages.

One other detail bothered him. There was some connection between Johnson and Abigail Chambers that he couldn't figure out. Since Jake's funeral, he'd seen the two of them outside Abigail's store more than once, and one evening, he'd observed Johnson heading to the Sagebrush—from Abigail's house.

Perhaps Johnson had set his sights on Abigail. She was at least five or six years older than Lily or the Harvey Girl Johnson had duped in Santa Fe. On the other hand, she had money. Her father had left her quite well off, and she had a successful business. Maybe Johnson was looking to the future, and hunting for a woman who could take care of him. Cody considered warning Abigail, but that would probably mean revealing Lily's secret. Besides that, she might take his attention the wrong way. No, he'd keep an eye out for Abigail's well-being, but he saw no way to outright warn her without risking her finding out Lily's history with the man.

He spotted the glint of obsidian in the dirt by his feet and knelt to dig out an arrowhead buried in the packed earth of the trail. Behind him, he heard hoofbeats coming up fast. He barely had time to scamper out of the way before horse and rider were upon him, passing him in a flurry of dust.

"Emma?" he shouted, unable to believe his eyes.

She managed to stop the horse a couple dozen yards down the road. The animal was already slick with lather, and Emma was breathing hard. As she started back toward him, Cody ran to meet her. "What's happened?"

She gasped out the details. Grace—pain—baby—doctor.

Cody whistled for his horse. "It'll take over an hour to ride back to town, get Doc—assuming he's at home—and come back here. We could have Grace on the wagon and take her there ourselves in half the time," he argued.

"I don't know, Cody. She's in a lot of pain. And the rough ride? She's got to be terrified."

Cody mounted his horse. "It's our best bet, Emma." He stretched out his hand. "Ride with me. It'll be faster."

"What about…" She glanced at the horse she'd ridden.

"He'll be fine. We're on Lombard land. One of the hands will find him and take him back to the ranch. Come on."

He had intended to have her sit sidesaddle in front of him, but to his surprise, she hitched up her skirt and straddled the horse's haunches, locking her arms around his waist. "Let's go," she said. Cody shook his head. These Harvey Girls were a breed to themselves. He spurred his horse to a gallop and headed cross-country, taking the shortest route back to the cabin.

By the time they got there, he had a plan all worked out.

Lily came running to meet them. "She's sleeping," she reported. "But…" She drew Emma closer, and Cody heard her whisper something about spotting.

"While I hitch up the wagon, you girls collect every blanket, straw mattress, and pillow you can find," he instructed them. "We'll line the wagon bed and make sure Grace doesn't get jostled around."

"We left one of the team back there," Emma reminded him as he headed for the corral where the other team horse was lapping water from a trough.

"We pair up my horse and this one. Now go." He shooed them toward the cabin, not wanting them to see that he was far from certain the mismatched horses would work. One was meant for riding and the other for pulling. But as if they understood the seriousness of the situation, the two animals cooperated.

Once he had them hitched up, Cody drove the wagon closer to the cabin where Emma and Lily had deposited a stack of blankets, quilts, and pillows on the porch.

Cody set the brake on the wagon and went inside. Grace was seated in a chair, watching the activity. "This is so unnecessary," she protested. "Nick will be back any moment now."

"We're doing this," Lily said through gritted teeth.

Cody pulled the mattress from the bed and carried it outside. Then he collected the stack of covers and pillows Emma and Lily had assembled and began padding the sides. He tied a rope from one side to the other, thinking Grace could hold onto that to steady herself.

"Okay, let's go," he said as he returned to the house and scooped Grace up. She was still fully dressed, and

Cody was glad of that. The layers of petticoats and clothing would provide additional padding. Gently, he laid her in the wagon bed, and as soon as he stepped away, Emma climbed in and settled herself next to Grace.

"Lily, you ride up front with Cody and keep an eye out for Nick in case he's already started back."

To Cody's relief, for once Lily didn't argue. Instead, she climbed up to the seat and turned so she could look back at Grace. "Are you all right?" she asked, twisting her fingers nervously.

Grace chuckled. "I can barely move with all this padding, not to mention Emma squeezed in next to me." Cody saw her glance up at Lily, and her expression sobered. "The pain is better, Lily, truly."

Lily gave a curt nod and faced forward as Cody climbed aboard, released the brake, and clucked his tongue to get the team moving. He tried to avoid holes and rocks along the trail but couldn't miss them all, slowing to a crawl at times to navigate his way around any barrier.

After they'd gone some distance this way, Lily let out a sound of pure exasperation. "This is going to take forever," she muttered. She continued to chew her lower lip and glance back at her friends.

"We'll get there," he promised, and when Lily looked at him, her expression filled with hope and trust, he knew this was one promise he couldn't break.

As they approached the outskirts of town where the trail was more beaten down and therefore smoother, Emma reported that Grace was sleeping. "That's good, right?" Cody asked, glancing at Lily.

She shook her head. "I don't know. I mean, what

if she's not really sleeping but instead passed out from the pain—or the bleeding?"

Cody reached over and covered Lily's knitted fingers with his hand—and didn't let go.

∞

"That's Nick's wagon," Lily said as they drove through town. "He's still here. Grace, Nick's here."

Grace moaned softly.

"Turn here," Lily instructed as if Cody didn't know the way to Doc's home and office. The minute Cody tugged on the reins and the wagon rolled to a stop, Lily scrambled down and took off running. "Doc! Come quick!"

A side door opened, and Sarah Waters peered out. She was dressed for evening vespers, already wearing her hat and gloves. "What on earth?"

Cody had cradled Grace in his arms and was carrying her to the house. "It's Mrs. Hopkins," he explained. "She's having bad pains. Is Doc here?"

"Right here." Doc squeezed past his wife, who was still standing in the doorway, and hurried forward. "Let's get her inside and have a look." He led the way to the entrance to his office, where Cody laid her on the examining table. Emma and Lily took up a vigil to either side.

"I'll go see if I can catch Nick before he starts for home," he said.

Lily watched him leave, realizing she always felt surer things might be all right when Cody was around. For one thing, he didn't wait to be told what needed doing. And for another, he always seemed to keep his focus on others. He clearly took his pledge to protect the citizens of Juniper and the surrounding area from harm seriously. That feeling someone might be there to make sure she was safe was new for Lily. It occurred to her it was something she could get used to.

Why was she allowing her fear of Victor to keep her from doing what her head—and heart—knew was best? Cody could certainly handle Victor. Cody would keep her safe.

Grace moaned softly as Doc probed her. Lily and Emma exchanged a look when Doc pulled free and they saw his fingers were stained with blood. Wiping his hands on a towel his wife handed him, he stepped away from the table. "Mrs. Hopkins, this child seems determined to come into this world ahead of schedule. In order for you to hang on as long as possible, you need complete bed rest—no housework or fixing meals for Nick."

"But…" Grace started to protest.

Doc held up a finger to silence her. "In fact, I'd be a sight more sure we can have things turn out for the best if you stayed right here in town, so I can be on call should you need me. Even a few more days could make a difference."

Emma stroked Grace's hair away from her cheek. "He's right, Grace. You're alone all day and sometimes into the night, and what if…"

Before Grace could say a word, the door to the outer office crashed open, and they heard heavy footsteps coming their way fast.

"Grace!"

Nick hurried to his wife's side, started to embrace her, but hesitated.

"Hug your wife, Nick," Doc said.

Grace held out her arms to Nick. "Doc Waters wants me to stay in town until…"

"You could lose this baby, Nick." Doc was nothing if not straightforward. Sometimes what he had to say was hard to hear, but Lily knew his patients appreciated the honesty.

Nick focused his attention on Grace. "We'll take a room at the Palace. I can go back and forth to the ranch and sleep over in the bunkhouse if necessary. The important thing is to make sure you get through this."

"No need for spending money on a room," Lily announced. "Grace can stay in Jake's old room where we can all keep an eye on her."

"Absolutely," Emma agreed. "And one of us can sit with you through the night and check on you throughout the day and—"

"Sounds like we've got a plan," Cody said. He'd followed Nick and remained standing in the doorway, observing the scene. He turned his attention to Lily. "Why don't you and Emma head on over to the hotel and get things squared with Aidan and Miss Kaufmann?"

"Yes," Emma agreed. "Come on, Lily."

Lily bent and kissed Grace lightly on the forehead. "It's all going to work out," she whispered.

"I'll come with you," Cody said as they left.

The three of them crossed the plaza in silence, the weight of Grace and Nick's situation making words unnecessary. When they entered the lobby, Cody suggested Emma and Lily go talk to the supervisor while he explained the situation to Aidan.

"Emma, you talk to Miss K," Lily said. "I'll get started setting up Jake's old room for Grace."

"She'll be in her office," Emma said as she hurried through the dining room.

Lily started for the kitchen, but Cody caught hold of her hand. "Lily? Doc's going to do everything he can."

"I know." She heard the tremor in her voice and realized she was thinking Doc's best might not be enough. She looked up at Cody, seeking reassurance.

"And if the worst happens, well, Grace has Emma and you to help her through it. I'd say that's pretty special."

"And you," she whispered. "What would we have done today without you, Cody?"

He swallowed as he ducked his head. "Glad I could—"

Before she realized what she was doing, Lily stood on tiptoe and kissed his cheek.

"Miss Travis!" Aidan Campbell glared at her from his position behind the front desk.

"Go on," Cody said softly. "I'll handle this." He strode toward the desk. "There's been some trouble, Mr. Campbell."

As she hurried on to the kitchen, Lily saw Aidan's expression of shock and disapproval shift instantly to one of alarm as he stepped away from the desk and approached Cody. The last she saw of them, the two men were walking to the reading room, heads bent close together.

She had just finished wiping down all the surfaces in the small room and storing the last of Jake's toiletries and uniforms in the narrow corner wardrobe when she heard male voices coming through the kitchen.

"This way," Aidan instructed as two men wrestled a bed frame past the stove and food preparation counters. Behind them, Cody carried a mattress, and behind him, Tommy balanced a stack of fresh linens and towels, topped by a bar of soap.

Aidan directed the exchange of Jake's cot for a bed Lily realized had been taken from a hotel guest room. "This will be far more comfortable," he said.

"Emma and Miss Kaufmann went back to Doc's to help with moving Grace over here," Cody explained after dropping the mattress in place.

As Lily took the linens from Tommy, she saw Aidan pay the two men he'd apparently recruited from off the street for their help, and they left. She hung the towel on the washstand and made the bed, aware that while Tommy had gone back to his post, Aidan and Cody lingered. Or rather Cody lingered, scanning the room as if looking for something out of place—something that might require his help. Aidan's stance, arms firmly crossed and his eyes on Cody, told her that he had no intention of allowing Cody to be alone with her.

"I've got everything under control here," she said as she snapped a sheet open, filling the room with the fragrance of soap and sunshine in the process. "Why don't you gentlemen see if Nick and Doc need any help bringing Grace over?"

Cody glanced at Aidan, who unfolded his arms and indicated Cody should precede him to the kitchen exit. "Let me know if you think of anything else Grace might want," he said.

"Flowers," she called. "Something to brighten this

dreary space." Once they'd left, she continued tucking in the sheet. Maybe things would be all right after all. Grace was a lucky woman to have so many people who cared so deeply for her welfare and happiness. Lily envied her.

# Chapter 9

ONCE GRACE WAS SETTLED AND NICK HAD TRANS-ferred their mattress and other belongings to his buckboard, Cody returned the rented wagon to the livery and reluctantly went back to his office. Grace needed rest more than anything else, and she had Nick, Emma, and Lily to make sure she got it. Other than hang around Lily—which was what he wanted to do—there was nothing he could offer.

He read through some reports from the territorial headquarters—another failed attempt to get Congress to approve statehood. Cody understood the issue. Congress was run by white men from states along the eastern seaboard, men who knew next to nothing about the West. In veiled language that still blatantly revealed their prejudice, they rejected bill after bill put forth by the territories in their bid for full statehood.

The very fact that the territory was called New Mexico scared them off. They imagined hordes of poor, uneducated, dark-skinned people who spoke Spanish better than they did English. And right alongside them were the native nations, tribes the federal government had finally subdued and was not about to give the right to vote. Cody hoped one day to be a part of changing their minds. The current territorial delegate to Congress from New Mexico was retiring, and Cody had given a lot of thought to seeking the position. Of course, that was before he'd gotten caught up in the chaos that was life around Lily Travis.

He pushed away from his desk, stood, stretched, and decided to make his rounds. He started by stopping in at the saloon.

"Quiet day," he commented when Sally joined him at the bar.

She shrugged. "Sunday. I never understood how some men can pretend to be so 'holier than thou' one day a week and spend the other six sinning like the devil himself."

The bartender set a mug of coffee in front of Cody. "Nature of the beast, Sally." Cody blew on the coffee. "Have you seen any more of that Johnson fellow?"

"He was in here last night, holed up back there in the corner with two others. I didn't get a good look at them, but they were rough-looking characters. Didn't seem to be his type, but he was clearly the one in charge of whatever was going on."

Cody drank the coffee and set the empty mug on the bar. "Do me a favor. If you see them again, send word."

"You expecting trouble?"

Cody grinned as he laid a coin next to the mug. "Always, Sally. That's my job." He tipped his hat to her and left.

Outside, he stood for a minute surveying the deserted streets of the town. The hotel was all lit up, but other than the two saloons, it was the only place that showed any sign of life. He walked slowly down the street, testing shop doors as he went to be sure they were secure. He wondered if Lily was the one sitting with Grace tonight. More likely, Nick had stayed the night and would head for the ranch at first light. He walked around to the back of the hotel and looked up to the window on the third floor he knew was the room Lily shared with Emma. The light was out.

"Sleep well," he whispered, then shook his head at such romantic foolishness. He was acting like a lovestruck kid. And besides, he still didn't have any answers about Lily's supposed marriage. "Tomorrow," he muttered. "First thing."

He was standing outside the post and telegraph office when Ellie Swift showed up.

"You're getting an early start," she commented.

"Realized I never checked the mail Friday. Anything come through?"

Ellie set down her belongings and shuffled through a stack of mail. She held out a letter. "This what you're looking for?"

The return address was the courthouse in Kansas City. "Could be," he replied as he slid his thumb under the flap and pulled out the single page. Some legal gibberish before coming to the point:

*No records of marriage for the time period requested found in Kansas City or the surrounding region for anyone by the name of Victor Johnson.*

Of course, there was always the possibility Johnson could have used a fake name, but Cody doubted that. Victor Johnson was an arrogant son of a gun, and in Cody's experience, such men always believed they were beyond the need for such ploys.

"She's not married," Cody muttered, rereading the letter to be sure he'd gotten it right. He fought a grin. He pushed down the urge to let out a whoop of pure joy.

"What's that you say?" Ellie asked, her back to him as she got things set for a day of business. "Speak up, Sheriff Daniels."

He hadn't realized he'd spoken aloud. "It's nothing. Just a friend who asked me to do some checking."

Ellie held up her hands to stop his babbling. "In other words, none of my business."

"Thanks, Ellie." Cody folded the letter and left. He wasted no time heading to the hotel. Victor Johnson had some explaining to do.

"He checked out last night," Aidan said when Cody stopped at the front desk, prepared to confront Victor once and for all.

Cody frowned. "Kind of sudden, wouldn't you say?"

"Between the two of us, I'm just glad he's decided to move on."

"You do know he left Santa Fe right before La Casita was hit?"

Aidan grinned. "Not a problem. I made sure he overheard me telling Miss Kaufmann that beginning immediately, the payroll would be held at the bank and employees were to collect their wages there. My guess is he decided Juniper and the Palace were not worth the trouble and he's moved on to some other town."

"Shouldn't let down your guard, Aidan."

"No, but it is a bit of a relief." He pasted on his welcome-to-the-Palace smile as he looked past Cody. Realizing there were hotel guests in need of Aidan's attention, Cody stepped aside to give them access. He glanced toward the lunch counter, where Nancy was back at her post. There was no sign of Lily.

Ducking into the reading room, he took a sheet of hotel stationery and scrawled a quick note before placing it in an envelope and sealing it. On his way out, he handed it to Tommy with a nickel tip. "See that Lily Travis gets this," he said. "Soon as possible."

When Grace insisted Nick go home, Lily and Emma had assured him his wife and baby would be in their competent care. Once Nick left, Lily settled in for the first shift, but she'd slept fitfully. The folding cot Miss Kaufmann had added to Jake's room was not the most comfortable bed she'd ever slept on. Of course, it also wasn't the most *un*comfortable, she reminded herself, thinking of the room she'd rented at the boarding-house back in Kansas City before joining the Harvey Company.

Emma had relieved her at four, and Lily made her way up the back stairs and fell onto her bed fully clothed, wanting nothing more than a couple of hours of solid sleep. The whistle announcing the arrival of the morning train woke her. This load of passengers would take their meal at the counter, but just before noon, there would be another train, and then two more after that, and each time, the dining room would be full. Lily stretched and yawned, blinking in the bright sunlight streaming through the window.

Footsteps approached her bedroom door, stopped, and then moved immediately away. Curious, she stood and saw one of the hotel's signature beige vellum envelopes on the floor. *Victor?* Her pulse racing, she picked it up and saw it was addressed to her—in familiar handwriting. Smiling, she tore open the envelope and removed the note.

> *Good news. VJ has checked out and left town. May I call on you tonight after your shift ends? I have other news to share, and I haven't forgotten those flowers for Grace.*
>
> Cody

Lily clutched the envelope and note to her chest and squealed. Victor was gone, and Cody wanted to see her—perhaps to tell her he'd discovered the identity of Jake's killer. It was going to be a very good day.

She smoothed Cody's note and scribbled her reply.

> *Yes—kitchen entrance at seven, and don't forget the flowers.*

She crossed out her name on the envelope, stuffed

the message inside, and hurried down to the lobby. "Tommy, please see that the sheriff gets this."

The boy grinned. "Sure will. Soon as I get the chance." He shoved the envelope in the pocket of his uniform.

Lily thanked him and headed through the kitchen to check on Grace and give both Grace and Emma the good news. Victor was gone. She felt as if a weight had been lifted, a physical weight she hadn't realized she'd been carrying ever since that night Victor had surprised her in the reading room.

As she expected, both Grace and Emma were delighted to hear her news.

"Oh, Lily, at last," Emma gushed, taking Lily's hands in hers. "I know how worried you've been."

"And now," Grace added, "perhaps you and Cody…"

Lily felt her high spirits plummet. "Nothing has changed, Grace. I mean, Victor and I are still…" She saw their disappointment and didn't wish to be the cause of diminishing their happiness for her. "On the other hand, there was a second part of Cody's message."

"Well, don't keep us in suspense," Grace said. "It's not good for my delicate condition," she added with a dramatic sigh that had all three women laughing.

"He wants to see me, tonight after work. He says he has something else to tell me. I'm thinking he's discovered who killed Jake."

Emma and Grace exchanged a look. "That's what you're thinking?" Emma asked.

"Well, what else could it be?"

Grace rolled her eyes. "Could be with Victor gone, the good-looking sheriff wants to let you know he's interested. More than interested."

"Could be," Emma added, "he's figured out how you can sever any ties you might have with Victor so the two of you can get better acquainted without any obstacles, if you catch my meaning."

Lily felt a blush become a roaring fire. "That's simply—"

"But if we're right," Emma interrupted, "promise us you'll open your heart to the possibility."

"Oh, my dear Emma," Grace said, eying Lily with a knowing look, "trust me. Her heart is wide open and waiting."

"You two are impossible," Lily huffed. "I need to wash up and change." She could hear their laughter following her as she raced up the stairs. But truth be told, she was grinning all the way.

Late that afternoon, Cody treated himself to a shave and even allowed the barber to talk him into a splash of some cedar-scented aftershave he claimed to have just gotten in stock. He ate a cold supper at his desk before heading over to the hotel. The sun was low in the sky when he remembered his promise.

*Flowers!*

Where the devil was he going to get flowers? He retraced his steps past the jail and Western Union and on to the edge of town where Abigail Chambers lived in a small adobe house with the garden that was her pride and joy. The shopkeeper was outside tending that very garden as Cody approached. She looked up, and her eyes widened in shock—and delight.

"Why, Sheriff Daniels, this is indeed a lovely surprise." She patted her hair and fussed with the collar on her dress.

Cody knew he was giving her the wrong idea, but he'd promised Lily flowers for Grace, and he would not go back on his word. Besides, this was an opportunity to gather more information about Abigail's involvement with Johnson.

"Evening, Miss Chambers. I expect you heard Grace Hopkins had to be brought into town yesterday. She's not doing well, and Doc wants to keep her close."

"Yes, the whole town is concerned. Grace is a lovely young woman, and she's been through so much. I do hope she recovers quickly." Her eyes narrowed at him as it must have dawned on her he hadn't come calling but rather to ask a favor on behalf of Grace.

"They've got her set up in a room off the kitchen at the hotel—no window, and she's pretty much confined to bed. I promised to bring her some flowers. Lift her spirits, you know." He was holding his hat in both hands, slowly turning it as he carefully chose his words.

"That's very kind of you." She considered the plantings in her yard, then snipped some small pieces of sage and cedar and handed them to him. "Hold these. They'll give the room a lovely fragrance. Now for color..." She tapped her forefinger on her chin as she surveyed her garden. "Ah, yes, perfect."

She cradled a lovely flower between the fingers of

one hand as she cut the stem. "Wild zinnia," she said, identifying the blossom.

Cody watched her move around her garden. "Couldn't help noticing you and Mr. Victor Johnson have struck up a friendship," he said.

"Why, Sheriff Daniels, don't tell me you're jealous," she said with a flirtatious giggle.

"It's just he seems to have moved on and is unlikely to return, at least from what I've heard. And nobody seems to know why he was here in the first place."

"He has an interest in our community," she replied matter-of-factly as she cut two more flowers and added them to the bouquet Cody held. "He's quite a success back east," she added.

"I see." Cody had learned sometimes the best way to gather information was to simply wait and allow the other person to fill the silence.

"If you must know, he originally approached me about buying my shop."

"Originally?"

Her cheeks reddened, and she ducked her head to hide a smile. "Since then, we have…he has…" She thrust the flowers into Cody's hands. "He has become a good friend to me."

"Are you planning to sell? Forgive me, but I can't see the ladies in town being comfortable buying a hat from Mr. Johnson."

"Oh, we'll operate the business together. He has some matters he must attend to back east, but once that is in hand, he'll settle here."

"Here in Juniper?"

"Victor intends to invest in Juniper and the

surrounding area. He says this is the future—a true boom town, he likes to call it." She relieved him of the flowers he'd been holding and arranged them into a bouquet. "Do you have a vase?"

"I expect the hotel can provide that." Feeling the need to warn her, he pulled his hat snug on his forehead and tightened his grip on the flowers. "I'd advise you to be cautious in dealing with Johnson," he said. "He's a big talker, but nobody seems to really know much about him."

"Well, I know a good deal about him, Sheriff. We've become quite…close."

"Just be careful," Cody warned as he turned to go. "Thanks for the flowers. I'll be sure to let Grace know you sent them."

"Let her know I'll stop to visit when she's feeling up to it," Abigail called after him.

Cody waved and kept walking, his mind on Johnson. He barely noticed the curious smiles of passersby as he strode through town to the hotel, scowling and clutching the bouquet.

Entering the kitchen, he nodded to Chef George and the other workers closing up for the night. Lily and Grace were talking as he knocked lightly on the partially open door to Jake's old room. He forced himself to put any thought of Victor and Abigail aside and smiled. Both women looked up when he opened the door wider and led with the flowers. "Heard a certain mother-to-be was in need of some cheering up," he said.

"Oh, Cody, they're beautiful," Grace exclaimed, accepting the bouquet and gently touching the delicate petals of the flowers. "The fragrance is wonderful."

"I'll get something to put them in," Lily said.

He caught the scent of her lily-of-the-valley soap as she hurried from the room. She barely glanced at him on her way out, but she was smiling. And that made him smile. He turned his attention to Grace.

"How are you faring?"

Grace laughed. "Well, the food is certainly plentiful. The accommodations, however, are not exactly to my taste. I miss Nick," she added.

"Has he been by today?"

"He wanted to stay the night. I persuaded him he should get to the ranch and tend to business there and then go home and get a decent night's sleep."

Cody chuckled. Nick Hopkins could be stubborn. On the other hand, the man would walk through fire—had literally walked through fire—for Grace. "Anything you need?" he asked.

"As a matter of fact, there is," Grace replied.

"Name it."

Grace's expression shifted to one of concern and pleading. "Be good to Lily? Do not hurt her. We both know she's a bit of a renegade, but then she's been through a good deal in her life, and until this business with that horrid man is over and done with—"

Just then, Lily returned, holding up a canning jar half filled with water. "Best I could do on short notice," she said as she took the bouquet from Grace and arranged it in the jar. She set it on the overturned orange crate to one side of Grace's bed. "At least you'll be able to pretend a little. The room already smells like the outdoors."

"It's perfect," Grace assured her. "Now if the two

of you don't mind, I'm getting tired. Emma will be here soon, so shoo."

Lily picked up a shawl draped over the back of the one chair in the room. "You're sure?"

"Go!"

"We'll be just around the corner on the veranda," she continued as Cody stepped aside to allow her to pass. "If anything happens, have Emma come and get us?"

"I'm right here," Emma announced. "Reporting for duty," she added with a military salute, her other arm holding a basket filled with yarn and knitting needles. "Hello, Cody. Please see that Lily is back by curfew." She stepped inside the room and pushed the door closed.

"Shall we?" Cody offered Lily his arm.

With a last worried glance back, she accepted his offer. "Now what's this mysterious news you have to share with me?"

Cody grinned down at her. "You're not exactly the patient sort, are you, Miss Travis?"

"I've *been* patient all day," she protested.

He led her to a pair of chairs in the shadows of the porch. He wanted her to himself without interruption or distraction, not that anyone else was around. The night air was unseasonably cool, and it looked like most guests of the hotel had opted to spend the evening indoors. They were quite alone. He took the shawl from her and draped it around her shoulders before indicating she should sit.

"First tell me why you've been so upset with me."

"Not fair," she protested.

"I need to know if I did something to offend you.

I'm trying to get this right, Lily, but you have to admit…"

"Did you say anything to Aidan about Victor bothering me?"

"Yeah. I know you asked me not to, but, Lily, it's Aidan's job to be sure you girls don't have to put up with that."

"Aidan said something to him, and he was very upset. He…he threatened me."

Cody felt his gut tighten. "I'm real sorry that happened, Lily, but I'm also pretty sure your days of worrying about Victor's threats are over." He removed the letter from Kansas City from the pocket of his sack coat and handed it to her.

"There's not enough light," she protested. "How do you expect me to read this?"

"It's for you to keep," he told her. "It's a response to an inquiry I made with the courthouse in Kansas City."

"About Jake?"

"About Victor Johnson."

"I don't understand."

He covered her hand with his. "I wanted you to know where things stood with you and Johnson. According to this letter, there is no record of him marrying anyone in Kansas City. Not three years ago or five years ago or six months ago. He tricked you, Lily."

Cody felt her hand tighten into a fist around the official letter. He wasn't sure what he had expected, but it wasn't this. Lily was shaking. "You gave your permission," he reminded her.

"I know, but this… I mean, I never thought you

could actually—this is my private life, Cody! If you can get this information so easily, what else…?"

His heart hammered in his chest. How could this have been a mistake? "Lily, I assure you, all I did was ask for some records to be checked. Your name was never part of it. I thought you'd be glad to know Victor has no claim on you."

"Claim?" she sputtered, then lowered her voice. "Understand that married or not, no man has a claim on me."

Cody bristled. This wasn't what he'd thought her response would be. He'd kind of thought she might be so grateful, she'd hug him. "Is any man allowed to fall in love with you, Lily? Because the thing is, despite your ornery ways and apparent determination to go through life on your own, I find myself caring a lot more than I apparently should." He released her hand and slumped back in his chair, staring out at the dark moonless night.

After a moment, Lily smoothed the envelope he'd given her. "I'm sorry, Cody. I thought you had news of Jake's killer. This—I was unprepared. You don't really know me, and the fact is I did spend the night with Victor. How can a man like you even think—"

He'd heard enough. More than enough. He stood and pulled her to her feet, wrapping his arms around her. "You don't get to decide what is and isn't right for me, Lily, any more than I have that right with you. So what do you say we spend some time getting better acquainted now that we no longer have the specter of Victor Johnson hanging over things?"

She didn't struggle or pull away. If she had, he

would have released her and found a way, somehow, to accept her decision.

"I suppose that might be all right," she said softly.

He traced her features with his forefinger. "And would it be all right if I kissed you, Lily?"

In the light spilling over the veranda from the lobby, he saw that she was trying not to smile. "I think that might be the perfect way to begin getting better acquainted," she said primly.

Cody cupped her chin and lowered his mouth to hers. Nothing he'd imagined all those nights he'd thought about what kissing her might be like came even close to reality. Her lips were full and soft, and she snaked her hand around his shoulders to cradle his neck. In spite of his coat, he felt the swell of her breasts pressing against his chest. He deepened the kiss, stroking her lips with his tongue until she opened to him.

When they finally pulled apart, she caressed his face. "Well now, Sheriff Daniels, that was all quite interesting, but I'm not sure I fully understood your point. Could we 'talk' some more?"

Cody's heart soared. What a woman! She would drive him mad, but he was sure the journey would be worth it. "Well, as I was saying," he murmured, and he settled his lips on hers again.

So this was what it felt like to be kissed by a man who truly cared, Lily thought as she savored the taste and touch of Cody's lips on hers. This was what it felt like to be held with respect and tenderness. It was all new to her, and she never wanted it to end. She treasured every detail—the way he smelled like cedar, the taste of peppermint on his breath, the touch of his fingers lightly stroking her skin. Lily's experience had always been that men took what they wanted. Cody was not taking anything. He was giving.

He pulled her closer, pressing her cheek to his chest. "Lily," he whispered. She felt the hard muscles of his body and heard the thunder of his heart beating in time to hers.

The front entrance to the hotel opened. Laughter spilled out as a trio of men headed for the saloon. Cody held her close to him until they had gone. Across the plaza, the church bells chimed eight times. Cody stepped back and linked his fingers with hers. "Come with me," he said softly.

At that moment, she would have followed him anywhere.

Hand in hand and without a word, they walked away from town. She had changed out of her uniform but was glad she still wore her sturdy shoes as he led the way up a rocky path, guiding her over obstacles she didn't even see, until after only a few minutes' climb, they came to an outcropping of rocks. He brushed away dirt from one large flat boulder and climbed onto it, holding out his hand to her. "I won't let you fall," he promised.

She took his hand, and he pulled her up to stand next to him, catching her in his arms. He turned with her and pointed toward the horizon. "Look," he said.

They were turned away from town, and as her eyes grew accustomed to the dark, she saw the mountains, their jagged peaks raised to the sky, the sheer magnitude of them breathtaking.

"I always knew they were there, of course," she said softly, "but, oh, Cody, aren't they magnificent?"

He was standing behind her, his arms wrapped around her, his face resting against her hair. "I come here sometimes. It never gets old."

She turned to him and looped her arms around his neck. "Tell me why you come here."

He shrugged. "Sometimes to work out a problem with a case. Sometimes just to remind myself there's more to life than the day-to-day routine. And lately, to think about you. About us."

"I think about you—us—a lot," she admitted. "I don't have a special place though. Just the hotel."

"I'll share this one with you," he said, "as long as you promise you'll only come here with me—not alone."

She smiled. "And just how am I supposed to think with you here to distract me?"

"That's kind of the point," he chuckled. "That and the fact that there could be snakes or other varmints sharing the space with you."

She ran her finger over his lips. "I don't like snakes," she admitted.

"Good. Maybe that will keep you from going it alone. Something I suspect you have a habit of doing far too often." When she had no sassy reply, Cody tilted her chin so she was looking at him, even though his face was hidden by the oncoming night and the brim of his hat. "Lily? I didn't mean—"

"Did it ever occur to you that once you know me, you might not like what you find out?"

"Whatever Victor Johnson did to you doesn't matter to me. I know none of that was your fault."

"And what if I told you there's more?"

She felt him tense. And just when she was sure he was about to lead the way back down the path and say a good night that would surely be goodbye, he sat cross-legged on the rock and tugged her down to sit facing him. "Okay, tell me."

She hesitated. Was she ready to reveal her past? All of it? Things she had not shared even with Emma or Grace? He reached for her, but she raised her hands and stopped him. If she told him her past and he rejected her, at least she wouldn't have to endure the pain of him physically releasing her. Still, she couldn't resist taking hold of his hand herself.

"My father died suddenly when I was eleven," she began. "A year later, my mother remarried. The man was the son of a wealthy businessman. He spent his days at his private club and his evenings at dinners and parties. Sometimes, he escorted my mother to these social events, but more often, he went alone. He was a stickler for wanting things just so. He pretended to be very devout. Said it was good for business."

"Sounds like somebody I wouldn't get along with," Cody ventured.

"My two older brothers had already gone on to lives of their own. We rarely saw them, so it was just my mother and me—and my stepfather when it suited him. There were servants, of course, a butler and valet and cook and personal maid for my mother. But life was lonely and dreary."

"When did you leave?"

She hesitated. It was a simple enough question to answer by saying something like "when I turned sixteen." But nothing about the life she'd known was that simple. Either she was going to trust Cody with all of it, or she needed to end any association with him here and now and without further explanation. She drew in a long breath.

"I left the morning after he came to my room for the third night in a row. He would lie beside me, covering my mouth with his hand, while whispering threats of what he would do to my mother if I screamed or called for help. He waited until I agreed—I had to nod—and then he'd let me catch my breath. Then he'd—" Her voice trembled, and she shivered violently. "And then," she whispered, shutting her eyes against the vile memories of those nights.

Cody scooted around until he was sitting behind her. He pulled her against him, his arms a comforting embrace meant to send a message of protection and shelter. "That's enough," he said softly. "There's no need to say more, Lily. It means a good deal to me to know you trust me to hear this."

She didn't pull away but looked up at him. "All of it? Because I think I need to finally tell someone the whole story. If you'd rather, I can tell Emma. I trust her. Either way, I realize it's time. If I don't tell someone, I'll never move forward."

"Why put yourself through the pain of those times?"

"Maybe I'm beginning to realize that facing all of it—my father's sudden death, the time with my stepfather, even believing Victor's lies—is the best thing.

If I stop running from it, it might help me understand why I seem incapable of finding true love. Real love."

Cody continued to hold her. "Maybe," he said softly, "it's not so much about finding love but more recognizing it when it comes along."

"You mean like Jake?"

"Not exactly. I reckon the kind of love you're talking about is the kind where both sides feel the same. Two people working together toward the same end."

She relaxed in his arms, listening to the night sounds as she considered what he'd said. "My stepfather was a horrid man, and so is Victor. But still, I allowed them to take what they wanted from me." She felt Cody tense. "Not all of it," she hurried to assure him, not wanting him to think any worse of her than her story already warranted. "Not even Victor got that."

"But you were married. Or thought you were."

"He was drunk and when he couldn't…when he failed, he forced me to satisfy him in other ways. The same ways my stepfather had demanded. And then he passed out."

Cody cupped her face with his large hands. "Lily, do you know what this means? The way you've blamed yourself, punished yourself, thinking you weren't—"

"Chaste? Pure? Innocent? Choose any word, Cody. It's not what I think. It's the truth."

"No, darling Lily, it is not. None of it was your doing."

She felt a kernel of hope. "What are you saying?"

"I'm saying now that you know Victor tricked you and there is no legal bond, allow yourself to find love, Lily. 'Real love,' as you put it." He kissed her tenderly. "And once you decide to follow that path, I'd really like to be considered as a prospect."

Her answer was to urge him to kiss her again.

The church tower chimed three quarters of the hour.

"I have to go," Lily whispered, making no move to leave.

"Tomorrow?" he whispered, sowing kisses along her temple, cheek, and jaw.

"Yes. I'll meet you here as soon as I can get away." She turned her face so their lips met.

Reluctantly, they pulled apart, and he stood and helped her to her feet. "Let me call for you."

"No. For now, Cody, I need us to find our way without the others watching it all. They mean well, but if nothing comes of this thing between you and me—"

He wrapped his arm around her as he led the way back down the trail toward town, taking care she didn't trip or stumble. "We'll do things your way, for now. As for nothing coming of 'this'? I'd say we've passed that point several kisses ago."

Lily couldn't seem to stop smiling. She'd told Cody the very worst of her past, and still he wanted to move forward. Was it possible that at long last, she had found a man who would love her the way she'd always dreamed? Was it possible she'd found a man she could love in return?

Once they reached the plaza, she kissed his cheek and, feeling as if she'd sprouted wings, ran the rest of the way to the rear entrance of the hotel just as the church clock chimed ten.

Cody watched her until she disappeared inside the back entrance of the hotel. He felt happy—more than happy. What filled his heart and mind was the kind of pure joy a man experiences when he knows another piece of the puzzle that is his life has just clicked into place.

It had been enough to know that Lily wasn't really married to that scoundrel Johnson. But now, to know that in spite of her stepfather's abuses and in spite of Johnson's trying to trick her, neither had managed to defile her was an unexpected gift. He was well aware that Lily carried a good deal of shame for what those men had done to her, taking the blame on herself. He would need to take whatever time was required to convince her that she carried no guilt for their actions. It would take patience and tenderness—and love.

While making his rounds, he planned their next meeting. Tomorrow, when she met him on the hillside, he should have a surprise for her. A box of sweets from Tucker's store, or better yet, he'd bring a lantern and a book of poetry. Women liked poetry, didn't they? Maybe after breakfast at the hotel lunch counter, he'd step into the reading room and see what he could find on the shelves. Maybe Aidan would have some ideas. He seemed like the kind of guy who might be familiar with poetry.

He'd need a clean shirt. The woman who did his laundry for him wasn't due for another two days. Once a week, she brought him freshly washed clothes and took away the dirty ones. He'd either have to buy a new shirt or wash out the one he was wearing. Except buying meant stopping at Tucker's and maybe running into other customers who would speculate on why the sheriff needed a shirt. Washing the one he was wearing made a lot more sense, so as soon as he finished his rounds, he stepped around to the back of the jail, removed his shirt, and washed it out in the tin pan of water he kept there for the drunks who were the usual occupants of the cells inside.

He scrubbed the neck and cuffs with a bar of lye soap, rinsed, tossed out the soapy water, and pumped fresh into the pan. It was a quiet night and unlikely any of the cells would get used, but he liked to be ready, just in case. Inside, he draped the shirt over the back of his desk chair to dry near the open window and was just about to turn in for the night when he heard the jingle of harness and the creak of a wagon passing his office.

*Unusual for this time of night*, he thought as he opened the door and looked out. Sure enough, a buckboard was just turning the corner of the plaza, headed south out of town. The driver was alone, dressed in dark clothing with a hat pulled low over his forehead. But in spite of the man's attempts to remain unrecognized, Cody was pretty sure he knew who the driver was.

*So Victor Johnson hasn't left town after all.*

# Chapter 10

LILY COULD BARELY CONTAIN HER EUPHORIA AS SHE hurried inside the hotel. From the small room on the far side of the kitchen, she heard voices—Emma and Grace. And then a third voice, Miss Kaufmann. Using a shiny saucepan as a mirror, she examined her face to be sure she looked presentable for an encounter with the head waitress. She crossed the kitchen and called out, "I'm back," as the clock in the lobby echoed the last of ten bells. She wanted to leave no doubt that she had returned within the limits of Miss K's strict curfew.

All three women looked at her expectantly.

"Did you have a nice evening?" Emma asked.

"Yes, thank you, but I'm here now. You should get some rest." She removed her shawl and set it aside. "Miss Kaufmann, good evening." She picked up the half-empty pitcher of water next to Grace's bed. "I'll just refill this."

They all continued watching her, their eyes bright with what she supposed was curiosity—curiosity she was not yet ready to satisfy. But to her surprise, what she'd viewed as curiosity turned out to be excitement.

"We have news," Grace announced.

Lily set down the pitcher. "The baby?"

Grace laughed and laid a protective hand on the mound of her belly. "The baby is fine. Emma has news."

Emma's cheeks flamed a bright, mottled pink. "Well, you see, Miss Kaufmann has decided to move back to Virginia to be closer to family, and she has asked me to be her replacement."

"Emma was the only possible choice," Miss K announced as if Lily had raised an objection.

"Of course she is," Lily said and hurried around Grace's bed to hug her dear friend. "I just knew this would happen one day. Didn't Grace and I tell you?" She was so happy for Emma that she broke the hug and turned to Miss K, taking the older woman's hands in hers. "You couldn't have chosen better," she exclaimed. "Emma will make a wonderful head waitress."

"And housemother?" Miss K lifted an eyebrow. "I have to wonder how the two of you will fare, Lily. I mean, you do have a rebellious streak that must be tempered. I sincerely hope Emma's promotion won't be a problem."

"We are friends first," Lily assured her.

"Yes, that's precisely my concern," Miss K replied before turning her attention to Grace. "I'm pleased to see you look far better than when you arrived, Grace. I know the circumstances are less than ideal, but clearly, Dr. Waters made the right decision having you stay here in town." She patted Grace's foot before turning to go.

"When do you leave for Virginia?" Lily blurted.

"Lily!" Emma whispered.

"Well, if we're to arrange a party, we need that

little detail, don't you agree? There are only so many Sundays, after all."

This time, it was Miss K who blushed. "There's really no need to make a fuss."

"Of course there is," Lily insisted. "Appreciation for all you've meant to the Palace Hotel staff as well as a celebration of Emma's promotion. It deserves a real fandango. Leave it to Grace and me."

"I suppose it would be nice to be able to say a proper goodbye," Miss K mused.

"And you'd be doing Grace a huge favor. Planning a gala for you and Emma will give her something to pass the time while she's confined here."

Miss K smiled at Lily. "I will say this once, Lily Travis, and deny it vehemently should any of you repeat it. You have this way of bringing us all alive. Your impetuous nature can be highly contagious."

Grace clapped her hands. "A party to plan. What fun!"

"I'll let you know my date of departure as soon as I've finalized my travel plans," Miss K promised. "And, Emma, in the meantime, I'll need to hold regular meetings with you in order to pass the baton, so to speak."

"Of course," Emma agreed. "Thank you so much for your confidence in me."

"Well, off to bed with you both," Lily said, shooing them from the room. "Our Grace needs her rest."

Grace groaned. "Rest is all I do these days."

"Then I need my rest," Lily countered with a grin. While she refilled the water pitcher, she could hear Emma and Miss K talking as they climbed the stairs, planning how to begin the change in leadership. Lily was so very pleased for Emma. For the first time in weeks, it seemed as if at least three Harvey Girls were all well on their way to better days.

The following morning, Cody went straight to the livery. Mick Preston was standing over an anvil, pounding a horseshoe into shape. He was a broad-shouldered, muscular man, maybe thirty, maybe older. He went about his work without bothering to socialize with his customers. If a man came to rent a wagon or horse, the deal was struck with a minimum of words. But Cody needed information this time and had little patience with Mick's usual reticence.

"I noticed Victor Johnson driving one of your wagons last night," Cody said after Mick had acknowledged him with a nod.

Mick gave the horseshoe a final tap. "Yup."

"He's back in town then?"

"Yup."

"Any idea for how long?"

A shrug.

"How long's he keeping the wagon and team?"

"Paid for a week."

Cody blew out a breath loaded with pure frustration. "Mick, I need information."

Mick glanced at him. "Why?"

"I can't really give you details, but don't you find the man's actions suspicious? He leaves town, then all of a sudden, he's back?"

"None of my business. He paid hard cash for the week. Long as he returns the wagon and team on time and in good condition, that's all I need to know."

It was more than Cody had ever heard the man say before. Maybe they were finally getting somewhere. "Look, Mick, I've had word to be on the lookout for trouble—trouble that could affect the whole town. And the first place I look for trouble coming is at strangers who come to town with no apparent reason and stay longer than a day or two. If that stranger makes a show of leaving, then comes back in secret, I get curious."

Mick appeared to ponder this for a moment. "Not my nature to get involved in the business of other folks," he muttered as if trying to convince himself he should make an exception. Mick met Cody's gaze, squinting into the sun that poured in through the open double doors. "I don't know what I can tell you, Sheriff."

"Do you know where he's staying?"

Mick shook his head, then snorted. "I reckon he's not the sort to enjoy sleeping under the stars."

Cody realized the blacksmith had nothing useful to offer. "Thanks, Mick. If you think of anything more, let me know." He started for the door.

"Had a fella with him," Mick called out. "The night he showed up here wanting the wagon. Scruffy-looking. Not from around here."

Cody paused. "I only saw Johnson driving the wagon."

"Other fella left on horseback while I was hitching up the team."

"Did they both go the same direction when they left here?"

"North," Mick replied.

"Thanks, Mick. Thanks a lot."

Back in his office, Cody stood staring at the large map of the area he had nailed to one wall. He ran his finger north from town, looking for reasons Johnson might have gone in that direction. Nothing up that way except mountains and desert…and an abandoned miner's camp, perfect for a couple of outlaws to hide out while they plotted their strike. Cody punched the map with his forefinger. "Gotcha," he muttered.

Only he didn't, not really. He had no proof that Victor was planning anything illegal. He might not seem the type to go exploring, but the stranger from the East had every right to rent a wagon and team and set up camp in an abandoned cabin. He had every right to travel with a sidekick. He had every right to be just outside Juniper.

Cody ran a hand through his hair. He checked his watch. He'd promised to see Lily after she finished her shift later that evening, but he needed cover of darkness to ride out to the miner's cabin and have a look around. And he also didn't want to alarm her by letting her know Victor was still in the area. Maybe if he simply told her something had come up—official business he couldn't put off—she'd understand.

He headed over to the hotel.

Aidan's assistant was at the front desk. "Mr. Campbell has gone to Santa Fe for the day," he replied in answer to Cody's request to speak to Aidan. "May I be of service?"

"No, thanks." Cody glanced toward the counter and then toward the dining room where other Harvey

Girls were setting things up for lunch. No sign of either Lily or Emma.

Hoping one or both might be sitting with Grace, he walked around to the rear of the hotel. The door to the kitchen was open, and he could hear George Keller barking out orders to his crew. Entering the busy kitchen, rich with the smells of food cooking and clouded by the steam rising from bubbling pots and skillets, he raised a hand in greeting to the men who glanced his way.

Doc Waters was just closing up his bag, and Nick was hovering near Grace, looking more hopeful than Cody had seen him since they'd brought Grace to town that Sunday.

"Now, don't go thinking you can dance a jig at this party you're planning," Doc warned Grace.

"Speaking of parties," Grace said, "I assume I'll be home in time for the one the Lombards are planning for Nick and me at the ranch?"

Doc scratched his beard but shook his head. "You're doing fine, but no sense tempting fate. In other words, I'd advise you to do your partying here in town for the time being." He pulled on his hat, picked up his bag, and nodded to Cody on his way out.

"Sounds like some good news at least," Cody said, removing his hat as he stood in the doorway.

"She's doing just fine," Nick said. "Doc says the baby might still come early, but every passing day is a victory."

Grace blushed. "Nick, I'm sure the sheriff didn't come here to hear the details of my confinement."

"Nope, came to see if you needed more flowers," he teased.

Grace laughed. "You mean you would actually go over to Abigail Chambers's garden and ask for more?"

"You heard about that, did you?"

"The entire town knows. Abigail has a huge crush on you, Cody, as if you didn't know. She has told anyone who would listen how you came to her, hat in hand, blushing and stammering…"

Cody groaned. "I've never given that woman a single sign of encouragement," he argued.

"Oh, Cody, she doesn't need signs. She makes up her own."

"Give the man a break, Grace," Nick said. "Nice of you to stop by, Cody, in the middle of the day and all."

Nick was probably one of the smartest men Cody had ever met. He clearly understood that Cody had not just "stopped by."

"Lily around?" Cody asked.

"She's over at Mr. Tucker's store, ordering things for the party," Grace replied, and when Cody raised an eyebrow, she continued. "Bonnie Kaufmann is going back to Virginia to be nearer family. Emma has been tapped to be her replacement, so Lily and I are planning a party that's part farewell to Bonnie and part celebration for Emma."

Nick continued to study Cody. "What's going on?"

"Victor Johnson is back in town," Cody said, lowering his voice and stepping closer to the bed. "I think he and a partner are holed up at that old abandoned miner's camp north of town. I plan to take a ride out there tonight and see what I can learn. Lily and I were supposed to… I was going to call on her tonight, except now that's an issue."

"I'll be sure she knows," Grace said, her brow wrinkling into a frown. "But, Cody, be careful, won't you? If they catch you spying on them, it would be two against one."

"I'll come with you," Nick volunteered. "Even the odds."

Grace looked at her husband with alarm but made no protest.

"I couldn't ask you to do that," Cody hurried to say.

"You didn't ask," Nick replied. "How about I have supper with my best girl here and come over to the jail after that?"

The truth was having Nick along would be a help. Two sets of eyes and ears were always better than one. Cody looked at Grace.

She let out a sigh. "Don't look to me to change his mind, Cody. In case you haven't noticed, my husband can be the most stubborn—"

Nick grinned and leaned in to kiss Grace's cheek. "I think the word she's looking for is 'adorable.'"

"You'll both be careful," Grace instructed. "No unnecessary risks."

"Yes, ma'am," the two men chorused.

Grace fixed her gaze on Cody. "In case you don't already know this, Lily would never forgive me if something happened to you and I hadn't done my very best to stop you from walking into danger."

Cody felt a rush of pleasure that must have shown in his expression. "I didn't know she cared that much," he said, unable to hide the silly grin he felt spreading across his face.

Just then, he heard Lily call out a greeting to the men in the kitchen. "I'm late," she announced as she hurried toward the stairs up to the waitresses' rooms. But when she saw Cody, she hesitated. "I'm late," she repeated, only this time, it was in a voice filled with regret. "I'll see you tonight."

She hurried on up the stairs. Cody saw George cross the kitchen, motioning him over. Cody said goodbye to Nick and Grace and met the chef near the stairs. He had to look down to talk—the man was half a foot shorter than Cody. "You and Lily?" George asked.

"Yes."

"Don't hurt her."

Why did everyone seem to think his intentions were less than honorable?

"I won't."

George nodded, then grabbed hold of Cody's elbow and steered him to a hollow space under the stairs. "Not a bad place to say a quick hello without being seen," he observed and then wandered back to his duties.

A moment later, Cody heard footsteps on the tiled stairs, smelled the scent of Lily's floral soap, saw her familiar white-gold hair, and waited. She was tying the sash of her apron when she passed and gave a little yelp as he gently took hold of her arm and drew her into the shadows.

"Cody, what on earth?" she whispered, but she made no move to pull away.

"I can't see you tonight. It's business—Victor's back." Although he'd considered keeping this news from her, something told him Lily had heard enough lies in her life. He felt her tense, and he wrapped his arms around her. "Not in the hotel. He's hiding out, but you still need to be careful. Promise me you won't go out alone, especially after dark."

She nodded. Her face was close to his in the tight quarters, her lips a kiss away. Not wanting to cause her any trouble, he made a quick survey of the kitchen and saw that George had called his crew to the far side to bark out orders, leaving their backs to Cody and Lily in the alcove. He grinned and turned his attention back to the woman in his arms.

"Are you going to kiss me or not?" she said, pushing his hat back further on his head.

"Why, Miss Travis, I thought you'd never ask." Taking care not to muss her hair or her uniform, he lowered his mouth to hers and realized as their lips met that she was smiling. He was too, and he stayed lost in that kiss until Cody heard George announce, "Ah, Miss Kaufmann! What kind of cake would you like for your party?"

"Plenty of time for such decisions," the head waitress said as she headed for her office. "At the moment, Emma and I have far more important matters to discuss."

Lily pulled away, checked to be sure the perky bow in her hair was on straight, touched her fingers to her lips and then his, and hurried on to the dining room. Cody lingered in the alcove until he saw Bonnie Kaufmann close the door to her office, then gave George a grin and a salute of thanks as he left, heading for the saloon. Maybe Sally could tell him something new about other strangers hanging around.

❧❧❧

All afternoon and into the evening, Lily served her customers with a genuine smile—one born of the knowledge that Sheriff Cody Daniels was sweet on her and she was head over heels for him. Love was a wonderful thing. For the first time in her life, she was sure she understood what Grace experienced every time she saw Nick. She *understood* that half smile that claimed Grace's lips whenever Nick's name was mentioned, and now she suspected she wore a similar expression when anyone brought up Cody.

Trains came and went, the dining room bustled and then was quiet, and the hours of work flew by. But later, when there was little to do but sit, it was as if time stood still. Lily had relieved Emma to sit with Grace late that evening. In the middle of telling Grace about her meeting with Mr. Tucker to order supplies for the party, she realized Grace kept jumping at every sound.

"Did you hear that?" Grace said, leaning forward, straining to hear something from outside. "Horses, don't you think?"

"I don't hear anything," Lily said.

"Shhh! Listen."

"Grace, what's going on? This isn't like you."

Grace closed her eyes for a moment. "Earlier when I tried to tell you Cody had said Victor was back, you said you already knew."

"Yes, he told me."

"Did he not tell you he and Nick were riding out tonight to try and find Victor and the man seen with him?"

Lily's blood ran cold. She could not manage words, just a shake of her head.

"It's been hours," Grace said. "Nick promised to come by the minute they returned." She made a move to get out of bed. "There," she whispered. "I heard something."

"You stay put," Lily said. "I'll go check."

"Be careful," Grace called as Lily tiptoed across the quiet, dark kitchen to the back door. Why she was moving so stealthily she could not have said, but the combination of silence and shadow seemed to call for it.

She pushed aside a curtain that hung over the window next to the door. Outside, she heard low voices and the soft whinny of a horse. The yard behind the hotel was deserted, and try as she might, she could not see around the corner of the building to catch even the smallest glimpse of the street and plaza. Perhaps what she was hearing was the last customers leaving the Sagebrush. Perhaps it was Nick and Cody returning at last. Perhaps it was Victor Johnson and his partner.

She jumped when Grace touched her shoulder.

"Anything?" Grace whispered.

The two women froze when they heard footsteps moving along the tiles of the veranda.

"Get back in bed," Lily whispered. "Go!" Grace scurried away while Lily glanced around the kitchen, looking for a weapon. She settled on a large iron skillet. Grasping the handle with both hands, she stood behind the rear door, watching as the knob turned. She slowly raised the skillet over her head as the door opened a crack.

"You coming in?" a male voice whispered.

"Probably shouldn't," another replied. "Give Grace my best."

*Cody.*

Lily felt such a rush of relief that she lowered the skillet, losing her grip in the process. It crashed onto the floor. Suddenly, both Nick and Cody were inside, guns drawn and aimed right at her.

"No," she heard Grace shout as she rushed from her room carrying the lantern. "My stars, Nick, you had me so worried." She managed to set the lantern on a counter before stumbling into her husband's arms.

"I'm here," he assured her, scooping her into his arms and carrying her back to the tiny bedroom.

That left Lily still huddled near the door and Cody still pointing a loaded gun her way. "I could have shot you," he managed as he holstered the gun and reached for her. "What were you thinking?"

"What were *you* thinking going off in the night that way?" She got to her feet, her legs still shaking. "You could have told me. Grace was worried sick."

He took a step toward her. "And you? Were you worried, Lily?"

"No, because I didn't know. I was going on about silly party details, oblivious to everything." She felt tears fill her eyes. "Don't ever do that again," she whispered as she reached for him.

He held her close. "It's my job, Lily."

"Then find another job," she grumbled and heard him chuckle softly.

*Men.* If she lived to be an old, old woman, she doubted she would ever understand them.

He kissed her hair. "I've been thinking about that," he said. "I'd thought it would be a year or two before I left this job, but maybe sooner is better than later."

Her heart beat faster, and she looked up at him. "Truly?"

He nodded, brushing the backs of his knuckles along her cheek. "I just want to get this business with Johnson finished."

"Why wait?" She wanted to know he was safe now, not next week or next month.

"Simply handing in my badge won't solve anything. He'd still be out there, a threat to the town—and you."

"He's nothing to me," she grumbled.

"I know that, darlin' girl, but you may still be something to him, and I won't take that chance."

Behind them, Nick cleared his throat. "Lily, I'll be staying the night. Grace is pretty upset with me, and I just want to make sure she calms down. Thanks for everything you and Emma are doing for us."

Lily stepped away from Cody and took hold of Nick's hands. "Good night, then. Doc Waters left some sleeping powders in case she has trouble nodding off, but with you here…"

Nick kissed her cheek and then nodded to Cody. "See you folks in the morning." He went back to join Grace, closing the door with a gentle click.

The lantern Grace had left on the counter cast a soft, golden light over the kitchen.

"I should go," Cody said.

"Not until you tell me what you found out tonight," Lily protested. "Did you eat anything?" she added, rummaging around until she found half a loaf of bread and a jar of jam. Not waiting for his answer, she set a kettle on the stove and got two cups and a tin of tea from a shelf.

Cody removed his hat and pulled up a stool. She felt him watching her prepare their snack.

"Talk to me," she pleaded. "Was he there? Were they both there?"

Cody pulled a carving knife from a wooden block and started slicing the bread. "They were both there. I recognized the other guy from a wanted poster Ellie Swift received just last week. Chances are he's the leader of the gang."

"You were gone a long time. What took so long once you knew they were both there?"

"We got close enough to hear them talking but not close enough to be able to make out what they were saying. Words here and there."

"What words?"

"Something about the bank and everybody being occupied."

Lily poured boiling water over a strainer of loose tea, filling their cups. "You think they're going to rob the bank?"

"That makes sense." He spread jam on a slice of bread and handed it to her before fixing one for himself. "Question is when, and are they working alone? Will it be just the two of them, or are they waiting for others? It's not uncommon to have a couple of men case the target and then a whole gang pulls the job. Seems to me that would fit Victor's style."

"Do you think they're waiting at that cabin for the rest of the gang to join them?"

He stirred his tea. "That would be my guess. I'd also guess Victor Johnson will be off somewhere establishing an alibi, so even if the others get caught, he's out of it. It would be the word of known outlaws against his."

They ate their bread and drank their tea, both lost in thought.

"Cody," Lily said after a while, "you heard them say something about everybody being occupied when they were talking about the robbery?"

He nodded.

"Everybody will be at the party for Miss Kaufmann." She saw his eyes widen and knew he understood the connection she was making.

"When is that?" he asked.

"We haven't set an exact date, but Grace and I thought a Sunday or maybe combine it with the Independence Day celebration. The hotel dining room will be closed both days."

"Independence Day sounds like a day they might choose. Most people will be busy with family and such. Businesses will be closed. I doubt Johnson knows anything about the party for Emma and Miss K, but that would certainly add to the distraction." He took the last bite of his bread, then licked jam from his thumb before grabbing his hat. "Do you think you can persuade the others to combine the two events?"

"I'm sure I can."

"Meanwhile, I'll start quietly rounding up a posse." He wiped his hands on his trousers and tugged on his hat.

Lily realized he was leaving. "Wait." She hurried around the table and took hold of his arm. "What are you going to do? To stop the outlaws, I mean?"

He cupped her cheek. "Nothing tonight, Lily. I just

need to start making some plans, and you need some rest." He leaned closer.

"I can help," she said. "Please let me help. For Jake, if not for myself."

"You've helped already, Lily. From this point on, you have to let me handle things."

"But—"

He kissed her before she could say more. It started as a kiss she knew was intended to distract her, to allow him to leave without giving her a chance to argue. But instead of pulling away, he moved closer. She cupped the back of his neck, prolonging the kiss.

"Let me be part of this, Cody. You know I'll just follow you to your office," she whispered, returning the kisses he feathered over her cheeks and lips.

"And risk incurring the wrath of Miss Kaufmann when she realizes you were out after curfew?"

"I don't consider this an unnecessary risk," she replied, running her tongue over his ear and rejoicing in the shudder of pure pleasure that elicited from him.

He tightened his hold on her. "You're playing with fire, Lily," he muttered, but he didn't back away. "All right," he said after kissing her so passionately, her legs threatened to buckle beneath her.

"All right?" She looked up at him.

"All right in that there's more to this than just stopping a robbery. There's also the need to clear Jake's name and prove he wasn't involved with Johnson's plans. You knew Jake possibly better than anyone. Maybe he said something you originally dismissed, or you saw something you've forgotten. Come with me and help me think this through. I'll make sure you're back well before dawn."

She didn't hesitate. Before Cody could change his mind, she grabbed his hand, and together, they slipped out the rear kitchen door and on across the plaza to his office. As she waited for Cody to light a lantern, she closed her eyes.

*We're going to find justice for you, Jake. I owe you that.*

# Chapter 11

ONCE THEY WERE INSIDE HIS OFFICE CODY DELIBER-
ately took his seat at the desk, indicating Lily should sit
across from him. But as usual, Lily did as she pleased,
and it pleased her to pull her chair next to his as he
laid out the notes he'd made after the meeting with
Ty Drake. The kisses they'd just shared still clung to
his lips, and he could still feel the light touch of her
tongue tracing his ear, feel the outline of her body
pressed to his as they'd hurried away from the hotel.
Add to that the fact that he could practically see the
flashes of desire that flew between them as she sat
only inches away, drawing their bodies closer, and he
understood how great a mistake he'd made in allowing
her to come here with him.

His bed was not ten feet away.

He stood so suddenly that Lily jumped.

"What?" she asked, her eyes wide with expectation.

He moved to the map of the territory, a safe distance from her, and pointed to the place where he and
Nick had spied on Victor and his crony. "When we
were in Santa Fe, Drake didn't give us anything really

solid. The break-in at La Casita was done at night with no witnesses." He tapped the map several times. "We know Victor and the other man are holed up here."

"Yes?"

"What we don't know is if there are already others perhaps camped out here—or here." With Lily in arm's reach, he couldn't think. His usually sharp mind was muddled. He had to come up with some way of getting Lily to agree to go back to the hotel before he started something they both might regret. "What I need to do is ride back out there and check the surrounding territory," Cody proclaimed, making things up as he went along.

He began making preparations, grabbing a saddlebag from a hook and packing it with jerky and extra ammunition. He wasn't lying to her, not really. Checking the area surrounding the abandoned cabin was the right move. He could hardly plan to thwart a robbery until he knew what he was up against. He was simply doing his duty—not running away from a pair of sparkling green eyes that had him thinking about the bed in the dark room just around the corner from where she sat.

"Tonight? You're going right now?"

"Night is best. If there is anyone out there, most of them will be sleeping." He added a couple of tin cans of beans and peaches to his bag, then took paper from a shelf and started writing a note. "I'll be gone for a day or two. It'll take at least that long to investigate all the canyons around there where men could hole up for a week or so. I'll stop by Frank Tucker's place on the way—he can handle things here in town. And here's a message for Aidan." He scribbled a note, folded and stuffed it in an envelope. "But not a word to anyone else, all right?"

He couldn't look at her. He knew she was confused, but he couldn't help that. "Come on. Let's get you back to the hotel." He strapped on his gun belt, then took out the weapon, broke it open, and checked the bullets.

Reluctantly, she followed him out into the dark night and walked at his side as they returned to the hotel. "You'll be careful," she said softly once they reached the door.

"Don't worry. There's no real danger. I'm just going to take a look around."

"If there's no real danger, then why look to be sure your gun is loaded?"

"Habit."

The only way he knew to shut her up, to stop her probing, was to kiss her—a kiss he figured had to last him a couple of days and nights at least. She clutched at his shoulders, tugging him closer, opening her mouth to his, pressing herself to him so that he felt the outline of her breasts against his chest.

He was the one to pull away, but he didn't release her, and she still clung to him. Their breaths came in ragged heaves in the dark of the night. "Lily, when I get back—"

"Yes," she whispered.

He pushed her hair away from her forehead. "Don't be so quick to answer," he murmured. "What I was about to say is…I love you, Lily, and the truth is I want you in every way a man can want a woman. When I get back, we have to…"

"Oh, Cody, is that why you have this sudden need to go somewhere away from me?"

He nodded. "A man can only fight temptation standing right in front of him for so long. Think on it, Lily. Once I get back, once this whole thing with the outlaws and Johnson is finished, I'd like us to think seriously about maybe—"

She placed her fingers against his lips. "Sheriff Daniels, that is possibly the worst proposition—or proposal—any girl has ever heard. You'll need to work on that, all right?" She raised herself on tiptoe and kissed his jaw. "Now go before I drag you back to that little room next to your office and have my way with you."

He couldn't help himself. He chuckled. The woman had a way of shocking him and making him laugh all at the same time. "Is that a promise?" he countered.

"Come back to me and find out," she teased, and then she was gone, letting herself into the dark kitchen and softly closing the door behind her. Cody stood in the yard and waited until he saw the curtain move in her third-floor window and Lily standing there, looking down at him. She blew him a kiss, and he walked away feeling like the luckiest man who'd ever lived.

Three long days and two longer nights Lily waited for Cody's return. She worked, she cared for Grace, and she tried—without success—to sleep. She had the room to herself on the nights Emma spent downstairs with Grace and was able to pace and sit by the window, listening for his horse or watching for any sign of his return. Once, she had seen a light coming from the jail, and her heart had leapt. But only a few minutes later, she'd heard Frank Tucker's gruff voice admonishing some cowboy to "sleep it off" as the shopkeeper made his way back through town to his living quarters above his store.

On the third night, she wearily descended the back stairs to relieve Emma.

"Grace is sleeping," Emma whispered as the two friends stood in the kitchen. Emma stirred the milk warming in the pan on the stove, her cure for sleeplessness that she'd insisted Lily try. "There's no reason you shouldn't get some rest as well. Honestly, Lily, you look awful—dark circles under your eyes, and… have you been eating? You look drawn and thinner than usual."

Lily smiled. "Emma, it's been only a couple of days since Cody rode out. Stop worrying."

"I worry about you, not him. When it comes to Cody Daniels, you're doing enough fretting for both of us. Now drink this down." She added a dash of cinnamon to the milk and handed Lily the cup.

"Lovely," Lily murmured as she sipped the sweet beverage. "Mr. Harvey should add this to the menu." She carried the cup to the door to Grace's room. "Good night, Emma."

Emma walked to the stairs but hesitated. "I could stay tonight and let you sleep."

"Good night, Emma," Lily repeated, raising the cup

of milk in a toast before slipping inside the small room and closing the door.

The lantern on the crate next to where Grace slept had been trimmed to a glimmer, but it was light enough for Lily to see clearly. She sat on the cot she and Emma used and sipped the milk as she looked around the room for something to pass the time. Her gaze settled on the wardrobe where she'd hastily tucked Jake's belongings the day they brought Grace to town. Gently, she opened it, the carton holding his things within easy reach. Milk or no milk, she knew there would be no sleep for her, so she reached for the box and pulled it onto the cot next to her.

Carefully, so as not to wake Grace, she lifted the items out, examining each of them. A knit hat Jake had worn in cold weather, a slender bundle of letters from his sister in Ohio that were tied with twine, a certificate from the Harvey Company citing Jake as an exceptional employee, and a sepia-toned picture of the staff of the Palace. They'd posed for it after Grace and Nick's wedding celebration. In the photo, Jake stood between Emma and Lily, his arms around their waists.

They had enjoyed so many happy moments, and Lily had simply assumed there would be more. She would not make that mistake again. She was going to live every day and treasure every friend from this moment forward. She studied Grace, sleeping peacefully, her hands cradling her unborn child, and thought of Emma upstairs, hopefully also at rest.

*And Cody?*

Where was he on this night? Sleeping under the stars or prowling around boulders and sagebrush, trying to spy on the outlaws? She squeezed her eyes shut, silently praying for his safe return.

Pushing her melancholy aside, she turned her attention back to the photograph. Bonnie Kaufmann stood straight and unsmiling at the end of the back row of employees. Now she was leaving, and although she and Lily had had their conflicts, Lily was sad to see her go. Emma would take her place, and Lily couldn't help but wonder how that might change their friendship. Certainly, she could no longer expect Emma to cover for her if she wanted to stay out past curfew with Cody.

With a weary sigh, Lily began replacing Jake's property in the carton. She picked up a uniform jacket, like the one he'd worn daily in the kitchen. How had it ended up with his personal effects instead of in the laundry with the tablecloths, napkins, and aprons? Folding it and smoothing out the wrinkles, she felt something in the pocket. She pulled out a sheet of hotel stationery and gasped as she held it to the lamplight.

The handwriting was familiar—Victor's handwriting.

*24 HOURS, COLLIER. SMOKEHOUSE.*

She turned the paper over. There was nothing more. The note was not signed or dated, but it was Victor's jagged scrawl—of that she had not the slightest doubt. And it was a threat, the *or else* implied and unnecessary. She refolded the note and tucked it back inside the jacket pocket. At first light, she would take the jacket to Cody's office and leave it there with a note.

*What else have we missed?*

She recalled Cody saying he had been through Jake's belongings, but he hadn't found this. She pulled everything from the box once again, this time going through every letter from Jake's sister, examining the knit hat for she didn't know what, and finally once again staring at the photograph. She removed it from the frame, hoping perhaps Jake had hidden an additional clue behind the picture, but there was nothing. Besides, why would Jake be thinking of leaving clues? How could he know he might die—or be murdered? She sank onto the cot in defeat, still staring at the image of her friend.

*Oh, Jake, what were you doing and why?*

Without the protection of a glass cover, the photograph was brittle. That was odd. It hadn't been that long since they'd all posed for it, and her copy was still pristine. Had Jake taken his out of the frame so he could study it more closely—study *her* more closely? For he had loved her, and she felt such guilt that she hadn't loved him in return. She ran her finger over his grinning face. "Jake, I'm so sorry," she silently mouthed as tears welled and one dropped onto the photograph—onto her face.

With her thumb, she wiped the tear away and noticed the paper beneath her touch was rough. Again, she moved closer to the light, peering closely at the photograph. Because she had known all the faces clustered together, she had not focused on any specific one before now—certainly not her own. But now, she saw that her image had been scratched. There was a small black mark that ran across it, and the paper had been rubbed as if someone had tried to erase the mark.

There were only two possibilities she could think of. First, that realizing she would never return his feelings, Jake had marked her face in a fit of anger or despair. Or second, that someone had marked her face as a warning to Jake. The first was so uncharacteristic for Jake that Lily simply could not imagine it. But she could see Victor doing something like this—finding something Jake prized and vandalizing it. He had stayed in the hotel, and if Jake was away after the kitchen closed, he would have had no problem going through things in Jake's room. Either way, she was fairly certain Jake had tried to repair the damage.

She replaced the photograph in its frame and wrapped it in the jacket. She would take both to Cody. It might not be much, but it was something. Or was it? To her, the message in the note was a clear threat. To Cody—or anyone else—it might be seen as simply confirming an appointment.

But why would Victor meet Jake in the smoke-house—a small adobe structure set well away from the hotel, where the cooks smoked bacon and other meats?

She thought about the night Jake had staggered into the yard, his face a bloody mess. He had come from the direction of the smokehouse, and when she held him, his hair had smelled of smoke.

Grace stirred. "Lily?"

"Right here."

Grace blinked. "Is Cody back?"

"Not yet."

"Tomorrow then," Grace murmured as she closed her eyes again.

*Yes*, Lily thought. *Tomorrow.* And prayed it would be so.

It had taken the better part of two long nights of searching, but Cody had found exactly what he was looking for—the outlaw hideout. There were half a dozen of them, near as he could figure, making eight once you added Johnson and the man staying with him at the miner's cabin. That man seemed to be the go-between as well as the gang's leader, showing up at the camp twice during the time Cody kept watch.

Gut instinct coupled with experience told him the gang was getting ready to strike. Sheer gut instinct told him Independence Day would be the perfect time. The payroll was scheduled to arrive on July 3 by way of the four o'clock train. The outgoing deposit was scheduled to leave on the first train on July 5. On the actual day of celebration, all that money would be in the bank. When the gang hit the hotel in Santa Fe, they got away with only the payroll. Getting both the payroll and outgoing deposit from Juniper held the promise of tripling their take.

As the sky lightened, Cody mounted his horse and turned toward town. He'd be back before the sun was fully up. After three days of little sleep and nothing to eat but canned goods and jerky, he was looking forward to a decent breakfast—and he was hoping just maybe Lily might be filling in at the counter. Once he'd seen her, he'd have all the energy he needed to get to work foiling Johnson's plan and putting the man and his gang behind bars. And once he did, he'd let headquarters know they'd be needing a new sheriff in Juniper.

Cody had other plans.

The kitchen staff started work before dawn, and the noise they made wakened Lily and Grace. Still fully dressed, Lily stretched and yawned. A light tap on the door told her George was there. She let him in, bringing a pan of water so Grace could wash up. He set the pan on the crate by Grace's bed and handed Lily a stack of clean towels.

"How're you doin' this morning, Grace?" he asked, looking everywhere but directly at the pregnant woman.

"Just fine, George, thank you. I do think folks are making far too much of this."

George chuckled. "Don't tell Nick that. Now how about I cook you two ladies up a mess of my famous huevos rancheros?"

"That sounds heavenly," Grace replied.

"Lily?"

"Not for me. I have an errand to run, and then I need to get ready for my shift later this morning." She picked up Jake's uniform jacket and clutched it to her chest.

"That for the laundry?" George asked.

"No." She cast about for some excuse. "I need to mend a rip. I'll take care of it." She didn't miss the way

Grace arched an eyebrow. Lily did many things well, but sewing was not one of them.

"You run along, Lily," Grace said. "The boys in the kitchen will be here if I need anything." She stared at the bundle in Lily's arms. "After you take care of that, please do lie down for an hour. You look completely done in."

"Promise," Lily replied and squeezed past George. "See you later."

Sunlight fanned over the plaza as she stepped out of the hotel. The day would be hot and dry. And the night would surely be perfect in their secret place in the hills rising behind the hotel. Lily smiled. *Tonight. Cody home safe. Cody holding her, kissing her…*

She had just stepped inside his office and was searching for paper to leave a note explaining the uniform, note, and photograph when she heard a rider stop outside and a voice speaking low. Then she heard the jingle of spurs approaching the door. She looked up as the door swung open and Cody stepped inside.

Her relief at seeing him was so overpowering, she ran to him and wrapped her arms around his waist. "You're back," she said, the words catching in her throat. He was covered in dust and in need of a bath, but she didn't care. He was there.

"Yes, ma'am," he replied, dropping his saddlebag and sweeping her off her feet in a hug that had her laughing with pure joy. He was laughing as well, his dimples etched deep in his cheeks.

She touched his face as he set her down but did not let go of her. As suddenly as they had given free rein to their happiness at being reunited, they now grew serious, searching each other's faces, silent questions asked and answered. Cody tossed his hat on the desk and lowered his lips to hers. "Never leaving you for that long again," he murmured. His kiss tasted of longing and desire and a need that crackled like a spark between them. He smelled of sweat and smoke from a campfire. She ran her palms over his chest and back, needing to assure herself he was real and unharmed.

"Tonight," she whispered. "Promise me tonight."

"Just try keeping me away," he said thickly as he kissed her again, this time trailing kisses down her cheek and the open collar of her dress.

*Touch me. Love me.* She wanted to scream the words, so great was her desire for this man.

But when the rise and fall of voices in conversation from people passing outside finally penetrated the haze of their passion, he reluctantly eased away from her and turned his attention to Jake's jacket. "What's all this?"

She told him what she had discovered, watching as he slid the note from the uniform pocket and read it, then stared at the photograph. "I was going to leave this for you and then go have a look around at the smokehouse. I mean, if we missed these clues, there might be something there."

"No, Lily. I don't want you involved in this."

"But I am involved," she protested. "I know it's slim evidence, but I think Victor was using a threat to me to get Jake to do something for him. Something Jake refused to do and that got him killed. I've been part of this from the beginning, Cody. I have to make this right. For Jake."

"I'll get justice for Jake, Lily. You need to stay out of it."

All her life, Lily had been around men who thought they had the right to determine what was right or proper for her. Well, no more! Not even Cody was going to decide what she could or could not do.

At the same time, she was smart enough to know challenging Cody's authority would get her nowhere, so she lowered her head for a second, hoping he would take the gesture for acquiescence, and then asked, "Did you find the outlaw camp?"

"I did. My guess is you were right about them planning to strike during the Independence Day celebration and that party you're planning for Emma, but we'll be ready."

"We?"

He nodded. "I'll round up some men here in town and from the ranches and deputize them, then fill them in on the plan."

"And just what is the plan?"

He grinned and tweaked her nose. "Nice try."

"Cody, I want to help."

He hugged her close, resting his chin on her hair. "I know, darlin', and you can."

She looked up at him. "How?"

"By staying out of it—making sure Grace is all right, since I'll probably be needing Nick's help."

"But—"

"Look, Lily, if we're going to foil this robbery and catch the culprits in the bargain, it's important that most folks here in town have no idea there's anything going on. Can't have them come rushing out if they happen to hear gunfire, for example. That's where you and Aidan and the other Harvey people come in. If the gang does strike during the celebration or the party, your job is to make sure everyone thinks it's just some kids setting off firecrackers or a dustup at one of the saloons."

There was no use arguing with him, so once again, she changed the subject. "You need to wash up, Sheriff Daniels," she said as she ran her fingers through his thick hair.

He chuckled. "Yeah, a couple of days on the trail can leave a fella smelling a little overripe, I expect." He backed away from her. "I've got some business to attend to first, but I promise when I see you tonight, I'll be smelling sweet as saddle soap."

She laughed. "And speaking of that, I have to get changed and to my station in the dining room."

He walked with her to the door. "How's Grace?"

"Better. She sleeps through the night most nights, and there's been no more bleeding. And she eats like every meal is her last."

"I reckon I could do with one of George's famous breakfasts. Do you know what's on special this morning?"

"I know he made Grace huevos rancheros."

Cody licked his lips. "Washin' up can wait. Lead the way, Miss Travis."

Together, they returned to the hotel. Cody stopped to say hello to Grace while Lily ran up to her room to change into her uniform. When she and Emma came downstairs not twenty minutes later, Cody was seated at the lunch counter, a plate of food in front of him and the coffee in his cup sending up a smoke signal of steam.

"Well, he's back," Emma said with a wink. "So what are you going to do with your nights now, my friend?"

"I have no idea what you mean."

Emma laughed. "You know exactly what I mean." She gripped Lily's arm, and her expression turned serious. "Just be careful. It was one thing for Grace to be with child before she finished her contract—she and Nick were already married."

"You know something, Emma? You're already starting to sound a good deal like Miss Kaufmann, and I have to say, it doesn't suit you."

"What is it Cody always says? 'Just doing my job.' That's it, isn't it?"

"And I have to remind you that you haven't started the job yet," Lily replied with a nudge. "So I'm assuming if I happen to be a bit late for curfew tonight, I can still count on my dear friend?"

Emma frowned. "You know I think you and Cody were made for each other, Lily. Just be careful, okay?"

Lily linked arms with Emma. "I'll take that as a yes."

# Chapter
## 12

As soon as he polished off his breakfast, Cody headed for the smokehouse. It was a long shot, to be sure—weeks had passed since Jake's killing. But he wanted to check. The building was small, square, and dark. The only light came from an opening in the roof that allowed the smoke to escape. Of course, if the meeting had been at the smokehouse, there was no reason to assume that meant inside the building. This setting, well away from the hotel, at night? Three men could have easily met without anyone seeing them, even if they stayed outdoors. Jake could have endured a beating that took his life without anyone hearing.

Cody ambled around the perimeter of the adobe building, noticing how a pile of sagebrush used to stoke the fire had been knocked awry. Something glinted in the sun, and he bent to pick up a button. He turned it over, looking at it. It was the kind of button that Harvey employees received when they'd been with the company for a certain number of years. Could be Jake's—or belong to somebody else from the hotel. It wasn't any use as proof that Jake had been there.

He bent and studied the ground the way he used to study trails when he worked as a scout. There, the marks of something—or someone—being dragged. And nearby, a stain in the darkened sandy earth that could be blood. And a tooth.

*Had Jake been missing a tooth when he died?*

Cody couldn't recall. The man's face had been such a bloody mess. But Doc would know. He dug the tooth from the ground with the point of his knife and pocketed it. *Come on, Jake. Give me more.*

Around the back of the smokehouse was a pile of ashes, no doubt dumped there when one of the kitchen staff came to tend the low-burning fire. Cody knelt and sifted through them, using the point of his knife again to collect bits of charred paper and set them aside. The smokehouse fire was built from sagebrush and mesquite, not paper. So why were the scraps there?

He intensified his search, spreading the ashes carefully as he hunted for anything that looked like a message or maybe a map. Having exhausted the ash pile outside, he entered the smokehouse and used a shovel leaning against one wall to fill a bucket with more ashes.

He sorted through the fresh supply—ashes that still held the heat of the fire and in some places continued to smolder. The search yielded four more bits of paper. Careful not to further damage the unburned parts, Cody laid out his clues, anchoring each slip or corner of paper with a small rock. Two showed numbers: *R3* and *12*. One was a bit of hotel stationery. Two more had markings like a map—or more like the layout of a building's interior.

After repeating the search with three additional buckets of ash that yielded nothing, he stood, folding his knife and putting it away. He never took his eyes off the puzzle he'd laid out on the ground as he tried to imagine what might have happened that night.

Jake had been summoned for a meeting—a meeting where he was expected to deliver information.

Cody stooped to pick up the pieces that looked like a hand-sketched map. A scribbled word trailed off into the charred edge.

*Fron…*

"Front?" Cody muttered. "Front desk?"

*Had Jake provided a map of the hotel lobby, showing the way to the safe?*

He picked up the pieces with numbers. *Combination for the safe in Aidan's office? But how would Jake know that?*

Carefully, he gathered the clues, laid them in a bandana he untied from his neck, and wrapped them before placing them in the pocket of his vest. He took one more look around before heading back to town and over to Doc's office.

"Yep. Jake's front teeth had been knocked loose, and one was missing," Doc confirmed after Cody explained his question.

"Thanks, Doc."

"Smokehouse makes sense," Doc added as Cody prepared to leave. "His fingers were burned pretty bad. He also had these bruises and cuts around his wrists, like somebody grabbed him real hard or held him down with something sharp enough to cut."

*The shovel.*

Cody imagined Johnson—or more likely his partner—forcing Jake's hands into the fire. He'd seen torture in his days working for the army, and fire was a favorite method for getting a man to talk. "Thanks again, Doc," he said as he headed to the mercantile. It was time to start drafting his posse, and as mayor, Frank Turner was the man he could trust to provide names.

With Cody safely back in town, Lily couldn't seem to stop smiling. As she served her customers, she thought about what she might wear for meeting Cody later. At least to herself, she couldn't deny her focus was as much on what she might wear under her shirtwaist and skirt as choosing an outfit from her limited wardrobe. His eyes had widened with admiration when she'd worn her dark-green wool skirt with the matching jacket, the day they'd gone to visit Grace. And she knew he liked her to wear her hair up, so he could remove the pins and comb his fingers through it. The fancy boots? Definitely. She imagined him cupping her calf as he pulled one off and then the other, and she shivered with anticipation. And then she was shivering with something far more sinister.

"You little hussy," she remembered her stepfather saying as he pushed her against the desk in his study, the morning he'd caught her running away. He'd kneaded her breast with one hand while the other tunneled under her skirt and petticoats in a failed attempt to pull down her pantaloons. Failed because she had fought back. Failed because she had bitten his earlobe and tasted blood. Failed because when he leapt back in pain, she had run.

"Lily?" Emma was staring at her with concern. "Are you unwell? You've gone quite pale."

Lily forced a smile. "I'm fine. Just a little tired. Between work and watching over Grace, you and I have been burning the candle at both ends. Sunday can't come soon enough. Nick will be with Grace all day, and we can get some sleep."

"Maybe you shouldn't go out and see Cody tonight," Emma ventured.

For an instant, Lily thought perhaps Emma was right. Except not because of her weariness—but because she realized she was unworthy. It didn't matter that she'd done nothing wrong, that she had never given in to the advances of her stepfather or Victor.

Eventually, her past would matter, so why continue a relationship that could not possibly end well? Cody had ambitions—political ambitions. She was hardly the proper wife for someone who might one day be the territorial representative and living in Washington, DC.

*Wife?*

"Lily?" Emma was watching her closely, her brow furrowed with worry.

"You may have a point, Emma," she conceded. "Perhaps I'll send him a note, beg off in favor of catching up on my rest."

Her decision certainly did not seem to satisfy Emma, who continued to look at her with concern. "I wasn't seriously suggesting you not see him. Cody's been gone for several days, and you were worried. Of course you should meet him."

Needing to disarm Emma's angst, Lily laughed. "And I was teasing you," she said with a forced smile. "Now I really need to get back to work."

She would meet Cody and break it off with him. She'd even suggest he take another look at Abigail Chambers. She was older, more respectable. She would make a perfect political wife.

As soon as her shift ended, Lily hurried upstairs to claim the bathroom. She washed her hair and braided it into one long, thick plait. Once back in her room, she pulled on black stockings, her plainest undergarments, and a dull gray skirt with a maroon jacket she'd not worn since arriving in Juniper. She was fastening her serviceable work shoes when Emma joined her in the room.

"That's what you're wearing?"

"Yes. Why?"

"It's June, Lily, and that's an outfit more suited to February."

Lily shrugged. "The nights can still be quite cool."

"I thought the idea was having Cody keep you warm," Emma said. "And please don't tell me you're going out in the night air with a wet head. You'll catch your death."

Lily shrugged again. Silence filled the room. Emma continued to watch her as she finished dressing.

"What's going on, Lily?"

She'd never been able to lie to Emma. Lily sat on her bed and stared down at her folded hands. "I like Cody—more than like him. I think I might love him. And he thinks he's in love with me, but, Emma, that simply cannot be."

Emma sat beside her, stroking her back. "Why on earth not? You two are perfect for each other. Please don't tell me you are still worried about that horrid man who tricked you."

"Cody is going places, Emma. He's planning to run for the position of territorial representative and head to Washington. One day, he might even be a state governor. A man like that—with those ambitions—needs a woman who is…who can…who isn't…"

"Lily Travis, you listen to me. You are as suited to a life as the wife of a powerful man as anyone I've ever met. You are smart and beautiful, and your training as a Harvey Girl will make you a wonderful hostess. You grew up in Chicago, meaning you're certainly no country bumpkin. From where I sit, you are the perfect representation for women all over the country as we enter a new century. In fact, it wouldn't surprise me one bit to see you hosting parties at the White House one day."

Emma's praise was so exaggerated that Lily couldn't help but feel a little better. She fought a smile and met Emma's worried expression. "The only way I'll host anything at the White House is if I stay a Harvey Girl for the rest of my days and some future First Lady hires us to serve."

"Fiddlesticks. And another thing. You would be furious if the shoe were on the other foot. You do not get to decide what's best for Cody any more than he gets to decide that for you."

Cody had once told her the same thing.

"But you don't know the whole story," Lily objected. "There are things from my past, men other than Victor Johnson. My stepfather—"

"I don't need to know the whole story, Lily. I know you. You can tell Cody about whatever it is that you've decided makes you unworthy, but my guess is he'll say the same thing I'm telling you now. Whatever happened in the past is just that—the past. The woman you've become may be stronger for those things, but no matter what, you are not to blame." She stood and went to the wardrobe they shared. Opening the double doors, she stared at the contents before pulling out the dark-green outfit Lily had first thought of wearing. "Now, get out of that sackcloth costume and put this on," she instructed.

Lily could not help but laugh. "Did I mention you are becoming quite bossy?"

"You did and I am. Now change. I'm going down to sit with Grace. Stop on your way out and say good night."

As usual, the talk with Emma had lifted Lily's spirits. Her friend was right. It was not up to her to decide for Cody. She had told him the truth—all of it—and now he would need to decide for himself. If he truly loved her, wouldn't he choose a future together over his political ambition? And what if he did? And what if sometime in that future, he regretted that choice and resented her?

"Stop this right now," she whispered as she fastened the last button on her jacket, then hurried down the stairs.

"Much better," Emma announced when Lily stopped in the doorway to Grace's room.

"You look lovely," Grace added.

Lily grinned. "Don't wait up, my dears." And the

last thing she heard as she hurried outside was Emma's admonition that she be back by ten.

*Maybe she would. And then again, maybe not.*

After Cody spoke to Frank, he rode out to the Lombard ranch and met with Nick and his boss. John Lombard chose three of his best ranch hands for the posse Cody was gathering and offered the names of neighboring ranchers Cody might want to contact as well. Their meeting ran later than Cody expected, and he was pushing his mount hard to make it back to town in time for his tryst with Lily. The last thing he wanted was for her to take matters in hand and go off on her own.

The sun was already behind the mountains, and only a pale hint of daylight remained as he rode into town. There—he spotted the silhouette of a woman climbing the path behind the hotel. Knowing what light there was would be gone in minutes, he left his horse with the blacksmith and headed for the cow path that would lead him up into the foothills.

"Lily?" he called when he was close.

She stopped and waited for him to catch up. "It got late, and I thought maybe I had misunderstood or that maybe you weren't coming," she said, hugging herself with crossed arms. "I thought perhaps—"

"I had to ride out to the Lombard place. It all took longer than I thought. I'm sorry, Lily." He had reached her and was unsure whether to hold out his arms or simply fold her into his embrace. In the end, it didn't matter. She took a step and so did he, and then they were together, her face turned up to his, her hands resting on his shoulders.

He kissed her and then took her hand and climbed the rest of the way to the outcropping. The boulders hid them from town and at the same time opened a vista of mountains and sky that made them both smile. Cody lifted her onto a large, flat rock so that they were face-to-face. "Do you forgive me?" he asked. "For keeping you waiting and for causing you worry?"

He stroked her cheek. She traced her thumb over his lower lip.

"Not yet," she said softly. "It'll take more than one little kiss to make amends, I'm afraid."

He grinned. "I see," he said huskily, and he feathered kisses along the line of her jaw. "Now?" He whispered the word against her ear and felt the shiver that rocketed through her.

She shook her head.

He climbed onto the rock and stretched out next to her, pulling her against him. Watching her for any sign of discomfort, he lightly traced the outline of her breasts with his fingers. She cupped the back of his neck, pulling him in for a kiss that made him forget everything except the feel of her body outlining his, the layers of clothing between them a barrier he would like to tear away with his bare hands. He shifted so she would not be aware of his erection pressing against her thigh. She tugged him back.

"Lily, you don't know…"

"Then teach me," she pleaded, and he realized she was as lost as he.

But she also wasn't a woman whose favors he might enjoy for a night. This was Lily, the woman he hoped to one day make his wife.

He hesitated, and that was enough. Suddenly, she pushed away from him and sat up, twisting away so that her back was to him. "Sorry," she murmured.

*Sorry? What did she have to be sorry for?*

"Lily, look at me," he said as he gently took hold of her shoulder, turning her toward him. "I want you. All of you."

"But?"

"But I love you, and if you love me in return, then we can wait until the time is right."

"And in the meantime, what am I supposed to do with all these…feelings?"

He didn't need to ask what she meant. "Well, maybe it's not ideal, but kissing seems to help and maybe some touching that doesn't get too…you know…"

"And what if something happens to you?"

"Like what?"

She let out an exasperated sigh. "You could be shot, Cody, the way you're determined to go off by yourself chasing down outlaws."

"Or I could round up a posse—as I did today—and put those outlaws permanently out of business."

"Or," she insisted, "you could be shot."

It dawned on him that she might be thinking of Jake, another man in her life who'd thought he could handle things without help.

"Lily," he said as he wrapped his arms around her. "This is my job. I know how to do this. I promise you…"

She was very still and silent, but at least she didn't pull away.

"Lily?"

"I love you, Cody," she whispered, "and if anything were to happen…"

He kissed her before she could finish that thought. She clung to him and opened her mouth to him, and he was lost. Too soon, she pulled back. "All right," she said.

"All right?"

"If there are ways we can…" She fumbled for words. "You mentioned touching?"

Given that encouragement, he slowly opened the buttons of her jacket. She kept her eyes on his fingers as each button was freed. Once her jacket was open, the blouse she wore beneath was exposed. The thin fabric allowed him to feel the heat of her skin as he ran his fingers over her breast. She gasped and leaned into his touch, her eyes closed, her breath fanning his face.

"Now you," she whispered as she pulled his shirt free of his trousers, opened it, and placed her hand against his bare chest. He sat up and removed his shirt completely and waited for her to decide her next move. Using her fingertips, she explored the ridges of his muscles, pausing at his nipples before moving lower until she was touching the waistband of his trousers.

Gently, he pulled her hand away. "No, Lily. Not there."

She hesitated, then opened her blouse and shrugged out of it. She placed his hand on her bare shoulder.

"Do you know how beautiful you are?" He touched her throat, then looped his finger under the strap of her camisole, easing it off her shoulder, tugging it lower until the mound of her breast was exposed. He kissed her there, and she gasped, her head thrown back, exposing the length of her neck. He trailed more kisses up to her jaw and back again, nudging the camisole lower with his teeth until he felt the nub of her nipple against his lips.

*Stop now.*

But Lily tangled her fingers in his hair, urging him closer. By instinct, he reached for the edge of her skirt, bunching it higher. When he eased his fingers between her thighs though, she stiffened. "No," she whispered, and then more forcefully, "No!" She pushed away from him, clutching her blouse to cover herself and tugging her skirt back down.

Dazed and confused, Cody stared at her, then shifted away to give her space. "What is it?"

But did he really need to ask? *Victor Johnson*, he thought, mentally cursing the man for what he'd done to her.

"Lily, I'm not him."

"I know," she said.

"Look at me, darling girl."

Reluctantly, she did as he asked. While there was no moon, their eyes had grown accustomed to the dark, and he could tell she was looking directly at him. "Talk to me, Lily."

She pulled her camisole back into place and shoved her arms into the sleeves of her blouse, her hands and shoulders shaking.

He pushed her fingers away and fastened the buttons for her. "Lily, there's nothing you can say that will change what I feel for you. But I can see you need to get it told, so I'm listening."

"After my father died, my mother remarried."

"So you've said. The man was wealthy but strict." He nudged her chin up with his forefinger so he could fasten the button at her throat. "He also came to your room, made you lie with him, but Lily, you said nothing happened."

"He didn't…I never allowed him to…" She shook her head vehemently. "He didn't do anything to me, Cody, but he insisted that I *pleasure him*." The last two words were a whisper of pure shame.

Cody wanted to wrap his arms around her, assure her no man would ever hurt her again, but she was clearly on the edge, so he settled for taking her hand between both of his. "It doesn't matter. He can't hurt you anymore."

It was as if he hadn't spoken. "The day I left, I snuck into his study to take some money I knew he kept there. I didn't realize he was in the house. He slammed the door, and when I tried to run, he grabbed my hair and twisted."

Her words came from somewhere cold and dead and not at all like Lily.

"He pinned me against his desk—my father's desk. He grabbed my breast with one hand, and as he leaned in to kiss me, I felt his hand…pushing my skirt higher, tugging at my… I knew then that this time, he wouldn't stop."

She stared off into the dark as if living the moment all over again.

Cody had never in his life wanted to kill a man the way he wanted to murder this stranger. He swallowed bile that stung his throat. "Lily? I'm sorry. Please forgive me."

"Don't apologize for him," she rasped.

"I'm not. I'm apologizing for my actions. For the coarse way I...for being no better than any man who allows his carnal urges to ride roughshod over his better self."

She released a long breath before facing him. "Cody, any way you look at this, I'm damaged goods. I love you, and for a moment, I thought my past might not matter after all, but it does, Cody. Inevitably, it will."

"Not to me," he grumbled.

She touched his cheek. "Let me finish. Your dream is to have a political career. I know some things about that life. My father was a state senator, and trust me, if his opponents could have dug up any scandals about him or my mother while he was alive, they would not have hesitated to use them."

"Lily, I don't care about any of that."

"My past could destroy your future, Cody. I won't be responsible for that."

He hopped down from the rock, leaving her sitting there. She watched him as he paced in circles, trying desperately to find the words that would persuade her to stop taking the blame for everything on her lovely shoulders.

"I'm not Jake," he blurted.

"I know that."

"Jake loved you, but you didn't share those feelings. You've said you love *me*. Was that a lie?"

"No." Her voice was barely audible.

"Okay, that's at least a place to start." He continued

pacing, then stopped. "And when we kiss, you feel something too. Something that obliterates everything and everyone but the two of us, right?"

"Yes, but—"

He held up a hand to stop her from saying more, climbed back onto the rock, and sat cross-legged in front of her. He took her hands. "Lily, the one thing we both know is nothing in this world is certain. All we have to work with is the here and now. So here and now, we love each other. We want each other in every way a man and woman can want since Adam and Eve first made love in the garden."

"That's all true, but…"

"Stop saying 'but' and give yourself a chance to be happy, Lily. Give us a chance to see where this love takes us."

She stared at his hands entwined with hers. "I'm afraid," she admitted.

"Afraid of what? Me?"

She shook her head. "Afraid to be happy," she whispered. "I've thought before that…"

He tugged her closer and wrapped his arms around her. "Lily, darlin', this is now. This is me." He felt her relax slightly, her face resting in the curve of his neck. "Will you think about it? About us figuring out life together? I won't push you, I promise."

Her arms snaked around his waist as she cuddled closer. "I'll think about it," she whispered.

For some time, they sat that way, their backs to a rounded boulder, their arms around each other, her head resting on his shoulder, as they watched the moon climb higher in the starlit sky.

"Cody?" she murmured after a while. She looked up at him. "I think this might be a good time for you to kiss me."

He heard the teasing tone in her voice, knew she was trying to lighten the mood, and recognized it for the peace offering it was. Before their conversation, he would have happily kissed her with all the pent-up passion he carried with him day in and night out. But this woman had been wounded, and he would not give in to his baser needs. Instead, he would start showing her what true love could be.

"I'd like that," he said and tilted her face so that he could touch her lips with his. When she opened to him, he slid the kiss to her chin, her cheeks, her closed eyes. "We should go," he whispered.

She nodded. "Thank you," she whispered as she held him a moment longer.

He stood, jumped down from the rock, and then lifted her to stand beside him. "No need to thank me, darlin' girl. The way I see it, tonight I just got permission to court the prettiest girl in all New Mexico, and I don't aim to mess that up."

Their arms wrapped around each other's waists, they made their way back to the hotel.

"Tomorrow?" he asked when they reached the kitchen door.

"Yes." She kissed his cheek and slipped inside. Cody stood outside the closed door for a moment. One day, his question would be not about a single day but the rest of their lives.

And with any luck at all, her answer would still be yes.

# Chapter 13

LILY AND CODY SAW EACH OTHER EVERY NIGHT FOR A week. At her request, they did not return to their special place. "Maybe one day," she promised, "but for now—"

"Got it," he said. Instead, they took walks through town, sat on the hotel veranda with Nick and Grace, and one night attended a concert on the plaza. On these occasions, Cody held her hand, kissed her good night when they parted, and asked nothing more of her than the opportunity to know her better.

"Do you have brothers and sisters?" he asked one night as they sat together on the veranda.

"Two older brothers. You?"

"A twin sister."

She laughed. "You mean there are two of you? I can hardly deal with one."

He laughed.

"Where does your sister live?"

"She married a man who has made a career in the army, so they move around a lot. Right now, they're at a fort in Colorado."

"Do they have children?"

"Yep."

"You're an uncle?" It was a detail that made her look at Cody in a new way. She imagined him with children of his own. He would be a wonderful father, kind and patient.

"I'm an uncle four times over," he replied. "What about your brothers? Married? Kids?"

"We lost touch once our mother remarried. They didn't approve of her new husband—they were right, as it turned out. They were older and left before the wedding. Garson went east for university and then stayed. He's a doctor now, married with two children."

"And your other brother?"

"R. J. is the adventurer in our family. He headed to California. I had a letter from each of them at Christmastime."

"So they know you're here?"

She shrugged. "They do, but I'm afraid none of us is much for writing."

He hesitated, then asked, "And your mother?"

Lily felt something harden in her chest. "She and I parted ways."

"Tell me, Lily," Cody said softly. "Let it out." He uncurled her fingers from the fist she hadn't realized she'd clenched and ran his thumb across her palm.

"The day he...the day I left, Mama was at church. She often went there even during the week. On my way to the train station, I stopped to tell her what had happened—why I was leaving. She'd become so quiet and withdrawn at home, I thought she would understand. I thought she'd come to realize the mistake she'd made."

She saw it all as clearly as if it had been yesterday. Her mother seated alone in the sanctuary. Lily sliding into the pew beside her, tears streaming down her face, her hair a tangled mess she hadn't stopped to repair, her blouse torn where he'd grabbed her.

Her mother had sat stock-still while she poured out her story. And instead of consoling her daughter, Marjorie Travis Worthington had continued to stare straight ahead, her fingers working the beads of her rosary. And when Lily clutched her mother's arm, the woman she thought was her refuge had shaken her off, stood, and left the church without a word.

"Once I arrived in Kansas City, I sent her a letter to let her know I was safe and how she could reach me."

"Did you receive an answer?"

Lily released a mirthless laugh. "Oh yes. Several pages long. She wrote that she had spoken to my stepfather, and he was sorry for having lost his temper. She wrote that he'd described my 'hysterics' and, after all, everyone knew that from childhood on, I had always been prone to lies and fabrications. Still, she said, my stepfather was a good Christian man and willing to forgive. If I could see the error of my ways and make a full apology to him, they would welcome me back with open arms." She turned to face him. "I did not send a reply, needless to say. And to this day, I have not heard another word from her."

Cody wrapped his arm around her, and she relished the warmth of his embrace, the simple act of a touch that held no demands, just comfort. She rested her cheek against his shoulder. "Tell me about your parents, Cody."

"My folks? Nothing unusual. They met while their families were headed west on a wagon train. They were really just two kids who fell in love. Eventually, they married and set up housekeeping in a little town outside Flagstaff. They opened a store, sort of like Tucker's mercantile here. We lived in town until I started working for the army and Molly met her soldier boy. Pretty basic."

"Sounds wonderful."

"Yeah. I always thought one day I'd follow in their footsteps—not the store, of course. I don't have the patience to run a shop." He chuckled, then shifted so that he was looking at her. "But the girl of my dreams and kids and a house filled with laughter and love? That part." He leaned in and kissed her, a long, sweet kiss. "Found the girl," he murmured. "Pretty sure the rest will come along."

She kissed one of the dimples that had been her undoing from the first day she saw him. "Pretty cocky, aren't you, Sheriff Daniels?"

He grinned and tightened his hold on her, drawing her against him. "I always get my man. Or in this case, Miss Travis, my woman." He nibbled her ear. "Lily?" he whispered.

"Hmm?" She was lost in the feel of his breath warm against her face, his arms holding her.

"I've filed the necessary papers to run for territorial representative. If I get elected, I won't be sheriff any longer. Even if I don't get elected, I was thinking I'd like to try some other line of work."

"If you get elected, you'll have to spend a good deal of your time in Washington," she reminded him.

"True. Sounds like it might get lonely."

She fingered the collar of his shirt, knowing what he was asking. Knowing what the next step would be. "Maybe not so lonesome if I came with you."

His heart beat steadily beneath her palm resting on his chest. In the times they'd spent together over the last week, Lily had come around to wondering if perhaps they might have a real chance at happiness.

"We'd have to get married, I reckon," he mused as if the idea had just struck him.

"That would probably be best," she agreed. She put aside any doubts she might still harbor about becoming the wife of a politician.

"Miss Travis, are you proposing to me?"

She snuggled closer. "What if I am?"

"I'd have to think about it," he said, his voice serious. And then before she could protest or pull away, he kissed the top of her head. "Okay, thought about it. Yes, Miss Travis, I would be honored to marry you."

She slapped his chest lightly, but she was laughing, and the truth was she could not recall a time in her life when she'd been happier than she was at that moment. For the first time in weeks, she forgot all about Victor Johnson and the threats he posed. Cody was here. He would make sure everyone was safe—her most of all.

"I guess the question is," he said softly as he knelt on one knee and took her hand in his, "will you marry me?"

With a delighted squeal, she threw her arms around his neck and kissed him. Nudging his lips apart with the tip of her tongue, she let him know in the only way she thought he might understand that she was ready to travel whatever road lay before them. No more doubts. Together, they would leave the past behind and build a wonderful future.

"I'll take that as a yes," he said.

Lily Travis might be a rebel and renegade when it came to what people might expect of a politician's wife, but she was going to be a breath of fresh air for Washington society. Cody couldn't seem to stop smiling whenever he thought of her. Even as he sat at his desk putting together his plan for stopping the robbery, he whistled a lively tune to himself. The community celebration and party for Bonnie Kaufmann was just one day away. By this time next week, he and Lily would be free to pursue their future. They hadn't really discussed details yet, but to his way of thinking, they'd be married before July was over. The election was in the fall, and since he was the only candidate on the ballot so far, there was no reason to doubt that he would be the next territorial representative. In between, he imagined the two of them taking an extended honeymoon. They'd visit his sister and her family, his parents, and maybe even Lily's brothers. Then they'd need to find living quarters in Washington—

"Sheriff Daniels!"

He looked up from the list he'd been making to find Abigail Chambers standing in the doorway to his office. "Miss Chambers, is there something I can do for you?"

"My property has been vandalized."

She seemed mighty calm to be making that pronouncement, but Cody knew better than to form an opinion without gathering facts. "Your shop?" he asked as he got to his feet.

"My garden," she replied.

He hesitated. "I don't understand."

"Come see for yourself." She didn't wait for him but walked down the boardwalk toward her house at the end of town.

Cody followed. Sure enough, her usually pristine flower beds were a shambles of uprooted plants, broken stems, and half-demolished blooms.

"Well?" she demanded, hands on hips.

"That's quite a lot of damage all right," Cody replied, stalling for time as he tried to figure out what to say. "May I?" he asked, nodding toward the iron gate half off its hinges. When she nodded, he stepped inside the yard and surveyed the damage more closely. "Miss Chambers, has it occurred to you this might be the work of a rabbit or mule deer?"

"Well, of course it has. I'm not a simpleton, Sheriff Daniels."

"Then I really don't understand why you need me."

Abigail burst into tears. "Who will repair the damage? Pay the cost of replanting? My garden is all I have! It's my pride and joy."

Cody was taken aback, and at the same time, his heart went out to her. "Let me see what I can do," he offered, although he had not the first idea of what that might be. "In the meantime, maybe we could replant some of these uprooted ones."

She glanced at a large overturned rosebush, then blinked her tear-soaked lashes at him. "Of course, my first thought was to ask Victor—Mr. Johnson—for help, but he's still back east."

*No, he's not.*

"This one looks like it could be saved," Cody said, kneeling to examine an uprooted plant that seemed otherwise undamaged.

"You would do that for me?"

He had all he could handle getting everything set to foil the robbery, but how long could it take? "Sure," he replied and found himself the recipient of a hug and slobbery kiss on his cheek.

"Thank you, Cody," she murmured.

He eased her arms from her hold on him and smiled. "I'll see to it first thing in the morning."

Her eyes widened. "Yes. Come for breakfast, and we can work before the day gets so hot."

Cody was a good judge of people, and something was not right. For one thing, Abigail kept glancing toward the house. For another, her hands were shaking. He surveyed the yard and for the first time noted the damage seemed confined to the area of the yard closest to the house—and farthest from the street. "I'll come in the morning around seven. Leave the shovel and pitch-fork out so I don't have to disturb you. Don't fret, Miss Chambers. I'll do some asking around and see what I can find out about who might have seen something."

"No!"

He knew panic when he saw it. "Miss Chambers, you want to tell me what this is all really about?"

She pressed her lips together, and tears filled her

eyes. "I...please. Can't we just keep this between the two of us?"

"Only if you agree to tell me what really happened."

"I told you—someone vandalized my garden. I'm humiliated that anyone would do such a thing. What will other people think?"

Knowing he would get no more information from her, Cody opened the broken gate. "I'll bring along something to repair this," he said. "See you at seven."

The strange episode with Abigail niggled at Cody. He couldn't get the idea out of his mind that the vandalism in her garden had been staged to appear to be more than it really was. He had an instinct for anything that might signal a trap, but in this case, he couldn't figure out what that trap might be. Either way, he had no time to figure out what Abigail Chambers might be up to. He had a robbery to prevent and Lily to protect.

Lily, Emma, and the other Harvey Girls worked long into the night decorating the dining room and hotel lobby for the festivities. Outside the hotel, townspeople were hanging bunting from the gazebo on the plaza. The next day, Mayor Tucker would make a speech from there, and everyone would join in singing patriotic songs and participating in traditional games and contests. Later, the hotel staff and some special friends, including Doc Waters and his wife and the mayor, would gather in the dining room to bid farewell to Miss K and celebrate Emma's promotion. It was going to be a busy day—busier than most people were aware. But Lily knew that in addition to the celebrations, there could likely be a deadly crime taking place just down the street.

Cody had stopped by for a quick supper with Lily and the rest of the staff after the dining room closed for the day, but he'd left soon after. His departure hadn't surprised her. She knew he was off somewhere making sure everything and everyone involved was ready for the following day. The key was to make sure innocent citizens were kept near the festivities on the plaza and well away from the bank. With Cody in charge, Lily was confident everything would go off like clockwork. Victor Johnson and his gang of outlaws would be behind bars before the party for Miss K's retirement and Emma's promotion got started. And she and Cody had one more surprise for their friends. Capping off a perfect day would be the announcement of her engagement to Cody.

"You're looking quite pleased with yourself," Emma noted as the two of them stood back to survey the results of their work.

"Tomorrow is going to be a wonderful day," Lily said as she linked her arm through Emma's. "Come on. Let's go see Grace. I have something to tell you both."

Nick had stayed in town, supposedly to be near Grace, but Lily knew he was also there to play his role in tomorrow's posse. She was glad he and Cody had formed such a close friendship. She and Cody might end up living miles away in Washington most of the time, but Cody had assured her, as territorial representative, he would need to have an office and living quarters in Santa Fe. She and Grace and Emma would be able to visit at least a few times a year. Everything was falling into place.

"We came to say good night," Emma said as they entered Grace's room.

Nick stood, kissed his wife's forehead, and stretched. "I'll just step outside for some air," he said.

As soon as he left, Emma sat on the foot of Grace's bed. "Lily has news," she said. Both women gave her their full attention.

"Cody…that is, I…well, we—"

"Oh, for heaven's sake," Grace said. "Spit it out, Lily."

"We're to be married." She couldn't seem to stop smiling.

"That's hardly news," Emma said, winking at Grace. "I mean, from the day you two met, it's been obvious you were meant for each other."

Grace held out her arms to Lily. "I am so very pleased for you, Lily. No one deserves happiness more than you."

Lily accepted the hugs first Grace and then Emma offered. "We could end up living in Washington if Cody is elected."

"Oh my stars," Grace said with an expression of feigned shock. "Do you really think Washington is ready for Lily Travis?"

"Lily Travis Daniels," Emma corrected. "Hmmm. How about 'First Lady Lily Travis Daniels'?"

"Stop that," Lily said, but she was giggling with delight. "I am so happy," she added and realized the admission came as a surprise. It had been so long since she'd felt such unadulterated joy.

"Would you look at the three of us?" Emma said, reaching out to each of them to clasp hands so that they formed a circle of friendship. "A baby on the way…a wedding to plan…and—"

"And," Lily interrupted, "my guess is with you taking over for Miss K, Aidan Campbell better watch his back. Emma Elliott could conceivably become the first female manager of a Harvey hotel."

Emma blushed.

Outside the door, Nick cleared his throat before walking in. "Sorry, ladies, but my wife needs her sleep if I'm to deliver on Doc's promise to let her take part in tomorrow evening's festivities."

Lily and Emma each kissed Grace's cheek before leaving. Arm in arm, they climbed the back stairs, the glow of their shared happiness making words unnecessary.

Later after they'd changed into their nightgowns and climbed into bed, Emma said, "Tomorrow is going to be such a joyous day." She trimmed the wick of their lamp. "Sleep well, Lily."

Lily sighed. *Tomorrow, and all the days to come.*

Something wasn't right.

For a moment, Cody considered going back to his office where he'd left his gun belt hanging on a hook next to his bed. He'd thought replanting Abigail's garden would be best accomplished without it, giving him more freedom to work the shovel and kneel to pack dirt around the plants. But as he stood outside her gate and saw no sign of activity, he figured he'd been right to suspect this was a lot more than shoveling dirt and repairing a broken gate. At the very least, he'd expected to smell bacon or sausage frying, given the way she was always inviting him for a meal. Or maybe the scent of cinnamon from some pastry she was baking.

The damaged hinges of the gate creaked as he stepped inside the courtyard and saw the front door was ajar. He knocked, listened for any movement from inside, then knocked again. "Miss Chambers?"

Stealthily, he moved toward the parlor window.

Through lace curtains, he saw Abigail tied to a chair and gagged, her eyes wild with fear.

A step sounded behind him. Before he could turn, something heavy came down on his head.

Everything went black.

Cody came to inside Abigail's parlor, his hands and feet hog-tied like a calf ready for branding. From his position facedown on the floor, his range of vision was limited, but he saw a man's boots moving around the room and heard Abigail's muffled protests.

"Shut up," the man growled, a voice Cody didn't recognize. A slap. A whimper. Then silence except for the man jerking the heavy velvet drapes closed, casting the room in near darkness but for sunlight coming from the kitchen down the hall.

Realizing he wasn't gagged, Cody shook off the dull ache in his head and said, "What's this all about?"

A voice he did know came from somewhere nearer

the door. "Ah, Sheriff Daniels, so sorry to spoil your little plan for today's holiday celebration."

*Victor Johnson.*

"Johnson, if you and your thugs know what's good for you, you'll move on before——"

Cody felt the breath rush out of him like a steam engine at the station when the second man kicked him hard in his side. But Cody wasn't done. "Let the lady go. She's no threat to you."

Steps.

Cody turned his head so that he could see Abigail's lower body and then Victor standing in front of her.

"I'm afraid Miss Chambers has served her purpose," he said. "Pity. We had ourselves some lovely moments. Didn't we, my dear?"

A choking sob came from Abigail.

"At least take out the gag," Cody said. "Even if she screams at the top of her lungs, there's nobody around this end of town to hear."

"You may have a point. Would you like to speak, my dear? Perhaps tell the good sheriff here how you have pined for him, how nervous you were when I suggested vandalizing your lovely garden as a way of enticing him into your little web? But look how nicely things have worked out."

A whimper was followed by coughing, and then Cody heard Abigail's high-pitched voice. "I trusted you," she whined. "I allowed you to——"

Johnson laughed. "Oh, Abigail, you allowed nothing. You gave, sweetheart. And I must say, although you are a bit long in the tooth for my usual tastes, I will give you your due. You have an enticing body, and you were a most willing student in the art of seduction."

Cody could hear Abigail sobbing now.

"Let her be, Johnson. It's me you want. Why torture her?"

Step. Step. And then Johnson was sitting on his haunches, his face inches from Cody's. "Believe me when I tell you, this is nothing compared to the plans I have for Lily. Now there's a seductress worthy of the name."

If Cody could have moved, he would have strangled Johnson with his bare hands and not thought twice. As it was, he strained against his bonds, bringing a laugh from Johnson as he stood and moved purposefully to the door. "You know the plan, Rusty," he said in a tone that was all business, and Cody realized he was giving last instructions to the other man.

"Got it, boss. Hold 'em 'til I get the signal, then—"

"Just make sure no one comes calling."

The front door opened and closed. Rusty struck a match, and Cody froze. Was the plan to set fire to the house? With relief, he heard sucking sounds and realized the man was lighting a cigar.

Abigail was still sobbing so hard, she was gasping for breath.

"The lady could use some water," Cody said.

To his surprise, their jailer left the room, and a minute later, Cody heard the unmistakable sound of a water pump being activated.

"Abigail," he whispered. "We're going to get out of this. I just need you to calm down and listen."

"He tricked me," she moaned. "He said he just

needed to speak with you privately, about that waitress. He told me she's his wife and…"

"She's not. He lied to her as well. Forget him for
now and concentrate." When Cody'd peered in at
the window, he'd seen more than just Abigail tied
to a chair. He'd noticed she was positioned next to
a table where two people had recently shared a meal.
Closing his eyes, he reconstructed what he'd seen on
that table—plates with half-eaten food, crystal glasses
partially filled with wine, napkins. One of which had
been stuffed into Abigail's mouth. And a knife stuck in
a cut loaf of dark, crusty bread. Dinner, not breakfast.
Abigail had been taken hostage sometime during the
night. His heart went out to her, thinking of the panic
and fear she'd already endured.

"We're going to get out of here. Can you take
hold of the hem of the tablecloth with your teeth and
gently pull it toward you?"

After some struggle, she did as he asked, and he
held his breath as the breadboard—and knife—inched
closer to her.

"Stop," he whispered when he heard Rusty coming
back down the hall.

"Your water, madam," he said before tossing the
liquid in Abigail's face and laughing. "Brought you a
whole pitcher, Sheriff." He stood over Cody and slowly
emptied the contents over the length of Cody's body.

*Thank you,* Cody thought. The moisture might
help stretch the ropes binding him. He'd been quietly
working his wrists back and forth and flexing his hands
to loosen the bonds. A plan of escape clicked slowly
into place. If all this had started during the night, as

Cody suspected, sooner or later Johnson's man would either need to relieve himself or he would fall asleep. Once he did, Cody would hopefully have loosened his ropes enough to untangle himself, or he'd be able to coach Abigail to retrieve the knife and cut herself free before releasing him. He would send her to raise the alarm while he disarmed their guard and locked him in a cell before heading for the bank.

Rusty paced back and forth, stepping quickly to the window to peek out when he heard any sound from outside. Time passed, marked by the click of the minute hand on Abigail's mantel clock. Outside, Cody heard laughter and the excited chatter of people passing on their way to the plaza for the mayor's speech and the start of the holiday festivities. Here and there, a firecracker popped. In the distance, a band played a Sousa march.

In spite of his absence, Cody hoped Nick and the others were moving ahead with the plan they'd worked out. Hopefully, they weren't wasting time trying to figure out where he was. At least Lily wouldn't be expecting to see him until later in the day, not until after it was all over.

Minutes became quarter hours. The good news was that, although his skin was raw and probably bleeding, Cody was close to being able to slip at least one hand free of the ropes. One was all he needed. He groaned. "Hungry," he muttered.

With a grunt of boredom, Rusty stood, stretched, and moved toward the table. He chuckled. "Hungry, you say?" He picked up the board with the knife stuck into the loaf of bread. Pulling the knife out and sending it skittering across the floor, he gnawed off a hunk of the bread and chewed it, then spit it out. "You ain't much of a cook, are you, lady?" he grumbled, tossing the remainder of the bread and the board on the floor.

To Cody's surprise, Abigail found her voice, shaky as it was. "I'm afraid not, but in the kitchen, there are fresh eggs and the cheese and chiles I planned to use in preparing breakfast for the sheriff and myself. If you would only untie me, I would be more than happy to cook them for you instead."

Rusty snorted. "You must think me dumber than a rock, lady." After a moment, he asked, "You got any whiskey around this place?"

"I most certainly do not," Abigail huffed, then apparently thought better of her response. "There is some sherry in the kitchen, however. I use it for cooking."

"Sherry? Guess it'll have to do." He started down the hall. "You two stay right there." His laughter was grating.

"Good work," Cody said softly. He freed his hand and contorted his body so that he could untie his feet. Once free, he retrieved the knife, using it to cut through Abigail's bonds. "Go to the hotel and find Aidan Campbell," he whispered as he helped her to her feet and steadied her until she had her balance. "Give him a message from me."

"What message?" she whispered, her whole body shaking with fear.

"Tell him things are in motion. He'll understand."

"I can't...what if Victor sees me?"

Gently, he led her to the front door. "You can do this, Abigail."

"What the…" Rusty came rushing at them from the kitchen.

Cody pushed Abigail toward the door before turning to take the brunt of Rusty's attack. He head-butted the other man as he heard the door swing open behind him. Sunlight flooded the hall. He could only hope Abigail would do as he'd asked and head for the hotel instead of the hills.

# Chapter
## 14

LILY HAD VOLUNTEERED TO STAY WITH GRACE WHILE
Nick joined the posse. The hotel was quiet now that
the guests were out on the plaza, where the staff had
set up tables of enough food to keep everyone well fed
throughout the day. The band playing and the cheers
of the crowd made her heart beat with excitement.
The occasional pop of a firecracker made her smile.
Later at the party for Bonnie and Emma, there would
be more food and speeches and music. There would
be dancing. She closed her eyes and imagined Cody
taking her in his arms as he led her around the floor in
a waltz. She did not doubt for one second that Victor
was walking into Cody's well-planned trap.

Grace made a low, whimpering sound.

From the moment Lily had arrived to relieve Nick,
she'd realized Grace was putting on a brave face for
her husband. Now as her friend bit her lip and stifled
a cry of pain, Lily rushed to her side. "I'm going for
Doc Waters," she said and started for the door.

"He was here earlier," Grace managed. "His daughter burned herself on some bacon grease—pretty bad

from what I gathered. He and Sarah have gone to Lamy to see about her. He promised they wouldn't stay long."

"But that could still be hours."

Grace shrugged and placed a protective hand on her distended stomach. "I didn't want him worrying about me with so much else on his mind. Besides," she said with a wan smile, "these things take time. Just stay with me, and we'll be fine."

"At least let me get Emma in here."

"She's got other responsibilities. George was telling me that two new waitresses arrived yesterday and Miss K has turned their training over to Emma." She patted the bed. "Come, sit with me," she said. "Tell me all about your plans—yours and Cody's."

Lily perched on the edge of the bed. She told Grace about Cody's idea that once he was sure the town was safe from the likes of Victor Johnson, he would resign his post. After a new sheriff was in place, she would resign her position with the Harvey Company, and they would be married. It seemed the more she talked, the less agitated Grace became. She no longer grimaced with pain, and her body was relaxed and calm. When her eyes closed and her breathing steadied, Lily stood and stretched with relief before walking into the deserted kitchen to refill Grace's water pitcher.

Suddenly, Abigail Chambers burst through the rear door of the hotel. "Where's Mr. Campbell?" she demanded. She stumbled in like someone who'd been drinking, checking the kitchen before moving on to the lobby. She looked a fright, her face blotched and mottled, her usually perfect clothing in disarray, her eyes wide with panic.

"I...he's..." Abigail was a gossip, and no one but those involved was supposed to know what was happening at the bank.

Abigail grabbed Lily's forearm. "Cody sent me to find him. That man—your husband—"

*Victor.*

"What about him?"

"He and his men are robbing the bank. Cody and I were held hostage until he was able to escape and free me. He told me to find Aidan and..."

"Where is Cody?"

"There's no time to explain," Abigail screamed. "I must give Aidan the message." And with that, she raced outside again.

"Lily?" Grace stood, clinging to the door frame. "I think..." Her voice faded as she slumped to the floor.

Lily ran to lift her and get her back to bed, a pool of clear liquid surrounding the place where Grace had collapsed. From outside, she could hear the innocent sounds of the celebration in the plaza. The band played, people applauded, children shrieked, firecrackers popped.

She froze. What if those weren't the popping of fireworks? What if the sounds she heard were gunshots? What if the robbery had begun and things had already gone awry? She knew enough of the plan to know Cody had situated his men both inside and around the bank. They were to hold their positions until the robbers were inside, and the posse could catch them in the act. But clearly, things had changed if Cody wasn't there to take charge of the operation.

*Hostage.*

Was Cody still being held somewhere?

Every muscle in Lily's body strained to run from the hotel and go in search of Cody, but Grace's grip on her tightened as she moaned, "The baby is coming. I can feel it. It's too fast."

*No*, Lily prayed. *Not now.* Surely Emma or Miss K or any one of a number of other women would be better suited to helping Grace than she was. Should she go to the plaza and cry out for help?

Grace gave a bloodcurdling scream, and her body went rigid.

"All right," Lily said, more for her benefit than Grace's. "We can do this." She ran to the linen closet and grabbed a stack of towels, dropping them at the foot of Grace's bed. Then she ran to the kitchen and got a pan of water, although she had no idea why it might be needed. It just seemed like the thing to do. Another scream sent Lily scurrying back to Grace's side.

She coaxed Grace to lie back, bend her knees, and plant her feet, then took a deep breath and lifted the hem of her friend's nightgown so she could see what was happening. The fine cotton was soaked with sweat, blood, and the fluids that had broken free. Never had she had such an intimate view of the female anatomy, and when it occurred to her that a child weighing at least several pounds with arms and legs flailing was supposed to make its way into the world through that narrow passage, she felt a wave of dizziness and nausea.

*Impossible.*

Grace drew in a breath, and once again, her body went rigid. With a keening cry that came through gritted teeth, she thrust her hips up.

Lily saw something start to emerge—dark, but not blood. *Hair.* "I see the head," she shouted above Grace's scream.

"The face," she added as the baby's head popped free. Instinctively, she cupped her hands to support the newborn. She turned it until a shoulder appeared, and then in one great rush, a fully formed but impossibly tiny child squeezed its way out and rested in her hands, slippery with mucus and blood and still attached to Grace by a long cord.

"Oh, Grace, you have a son." She held the baby up for Grace to see before laying the child on one of the towels. That's when she realized he was neither crying nor moving.

Panic seized her. "Grace, he's not breathing. Tell me what to do. You lived on a farm—you must have seen baby animals born. How different can it be? What do I do?"

Weakly, Grace tried to push herself higher so she could see. "Use your pinky finger to clear his mouth."

Lily did as instructed, and to her relief, the baby stirred, then hiccoughed and let out a cry, then another, stronger cry. Lily grinned at Grace.

"What do we do about this?" Lily pointed to the cord.

"String," she said. "You need string and scissors."

"What on earth for?" Lily demanded, looking wildly around the room for the items Grace mentioned.

"You have to cut the cord. Go look in the kitchen for the cord George uses to tie meat. Bring a length of that and the scissors."

Gently, Lily transferred the baby to Grace's arms

and ran to the kitchen. She rummaged through every drawer until she located the scissors then cut a length of cord from the skein George kept on a spindle at one end of the butcher block. By the time she returned, Grace was still holding the baby, but she was grimacing again, her body starting to contort.

*Twins?*

But what emerged this time was a blob of blood and mucus with no resemblance to a baby. Lily was unable to conceal her horror.

"Afterbirth," Grace told her, collapsing.

"Oh." *Childbirth is certainly a messy, painful business.* But when she looked up and saw the way Grace was smiling at her son, Lily had to admit that apparently, somehow, it was all worth it.

Grace told Lily how to wrap the string around the cord and then how to cut it so mother and child were separated for the first time. "He doesn't feel it," Grace assured her when she hesitated.

The baby let out a cry that to Lily sounded like a cross between protest and jubilation. Grace looked at Lily, and they both burst into tears and peals of laughter. They had done it.

Wiping her eyes with the edge of one of the towels, Lily understood why the doctor always brought water and so many towels. "Let's get you and young Master Hopkins cleaned up, and then I'll go leave a note for Doc. Not that we need him now."

The two of them giggled.

Lily helped Grace move to the cot where she and Emma usually slept, and she changed the linens while Grace washed herself and the baby. After helping

Grace back to bed with a fresh nightgown for herself and a clean towel for the child, she bundled the soiled linens and placed them in the outgoing laundry basket near the back door in the kitchen. From outside, she heard a whistle and shouts of encouragement and knew the games and races must be in progress on the plaza. The day there would end with ice cream sundaes. She also heard horses on the move and shouts coming from the direction of the bank.

She ran to the hotel lobby just in time to see Cody and Nick riding hard after two other men on the way out of town. *No.* Cody had managed to get away but was now going after the outlaws. She clenched her fist to her mouth to stifle her protest. A moment later, she saw Ty Drake and some other men Cody had told her would be coming from Santa Fe follow. Clearly, the robbers were getting away. She heard the clang of the fire bell mounted in a tower at one end of the plaza— the bell used only in the event of an emergency. The band stopped playing in midsong, and for an instant, everything went still. Then people were running and shouting and Mayor Tucker was calling for women and children to take shelter while the men mounted their horses and rode off after the posse.

Guests and townspeople crowded into the lobby, seeking shelter from the gunfire. Miss K shouted for calm, but no one seemed to be paying her any mind.

Lily hurried back to the kitchen where the rest of the staff from the hotel were gathered, all talking at once, their voices shrill with panic. Why was Aidan there? Wasn't he supposed to be at the bank?

"Something went wrong," Aidan said when Lily

ran to him first, knowing he'd been part of the plan to stop the robbery. He was breathing hard and clutching his shoulder, Emma by his side.

"He's been shot," Emma said. "Get some towels and water, Lily. Tommy's gone to fetch Doc Waters."

"I…Grace…Doc isn't here. He and Sarah have gone to Lamy."

The baby's wail silenced the room. Everyone held their position as if playing the children's game of statues, all heads turned toward Grace's sickroom.

"Oh yeah," Lily said, taking advantage of the sudden quiet as she collected more towels. "While you were all out celebrating, Grace had a baby boy."

For a moment, the robbery and the danger were forgotten. The other waitresses took turns crowding into Grace's room, and their coos were a welcome reprieve from the distress of before.

"How on earth?" Emma murmured, staring at Lily. She glanced toward the room. "Is Doc Waters in there?"

"Doc's gone to see about his daughter. She suffered a bad burn."

"So you…?"

Lily shrugged. "Grace did most of the work," she said as she handed Emma the towels and went to get water.

"It's nothing," she heard Aidan tell Emma. "No more than a scratch."

But when Lily came back with the pan of clean water, she saw that Aidan was quite pale, and he grimaced as Emma removed his jacket. His shirt was soaked with bright-red blood.

"Let's get you sitting down," George said as he gently eased his arm around Aidan and half carried him to a chair. Then he unceremoniously ripped the shirt open at the shoulder, held out his hand for a towel, and pressed hard against the wound. "We'll need alcohol to clean this, and then iodine and bandages." Emma hurried off to gather the necessary supplies.

From the lobby, they could hear Miss K taking charge, giving directions for women and children to gather in the dining room and instructing the musicians to play something soothing.

"What happened, Aidan?" Lily asked.

Aidan shook his head. "We couldn't find Cody, so we went ahead and took our positions as we'd discussed. It all went like clockwork at first—we were in place, watching every possible exit. The gang came in through a rear entrance as we expected."

George took up the story. "I was inside and saw them set dynamite to blow the safe open. I sent Tommy to alert those waiting outside, and we started to move in."

"That's when Abigail came running to warn us," Aidan said. "But it was too late."

"I don't understand," Lily said.

"There were outlaws inside the bank, but what we didn't realize is there were outlaws watching us on the outside as well. When we started to move in, that's when they opened fire."

Lily closed her eyes. She'd seen Cody take off after the escaping outlaws. "Was Cody hurt?"

Aidan hesitated. "Hard to say. There were a lot of shots fired by both sides. All I know is that he and

Nick and some of the hands from the Lombard ranch rode off after them."

All during this conversation, Emma and George were working together to treat and close Aidan's wound. "What about Victor Johnson?" Emma asked.

Aidan looked surprised. "Come to think of it, I didn't see him. Not before, during, or after."

Emma glanced at Lily, who understood they were both thinking the same thing—Victor was still out there somewhere.

Cody and Nick rode side by side. They'd lost sight of the outlaws, who had probably found shelter in one of the many canyons along the way. "Let's split up," Nick shouted.

Cody shook his head and motioned for Nick and the others to follow him cross-country. "Got a better idea," he yelled back. Alongside Nick, Cody had chosen his posse with care—Ty Drake and two of his deputies, in addition to three of Nick's ranch hands. With any luck, they could get ahead of the gang and surround them. Rather than the canyons, he figured the outlaws were headed back to their camp. That was the most likely landmark they'd have used as a meeting spot should they get separated.

And if so, then Johnson should meet them there to oversee the split of the money before they all scattered. There was no sign of anyone watching the posse this time, but to be cautious, he used hand signals to post Drake and his deputies on high ground around the camp. He and Nick dismounted and climbed down to the sole entrance—a narrow slit between high walls of granite.

He tossed Nick one end of his rope. "Tie it around that boulder," he instructed as he did the same with the other end. Working quickly, he and Nick set a trap for the gang. If they came riding in fast, even if the horses noticed the barricade set just below a horse's knees, by then it would be too late. The horses would panic and rear, throwing their riders to the ground—or at the very least leave the riders fighting for control, unable to react to the posse quick enough.

"Let's go," Cody shouted after checking the tension and security of the ropes a second time. Nick followed him up the steep incline to a position just above the entrance. Cody signaled Drake and the other men, and they took their positions. While they waited, Cody studied his surroundings. *Where was Johnson?*

Nick nudged him. In the distance, they heard riders, coming fast. Cody drew his gun and held it up, a signal to the others to be ready. Ty Drake grinned from his post.

The capture went off exactly as planned. The horses panicked, as did their riders, and within minutes, Cody, Drake, and the others had them surrounded, disarmed, and tied together with the rope that had been their undoing in the first place.

"Got this under control, Daniels," Drake said as one of his men loaded the saddlebags containing the bank's money onto Cody and Nick's horses. He glanced at Nick. "You two best head on back to town. I hear this man's to be a father one day soon—wouldn't do to have the little lady worry unnecessarily." He clapped Nick on the shoulder, then shook hands with Cody before turning his attention back to his prisoners. "Well now, look at that," Drake drawled. "Seems to me we got more men than horses. Likely some will have to walk." He rubbed his beard and studied the horizon as if considering the choice. "Ten—maybe twelve miles—to the fort." He climbed into the saddle and instructed his deputies to do the same. "Let's head out, boys," he shouted.

Cody and Nick watched them go, Drake and his deputies riding while the outlaws shuffled along behind, trying to keep up with the pace Drake set for them.

"Good work, Nick," Cody said as they rode back to Juniper.

"But it's not over, is it?"

"Sure it is. We got the money back, and the robbers are under arrest."

"What about Victor Johnson?"

"I'll get him," Cody said through gritted teeth and spurred his horse to a faster pace. "Come on, Hopkins. You need to let Grace see you in one piece."

"And I reckon you might be hoping Lily will coming running to welcome her hero home?" Nick laughed as he galloped ahead of Cody, sending up a cloud of dust that had Cody swearing even as he grinned.

The mood inside the hotel was tense. Everyone had been cooped up for too long, children complaining as their pleas to be allowed to play outside went unaddressed. Worried parents hovered around Aidan and Frank Tucker, the streets outside the hotel unusually quiet and deserted. In one corner, Abigail told and retold her ordeal to anyone willing to listen. By now, it sounded as if she had rescued Cody rather than the other way around. Everyone was waiting to learn if the outlaws were still in the area or if the posse had won.

Lily stood near one of the lobby windows, watching for any sign of Cody's return. Grace sat nearby, having insisted on being moved out of the back room so she could be part of whatever was going on. Her newborn son slept peacefully in a makeshift cradle Miss Kaufmann had concocted out of a wash tub layered with pillows. Emma sat with Aidan, his shoulder bandaged and obviously painful, while Miss K tried without much success to assure the masses of people crowded into the lobby and dining room that everything was under control.

"They're back," Lily shouted as she ran to the door, ignoring warnings of possible danger. Leaving the door open, she ran the length of the veranda and on down the street to meet Cody and Nick. They had stopped outside the bank and were handing saddlebags to the banker and his assistant.

"Cody!" Lily shouted, not caring in the slightest how it might look for her to be running down the middle of the street calling his given name.

Cody slid from his saddle and held out his arms to her. "We got 'em, Lily," he said as he gathered her close. "It's over."

"Victor?"

She felt him tense and had her answer. Victor was still out there somewhere.

She stepped back so she could look up at him. "Are you hurt?"

"Not a scratch. How's Aidan?" He wrapped his arm around her shoulders as they walked toward the hotel together, Nick already on the veranda ahead of them.

"He's fine. Grace had her baby! It's a healthy boy."

Her news was confirmed by a whoop of pure joy coming from the hotel, followed by laughter from those gathered there.

"A son," Cody murmured. "Well, that's good news. Doc was back in time, then."

"Not exactly."

A wagon's approach from the opposite end of town caught Cody's attention. Doc and his wife rolled slowly into town, clearly mystified by the empty plaza. Cody glanced at Lily.

"If Doc wasn't here, then who delivered the baby?"

Lily shrugged. "Good thing Grace grew up on a farm and had some idea how these things go. I couldn't have done it without her."

"*You?*"

"Well, you don't have to sound so surprised," she said, giving his chest a playful slap and grinning. "Not that I plan to make a habit of it, but if I do say so myself, Grace and I managed just fine. Come see for yourself."

She tugged his arm as she led the way inside the hotel. Nick was holding his son and grinning like a man who'd just discovered gold. "It's a boy," he announced when he saw Cody. "Born on the Fourth of July! That has to be special, don't you think?"

Cody grinned. "Congratulations. Grace, are you doing all right?"

"Thanks to Lily, we're both just fine."

"I'll be the judge of that," Doc muttered as he stepped past the circle of people surrounding Grace and Nick and set down his bag.

Leaving Doc to examine the newborn and Grace, the throng of townspeople surrounded Cody, who kept one arm firmly around Lily's shoulders. "It's over, folks. Go enjoy your celebration," he announced. "I understand there's ice cream?"

With a whoop, the children raced for the door. Unconvinced the danger was completely over, their mothers followed close on their heels, admonishing them to be careful. The men stayed, clearly hoping for details of the chase and capture. They ignored Lily as they pelted Cody with demands for details.

She couldn't help but be impressed with his patience and the way he answered the same question again and again. But at the same time, what she wanted—*needed*—was to be alone with him. Between the robbery and the unexpected arrival of Grace's baby, it had been quite a day, and they still had Miss Kaufmann's farewell party that evening.

"Excuse me, gentlemen," Lily said when she heard a fourth man ask for Cody's assurance that their money had been returned to the bank. "I believe Sheriff Daniels has answered your questions."

The men glanced at each other and then at Cody.

One man grinned. "Sorry, Sheriff. Just wanted to be sure." He shook hands with Cody and then herded the others back outside to join their families. Lily heard the band start playing again, the music mixed with the laughter of children. Nearby, Doc had his stethoscope pressed to Grace's chest while Nick studied the baby in the washtub as if he couldn't quite believe what he was seeing.

"Come on," Lily said, taking Cody's hand and leading him through the kitchen and on into the yard behind the hotel. "Alone at last," she said with a nervous laugh. Suddenly, she was shy. She wanted so much for him to kiss her, but here in broad daylight?

He stepped closer, his palm smoothing her hair away from her forehead. "You are one amazing woman, Lily Travis," he said, his voice low and raspy with emotion. "Have I told you lately I love you?"

"Not lately enough," she replied, cupping his cheek with her hand.

He leaned closer, his lips brushing her forehead. "I love you," he whispered.

"Sorry? I'm not sure I heard that."

He chuckled. "I love you."

Her heart hammered. There was nothing she wanted more than to spend the rest of her life with Cody. But Victor was still out there somewhere, and now that Cody had foiled his plans, he would want revenge. She knew him that well, at least.

As if he'd read her thoughts, Cody tilted her chin so she was looking at him. "Lily, don't let Victor spoil things for us."

"But…"

"No," he murmured as he kissed her. It was a kiss that left her knees shaking and made her cling to him for balance. "At that party tonight, I'm claiming every dance, okay?"

She tipped his hat back so she could see his face more clearly. "Whatever you say, Sheriff Daniels."

He laughed. "Well, there's a first—Lily Travis taking orders from me?"

"Maybe in the past you gave the wrong orders."

He narrowed his eyes at her. "I see. Well, how about this one. Kiss me, Lily."

Uncaring of who might be watching, she raised herself on tiptoe and fit her lips to his, pressing her tongue to his teeth until he opened to her.

"Anything else?" she murmured when they parted, their breaths coming in gasps of desire.

"Marry me."

"Yes," she whispered. She touched her fingers to his throat and felt the beating of his pulse. Or perhaps it was her own heart she felt—or could it be both their hearts beating as one?

# Chapter 15

THE CELEBRATION FOR EMMA AND MISS KAUFMANN
was subdued given the events of the day. While no
one had died, Aidan and two others had been injured,
reminding everyone of the fragility of life on what was
still the frontier.

Ty Drake had sent a wire telling Cody that the
outlaws had been placed in the custody of the Army
and were being held in Santa Fe to answer for
crimes they had committed throughout the territory. There had been no sign of Victor Johnson, and
Drake had been unable to gather any information
from the gang leader.

Putting all that aside, Cody set his mind on the
evening's festivities. Lily wore a pink calico dress, and
she'd pinned up her hair in a way that made him long
to pull the combs holding it free and let it spill into
his open hands. He had never seen her looking more
beautiful—or more happy. As others congratulated
her on her role in delivering Nick and Grace's baby,
she blushed and smiled in a way that made her glow.
Cody stood near the refreshment table watching her,

knowing she hadn't yet realized he was there, enjoying this moment to observe her unawares.

Emma at her side, Lily fussed over Grace and the baby, making sure both were protected from the summer breeze drifting in through the open windows. At one point, she lifted the baby, showing him off to others gathered around and teasing Nick about the need to give the child a name. The image took Cody's breath away, for what he saw was Lily holding their child—and the future he was determined to have with her.

She looked up then, and as if her gaze was pulled by an invisible cord, saw him. Her smile faltered, replaced by an expression he knew was mirrored on his face—longing, desire, love. He crossed the room, threading his way through other guests, but never taking his eyes off Lily.

"You look…" They said the words in unison and then smiled.

"You first," she said.

"Why, Miss Lily, are you fishing for a compliment?" he teased.

She arched an eyebrow. "Forgive me, Sheriff Daniels, I was under the impression you were about to offer one."

He found he had no patience for banter. He held out his arms to her. "Dance with me?"

She stepped toward him, and they joined other couples who swirled around the center of the dining room that had been cleared for the occasion. She looked up at him, one hand linked with his and the other resting lightly on his shoulder. She was smiling, her eyes shimmering like a deep pool of water after a spring rain. He could hardly believe his good fortune.

Nearby, Nick danced with Emma while Grace rocked the baby and looked on approvingly.

"No doubt Grace insisted Nick ask Emma to dance," Lily said. "I do wish Aidan would realize what a jewel she is."

"I thought he promoted her to take Bonnie Kaufmann's position," Cody replied.

"Oh, he knows Emma is the best choice for that. I just wish he would realize she's also the best choice for him."

Cody grinned. "Matchmaking, are you?"

"Grace has found happiness, and so have I. It seems only fitting that Emma should as well."

"You're happy, then?" He really didn't want to talk about Grace and Emma.

The slight frown that had marred her forehead eased. She met his gaze. "I am happier than I ever thought possible," she said softly.

He tightened his hold on her. "Let's take a walk," he suggested.

"Why? What's happened?" The frown was back, and he realized his own expression had sobered, alarming her.

"Because I can't very well kiss you the way I want to here in front of all these people, and frankly, Lily, if I don't kiss you in the next few minutes, I won't be responsible for my actions."

"Oh," she said, her frown changed to a shy smile. "Well, in that case..." She linked her arm through his as they walked toward the front door.

The minute they were outside, he grasped her hand and pulled her into the shadows. It was impossible to say who made the first move. All Cody knew was that she was there in his arms, her mouth open under his, her tongue and his engaged in a dance far more satisfying than the one they'd shared moments earlier.

"Lily," he murmured as he pressed her to the wall, allowing his body to outline hers. Suddenly, he realized that her cheeks were damp beneath the kisses he feathered over them, and he tasted tears. He stepped away. "Why on earth are you crying?"

"I could have lost you today," she said, her voice shaking. "We might never have had the chance to…"

He held her close, his chin resting on her soft hair. "Shhh. I'm right here. I've already spoken to Ty Drake about one of his deputies taking over as sheriff here, and I've filed the papers to run for the position as territorial representative. So as soon as I know Victor Johnson is in custody and no threat to you or anyone else, we can—"

"I don't want to wait," she admitted.

"Lily, I can't marry you until—"

"You mean you won't." Her expression was defiant.

Cody took half a step away from her. "I won't put you in needless danger. Victor Johnson is still out there somewhere."

She blew out a frustrated breath and leaned against him. "I know," she murmured.

"He's not just a threat to you, Lily. Think of what he did to Abigail and that waitress in Santa Fe. He's dangerous, even more so now that we foiled the robbery."

For a long moment, they were silent.

"And what if we don't wait? What if…" she said.

He tightened his hold on her, knowing what she was suggesting. "I want you, Lily, more than you can possibly imagine. But we shouldn't. Your reputation could be ruined."

"Isn't it my choice to make?" She stepped back so that she could look directly at him. "Cody, I am fully aware of what I'm suggesting. Certainly my stepfather and Victor made sure I was educated in that arena, even if it was against my will."

"I am not those men," Cody growled.

"I know that," she hurried to assure him. "Don't you understand? They only knew how to take what they wanted, and in the process, they robbed me of my ability to trust. But what I feel for you is so different from anything I've ever known.

"And yet, what if we marry and I find I simply can't…that the memories of what they did are too ingrained in me to ever allow someone good and kind and loving like you…" Her eyes glistened with unshed tears, and her lower lip trembled. "You must think me horrible."

"I think you are anything but horrible, Lily. You are brave and caring and scared." He was so torn, wanting to protect her and make sure no man—especially not him—ever caused her pain again. At the same time, he wanted to show her what real love might feel like, how the act of true love might be the balm needed to erase all those painful memories. Cody wrestled with what his head told him might be a mistake but his heart begged for him to consider.

"Look, ever since Jake died, things have been anything but normal for us."

"I know," she agreed. "It seems like maybe it's time for a new normal. I feel like one is out there but just out of reach."

"Honey, today was full of upsets."

"But that doesn't change anything. It only makes me want us to be together more."

The door to the hotel opened, and another couple found a place in the shadows on the opposite end of the veranda.

"Come on. Let's walk over to my office. At least there we can talk this through without worrying about being interrupted."

She nodded.

Hand in hand, they crossed the plaza. He opened the door and allowed her to go ahead of him into the dark space. Once he'd shut the door, he was at a loss as to what he might do next. He reached for the lantern. She covered his hand to stop him.

"There's enough light from the street," she said as she perched on the edge of the single chair near his desk.

"I could make tea," he offered with a nervous laugh. "Might calm our nerves."

"Or you could kiss me," she replied, giving him a light tap on his lips, but immediately after she did that, all pretense of teasing disappeared. "Today taught me one hard lesson—we may not have tomorrow."

He drew her to her feet and slowly removed the combs and pins from her hair, drawing in a breath as the mass of its platinum beauty tumbled down over her shoulders. He placed the hair ornaments on his desk and cupped her cheeks in his palms. "I love you so much, Lily," he whispered as their lips met.

The kiss was sweet and lingering, full of a new kind of curiosity. They had time, Cody thought. They had all night. And when he took her hand and led her to his bedroom, she did not protest.

Lily knew Cody's living quarters were part of his office. Once when she'd come there to seek his help, she'd glimpsed the rumpled covers on a narrow bed. Now they stood next to that bed.

"Lily, I—"

She placed a finger to his lips to silence him. She was done talking or analyzing the right or wrong of this. She eased the suspenders from his broad shoulders and began opening the buttons on his shirt, pulling the tails free as she worked her way from top to bottom. She placed her palms flat on his bare chest, feeling the heat of his body, the thunder of his heartbeat. She traced her fingers over the hair that tapered to the waist of his trousers, then straightened and reached for the first button at the neck of her dress.

"May I?" he asked, covering her hand with his.

For an answer, she slid her hand away, leaving his touching the buttons. With agonizing slowness, he opened each one, his face half in shadow and half illuminated by light from outside the single window. Finally, he released the last button. Watching her closely, he eased the upper half of her dress from her shoulders.

She shrugged her arms free before pushing his shirt

open. He let it drop to the floor as he leaned in to kiss her bare shoulders, her exposed throat. Her breasts swelled with desire, her nipples pressing against the soft linen of her camisole. It seemed only natural to kiss his nipples and then to go a step further, laving them with her tongue.

He shuddered and looped a finger through the strap of her camisole, tugging it down. She drew in a breath. He bent to kiss the swell of her breast. She tangled her fingers in his hair and pressed him to her. Through the thin barrier of fabric, she could feel the nip of his teeth, the open-mouthed kiss, and a current coursing through her lower body that cried out for him to take her to his bed.

He stepped away and closed the door separating his private quarters from his office. He continued to face the door. She stepped closer, running her hands over his back. "I want to try, Cody," she whispered. "At least then we'll know."

He turned to face her. "There are ways we can be together without…"

"Teach me," she said. "Love me," she whispered as he lifted her and laid her gently on the bed.

His hands trembled as he lifted her skirt to pull off her shoes and stockings. He took his time, cradling her calf in his palm and leaning in to kiss her bare skin once the task was done. He sat on the side of the bed and removed his boots, then knelt before her and ran his hands over her legs, up and under her skirt to her thighs. When she thought she might explode from the desire coursing through her, he withdrew his hands, smoothed down her skirt, then lay beside her and began undoing the ribbons of her camisole. He spread the fabric, exposing her naked breasts—breasts he cupped and nipples he caressed with his thumbs.

She closed her eyes tight, thrilling to the exquisite pain of it all. She struggled to sit up, and he took it as rejection, moving away at once and turning to face the window.

"It's all right," he said. "I understand."

"Look at me, Cody." He glanced at her over his shoulder. She stripped off her camisole and began unfastening her skirt. She stood by the bed and let both it and her petticoat fall to the ground. He was facing her now, and when she unbuttoned her pantaloons and eased them down her legs, she heard him suck in a breath.

She had gone too far—he would see her as some wanton woman and be disappointed. Lily turned back to the bed and reached for the quilt to cover her nakedness. "I'm sorry," she whispered.

He covered the chasm between them in two steps, unbuttoning the fly of his trousers as he did. Gently, he pulled the quilt away and dropped it back on the bed. His eyes never left her as he stepped out of his trousers and kicked them aside. Cody lifted her, one arm under her hips urging her to wrap her legs around him. She felt the fullness of his erection pressing against her through the fabric of his undergarment and wanted to cry out with her desire for him.

Clinging to one another, they toppled onto the bed, their legs intertwined.

"Lily?" His mouth was next to her ear, his breath warm. "Whatever we do from this moment, know you can stop at any time. If it's too much—"

For an answer, she ran her finger down the center

of his chest until she reached the band on his undergarment. She did not stop. Instead, she tunneled her hand under the fabric until she could hold him. When he startled like a newborn colt, she started to pull away, but he rolled toward her instead of away. His fingers threaded their way between her thighs, until he was touching the very core of her need.

They both froze, their eyes open—his seeking permission, hers pleading for him not to stop whatever this new sensation was.

He struggled out of his undershorts and straddled her. Tenderly, he positioned her bent legs to either side of him. She felt the tip of his penis seeking entry and grasped his bare hips, urging him on, giving him permission—and still he hesitated.

"Cody, yes," she whispered.

Slowly, he eased into her. Surely, her body was too small to hold him! And yet she believed with all her heart that their bodies were meant to fit together in this way. She smothered a cry when something inside her seemed to give way, allowing him full entry. Any hint of pain was erased as he began to move within her, and instinctively, her body responded.

And then without warning, he pulled out and rolled to his side, his breathing labored.

"It's all right," he managed, but he turned away from her, and for one awful moment, she felt rejected and used. She pulled the covers tight around her and started to sit up. But then he was facing her again, stroking her shoulder. "Lily, it's not what you think. Please, Lily, look at me."

She was fighting tears of humiliation, but she turned

to him, tossing her hair away from her face. "There's no need for apologies, Cody. Here we thought I might be the one to reject *you*—"

He let out a growl of pure frustration. "I pulled out because I don't want you getting pregnant before we can marry."

Her heart skipped a beat as she realized this man—this incredible man—had foregone his own pleasure to protect her.

"Oh," she said, the only response she could find. All the tension seeped out of her.

"Will you stay tonight?" Cody's hand rested on her shoulder.

"Maybe it would be best if I went home."

"Please stay, Lily. I've lost count of the nights I've spent lying in this bed alone, staring at the ceiling and imagining you here beside me. And I'm talking way before we started stepping out together."

She wanted to stay more than she'd ever wanted anything. She wanted to spend the rest of her life lying next to this man. "Maybe, if that cup of tea is still available…"

He laughed. "Wait right here." He got up and pulled on his trousers. Moments later, she heard him in the other room, clanging the lid on the wood stove as he stoked the fire, followed by the clink of a spoon against crockery. She wrapped herself in the quilt and watched him from the doorway.

He caught her looking and grinned at her. He was shirtless and barefoot as he puttered around gathering a tin of loose tea and a bowl of sugar while the water heated, and she was pretty sure no man had ever looked more desirable.

"Cody? I've been thinking."

"I've discovered that can be dangerous when it comes to you," he teased.

"I'm serious. I'm sure Victor is long gone and can't hurt us or those we care about anymore. What if we don't wait—to be married, I mean?"

He continued pouring steaming water into a teapot, then set the kettle back on the stove and turned to face her. He was frowning. "Letting Victor get away will not end this, Lily. He'll always be there. Maybe not physically, but we both know he had something to do with Jake's death. And we both know what he did to you. Not to mention the other girls he'll take advantage of."

She knew he was right. Justice for Jake had been the one thing driving her for weeks now. Letting Victor walk away from that was simply not possible.

She took the mug of tea Cody offered and headed back to his bedroom. She sat on the side of the bed, pulling the quilt around her. When Cody followed, he tucked the cover more securely around her before pulling up a chair and straddling it. "Are you all right?" he asked, watching her sip her tea. "I mean, do you understand how much I wanted…"

"Cody, I'm very all right," she assured him.

He ducked his head, suddenly shy.

They drank their tea, the silence between them feeling as normal to Lily as if they'd shared such moments countless times.

"Cody, how can we stop Victor? How can we prove he was behind Jake's death and the robbery and everything else?"

"*We* don't do that, Lily. I'll handle it. You need to stay out of it."

"No."

His head shot up, and he scowled at her. "No? Lily, I can't be worried about your safety at the same time as I'm tracking Johnson."

"I want to help. And I will, with or without your permission." She set her mug on the floor and rummaged around for her undergarments. It was difficult to make her point when she was wearing nothing but a quilt. She found her camisole and put it on. While tying the ribbons, she felt Cody watching her.

"Stop that," she said without meeting his gaze.

"Can't," he replied as he set his mug on the floor next to hers and stood. He was giving her that devilish grin that was a surefire way to get her heart racing. "Need some help?"

When she risked a glance his way, he was holding her pantaloons. She snatched them away from him and put them on. "You're impossible," she muttered, but she couldn't help but smile when next he held up her petticoat.

"Put your shirt on," she grumbled.

He chuckled and did as she asked. She finished dressing and went to his desk to retrieve her pins and combs to put her hair back up. Cody came up behind her and wrapped his arms around her. "Leave it down," he said as he kissed the nape of her neck.

"I have to get back to the hotel."

"I know, but we've got a little time."

She turned to face him, leaving the combs and pins on his desk and wrapping her arms around his neck.

"If anyone had told me I would fall in love with a lawman, I would have laughed," she said.

"And yet?"

"And yet here I am," she murmured as their lips met. In spite of everything she'd endured in the past, her future with Cody promised to make up for it all. "Cody, promise me you'll do everything possible to prove Jake's innocence."

He was still holding her close, kissing her temples and forehead. "I'll do my best, Lily, but we both need to face the fact that Jake may have been involved at the beginning. Perhaps he had a change of heart."

"Well, he didn't have to die for a change of heart. What if he was trying to do the right thing? What if he wanted only to protect me?" As was always the case whenever she thought of Jake, Lily felt sadness overwhelm her. She had taken his friendship and devotion to her for granted. "I just want to do whatever I can to make sure Jake rests in peace and his good name is restored."

"I know. All I ask is for you to let me do my job—a job that may involve my having to leave town for a while. Promise me you won't make any moves on your own while I'm gone."

She looked up at him. "You're going after Victor?"

"I'm going to Santa Fe to see what I can find out from the gang members being held there. Depending on what they have to say, I will follow the trail wherever it may lead. But I can't do any of that if I'm worrying about you, so promise me—"

"I'm hardly likely to—"

"Promise," he growled.

She bit her tongue, knowing he was right. She would not add to his danger by causing him unnecessary worry. "I promise," she said.

He let out a long breath of relief and picked up her hairpins. "Time to get you back to the hotel." He placed the pins in her hand.

She twisted her hair into a knot and stabbed it with the pins. "I don't want to go," she admitted.

"If I could, I would keep you here all night, but you were right earlier, and we both know it can't happen." He touched each button on the front of her dress. "But when I return…"

"When you return, Sheriff Daniels, it had better be with the intent of marrying me as soon as possible."

He grinned. "That's a promise I can make—and keep," he said as he placed his hand against her back and steered her toward the door. Just before opening it, he pulled her close and kissed her, a kiss that left them both breathless.

"I guess that'll have to hold me until I get back," he said. He reached for the door and then once again turned back. "One more thing," he said. "Next time we make love? Nothing will stand in our way, okay? No Victor, no curfew, and definitely no need to be careful. Agreed?"

He looked so intense that all Lily could do was smile. She brushed his hair away from his forehead. "Agreed," she said. And when he turned for the third time to open the door, it was Lily who stopped him. "You know that kiss? The one that's supposed to last us?"

He grinned. "Not enough?"

"Not by a long shot," she said as she stood on tiptoe and wrapped her arms around his neck.

# Chapter
## 16

THE RIDE TO SANTA FE TOOK LONGER THAN PLANNED. A sudden dust storm rolled across the desert, and Cody had to stop and find shelter for himself and his horse. Like the thunderstorm he and Lily had endured, the pillar of swirling dirt and debris seemed to come out of nowhere. One minute, the sky was as clear and blue as the cornflowers that had grown on the lane leading to his parent's place, and the next, everything went dark as granules of sand and dirt stung his eyes and skin. He made it to an arroyo at the base of a mesa where he and his horse were protected from the brunt of the passing storm by the high walls to either side.

It certainly didn't take a dust storm or memories of a thunderstorm to start him thinking about Lily. He'd had nothing else on his mind since leaving her the night before. He reminded himself repeatedly on the road of the need to keep his focus on the work at hand. He couldn't help worrying that Lily might go off on her own though. If she discovered anything she thought might clear Jake, she wouldn't hesitate to follow that lead regardless of the danger. So the sooner he caught up with Johnson the better.

He'd thought about speaking to Aidan, asking him to keep an eye on Lily, but he knew she would be furious if she ever found out. He'd also considered leaving a note for Emma with the same message but again knew Lily's fury would not just be directed at him but at her friend as well. He'd figured out that trust was a big issue with Lily. A person had to earn that. After last night, he figured he was on pretty solid ground, but with Lily's history of having her trust broken, it was probably best not to take anything for granted.

The storm finally passed, and Cody headed for the jail. He knew the military officers in charge of the prisoners from serving with them when he was working with the army as a scout and guide. Captain Troutman personally walked Cody to the wing of the jail where the outlaws were being held.

"We can't get anything out of them. You might have more luck," he said. With a jerk of his head, he dismissed the two soldiers on guard duty. "I'll leave you to it, Cody. Keep your distance from the cell doors—last thing we need is a hostage situation. Guards will be just outside here."

"Thanks," Cody said and nodded to the guards before entering the dim corridor that ran the length of the building. There were four small cells, three occupied by two men each and the last by a familiar, lone outlaw.

*Rusty.*

Cody leaned against the rough clay wall outside the gang leader's cell, folded his arms, and simply stared at the man who had held Abigail and him captive.

"What do you want?" Rusty sneered, but he backed away from the bars, and his voice shook slightly.

"Depends," Cody replied.

"On what?"

"On whether you and your friends here want to take the full brunt of paying for what happened back in Juniper—and the job a few weeks ago in Santa Fe."

"You got no say in that."

"I'm a witness, and I know several others willing to testify against you. I reckon that might be enough to see you all hang." He heard murmurs from the other cells and was aware the other men were listening to everything he said. That was his intention, so he waited a long beat before adding, "Of course there might be a way 'round that."

"Such as?"

"We both know who was the actual brains behind these robberies."

Rusty moved a step closer. "You sayin' I don't have the smarts to put something like this together?"

"That's exactly what I'm saying."

Snickers came from the other cells.

Cody shifted his position, cocking an ear. "You boys hear that?" From outside came the unmistakable sound of hammering. "Sounds like the captain might be having his men get a head start on building that gallows. Shouldn't take long."

"We deserve a fair trial," one of the other men shouted.

"That's true. Doesn't change the likely outcome, since you were caught with the goods, but you'll have your day in court," Cody replied, never taking his eyes off Rusty. "Of course by then, it'll be too late."

"Too late for what?" Rusty snarled.

"To make a deal."

"What kind of deal?" a man from two cells down demanded.

"Shut up, Snake," Rusty yelled. "Who's runnin' this?"

More murmurs of discontent from the others, but no one openly challenged Rusty's claim.

"I'm listenin'," he said.

Cody propped one foot on a small wooden stool and counted out the details on his fingers. "One, you tell me what Jake Collier had to do with any of this. Two, you tell me everything you know about Victor Johnson's part in this business. And three, you tell me where I'm likely to find Johnson."

"In exchange for what?"

"Me sharing that information with Captain Troutman and persuading him to talk to the judge about sparing your sorry lives. No guarantees, but thankfully for your sakes, nobody died on this job—except Jake."

"That was an accident," Snake called out. "We was just supposed to scare him and rough him up some."

"And yet he died of the injuries you and your friends inflicted," Cody said, keeping the fury that filled his chest in check. "A good man died for no reason."

"That was all Johnson," Rusty muttered.

"Meaning?"

Rusty looked up. "If I tell you what you want to

know, how do I know you won't go back on your word?"

"It's a fair question. Guard!"

One of the soldiers came running, gun drawn. The other prisoners moved to the backs of their cells.

"Would you ask Captain Troutman to come?" Cody instructed. "I believe these men are in a mood to talk."

The kid took off at a run.

Troutman had obviously stayed close by, because it wasn't a minute before he stepped inside the narrow corridor outside the cells. He was accompanied by his assistant, who held a notebook and pencil. "Okay, let's hear what you have to say," the captain demanded.

Cody laid out the terms he'd offered Rusty and his men.

Troutman moved closer to Rusty's cell. "You give me the evidence necessary to arrest Victor Johnson, and I'll do what I can with the judge. That's the best I can offer."

Rusty hesitated.

"Way I see this, Rusty," Cody said, "if you refuse to talk, you hang for sure. If you give the captain what he needs, you and your men have a fighting chance."

Snake wasn't about to wait for Rusty to make a choice. "Johnson was threatening Collier. Told him either he got the combination to the hotel safe for us or that waitress Collier was sweet on wouldn't be so pretty anymore."

Cody's gut clenched. "What happened the day Jake was beaten?"

"Tell them, Rusty. You was there," Snake demanded.

"Johnson sent word for Jake to meet us at the smokehouse and bring the safe combination and a map showing where to find it. When he got there, he wanted some kind of guarantee the girl wouldn't be harmed. Johnson had me and the other boys rough him up some, making the point he wasn't in no position to name terms."

The captain's assistant was writing down every word, his pencil flying across the page.

"Jake was mad. After we punched him a few times, he pulled a paper from his pocket—looked like the map. Anyway, he just stood there, nose bleeding and all, and he was grinning. He tore the paper in little pieces and tossed it on the smokehouse fire. He sez, 'There's your map and your combination, Johnson. You touch Lily and I'll kill you.'"

It felt like no one was breathing inside the jail. The only sound was the distant rhythm of the hammers.

"So that's when you beat him so bad he died."

"No!" Rusty clutched the bars of his cell. "Jake started to walk away, and that's when Johnson picked up a shovel and came after him, cut him off at his knees, and then made us drag him back to the fire. Then he stood over him, demanding Jake pull out those pieces of paper, telling him he was going to kill that waitress and take his time doing it, and all the while he was holding Jake's hands in the fire with that shovel."

The threat made Cody's blood run cold. "How did Jake get away?" Cody asked.

"He musta passed out. We all thought he was dead.

Johnson gave him one more whack with the shovel, and we got outta there."

Cody's mind raced to make sense of the confession. Jake must have regained consciousness and somehow managed to stagger back to the hotel in an attempt to save Lily.

And she was still in danger. It didn't matter that keeping the payroll at the bank made the location and combination of the safe useless. It didn't matter that Jake was dead now.

To a man like Johnson, his promise to kill Lily was a promise to be taken seriously.

"You got all this?" Cody asked Troutman's assistant, who nodded. Cody moved to the cell where Rusty still clung to the bars. "Where did Johnson go when you hit the bank?"

Rusty gave him a snaggletoothed grin. "He was right there all the time," he said. "Right under your nose. The old codger we was using for a shield when we left the bank and ran for our horses. That was him."

Cody closed his eyes, reliving the scene. There had been gunfire, and then one of the masked outlaws had grabbed an old man passing by, prodding him along as the gang ran for their horses. As they mounted up, the gang leader—Rusty, no doubt—had shoved the man aside. Cody and Nick had ridden after them, figuring someone would attend to the old man.

"Where were you supposed to meet up?"

Rusty shrugged. "Don't matter, 'cause he ain't there. Way me and the boys figure it, he got away clean. Probably back to the miner's cabin, packing up and heading back to that fancy place he lives out east."

Knowing he was unlikely to get more, Cody turned to the captain. "I've got to go," he said. "If anything changes, send me a wire."

Troutman followed him into the compound. "Don't go after Johnson on your own, Cody. A man like that…"

Cody just kept walking until he reached the hitching post where his horse waited. "I'll keep in touch," he said as he swung up and into the saddle and spurred his horse to a full gallop. Time to take out a warrant for the arrest of one Victor Johnson—wanted dead or alive.

Lily could not recall a time when she had been more unsettled. The morning after the party, Grace and Nick had returned to their cabin with the baby, so once her shift ended in the dining room, Lily's evenings were free again. Two days after the party, Bonnie Kaufmann had boarded the afternoon train, and after seeing her off, Lily and the other girls had surprised Emma by moving her things into the head waitress's old room. So now the room Lily had once shared with Grace and Emma was hers alone—at least until a new girl arrived.

At first, Lily had walked down the hall to Emma's room in the evenings, where the two of them shared the latest gossip and their hopes and dreams for the future as they always had. But after a couple of days, some of the other girls complained to Aidan that Emma was showing favoritism, and he had put a stop to their nightly chats.

It wouldn't matter for long. Once Cody had found the evidence he needed to clear Jake's name and Victor was under arrest, she would be moving on as well. Her thoughts were full of her plans for the future—a wedding in Juniper, and then she and Cody would find a place in Santa Fe. In the fall, she had little doubt he would start his new job as territorial representative and she would… What would she do? Cody's position would require him to travel to Washington, sometimes for long periods of time. She could go with him, but what would she do there? Of course eventually, they would have children, and her role would shift yet again.

In the meantime, she found herself spending much of her free time alone, especially in the evenings when she often sat on the hotel veranda, hoping perhaps she might see Cody come riding into town. Victor was still out there somewhere, but she couldn't bring herself to believe that he had any interest left in her. She told herself he'd be a fool not to have gone back east following the debacle on Independence Day. It made sense that he would want to put as much distance as possible between himself and the activities of that day. Besides, in her off times, she made sure to choose a place to sit that was close to the entrance to the hotel where guests were always coming and going and Aidan or his assistant were within hearing distance should she cry out.

Cody had been gone for nearly a week. Surely, he would return any day now. Her restlessness getting the better of her, she paced the length of the veranda and back again.

"Lily?" Aidan stood at the entrance to the brightly lit lobby. "Telegram for you," he said. "It arrived earlier today." He handed her the envelope and turned to go.

"It's from Cody," she said, and Aidan hesitated while she scanned the brief message, reading it aloud. "Been to Santa Fe. Good news about Jake. Back soon." She clutched the paper to her chest. "He's coming home," she repeated and gave a whoop of joy and kissed Aidan's cheek.

Aidan fussed with the cuffs of his coat as he said, "Really, Miss Travis!"

He was embarrassed, but Lily was pretty sure he was also smiling. "I have to tell Emma," she said and then remembered that their stations had changed. "Of course, I can wait until I see her in the normal routine of our day."

Aidan let out a long sigh. "Go," he grumbled. "Just don't make a habit of such late-night visits. The other girls—"

"—need to get over it," Lily said as she ran through the lobby and kitchen and on up the back stairs. "Cody's coming home."

But two days passed with no further sign. Each day, Lily walked to the Western Union office. Every day, Ellie Swift regretfully shook her head. "Not a word," she said on the third day. "I'm starting to worry."

"*You're* starting to worry? I can't sleep or eat, and my Harvey Girl smile is painful. Where could he be?"

Ellie patted her shoulder. "Perhaps he stopped to investigate something related to the robbery."

"And perhaps he's out there somewhere, his horse crippled or him shot or…"

"You cannot think such things, Lily. Let's talk to Frank Tucker. As mayor, he can organize a search party to cover the area between here and Santa Fe." She turned the sign on the door to closed and then took hold of Lily's arm as the two of them walked to the mercantile.

"Way ahead of you," Frank said when Ellie explained why they were there. "Captain Troutman sent word Cody had left the jail, and he was worried he'd gone off to find Victor Johnson on his own." He looked at Lily. "You need to watch yourself, young lady. If Johnson is still around, you might be in danger."

"I have nothing he wants," Lily said. "Can we send men to search for Cody?"

"Yes, of course. But in the meantime, I need you to stay put, understood?"

Lily wasn't about to make promises she had no intention of keeping. She had promised Cody not to go after Victor on her own, true, but this was different. She wasn't trying to find Victor. She was trying to find *Cody*.

"I have to work," she said, giving the mayor her most innocent smile. "In fact, my shift starts in half an hour." She clasped Ellie's hands in hers. "Thank you," she said, then shook Mr. Tucker's hand before hurrying back to the hotel to change into her uniform and take her place in the dining room just as the first train pulled into the station.

Throughout her shift, her mind raced with ideas she considered and rejected for how she might join the search for Cody. If she were Grace or Emma, it would be a simple matter of securing a horse and taking off, but Lily was a city girl and had never learned to ride. The one time she'd been on a horse had been during a picnic Aidan had arranged for the staff, and she'd been terrified the entire time. She'd never realized how large and broad—and far from the ground—horses could be.

She kept a smile in place and went through the motions of serving the customers that came and went in a steady stream from noon until the dining room closed at six. Afterward, she joined the other girls in cleaning the dining room, resetting the tables, and finally gathering in the kitchen for their supper.

Fortunately, a church social planned for the weekend had all the others engrossed, and Emma was occupied planning the schedule for the new girls who would arrive the following week. As long as she smiled and nodded occasionally, no one paid much attention to Lily, as she continued to rack her brain for ways she could get away.

"Beef delivery!" George shouted out the words directed at the men who worked for him in the kitchen, reminding them their work was not finished. Grumbling, they downed the last of their meals and headed outside to unload the meat from the Lombard Ranch.

Lily perked up and moved closer to the door that led out to the yard. Nick and one of his men were standing at the back of the wagon. They unloaded sides of beef while the hotel staff wrestled them inside to be slammed onto large tables where they would be carved into roasts and steaks. It occurred to her that the Lombard Ranch was on the way to Santa Fe. It also occurred to her that she might not be capable of riding a horse, but she could stow away in a wagon.

Should she leave Emma a note? She wouldn't want her friend to worry, but there really wasn't time. This was her moment—now, when all the men were distracted as they carried the heavy sides of beef inside. Now, when no one seemed to be paying her any mind at all.

She stepped aside to let them pass, nodded to Nick, and then eased her way out into the yard and around to the back of the wagon. She watched as the men unloaded the last of the cargo but did not follow them back to the kitchen.

Several burlap sacks had been tossed into a corner of the wagon bed. Looking around to be sure no one saw her, she removed her white apron and hair bow, wadded them into a ball, and stuffed them inside one of the burlap sacks. Her black dress, shoes, and stockings would be better camouflage. She climbed aboard and made herself as small as possible under the sacks, taking care to arrange them around and over her to conceal her head and the platinum-blond hair Cody had once told her caught the moonlight.

From inside the kitchen, she could hear Nick and George talking. The men would be enjoying a beer before Nick and the other cowboy made the trip back to the ranch. Every minute they delayed gave her a little more protection as the sun disappeared and darkness began to fall. She'd left herself enough of a peephole to be able to see the back entrance to the hotel. When she saw Nick and his ranch hand approach the wagon, she held her breath, but to her relief, they simply climbed aboard, calling out their farewells as they turned the team and headed out of town.

*Now what?* Lily hadn't really planned beyond finding some way to follow Cody's trail. As the team of horses plodded along, she realized how foolhardy the whole thing was. Once they reached the ranch, she decided she would reveal herself to Nick. By then, they'd be too far from town for him to send her back at least before morning. The ranch was halfway to Santa Fe, the last place she knew Cody had been. No doubt Nick would take her home to Grace, hoping his wife could talk some sense into her.

Lily smiled. Too bad Emma wasn't along for this adventure. Between the three of them, they would come up with a plan. Satisfied she'd accomplished at least the first step in her determination to find Cody, Lily settled back and let the sway of the wagon and the low voices of the men up front soothe her. Her eyes drifted shut.

"What the—!"

Lily woke with a start.

Nick was standing in the bed of the wagon, a broom in one hand. The horses were unhitched, and the other man was nowhere to be seen. As she rubbed sleep from her eyes, Lily saw they were at Nick and Grace's cabin. It was still night.

"Hello, Nick," she said calmly as she shrugged off the burlap sacks, stood, and picked straw from her hair.

"Grace!" His bellow had Grace running from the cabin to see what had happened. She was holding little Jimmy, named for her father. She stopped short, her mouth open.

"Lily?"

"Evenin', Grace." Lily climbed down from the wagon and shook out her uniform.

"What are you doing here?"

"She hid out in the wagon while we were delivering the beef," Nick said. "You're a little old to be running away from home, Lily."

"It's Cody. He was supposed to be on his way back to Juniper from Santa Fe, but he hasn't arrived, and no one has heard from him. I think something may have happened. Mr. Tucker is organizing a search party, but by the time—"

"Come inside," Grace said, casting a glance over her shoulder to include her husband in her request.

Inside, Grace laid Jimmy in his cradle and scurried around pouring coffee for them all. She set a plate of biscuits and jam on the table. While they ate, Lily told them about Cody's telegram.

"Aidan was worried," Nick said. "He says it's not like Cody to say he's going to do something and not follow through."

"It's been two days since he sent that wire," Lily added.

The three of them fell silent, sipping their coffee. After a long moment, Nick stood. "I'll head down to the ranch and round up some of the men. If Tucker and his party start from Juniper and we head toward Santa Fe…"

"You've had no sleep," Grace said, stroking his cheek with the back of her hand.

He smiled and leaned into her touch. "I'll be all right. Wouldn't sleep anyway for worrying about Cody."

Lily felt a rush of jealousy, seeing the two of them. It was as if they were alone in the room and no one else mattered. It was the way she felt when she was with Cody. She cleared her throat and stood. "I'll go with you," she said.

Nick chuckled. "And do what? As I recall, you don't ride, and if we have to tend to you, we won't be looking for Cody."

"Stay here with me," Grace urged. "Did you leave a note for Emma or Aidan? Do they know where you are?"

"I should have, but there was no time."

Nick sighed. "Mr. Lombard has a telegraph on the ranch. I'll send a wire and let everyone know you're here with us."

"I'm sorry," Lily blubbered, suddenly overcome with the way her rash actions were causing trouble for her friends. "I just…Cody might…" She slumped back into the chair and buried her face in her hands.

"We're gonna find him," Nick said softly.

Grace stroked Lily's back. "Of course you will, and in the meantime, Lily, you should get some sleep."

While Grace saw Nick off, Lily splashed water on her face and washed her hands. She removed the pins from her hair and used her fingers to comb through it. "I'll take the chair," she said, pointing to a leather armchair near the front door.

"You should lie down," Grace said. "I can take the chair."

The baby stirred, arms and legs flailing in a dream. Lily saw the cradle was within easy reach of the bed.

"Jimmy will need you, so no more discussion. Let's get some sleep."

Grace brought Lily a light blanket and tucked her in. "Try to sleep," she advised. "It's all going to work out."

Lily wasn't so sure. She closed her eyes, heard Grace return to the bed she shared with Nick, and heard the slight squeak of the cradle as the baby shifted. Soon, everything was quiet, the only sounds Grace's even breathing and the call of a night bird. But inside Lily's head, there was noise. She imagined gunshots and Cody's horse rearing, throwing him to the ground. She imagined him lying there, calling out for help, unable to stand. She imagined—

She froze, her senses on full alert as she heard footsteps on the porch. Had Nick returned so soon? Had she slept and it was now hours later? A shadow passed the window—large and male. Slowly, she set the blanket aside and crossed to stand next to the bed.

"Grace," she whispered, and her friend came instantly awake. Lily signaled silence and then with jerks of her head and hands tried to convey the situation. Grace nodded and pointed to a rifle mounted over the door, signaling Lily to take it down while she moved Jimmy and his cradle to a protected corner of the cabin away from the door.

Just as Lily reached for the rifle, the door slammed open, and the large shape of a man holding a gun filled the doorway. "Evenin', ladies," he said.

Lily shuddered. She knew that voice.

*Victor Johnson.*

Only this man was not the dapper businessman she had known. This man's clothes were covered in dust, and he was unshaven and wild-eyed. Everything about him screamed desperation. His hand shook as he waved the gun at them. "Please be seated," he instructed as he arranged two of the kitchen chairs back to back and removed a coil of rope from his shoulder.

"Where's Sheriff Daniels?" Lily demanded even as he wrapped the rope tight around their upper bodies, pinning them to the chairs.

"Lover boy is fine," he replied. His breath was foul and smelled of liquor. Once he had them bound, he stood and glanced around. "Where's the kid?"

Lily felt Grace stiffen.

"Why?" Lily demanded.

Victor leaned in close to her face, his fingers pinching her cheek. "Because, Lily, the kid is my insurance. Your friend's husband is going to find lover boy where I left him and bring him back here, and that's when we start negotiations."

Never in her life had Lily wanted to break one of the commandments more than she did in that moment. Her gaze shifted to the rifle, lying now on the floor where it had fallen when Victor broke in. Mentally, she imagined the steps it might take to get to the weapon, cock it—did it need to be cocked? Oh, she was hopeless.

"How did you know I was here?"

"I didn't. Thought I'd get to you later." He checked the tightness of their bonds and, apparently satisfied, went to the table and helped himself to a leftover biscuit. Then a sound outside made him freeze until he realized it was nothing more than the call of a night bird.

Lily cast about for some way she might calm him and perhaps distract him from his determination to take the baby as his hostage.

"Victor," she said sweetly. "There's no need to harm the child. You have time to get away. There's a horse in the barn and plenty of time for you to get to Santa Fe and catch the morning train. Everyone is out looking for Cody, so no one will notice. If you clean yourself up a bit, keep the whiskers—"

The backhanded slap would have knocked her to the floor had she not been tied to the chair. She heard Grace cry out in protest, and then the baby started to cry.

Victor followed the sound and, seconds later, turned to them. He was grinning and holding the snugly swaddled baby under one arm like a sack of flour. Lily realized in that moment that Victor was more dangerous than she had first thought. He appeared demented, and she was certain he'd been drinking.

Unable to communicate with Grace, Lily bit her lip, forcing herself to remain silent and watching Victor while she tried to figure out what to do next. He juggled the baby as he set the bottle and then the gun on the table and then scoured the cabin for food. It occurred to Lily that he'd been on the run since the robbery, and Victor was not a man accustomed to living off the land. She kept her eyes lowered so as not to rile him but saw him stuff biscuits in his mouth and wash them down with water he pumped into a canning jar.

Lily tried again. "Why didn't you just go home?" she said. "Surely, you didn't need the money from the robbery."

"How would you know what I need, Lil?" He sneered at her and pulled a half-empty pint of whiskey from his pocket. He took a long swallow. "Gone," he muttered, staring off toward the window, where the gray of predawn was starting to lighten the sky.

She wasn't sure what "gone" meant. All she knew was that Victor was getting more upset by the minute.

After a while, he swiped the back of his hand across his mouth and looked down at the wriggling child as if just remembering he was holding him. With the toe of his boot, he dragged the cradle closer to Grace and all but literally dropped Jimmy into it. "Kid stinks," he muttered as he sank into the leather chair where Lily had slept.

He stared at her. "As I believe I mentioned, I didn't know you would be here," he said. "Planned to get to you later."

"Why Grace and the baby?"

"Blame your lover boy, Lily. Daniels is a man of honor and duty. He'd trade his life for that kid's or hers." He jerked his head toward Grace, then he grinned. "Occurs to me now he'd do just about anything for you too, Lily."

"Like Jake?"

He snorted. "He tried to double-cross me. Nobody pulls something like that with me."

"You made him pay," Lily said quietly, hoping to hear him confess his part in Jake's death.

"He ruined the whole plan. Everything was going like clockwork until he decided to play the hero."

"He brought you the information you needed?"

"Yeah, he brought it. Then tore it up and tossed it

on the smokehouse fire. Well, that was a mistake. He paid for that one."

"You hit him."

"Rusty and his boys hit him first. He was already down. I asked him nicely to recover the information, but he refused, so I gave him a little help. Fortunately, there was a shovel handy."

Lily winced, imagining Jake on his knees, being forced to reach into the fire.

"He wasn't of a mood to cooperate even after I held his fingers to the fire, so I hit him with the shovel. Like I said, nobody double-crosses me. All he had to do was follow orders and he would have been fine." He shook his head sadly, then he looked at Lily and grinned.

"He didn't though, so you killed him."

"He was of no use to me, and I couldn't have him ruining the plans I had for you."

Lily swallowed a mass of bile. "Which were?"

The laugh that filled the room was pure evil. "You shall see, my dear." He went to the window and lifted the curtain.

"Lily, be quiet," Grace whispered.

But words were their only weapons. Lily was sure their only chance was to keep Victor talking until Cody and Nick returned. *Please*, she thought, *let them come soon.*

As if reading her mind, Victor returned to the chair. "Your men should be back before long, ladies. I left a real good trail. Until then, I suggest we all get some rest."

It was so typical of Victor to believe he was in full control. Within minutes, he was snoring, the gun on the table within Lily's reach if she'd been free to pick it up. Her hand twitched, and she realized that while her upper body was bound tight both to the chair and to Grace, from the elbow down, she had movement.

"Grace," she whispered. "I think I can get the gun."

"Be careful," Grace whispered back.

Lily strained against the ropes, her fingers reaching for the weapon. "Push us closer," she instructed and felt their combined chairs inch forward.

Victor snorted and stirred, and they froze. He was behind her, facing Grace, so what good was it for her to get the gun when she couldn't see him? She leaned back. "Stop pushing," she said. "I can't reach it." It was a lie, but until she could get a proper plan in mind, she didn't want to raise false hope.

The baby stirred and fussed.

"Shhh," Grace murmured.

"Trying again," Lily whispered as she closed her fingers over the barrel of the gun. At least if she was holding it, Victor wouldn't be. Of course there was still the matter of Nick's rifle on the floor. "Got it."

*Now what?*

She'd never fired a gun before—she'd never even held one. She stared at the glinting metal of the barrel and the intricate workings of the trigger and chambers where she could see bullets. Her movement was too limited for her to manage to hold the weapon and hide it in the folds of her skirt at the same time. She could either hold it or hide it.

*Or unload it!*

"What kind of gun is it?" Grace whispered.

Lily examined the markings. "Smith & Wesson. I need to remove the bullets."

"It's a .44 caliber like Nick's. To unload it, break it open between the cylinder and the barrel."

Lily remembered the night Cody had checked his gun to be sure it was loaded—the way he'd grasped the barrel and handle. "I've got it," Lily whispered. The bullets fell into her hand. With agonizing slowness, she folded her fingers to hold onto the bullets, closed the gun again, and pushed it back onto the table.

"What's happening?" Grace whispered.

Just then, Victor groaned and smacked his lips, and Lily heard him get to his feet. He moved to where she could see him, picked up the gun, and went to the window. "Shouldn't be long now, ladies," he said as he used the barrel of the gun to lift the lace curtain and peer out.

Little Jimmy started to wail.

"Shut that kid up," Victor snarled, waving the gun at Grace.

"He's hungry," Grace replied calmly. "If you could hand him to me and loosen my bonds, I could feed him."

Lily saw the exact moment Victor realized what feeding the baby entailed. His smile was so malevolent, Lily was afraid for Grace.

"Well now, missy," he said as he approached Grace. "Maybe you and me can work something out."

"Thank you," Grace said primly, her innocence making Lily clutch the arms of her chair.

Lily felt the ropes that held them loosen, although they remained tight enough that she really couldn't do much. Then she heard fabric ripping and Grace's gasp, followed by her pleas for Victor to stop. Lily closed her eyes, wishing she'd left the gun loaded. Never had she wanted to shoot a man more than she did now. She struggled to free herself while Jimmy continued to scream from his cradle and Grace continued to plead, sobbing now as Victor assaulted her.

"Need to prime the pump, missy," he said. He was standing over Grace, so close Lily could smell the fetid sweat of his clothing. "Let's have a feel, darlin', and maybe a taste."

"Stop!" Lily demanded when she was finally able to wriggle free of the loosened ropes and stand. "If you must indulge your vile urges, I'm right here."

Lily took in the scene. There was a moment when everything seemed to stop. Even Jimmy seemed to be holding his breath. Grace's dress ripped open, Victor's hand still kneading her exposed breast as milk leaked down her chest.

Lily's eyes flew to the gun. He followed her gaze and grinned as he released Grace and picked up the gun. "I'll get to you, Lily. Don't you worry."

The blessed sound of hoofbeats coming closer made him turn back to the window. "Well, well, well," he chortled. "Party's about to begin."

Grace freed herself and ran to comfort her child, holding him close as she sat on the bed.

Voices, low and urgent.

Cody. Nick.

Footsteps on the porch.

Victor waved the gun, instructing Lily to sit.

She faced him defiantly and started toward the door.

But while she might have removed the bullets, she quickly realized the gun was still a formidable weapon. Victor stopped her advance by whipping the butt of it across her cheek. She crumpled to the floor in pain.

"Lily!" Grace screamed.

The door burst open.

Victor wheeled around, aimed, and fired.

*Click.*

*Click.*

*Click. Click. Click.*

Cody and Nick were on him in an instant, both men seemingly intent on beating him the way he'd beaten Jake.

"No!" Lily shouted, staggering to her feet. To her way of thinking, dying was too good for Victor Johnson. She wanted him to live a good long life—in prison. *That* would be justice.

From outside came the sounds of more horses, more men's voices. Suddenly, the small cabin was filled with men—men in work clothes and men in uniform, Frank Tucker and Aidan among them.

"We got this," a uniformed soldier who seemed to be in charge announced. "See to the ladies," he added as he directed his men to take Victor into custody.

Nick looked around, spotted Grace clutching their son, her clothing torn, and with a feral growl, he went after Victor again. Cody restrained him. "It's over, Nick," Lily heard him say as he guided Nick back to where Grace stood, the baby on one hip, her other arm stretched out to embrace her husband.

Cody let out a breath and turned to face Lily. In two steps, he was beside her, his strong arms pulling her close, cradling her head and bruised face against his shoulder. "What am I going to do with you, Lily?"

"Marry me?" she croaked.

"Looks like I'll have to if I have any hope of keeping you out of trouble."

Frank and Aidan stepped back inside the cabin. "You folks need anything?" Frank asked. "Want me to go for Doc? Take Lily back to the hotel?"

"We'll be fine," Grace said. "Unless...Lily?"

She realized she was still clutching the bullets. "Perhaps somebody could take these," she said and opened her hand. "They're from Victor's gun."

"Well, I'll be jiggered," Frank muttered as he held out his hand for them. He glanced at Cody. "Got yourself quite a woman there, Sheriff."

"Don't I know it." Cody tightened his hold on Lily.

Aidan stepped forward. "Lily, whatever possessed you to go off on your own? Emma—Miss Elliott has been frantic."

Lily caught Grace's eye at Aidan's slip of the tongue. Maybe Aidan Campbell was finally beginning to see what had been right there in front of him all the time. She couldn't help a smile, even though it came with a good deal of pain. "Sorry, Aidan, I meant to leave a note."

Aidan rolled his eyes and threw up his hands. "Impossible," he muttered as he stalked back out to the porch.

"Cody, you should get Lily to the doctor," Grace said.

"Agreed." He turned to Nick. "Everything all right here?" he asked.

"We'll be fine," Nick said, and the two men shook hands.

"Thanks," Cody said, "I walked straight into a trap."

"Could have happened to any one of us," Nick assured him.

Cody retrieved his hat from where it had come off while he and Nick subdued Victor and tipped his fingers to the brim. "Grace, you take care of that boy," he said.

Lily knew he was really admonishing her to take care of herself, but he was a man, and sometimes they spoke in a language all their own.

Outside, Cody whistled for his horse and mounted, then stretched out his hand to Lily, pulling her up to sit sidesaddle in front of him, her head resting against his chest. Slowly, he turned the horse and started down the trail.

That was when Lily realized the tears she'd held in check ever since Victor had appeared at the cabin were falling free, soaking the front of Cody's soft cotton shirt.

"Shhh," he said softly. "It's over, Lily." But she noticed his voice was raspy, and when she looked up at him, she saw that those long lashes were damp.

## Chapter 17

ON THE RIDE BACK TO TOWN AFTER VICTOR'S ARREST, she had insisted Cody tell her what had happened— how Victor had managed to overpower him.

At first, he'd refused.

"It's over, Lily. Let it go."

"No. Tell me. I need to know it all. Whatever you have to say could not possibly be worse than what I've imagined."

With a sigh of resignation, he did as she asked.

"Ty Drake had come across solid evidence Johnson was still in the area. The day before I reached Santa Fe, Johnson sold that gold ring of his to a local jeweler."

"He told me that ring had belonged to his father," Lily said. "He must have been truly desperate to part with it."

"I figured he'd holed up at the miner's cabin again, so I headed there. There's a trail down to the cabin that follows the side of a steep cliff. It's narrow and slippery, the rocks are loose, and it's washed out in places, making the journey even more difficult. My plan was to get as close as possible and then go the rest of the way on foot. I could see smoke rising from the chimney, so I was pretty sure I was on the right track."

"Your horse slipped?"

Cody shook his head. "Victor came outside. He had binoculars and was scanning the area when he spotted me."

"Why didn't you just shoot him?"

"I thought about it, believe me. But I knew I was too far away and the terrain was too unsteady to get off a good shot." He hesitated. "You're sure you want to hear this?"

For an answer, she looked up at him. "Tell me all of it," she said, stroking the side of his face with the backs of her fingers. "I need to know."

"I navigated a tricky patch of the trail that took me around a stretch of boulders and out of sight of Victor. When I reached the open again, I saw Victor watching for me, sawed-off shotgun aimed right at me. He fired."

"And missed, obviously," Lily said with a satisfied nod of her head.

"He didn't miss, Lily. He shot my horse."

Lily gasped, imagining the horse shrieking as it lost its footing and went tumbling over the cliff's edge, Cody powerless to stop it. She sat up and tried to examine Cody for signs of injury.

"I'm okay," he assured her, pulling her close again and kissing her temple. "We're okay." There was a catch in his voice.

She snuggled a little closer to him. "Tell me the rest, Cody."

"Fortunately, the horse and I weren't too far from

the base of the trail, so the fall wasn't nearly as bad as it might have been. We landed hard, and my horse was still thrashing around in pain and panic. I had all I could do to dodge being kicked when I heard a second shot—closer—and the horse went still. When I looked up, Victor had the gun barrel inches from my head, and he ordered me to get up."

He didn't say anything for a long moment, and Lily began to regret forcing him to relive his ordeal. "It's okay," she whispered. "That's enough for now."

"Might as well get it told, and then, Lily, we leave it."

She nodded.

"I got to my knees and closed my fist around a handful of loose dirt, intending to fling it in his face, but he musta seen what I was planning. He hit me hard with the butt of the shotgun, and I blacked out. When I came to, Victor was gone, and so was my gun. I'm not sure how long I'd been out, but it was coming on dark, and I figured I'd best seek shelter. I managed to get to the cabin, and that's where I spent the night."

"How did Nick and the others find you?"

"When I woke that morning, I started several campfires around the place, hoping the smoke would draw somebody in so I could borrow their horse and go after Victor. Nick knew about the cabin—it was near a piece of land he'd once tried to buy—and when he saw the smoke, he had a hunch I'd gone there."

"And how did you know Victor was headed to find Grace?"

"I found a map in the cabin, something he'd drawn out while he was staying there. It showed the miner's cabin and Nick and Grace's place. My name was next to the miner's shack, but next to their place, Victor had written *Hopkins's wife and kid*. And I'll be honest—seeing that made my blood run cold."

"But he didn't even know them."

"He knew they meant something to both of us. Who knows what goes on in the mind of a monster like that? He was desperate."

"But why not come after me directly?"

"I expect that was to be the next part of his plan. Finding you there with Grace must have seemed like a real bonanza." He hugged her closer. "None of it matters now, Lily. The only things that matter are you're safe, he's locked up, and we're together."

She couldn't argue with that. "I must look a mess though," she fumed, gently touching her injured face. To her surprise, he reined in the horse and dismounted. "Why are we stopping?"

"Because I will not have you fretting over this." He held out his arms, grinning up at her.

She placed her hands on his broad shoulders, and he lifted her to the ground. "Never could resist those dimples," she said when he continued to hold her close.

"Countin' on that," he said as he gently cupped her face in his large palms and kissed her. "Lily Travis, the first time I set eyes on you, I thought you were the most beautiful woman God ever made. At the time, it was your face and those incredible green eyes and that halo of hair that made you look like an angel."

She looped her arms around his neck. "And then you got to know me and realized I was no angel at all," she teased.

He chuckled. "I'll admit I had some doubts you and

me might ever find the road leading us together. But when it comes to something I want, I can be pretty stubborn."

"And am I something you want, Cody? Messed-up face and all?"

"What I want is a life with you, Lily. And what I see when I look at you now that I know you is a woman who is more beautiful on the inside than she could ever be on the outside. Any man would count himself the luckiest cowboy alive to have you say yes."

She pretended confusion. "Yes to what? I didn't hear a question."

He released her and dropped to one knee. He held her hands in his and looked up at her. "Lily Travis, will you do me the honor of becoming my wife?"

Her heart swelled with joy. "Yes," she said, barely able to believe what lay in her future. She'd made mistakes, and she'd survived abuse, and now at last, it was her turn for happiness. She tightened her hold on his hands. "Yes," she repeated.

He stood and whistled for his horse. "Let's go home," he said, wrapping his arm around her shoulder.

*Home.* Right now, it was a small room on the third floor of the hotel for her and a similarly small room at the jailhouse for him, but in time…

The following morning, Lily studied her face in the bathroom mirror. One side was swollen and bruised where Victor had hit her with the gun. She could hardly show up in the dining room looking this way.

But how could she not? They were fully staffed, true, but Emma was a little overwhelmed with the new girls as she tried to train them and do all the other duties required of a head waitress and housemother. Still, she had insisted Lily take time off to recover.

Everyone had been so sweet and caring once Cody brought her back to the hotel. The kitchen staff had prepared her special meals of soft foods, and the other girls had taken turns checking in on her through the evening and refreshing the ice pack Doc had instructed her to keep on her cheek and eye to reduce the swelling. Of course the only person she'd really needed was Cody, but Emma had been firm on that point.

"No men upstairs," she'd announced. "You know the rules, Lily."

She'd had to be satisfied with standing at the window while Cody waited below in the yard. She blew him a kiss that he pretended to catch. Later on, Emma had delivered a note from him.

*Sleep well, knowing you and everyone you care about is safe. I'll be gone for a few days—to Santa Fe to give my testimony.*

*Love, Cody*

A light tap at the bathroom door roused Lily from her daydreaming.

"Lily? It's Emma."

Lily opened the door. She was dressed in her full uniform, but she gingerly touched her face. "I insist on doing my part, but I simply can't appear in public looking like this, Emma. I'll scare the customers."

Emma's mouth worked the way it did when she was trying to come to a decision. "I won't deny we could use the help." She smiled. "I have an idea," she said as she took Lily's hand and led her toward the back stairs. "The new girls are working the counter. What if we station you just out of sight where you can observe them? You can help if they need someone to tell them what to do or where to find something. Then that will free me to work your shift in the dining room."

Lily smiled and then grimaced. Smiling was still painful. "Brilliant," she managed as they went downstairs. "You know, you make a very good boss lady, Emma Elliott."

Emma's cheeks flushed, and she ducked her head. "Flatterer," she muttered, but she was smiling as she instructed one of the kitchen workers to set Lily up with a stool, paper, and pencil near the kitchen entrance to the lunch counter.

"You want me to take notes?"

"I want you to jot down anything you think might help with training in the future. Where do the new girls seem to struggle? Is there a better way of organizing things behind the counter to make the work more efficient? That sort of thing."

"Got it." Lily realized she was glad to have something productive to occupy her and keep her mind off her injuries—and Cody.

For the truth was, even with Victor in jail and the absence of any further threat to either of them, she could not help jumping at every unidentifiable sound.

And she couldn't stop thinking about how close they'd come to losing each other before they'd had a chance to start the happy life they both dreamed of. But the past weighed on her, and she found it hard to believe she had nothing to fear. Anything might happen.

*But it won't*, she told herself. She and Cody were safe, and they deserved to be happy. And she vowed she would spend every day of whatever time they might have together making sure they were.

At the jail in Santa Fe, Cody met with Captain Troutman and gave him all the details of what had led to Victor's capture.

"Do you want to see him?" Troutman asked.

It was a strange question. "Why would I?"

Troutman shrugged. "Let's just say that after everything you told me—what he did to Miss Travis and her friend—I could make sure you had a few minutes alone with him."

*Revenge*. That's what Troutman was suggesting. The opportunity to torment Victor for what he'd done to Lily, Grace, and Jake. He considered the idea. Maybe he should. Then he'd be able to tell Lily he'd gotten his own brand of justice for her friend.

"Sure. I'll see him."

Troutman smiled and led the way to the cells. He dismissed the soldiers on guard. The other outlaws had been transferred to the courthouse that morning to stand trial, leaving Victor as the sole occupant of the jail.

"I'll be right outside here," Troutman said as he handed Cody the keys.

Cody stepped inside the shadowy interior of the building. The first two cells were empty, the doors standing open. The door on the third cell was closed, and Victor stood near the small, barred window high on one wall. He'd cleaned up some—shaved and combed his hair—and when he turned to face Cody, his eyes widened in surprise before narrowing in suspicion. He saw the ring of keys in Cody's hand and took a step back.

"What do you want?" He delivered the question in the dismissive tone of someone in charge.

Cody smiled.

"I want a full confession, Johnson. It's just you and me now. Admit you're responsible for the murder of Jake Collier, and I'll go."

Victor smiled and turned back to the window. "You must think me stupid, Sheriff Daniels. Right now, I have a chance of beating the charges against me, and you want me to tie the noose for my accusers?"

"Actually, I want you to live. So does Lily."

He saw the other man's shoulders tense at the mention of her name, but then he gathered himself and turned to face Cody. "I must admit I've never quite understood the fascination good men like you and Collier have for that woman. She's not worthy of either of you, and she was the one who got Collier killed."

Cody felt the keys dig into his palm as his fist tightened. He'd never wanted to smash that fist into a man's face more than he did now. He was tempted to unlock the cell and drag Johnson out, beat him the way he'd allowed Jake to be beaten, cripple him for what he'd personally done to people Cody cared about. He wanted to see the man bleed and suffer and hear him plead for it all to stop, admit to anything just to save his own skin.

But he knew in some way that's what Victor wanted—for Cody to lose his temper and surrender to his baser instincts. For Cody to come down to his level. He wouldn't give the man the satisfaction.

"I knew you were a coward, Johnson, but I never thought you'd stoop so low as to hide behind a woman."

Johnson spat a glob of saliva on the ground. "If you think I'm a coward, unlock this cell and let me show you."

Cody laughed. "I don't want to fight you. I don't even want to touch you."

"Think you're a better man than me? I could buy and sell you three times over."

"I doubt that. According to the authorities back east, you've piled up quite a bit of debt. Your fancy house is gone, and your bank accounts are empty. Probably doesn't matter, because you're going to prison, where money—even if you had it—won't do you any good at all. And you are scum. Any man who relies on others to do his dirty work, any man who torments babies and innocent women—"

"Innocent?" Victor hooted. "Lily Travis is no more…"

Cody took one step closer to the cell and held up the keys. "You mention her name one more time and I'll open this cell, throw you out, and shoot you, and Troutman and his men will agree I did it in self-defense."

"Don't kid yourself, Daniels. Lily wanted everything she—"

In a split second, Cody had the cell unlocked and Victor backed up against the wall, his arm pressed against the man's windpipe.

"You need to listen to what I'm saying," he said, his spit landing on Johnson's cheek. The man's face was almost purple with the effort to breathe. He clutched at Cody's arm, trying to free himself, his eyes bulging with fear.

Cody pressed harder, so tempted to finish him, but then he let go. While Johnson collapsed to the dirt floor, coughing and gasping for air, Cody walked away, clanged the cell door shut, and relocked it before heading for the exit.

"That's it?" Victor taunted, still choking on the words. "Who's the coward now, Daniels?"

When Cody stepped back out into the sunshine and handed Troutman the keys, the captain gave him a puzzled look. "You're done?"

Cody grinned. "Pretty sure it's Johnson who's done. Me? I'm just getting started." He tipped his fingers to his hat, mounted his horse, and rode away. Back to Juniper and Lily.

# Chapter 18

"HAVE YOU AND CODY PICKED A DATE FOR THE WED-ding?" Emma asked a few days later as she and Lily finished cleaning the closed dining room.

Lily did a little dance as she quoted a popular rhyme. "You know what they say:

> Marry on Monday for health,
> Tuesday for wealth,
> Wednesday the best day of all,
> Thursday for crosses,
> Friday for losses, and
> Saturday for no luck at all."

Emma laughed. "So Wednesday, then?"

"Best day of all," Lily said, then she bit her lip. "Of course, it's also a work day, and everyone we want to be at the wedding will—"

"Be there," Emma finished. "If you think anyone will miss seeing you and Cody finally tie the knot, you haven't been paying attention. I'll speak to Aidan and see what we can work out."

Tommy cleared his throat, shifting from foot to foot in the doorway. He was wearing a uniform that Lily suddenly realized was tight on him. "Tommy, you must've grown a foot over the last couple of months," she said.

The bellboy blushed and ducked his head. "Only a couple of inches," he murmured.

"Even so, we need to make Mr. Campbell aware of your need for a larger size in that uniform." She walked around him, gesturing measurements with her hands.

Emma took pity on the boy. "Tommy, was there something you needed?"

"I brought a telegram for Lily," he replied, handing Lily the envelope.

Eagerly, she took it from him. Even though telegrams often brought bad news, Lily was confident nothing could spoil her happiness. She ripped open the envelope and scanned the message—then read it again, her hand shaking so much the paper rattled.

"Lily?" Emma stepped to her side. "What is it?"

"It's from my mother." The mother she had not had a word from since their exchange of letters after Lily left Chicago. "My stepfather died."

"Oh."

Lily glanced at her friend, who looked at her with confusion. "I know, Emma. He was a horrid man, and she knew how I felt, so why hunt me down to deliver the news?"

"Perhaps she's had a change of heart?"

Lily thought of the woman she'd known before her father died—a true lady of grace and beauty, a devoted mother, and loving wife. But all that had changed.

Lily's stepfather had demanded her complete devotion. He had been possessive and controlling. Lily's brothers had left not long after the marriage and so had never experienced the darker side of their mother's new husband. But Lily knew better.

"Does she say anything else?"

Lily reread the message. "She's selling the house." She crumpled the telegram in her fist. "So that's that."

Emma chewed at her lower lip. "Lily, she's reaching out to you. Otherwise, why write you at all, knowing how you felt about him?"

Lily fought a stew of anger, sadness, and confusion. She had adored both her parents and always hoped to find the kind of love they had shared. Now that she had, she didn't want to think of those dark times after her stepfather had moved into the large house on Michigan Avenue, the home that had once rung with laughter and been filled with love.

She smoothed out the telegram.

"At least write to her, Lily," Emma urged. "Let her know you're safe and happy and about to be married. Give her that peace."

Lily snorted. "You are a better person than I am, Emma," she said softly.

"At least think about it." Emma squeezed her hand. "I'm going to speak to Aidan about the wedding date. I'll see you upstairs."

Still clutching the telegram, Lily climbed the back stairs. Once she reached her room, she removed her uniform and changed into the pink calico dress that was Cody's favorite, brushed out her hair, and caught it in a barrette at the nape of her neck. She heard

Emma's unmistakable quick steps coming down the hall and turned as her friend knocked and then entered the room. Emma was smiling broadly.

"Aidan says you should pick whichever Wednesday you want and we'll make it all happen."

Lily felt a lightness of spirit flicker and then flare back to life. "I'll talk to Cody tonight," she said, taking one last check of herself in the mirror and stuffing her mother's telegram in her pocket. "Thank you, Emma," she added, kissing her friend's forehead before hurrying down the hall. "I won't be late."

Emma laughed. They both knew she probably would be.

Cody read the message Lily's mother had sent, then laid the telegram on a side table in the hotel reading room and held out his arms to her. She came to him. "So at long last, both the men who wronged you are no longer a threat. It is truly over, Lily. Time to grab onto happiness."

She tightened her hold on him. "Got it right here," she said, "and not about to let go."

Voices from the lobby made them step apart. "Let's go outside," Cody said.

They sat in a swing that hung from the wooden rafters on the side of the hotel. The night air was as hot as midday in August back in Chicago. "What should I do about Mother?" she asked.

Cody hesitated. He didn't know Lily's family beyond what she had told him about the day she left home and the encounter with her mother at church. "I don't know, darlin'. She's your mother, and where I come from, family is everything."

"You think I should write to her?"

He considered his next words carefully. "I think we need to set a definite date for the wedding and then let your family and mine know they are welcome. And see what happens."

"You know your parents will come. I've already had a letter from your mother welcoming me to the family, and she's never even met me."

Cody grinned. "I wrote her all about you."

"You're biased."

"Maybe, but I'm also right. Now when are we gettin' married, lady?"

She grinned. "Wednesday."

He felt his heart race. "Day after tomorrow?"

She shrugged. "Any Wednesday."

"Okay, a Wednesday. Got a month in mind?"

"September?"

"That works. First Wednesday in September."

"First *day* of September." She rested her head on his shoulder. "We're going to be happy, Cody."

"Yes, we are." He waited a beat. "So how about you write your mother and ask her to be here?"

"She won't come."

"You don't know that. Truth is I'd like to thank her."

Lily sat up. He could feel her staring at him in the dark. "Thank her for what?"

He touched his forefinger to her lips. "For you, Lily—for this remarkable warm and funny and beautiful inside and out woman who has agreed to be my wife."

She was so quiet and still that under other circumstances he might have thought she'd dozed off. But he knew she was sorting through the myriad thoughts racing through her brain. He had learned she needed to come to decisions in her own time, so he wrapped his arm around her. "Come on," he said. "It's been a long day for you, and I've got rounds to make."

They had decided to abstain from making love until their wedding night. "I want it to be special," Lily had told him, and he had every intention of making sure her wish came true.

They had a date, and now what Lily needed was the perfect gown. One morning before reporting for her lunchtime shift in the dining room, she walked over to Mr. Tucker's store to examine his selection of fabrics. In recent years, brides had taken to wearing white for their special day, but somehow white did not seem right for Lily.

"With my hair and fair skin, I'll look like a ghost," she'd told Emma.

Now she scanned the bolts of fabric in the mercantile, most of them practical calicos and serge. And then she saw it—a heavy silk in a deep purple that reminded her of wine. She wrestled it free of the stack, praying there would be enough fabric for a proper wedding gown left wound around the tattered cardboard.

"Lily?" Mr. Tucker came to help her take down the fabric. "Best check that over carefully. It's been up there since well before Mrs. Tucker passed on—got to be ten years or more now." He carried the fabric to the large wooden counter and began unrolling it, spreading it out so they could examine it for damage.

"It's perfect," Lily said softly as she ran her palms over the smooth surface. But was there enough? As if reading her mind, Mr. Tucker began measuring the length. Lily silently counted off the yards.

"Eight and change," he announced, looking up at her.

"I'll take it."

"You don't want to know the price?" Mr. Tucker started folding the silk back onto the bolt.

"It's perfect," she repeated as if that alone should answer his question.

Mr. Tucker smiled. "Got some fancy trimmings over here," he said once he'd set the silk aside. He pulled down a smaller bolt of heavy lace and placed it on the counter.

Lily fingered the intricate design and mentally calculated her budget. She had her salary for August plus tips, but would it be enough? "How much for the silk plus a yard of the lace?"

Mr. Tucker checked the price tags, then pulled a scrap from the roll of brown wrapping at the end of the counter. He wet the tip of a pencil with his tongue and wrote down figures, then crossed them out and tapped the pencil against the counter before starting to write again. Lily held her breath and kept her hand at her side, fingers crossed.

"Silk," he muttered and shook his head before taking a second look at the tag on the lace. Finally, he heaved a sigh and pushed the scrap of paper toward her.

$$8 \times \$2 \ yd + 1 \times \$.75 = \$16.75 \text{---wedding present} = \$0.00$$

Lily read the figures twice before looking up at the older man. "I couldn't," she whispered.

He shrugged. "You'd be doing me a favor, taking this off my hands. That silk has sat up there for years now. As for the lace, well, it makes a mighty fine collar, don't you think?" He draped a length of the trim around his neck and grinned.

Lily hurried around the counter and kissed Mr. Tucker's cheek. "Thank you," she said. "Thank you," she repeated, kissing him again.

Beneath his white beard, his skin flushed, and he chuckled. "Well now, Lily, I reckon you've earned your time for having some happiness." He gave her a one-armed hug, then turned to the task of measuring and cutting the lace. "You got somebody in mind for sewing up this dress for you?"

Lily had to admit she hadn't given that a thought. She could see the gown in her mind, but actually putting it together?

"Abigail Chambers is right handy with a needle, and she's got a sewing machine you might find useful," Mr. Tucker continued. He pulled a length of the wrapping paper and set the fabric in its center. "She's right embarrassed for getting fooled by Johnson, thinks it's partly her fault you all had to suffer." He pushed the package across the counter. "She could use a friend."

Lily fingered the string holding her package together. "I doubt…"

"Give it a try, Lily," Mr. Tucker said.

So clutching the package, Lily left the mercantile and, instead of heading for the hotel, walked two doors up the boardwalk to Abigail's hat shop.

"Hello?" she called when the proprietress did not immediately appear in answer to the jingle of the bell over her shop door. "Miss Chambers? Abigail?"

Abigail stepped out from behind the curtain, and Lily swallowed a gasp. Lily had never seen her out in public unless she was perfectly groomed, but now dark circles rimmed the undersides of Abigail's eyes, and her hair was a bird's nest of frizz and tangles.

"Yes?" she demanded, her eyes defiant.

"Hello, Miss Chambers. Mr. Tucker suggested I might…that is, I purchased this beautiful fabric for my… I need help," Lily finally blurted.

Abigail's hard gaze softened slightly. She held out her hands for the package and opened it, smoothing her hands over the silk. "For your wedding?"

Lily nodded, thinking this had been a mistake. She was causing the hatmaker more pain.

Abigail fingered the fabric lovingly, as Lily had. "It's truly beautiful," she murmured. She looked up at Lily. "Do you have a design or pattern?"

Lily gave her a weak smile. "In my head?"

Abigail hesitated, then handed her a pad of paper and pencil. "Can you sketch it?"

"I think so."

Abigail indicated a small table where customers usually sat to try on hats. As Lily drew, Abigail stood behind her, watching. From time to time, Lily glanced up at their reflections in the mirror. She could practically see the wheels turning in Abigail's head.

"What if we use the lace here and on the cuffs?" Abigail hurried back to the counter and returned with a catalogue. She flipped through it until she found what she wanted. "Like this," she said, showing Lily the picture.

"Yes," Lily agreed. "And maybe the upper sleeves could be—"

"—puffed out. It's the latest thing." The shopkeeper was definitely getting caught up in the excitement of creating Lily's gown.

Lily altered the sketch and showed it to Abigail, who smiled and pulled the tape measure from around her neck. "Let's get started," she said with a genuine smile as she led Lily to a full-length mirror and began taking and recording measurements.

Back at the hotel, Lily could hardly wait to tell Emma about her morning. "And Abigail has already started making a pattern. She's insisting on doing the dress in muslin first to be sure everything is perfect and—"

Emma cocked an eyebrow. "Abigail? Abigail Chambers?"

"Oh, Emma, she's really nice once you get to know her."

"You do recall she's been chasing Cody since the day he arrived?"

"The chase is over. Actually, I was thinking she and Frank Tucker would make the perfect pair. I mean, think of it—her business and his go so well together, and they are both lonely. Why not?"

Emma chuckled. "Why not indeed."

Back in her room, Lily ignored the letter she'd started writing to her mother. She had no idea what to say. What surprised her most was the feeling of grief she had for the life her mother had lived since Lily's father died. Their romance had been as much a fairy tale as Lily and Cody's. Had the ensuing years erased all the memories of happy times, or could they be rekindled? Lily sat near the window that overlooked the hotel's rear yard and started fresh.

*Dear Mama,*

*I wanted to let you know I received your wire and share some news. I am to be married next month, to a man who reminds me so much of Papa, and so I have thought often of you and those happy days when our family shared so many good times. He is the sheriff here in Juniper, but soon he will take up a new position as territorial representative for New Mexico. We will live in Santa Fe and Washington, and it promises to be the life of adventure I always longed for. Cody Daniels is a good man, kind and caring. His family will be here for the wedding, and I thought perhaps you might consider coming as well.*

She paused, surprised at having written those last words. Tears welled as she stared at the page, realizing that her hand had written what her heart had not allowed herself to acknowledge. She wanted her mother with her on this important day of her life.

Quickly, she added the practical details for traveling from Chicago to Juniper and the dates and signed off with "Your daughter, Lily" before folding and sealing the envelope. She hurried downstairs to the front desk, placing the letter with other outgoing mail before she could change her mind.

When she looked up, Cody was standing in the hotel entrance, backlit by a setting sun. Her breath caught. She had to be the most blessed woman in the world.

The minute Cody saw Lily tuck the envelope in with other mail on the front desk of the hotel, he knew whose address would be on that letter. The question was, what had she said?

"You wrote your mother?" he asked when she joined him and they headed outside to the swing where they spent every evening now.

"I did. I invited her to come for the wedding."

"I'm glad."

"She might not come," Lily said, her voice unsteady with the realization.

"Or she might," he replied. "Either way, you've made the attempt at reconciliation."

"Seems to be the order of the day for me." She told him about her time with Abigail and how Frank Tucker had insisted on making a present of the fabric.

Finally, she leaned back and let out a sigh. "It's been a wonderful day," she said.

He wrapped his arm around her and kicked the swing into motion. "I have some news of my own," he said. "I got word today that with no other candidates in the running and the current representative's health failing, the governor has appointed me to the position sooner than we expected. I gave Mayor Tucker my resignation this afternoon."

"That's wonderful, Cody."

"So how do you feel about a wedding trip to the nation's capital?"

"Washington?"

He chuckled. "Unless they moved it and didn't tell anyone."

Lily squealed with delight. Then she sat up. "I haven't a thing suitable for wearing in Washington," she fumed. "I have to…"

"They have shops there," Cody assured her. "Sounds like this dress you and Abigail are cooking up for the wedding might be perfect for the trip itself, and once there, we'll go shopping. I reckon my wardrobe will need a bit of sprucing up as well."

"But some things you'll keep," Lily said, her tone worried. "Your hat and boots, and definitely no stiff collars and ties for you," she added. "I won't have it. Those stuffed shirts in the capital need to see that there's a new time coming and we are the face of it."

Cody laughed. He felt a little sorry for the men and women of Washington. They had no idea that a sudden storm in the form of Lily was coming their way. She would undoubtedly change things in ways they hadn't even begun to imagine.

Later, after Lily had gone in for the night and he'd made his rounds, Cody had an idea. He stopped by the hotel. The mail was still on the front desk, ready to go out with the morning train. He found Lily's letter to her mother, saw she had used her father's surname in the address rather than that of her stepfather, and copied the information down. Then he went back to his office.

*Dear Mrs. Travis,*

*My name is Cody Daniels, and as Lily tells you in her letter, we are to be married. Lily has often spoken of you and her father and the happy childhood she and her brothers shared before Mr. Travis passed. I wanted you to know that in spite of some difficult times that followed, Lily is a woman much beloved by all who know her. She is high-spirited, to be sure, but her devotion to those she loves is rock solid. It is my great honor that she has agreed to become my wife and join her path to mine. I love her with all my heart, and my promise to you is that I will make sure she is safe and happy every day of our lives together. I know that your presence would add a special blessing to our wedding day. Please come.*

He had no idea how to sign off, so he just added his name. The following morning, on his way to have breakfast at the counter, he added his letter to the stack of mail at the front desk.

As Lily came downstairs for work the day before her wedding, George motioned her into the kitchen. "We need to decide on your cakes, Lily."

"Cakes? As in more than one?"

"Tradition requires three. One each for the bride and groom, and a third for the guests."

"Grace had one cake," she reminded him.

"Grace's situation was different. Now, I have in mind a fruitcake with white frosting for Cody. For you, something very special—a lemon cheesecake with charms."

"Charms?"

"Small good-luck tokens for the wedding party. I place them on top of the cake, each attached to a ribbon. Then members of the wedding party pull the ribbons to collect their charm."

"Sounds like a mess," Lily noted, but she could not deny the idea was appealing. "What's your idea for cake number three?"

"Traditional. The pieces are boxed for guests to take home and enjoy, so the cake has to be sturdy— layers of white cake separated perhaps by some fruit jam?"

Lily touched George's sleeve. "I leave it all in your very capable hands, as I doubt I'll recall a single detail of the day. I'll be far too excited."

She hurried on to the dining room. She had a gown and now the proper wedding cake—*cakes*. She had sent letters to her brothers and received telegrams saying they would not be able to attend but wished her every happiness, and they urged Cody and her to visit while on their wedding trip.

And she had written her mother. Whether or not there would be a response from her remained to be seen, but Lily refused to allow anything or anyone to dampen her excitement as her wedding day approached.

"Final fitting for your gown tonight," Emma said, as if she needed reminding.

"Also my final day of work," Lily said and was surprised at the feeling of melancholy that accompanied that statement. "I'm going to miss it, you know," she added.

"Not nearly as much as I'll miss having you here," Emma replied.

The two friends hugged each other and blinked back tears as Aidan opened the dining room's double doors in preparation for the arrival of passengers from the morning train. The hotel manager cleared his throat, and Emma and Lily gave each other one more squeeze and hurried to their stations.

That evening, Grace and Emma accompanied Lily to Abigail's shop. Grace and Nick were staying at the hotel until after the wedding, and Nick had volunteered to care for the baby while the ladies were out. Cody, on the other hand, had not seen the need for an entire evening devoted to trying on a wedding dress.

"It's only a dress," he argued, "and you keep saying I can't see you the day of the wedding. Tonight's our last chance."

Lily laughed. "Cody, we have the rest of our lives. What's one night?"

"Too much to ask," he grumbled.

"Well, since I officially ended my employment with the Harvey organization today, I have no curfew."

She let that sink in and knew the minute Cody understood what she was really saying. "We have all night?"

"Be outside Abigail's shop at nine." She stood on tiptoe and kissed him. "Now shoo."

Upstairs, she changed out of her uniform for the last time, recalling the first time she'd tied that pinafore apron in place. It was after Victor had left her. She'd had no money, was about to be evicted from her rented room, and the Harvey Company had saved her. Then because of her work, she had met Emma and Grace—the two best friends any girl could ever hope to have.

And she had found her true love.

She hung up her uniform and changed into Cody's favorite pink calico dress. She reached for her work shoes and then smiled as she set them aside and put on her fancy boots instead. When Emma and Grace tapped on her door and stepped into the room, Lily lifted her skirt and pointed with glee.

"You are not wearing those with your beautiful wedding dress," Emma announced.

Lily grinned and ignored her friend's edict. "Shall we go?" She locked arms with both women as they walked to Abigail's shop.

"Remember that first day?" Grace asked.

"You were such an innocent," Lily teased.

"That changed," Grace replied. "Changed for all of us."

They walked on, tightening their hold on one another as the memories washed over them.

When they reached the shop, Lily was surprised to see Cody waiting there. "Cody," she said, shaking her finger at him in mock anger, "I told you we would be done at nine."

Cody ducked his head. "I know, but there's somebody here who'd like to be part of your evening—if you agree." He turned and motioned to someone Lily hadn't seen behind him, standing in the shadows.

"Hello, Lily."

Lily's mother stepped up beside Cody. She looked older and smaller. She fidgeted with her hands as if not knowing what to do or say beyond that greeting.

"Hello, Mother," Lily whispered as she felt Emma and Grace loosen their hold on her without entirely letting go. "You came," she added.

"May I stay?"

Lily felt tears fill her eyes. It was as if time stood still. In that moment, she saw a helpless woman standing before her and realized she'd seen that face before. This was the same nervous woman who had turned away from her that day in the church.

She stepped forward and opened her arms. "Of course," she managed, and her mother practically collapsed in her embrace. Both of them were crying.

"Well," Cody said, his voice shaky, "how 'bout I leave you ladies to it? I'll be back at nine, Lily, like we planned."

Emma and Grace moved closer as Cody left. They introduced themselves and then Abigail as she opened the door, no doubt drawn outside by the commotion.

"And this is my friend Abigail, Momma," Lily said. "Wait until you see the dress she's made for my wedding." She wrapped her arm around her mother's shoulders and led her inside.

"Wait," her mother said, turning back. She picked up a small valise. "I brought something I thought maybe…" She opened the bag and took out a bundle of netting trimmed in ivory lace. "It's the veil I wore when I married your father," she said, handing it to Lily. "I thought perhaps…"

"Oh, Momma, yes. Thank you." She shook out the folds and draped the veil over her head.

"It's perfect," Abigail said. "Just perfect."

"Where's my gown?" Lily danced around the shop, wearing the veil. "I want to see it all together."

"Step this way," Abigail invited as she held open the curtain that separated the shop from her workroom. "Ladies, please feel free to try on the hats while Lily changes. They're all for sale," she added with a wink.

# Chapter 19

LATER THAT EVENING, AFTER THEY'D SEEN LILY'S mother back to the hotel, Lily and Cody sat on their favorite rock, staring at the outline of the mountains against a star-studded sky. Cody inhaled the sweet scent of her and thought himself a lucky man.

"Never would have thought you and me…"

She linked her fingers with his. "Neither did I."

"Jake did," he said softly. "He told me he hoped we would be together one day."

"I miss him," she whispered.

They sat in silence for a long moment, and then Cody got to his feet and held out his hands to her. "Come on," he said.

"But there's no curfew," she protested.

"Not worried about that. Just come with me."

He led her over the rough terrain down to the town cemetery that sat just below the hillside. He opened the low wrought iron gate and, placing his arm around her, walked on to Jake's grave. They stood there a moment, and then Cody cleared his throat.

"Well, Jake, you were right, so we've come to

thank you. I promise you I will love this woman until my dying day. I'll love her with all the devotion and care we both know you gave her in life."

Lily knelt to rearrange the bouquet of fresh greenery she knew George and the kitchen staff replaced several times a week. She stayed there, her fingers tracing the carved words on the wooden cross that marked his grave. "I did love you, in my way. You taught me how to trust again when you gave me your friendship and support without any strings attached. I will never forget you, Jake." She kissed her fingers and touched them to his name. "Rest in peace," she whispered.

Cody backhanded a tear coursing down his cheek and knelt next to her. He bowed his head as she did hers. After a moment, he said, "Lily? How 'bout we name our first son after him?"

"Yes," she whispered. "Jake would love that."

The day of the wedding dawned clear and hot. The ceremony was scheduled for late morning, followed by a reception in the hotel dining room.

Cody was nervous.

"What can go wrong?" his father asked. "Looks to me like Lily's got this thing well in hand."

His parents had arrived early the morning of the wedding, and Cody had pressed his father into service as best man. And now they stood in a small anteroom next to the church sanctuary, waiting for the start of the ceremony.

"I just want everything to be perfect for her," he

said as he ran a finger under the buttoned collar of his shirt.

"Nothing about life is perfect, Son. You know that better than most with all you've seen as sheriff. Speaking of which, have they found your replacement?"

Cody nodded. "Ty Drake's deputy is taking the job."

"And you and Lily are headed for Washington." Joe Daniels shook his head in wonder. "My boy, sitting in the Capitol Building with a bunch of bigwigs."

Cody grinned. "Pretty sure I might raise a few hackles once I get started pushing for them to reconsider statehood."

"Just remember not everyone is in favor of that, Son, even here in the territory. Take care."

A knock at the door interrupted their conversation. Cody's mother, Ginny, smiled broadly as she stepped into the room. "Don't you look a picture," she said as she smoothed the lapel of his suit jacket and pinned a sprig of spruce to it.

"Is Lily nervous?" he asked.

"Not as nervous as you," his mother replied. "She's a lovely young woman, Cody."

His father chuckled. "You'll have your hands full with that one," he added. "My guess is she'll set Washington on its ear."

Cody grinned. "That's the plan," he said just as the church organist started playing.

"That's our signal," his father said and led the way out to the sanctuary.

Cody took his place and turned to face the long aisle. Lily would be walking down it any minute, with Aidan Campbell escorting her.

"You got the ring?" he asked his father for the third time as George Keller led both Lily's mother and Cody's to their places.

"Asked and answered," his father said and nudged him as the organist struck up the prelude to the wedding march. Everyone in the packed church stood.

Grace and Emma led the procession, wearing their Harvey Girl uniforms. Cody gave each of them a nervous smile as they took their places opposite him. Then he heard an excited murmuring and looked to the back of the church where Lily stood with Aidan.

She wore a dress in a deep purple that reminded him of the night sky just after sunset. Her hair was done up in a loose pile, curls framing her face, and the way the morning light streamed through the church windows, he could have sworn there was a halo around her head. She caught his gaze through the sheer veil that covered her features and held it as she made her way to the altar.

Aidan stepped aside to stand with Cody's father, and as the music ended and the congregation sat, there was a moment when Cody could swear only he and Lily occupied the church.

Even as the minister intoned the words of the ceremony, Cody heard and saw nothing but Lily. He assumed he had played his part properly, for all too soon the minister was calling for the ring.

"Lift the veil and then take the ring," the minister whispered.

His hands were shaking as he followed the instructions, the gold band with their initials and the date engraved on the inside warm in his hand. *Don't drop the ring.*

His mouth was dry as he repeated the words dictated by the minister. "With this ring…"

But Lily's smile and those big green eyes sparkling with love and pure joy gave him the strength he needed. He slid the simple gold band onto her finger. Lily was his wife now. Together, they would build a life of laughter and love, meeting any challenge that came their way.

"I now pronounce you man and wife," the minister proclaimed. The music swelled as Cody and Lily looked at each other.

Both their mothers had been very clear about the proper style of wedding kiss—they might share a light peck on the closed lips, but certainly no more. Then they would walk to the exit without interacting, either by touch or eye contact, with any of those attending. Lily had rolled her eyes at this.

"Well, Mr. Daniels, are you going to kiss me or not?" she said softly.

He grinned, "With pleasure, Mrs. Daniels." He cupped her face with his hands and kissed each closed eyelid. "I love you, Lily."

She wrapped her arms around his neck and kissed him on the mouth. Behind him, Cody heard the congregation gasp. Then with a grin, Lily grabbed his hand and started up the aisle, stopping to hug her mother and then his parents, and then, entirely against all instructions for proper etiquette she'd been given, greeted guests along the way.

That was Lily, Cody thought. *His* Lily.

As she and Cody walked up the aisle, Lily felt as if she were lighter than air. Music and sunlight filled the church. All around her, people were happy. And Cody held her hand like he would never let go. Once they stepped outside, they saw Nick waiting with a buggy to take them to the hotel. They could have walked, but riding all the way around the plaza only added to the romance of this day. Nick took his time with the circuit, giving their guests time to reach the hotel on foot. She could not seem to stop smiling, and it delighted her to see that Cody appeared to be in the same state of euphoria she was.

At the hotel, the Harvey Girls were lined up in two facing columns outside the closed entrance to the dining room. Grace and Emma stepped to the double doors and swung them open to reveal the wedding guests gathered inside. Aidan stood just inside the entrance and tapped a fork against a crystal glass to gain everyone's attention.

"Ladies and gentlemen, it is my great pleasure to welcome Mr. and Mrs. Cody Daniels."

A cheer went up along with applause as Lily and Cody crossed the large room to their place at the head table. Cody's parents and Lily's mother were already seated there and appeared to be getting along famously. Grace, Nick, Emma, and Aidan took their places as well. Harvey Girls sent for the occasion from the La Casita Hotel in Santa Fe circulated among the tables, filling champagne flutes with their usual efficiency. George and his staff emerged from the kitchen carrying large trays filled with individual servings of huevos rancheros that the girls quickly delivered to the tables.

In addition to the entrée, each table had baskets filled with muffins and bowls of cut fruit. Once everyone was served, the waitresses patrolled the room, filling coffee and tea cups and responding to any request.

Lily saw it all as if her wedding veil still covered her face. Nothing seemed real. How could it be that she was here with Cody—and her mother? She took hold of her mother's hand and squeezed. "I am so glad you came," she said softly.

"With food like this, I may just decide to stay," her mother replied with a laugh that quickly sobered. She touched Lily's cheek. "I am so proud of the woman you have become, Lily. In spite of my—"

Lily interrupted her. "That's all in the past, Momma. From this moment on, we only move forward." She lifted her champagne glass in a toast, and her mother returned the gesture.

Cody leaned closer, drawing her attention back to him. "The train will be here soon," he reminded her.

"Emma and Grace have everything under control," she assured him, and on cue, her two friends stepped forward to place two cakes on the table in front of them—a bride's cake for Lily and a groom's for Cody. The bride's cake was bedecked with ribbons and tiny metal tokens.

"Come," she called as she stood and pulled Cody up beside her. She distributed ribbon ends to Cody's father, Aidan, Emma, and Grace. "Okay. Now pull," she instructed. Everyone was laughing, and others had gathered round to watch the fun, while Lily only looked up at Cody. She was sure she would never get used to the idea that this gorgeous man was her husband. She saw a future filled with adventure and children and so much love—the kind of love she had known before her father died.

Cody caught her watching him and smiled, revealing the dimples that had drawn her to him from the start. They each cut a slice from their cakes and fed it to the other. Cody wiped a bit of frosting from her lips with his thumb, and the desire she saw burning in his gaze made her legs weak.

"We need to go, Lily," he said, and Lily heard the distant whistle of the train moving closer. Cody turned to kiss his mother and shake hands with his father, then kissed Lily's mother on the cheek. "Thank you," Lily heard him whisper. "Thank you for trusting me with your beautiful daughter."

Her mother patted his hand, tears brimming. "Be good to her," she said.

Cody nodded, then took hold of Lily's hand. "Thanks, folks," he shouted. "It's been a special day, but Lily and I have a train to catch."

As they made their way through the room, Lily saw Emma and Grace handing out small bags of rice to the guests. She kind of regretted not having had the chance to fully enjoy the cake, but when she looked up at her husband, all thoughts of food disappeared. She stopped in the lobby to remove her veil and put on the hat Abigail handed her, while Cody picked up the luggage they had packed the night before and stashed behind the front desk.

"Goodbye," Lily called as she hurried outside.

Nick took the suitcases from Cody and led them down the path to the station. The wedding guests trailed behind them, tossing handfuls of rice in their direction and shouting their good wishes. Cody hopped aboard ahead of her and then held out his hand. Lily lifted her skirt and saw him notice the boots. He rolled his eyes, and she grinned at him as he pulled her up onto the platform at the back of the train. They held tight to each other and waved to Juniper as the train slowly pulled away.

The shouts and cheers faded, and they were left standing alone, the wind in their hair and the rhythmic sound of the train's progress the only music. She smiled up at him, loving the way he was looking at her. As if he too could not quite believe they were standing there. Involuntarily, she shivered.

"You're cold," he said and, without waiting for an answer, ushered her inside the first-class car.

They smiled at the few other passengers who greeted them with nods and murmurs of congratulations as they made their way to their private compartment. Once inside, Cody tossed his hat aside and wrapped his arms around her waist. "Happy?"

"Delirious," she replied and kissed his jaw.

"Afraid I'll need more than a peck on the jaw," he said.

Lily felt as if she could happily drown in the kiss they shared and hoped it might go on for much longer, but a light knock at the door had them pulling apart too soon. Cody opened the door, and Lily broke into a smile.

"Ollie!"

The conductor she had met on the train to Juniper just a year earlier grinned at her. "Got some wedding cake out here," he said as he pointed to a metal cart set with two glasses and a bottle of champagne in an ice bucket. Cody stood aside to allow Ollie to roll the cart into the compartment.

"Ollie, this is my husband, Cody Daniels."

"Pleased to know you, Mr. Daniels. And *Mrs.* Daniels."

"Ollie was on the train that brought Grace, Emma, and me to Juniper the first time," Lily explained, and Cody broke into a broad grin.

"Well, let me shake your hand, sir," he said.

Ollie accepted the handshake with a shy smile. "Compliments of Mr. and Mrs. Hopkins," he said as he popped the cork and filled the glasses, then he backed out the door. "You folks enjoy now, and when you're done, just set the cart in the corridor. I'll see to it nobody disturbs you again." On his way out, he lowered the privacy shade on the door to the compartment, and Lily was pretty sure he winked at Cody as he left.

"If people keep serving us champagne, I'm going to need a nap," Lily said. She sat on the upholstered seat and raised her glass to Cody.

"To us," he said, touching his glass to hers. They each took a sip, and then Cody set the glasses back on the cart and wheeled it out.

Lily stretched, removed her hat and gloves, and pulled off her boots. Cody closed and locked the door before collapsing onto the seat with her. She tucked her legs underneath her and curled into his arms. Without the necessity of words, they watched the world fly by out the window.

After a few moments, he kissed her temple and said, "Do you know what I wish?"

"What?"

"My wish for us is that every day we share will be better than the one before."

She twisted around to face him. "That's a tall order."

He tweaked her nose. "I think we can do it. We're just going to have to work really hard."

Lily had almost dozed off when Cody stood and removed his jacket. He remained standing as he considered the furnishings of the small cabin. "There's got to be a way to make this thing into a bed," he mused.

"Cody! It's not even noon."

He shrugged as he fiddled with the seat opposite them. All of a sudden, it slid forward, and the back flattened. "Looks like a bed to me, Mrs. Daniels." He opened an overhead storage bin and produced two pillows and a blanket, his grin infectious. "I don't know about you, but I could use a nap."

How could she resist this man?

She shrugged out of her jacket and took off her skirt and petticoat, then faked a yawn. "Sounds like a good idea," she replied as she curled onto the bed and tugged the blanket over herself. She closed her eyes, pretending sleep, but frowned and peeked when she heard him still moving about.

"Cody," she gasped when he lay down next to her, turned onto his side, and raised up on his elbow so he could see her. The man was stark naked.

"You gonna share that blanket, Mrs. Daniels?"

"No," she teased, clutching it tighter.

"Guess I'll just have to lay claim then," he said, and she noticed his voice was raspy and the teasing glint in his eyes had been replaced with something far more intense. He pulled the blanket away and tossed it aside. "You're overdressed, lady."

He kissed her and tunneled his hand under the waist of her pantaloons. She couldn't decide what felt better—the rhythmic stroking of his tongue inside her mouth or the massage his fingers gave her inner thighs, edging ever closer to her most private areas. She had her answer when he found her core and filled it with his fingers. Her hunger for him was insatiable. She moaned when he abandoned her mouth and used his teeth to pull free the ribbon ties of her camisole.

She tugged at his shoulders, clawed at his back, sending whatever signal she could to demand more from him—much more. She could feel the fullness of his erection pressing against her and recalled the night they had started to make love and he had pulled away.

*Not this time.*

She twisted away, struggling to push her pantaloons down her hips. "Help me," she pleaded, nearly beside herself with the desire to have him inside her again.

He half sat up and undressed her with a tenderness that was breathtaking. As he removed her camisole, he kissed her breasts and then moved lower, kissing her stomach as he pushed her undergarment down and off. Finally free of the bonds of clothing, she urged him up so she could see his face, wanting to know if he shared what she felt.

He gazed down at her. "This time, there's no going back," he whispered as he slid into her, filling her.

There was a heartbeat when he stayed very still, watching her, his gaze seeking her permission to complete their union. Instinctively, she wrapped her legs around his hips, urging him deeper. He sucked in a breath and then began the lesson only he was allowed to give her—the lesson of making love.

Afterward, they lay curled together under the blanket as their breathing slowed, listening to the clack of the wheels against the tracks. Cody knew he would never have enough of this incredible woman.

"Hungry?" he murmured, realizing neither of them had ever gotten around to consuming the wedding breakfast.

She giggled and lightly bit his earlobe. "What are you suggesting, Mr. Daniels?"

"Well now, there's hunger that can be satisfied with a good solid meal, and then there's hunger that requires something entirely different."

She shifted so that she was atop him, her long, white-gold hair a curtain that surrounded them. "I'll take that one," she whispered as she ran her palms over the ridges of his chest and bent to kiss his stomach.

"So soon?"

"I want to make sure," she replied, her voice muffled as she moved lower, her mouth within a fraction of finding trouble.

"Sure of what?" He pulled her back to face him.

"Sure that we've done a good job of getting started on our firstborn. We've wasted a lot of time, Cody, with me being too stubborn all those months to see what was right in front of me and you having all these rules and constantly chasing after bad guys. I mean, you do want children, don't you?"

"Yes, ma'am," he replied with a grin. He lifted her so that she remained sitting on top of him as he entered her. Her eyes widened in surprise, and then she smiled.

One thing was certain, Lily would only play by the rules that made sense to her and question everything else. He'd known from the day he met her that she was a renegade—now she was *his* renegade.

# Author's Note

The hotels named in this story are fictional, but there are still hotels around that were once part of the Harvey Company. One well worth visiting is La Fonda in Santa Fe, where you can take a step back in time and imagine meals served by smiling young women dressed in black with white pinafore aprons "setting your cup" and serving you a delicious meal.

While Fred Harvey and his sons eventually became famous for hotels and restaurants and even guided tours that helped the West become a major destination for travelers, it was his eating houses along the Santa Fe railway that started it all. Throughout the story, I have mentioned dishes made famous by the Harvey Company. Thanks to George H. Foster and Peter C. Weighlin, many of those recipes have been preserved in *The Harvey House Cookbook* (Atlanta: Longstreet Press, 1992).

With the publisher's permission, here are two of those delicious recipes:

# Huevos Rancheros

- 1 cup pinto beans
- 1 tablespoon red chili powder
- ¼ cup cold water
- 4 tablespoons minced onion
- 2 tablespoons butter
- 2 eggs
- ½ to 1 teaspoon finely minced green chili pepper
- 1 teaspoon butter

Wash beans, cover with cold water, and let soak overnight.

In the morning, heat to boiling, then reduce heat and let simmer, covered, until beans are tender, three to four hours. Cool.

Add red chili powder to the cold water and let soak one hour. Sauté onion and finely minced green chili pepper in 2 tablespoons butter very slowly until tender but not browned. Add beans, which have been broken up coarsely with a fork, and heat through. Add ¼ to ½ cup hot water if beans are too dry.

Transfer beans to a well-buttered ramekin or individual casserole dish. Make two depressions in top of beans using back of tablespoon and drop an egg in each depression. Pour two

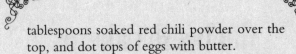

tablespoons soaked red chili powder over the top, and dot tops of eggs with butter.

Bake in a moderate oven (350 degrees) for 20 to 25 minutes or until eggs are set. Serves one.

# Cheese Cake

- 2 cups fine graham cracker crumbs (25 crackers)
- 1½ cups sugar
- ½ cup melted butter
- 4 eggs
- 2 tablespoons all-purpose flour
- 2 tablespoons cornstarch
- 1 teaspoon salt
- 2 teaspoons grated lemon peel
- 1½ teaspoons lemon juice
- 1 teaspoon vanilla
- 1 cup heavy cream
- 1½ pounds dry, small curd cottage cheese

Mix crumbs with ½ cup sugar and the melted butter; reserve ¾ cup of crumb mixture for topping. Press remaining crumb mixture into a 9-inch springform pan, lining bottom and sides, building up sides to 1¾ inch height.

Beat eggs with remaining sugar until light; add flour, cornstarch, salt, lemon peel, lemon juice, vanilla, cream, and cheese. Beat thoroughly.

Pour into crumb-lined pan; sprinkle with remaining crumbs. Bake in moderate oven (350 degrees) for one hour. Cool, then remove from pan.

# Read on for an excerpt from
*Last Chance Cowboys: The Drifter,*
also by Anna Schmidt

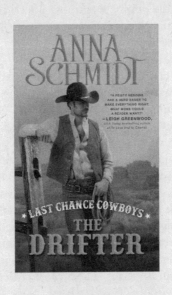

# Chapter 1

*Arizona Territory, June 1882*

CHET HUNTER TUGGED ON HIS HORSE'S REINS AS HE paused on a flat mesa and studied the terrain below. His dog, Cracker, glanced up at him. Their journey had already taken them hundreds of miles from Florida, traveling across territory that was a far cry from the tropics they'd left behind. He eased a speck of the never-ending dust from his eye with the knuckles of one hand and surveyed his surroundings.

Below was a river, a cluster of trees—most likely cottonwoods—some scrubby mesquite, and miles of open grassland as far as he could see. The river was low, but that was the only clear evidence of the drought that had followed him from West Texas and into the semi-arid landscape of New Mexico and Arizona. For days, he'd picked his way through open range that had been overgrazed until the grass he'd been told could grow as high as seven feet was little more than stubble. He'd crossed dried-up creek beds and rivers with waters that barely reached his boot tips.

The scene below looked about as close to paradise as he ever thought he'd see in this part of the country.

Maybe it was one of those mirages he'd heard about. From what he'd always figured, Arizona Territory was desert and rock with cactus plants tall as any man providing the only hints of green…and the only relief from the unrelenting sun that scorched the land from morning to evening. But here the white light of the noonday sun made the land stretch out flat, and the mountains in the distance jutted up from a purplish-blue haze. Beyond the river, he saw what looked like hundreds—no, more like thousands of cattle grazing. The herd stretched out for miles, and that could mean the work he needed to shore up his savings and eventually get him to California—not to mention the chance of a decent meal.

And if he couldn't find a likely ranch before sundown, the area below the mesa looked like it might be as good a place as any to set up camp. For one thing, he could bathe in the river that had more flow than any he'd seen in a while. It would feel mighty good to wash off the layers of dust and sweaty grime that clung to his clothes and skin. Cracker could take a bath as well and cool off some. But as he zigzagged his way along the terraces that led down to the valley and to what, from above, had seemed to be open land in all directions, he realized that the way to the river was blocked. Barbed-wire fencing stretched on as far as the eye could see with signs warning that the land was property of the Tipton Brothers Cattle and Land Company and there was to be No Trespassing.

"Come along, Cracker," he murmured, although

the instruction was not necessary. The brown-and-white collie, her fur matted with dirt and debris, had an instinct for knowing what Chet might need, especially now that the two of them had traveled halfway across the country with pretty much just each other for company. In a lot of ways, Chet felt as if he and the dog had melded into a single being. Cracker picked her way over the rutted path that ran parallel to the fence—a fence that appeared to stretch on all the way to the horizon.

Nope. No free range here.

He rode along the fence, studying the land on the other side. Now that he was level with the grass, he saw that it too was stunted and parched, but that was to be expected, given the heat and obvious lack of rain. At least here there was grass—not like the barren landscape he'd left behind in Texas. On the Tipton side of the barbed-wire barrier, he spotted some skeleton remains of steers left to rot, their bones bleached by the sun. Cracker saw them too and pressed her nose between the strands of wire, then let out a yelp.

"This way, Crack," Chet said as he turned his horse away from the fencing. By contrast, the land where he was riding showed signs of new growth in spite of the drought. Of course, he also had not seen any cattle on this side of the fence. But he figured that if the fence marked a boundary for the Tipton Brothers Company, then outside the fence must be land owned by some independent rancher or farmer—land that Tipton's owners had not yet swallowed up. Chet crossed a running creek and climbed back up to higher ground. As he followed the mesa, he spotted another herd—much smaller than the first—in the distance, grazing on open land. There had to be a ranch somewhere around—maybe two or three smaller places. Plenty enough work to be had for a drifter who knew his way around a herd.

∽

Maria Porterfield had had almost no sleep and the last thing she needed was a confrontation with the ranch foreman. But like it or not, Roger Turnbull was striding toward her, and every muscle in his body told her he was not happy.

"Cyrus Cardwell said you went to the bank asking for a loan, Maria."

She took another sip of her coffee and gazed out at the horizon that marked the boundaries of the Clear Springs Ranch. "And just why would Mr. Cardwell be discussing my family's personal business with you, Roger?" Behind him, she saw a trio of hired hands who worked for her family pretending not to listen. She acknowledged them with a wave, which made Roger wheel around to face them.

"Go check on the horses," he ordered. "I'll be along directly."

When the men pushed themselves from the corral fence and sauntered away, Roger turned back to Maria. "I am trying to do my job."

"I fail to understand how the financial affairs of this ranch are part of your job."

"Maybe that was true before your father died and your brother took off, instead of staying and running this place like a man should. But things are different now. What do you expect?"

"I expect you to trust that I know what I'm doing."

Roger removed his hat and looked down at her with a glint in his eyes that told her he was about to try to sweet-talk her into seeing things his way. If she lived to be a hundred, she would never understand why men thought women couldn't see straight through such tactics.

"Now, Maria, everybody here knows that you are as good as any man when it comes to certain things, but—"

"My father taught me and my brother everything we needed to know to take over the running of this ranch, Roger. Jess isn't here, so it falls to me."

"But I am here, and with all you've got to worry about, taking care of your mama and sister and young Trey, letting me run the business end of things is exactly what your pa—"

She took a step closer to him, her chin jutted out in anger. "Do not presume to think you know what my father would want, Roger. You've made it clear you know nothing about him. He would *not* want to sell out to the Tiptons—as you have repeatedly urged me to do since the day he died."

Roger's eyes narrowed. "Well, if you keep borrowing money you can't repay, you won't have to sell, Maria. You'll lose this place for sure and not have a dime to show for it."

The fact that he had a point just infuriated her more. A big part of what kept her awake at night was worrying that she might make a mistake. Asking for a loan from the bank was just one example. "We need that money to see us through until we take the herd to market," she said.

"Face facts, Maria. The men haven't been paid in a couple of weeks, and I haven't taken anything for the last month."

"They have food and a roof over their heads, and are free to move on and seek work elsewhere—as are you," she blustered. "I understand the Tipton brothers are hiring."

The minute the words left her mouth, she knew she had gone too far. Roger Turnbull was a good man—a man her father had trusted. On top of that, she was well aware that he had feelings for her. She might not return those feelings, but she had certainly relied on Roger a good deal since her father's death. Perhaps too much. "Roger, I didn't mean—"

He slowly put on his hat and stepped away. "Guess if that's the way you feel, then I'm wasting my time staying. I'll be out of your hair in an hour." He turned and walked away.

"Roger, no." Panic filled her chest as she watched him just keep on walking. But she knew from experience that trying to argue further would do no good when his pride was stung. Maria turned away, frustrated. Now she was really in trouble. She was short of money and short of help. Maybe asking for the bank loan hadn't been a mistake, but losing Roger—and any of the hands who might defect with him—surely was.

She took a deep breath and let her eyes roam over the land—her family's land that stretched as far as she could see and beyond. She needed to get away from her own crushing worries for a time; she needed to ride.

She slapped her father's battered hat over her long braid and whistled for his favorite horse, Macho. Once the animal was saddled, she mounted and rode slowly out of the yard. But when she reached open land, she urged Macho to a full gallop, relishing the hot, dry air that stroked her face and the wild freedom of knowing that she could ride like this for an hour or more and still be on Porterfield land.

Roger, his cronies, even her own brother might desert her and her family, but with or without them, she would find a way.

❧

The sun was low on the horizon and streaking the sky with purples and oranges by the time Chet spotted a small house, a few rough but well-maintained outbuildings, and a thin stream of smoke from a cooking fire rising up toward the sky. The house—built in the Spanish style—was a low, rambling single-story structure with a tiled roof, adobe walls, and trees shading the courtyard that marked the entrance. In addition to the cluster of outbuildings, he noticed some fenced pastures. But this was fencing that was intended to divide the land into areas for dedicated use. It was fencing intended to keep animals in, not people out. He saw several dozen beef cattle grazing in the largest area and a smaller group of dairy cows in another. Beyond the house, he could see trees and a stream that was probably an offshoot of the river he'd seen on the Tipton property.

He watched as a couple of men rode slowly up the dirt road and on past the house, where they

dismounted and unsaddled their horses before turning them loose in the corral. If he had to guess,
these men were coming off the trail, where they'd
probably spent twelve to fifteen hours circling the
herd along with hands from other small ranches.
Others would take the night shift. Suddenly, a third
horse and rider galloped into the yard, stopping near
the house. The rider slid down from the saddle and
tossed the reins to a kid, then walked determinedly
across the courtyard, headed for the house. He
figured the rider was a woman by the way she
moved and her size, although she was dressed like a
man—trousers tucked into boots, a vest worn over a
long-sleeved shirt, and a hat. She disappeared inside
the house. Chet waited to see what might happen
next, and a few minutes later, he heard the clang of
a bell and several men emerged from a bunkhouse
and ambled across the yard.

"Chow time," he said, and Cracker started down
the almost nonexistent trail. Chet gave a whistle and
the dog returned. "Not for us," Chet corrected. "Not
yet." He leaned one elbow on the horn of his saddle
and kept watching the activity below. He was dead
tired and the thought of a home-cooked meal and
maybe a chance to wash up had him staring so hard
that his vision blurred, and once again he wondered if
maybe the whole business was nothing more than some
mirage. But he had heard the clang of the dinner bell,
he saw the men making their way over to the courtyard, and he could practically *smell* the stew a short,
squat woman was serving up. He was down to his last
tin of beans—which he had saved for times when there

were no jackrabbits or friendly prospectors. He needed a bath, a decent meal, and work—work that paid.

He'd left Florida in a hurry, but he'd been pretty sure that he could make it to Texas in time to hire on as an extra hand for the calving and branding season. Only, by the time he reached West Texas, he'd had to face facts. No one was hiring. The grasslands there were barren and the cattle that hadn't been moved farther west were scrawny and underfed. So he had pushed on. Somebody had told him about a big cattle company in Arizona that might be hiring—clearly the Tipton Brothers—so he'd kept on riding. Tomorrow he would see if he could find their offices. Based on the fencing and No Trespassing signs, he doubted the men who owned Tipton Brothers would be the sympathetic sort. But work was work, and given a chance, Chet could outwork the best cowhand anywhere.

Cracker barked, ran in a circle around Chet and his horse, and barked again. "Okay, Crack, let's go see if those folks will give us supper and maybe let us camp out in their barn for the night. If nothing else, they'll be able to give us directions." Chet straightened in the saddle and clicked his tongue to urge the horse forward.

ᴄᴑ

"Rider coming, Miss Maria."

Maria stepped into the courtyard and followed ten-year-old Javier's pointing finger to the eastern horizon, where a lone rider sat motionless at the top of a rise before he slowly started down the trail, a mangy-looking dog leading the way. After the day she'd had, the last thing she needed was more trouble. But the man was taking his time, which could be a good thing. If he'd been riding hard, she would have steeled herself for yet another bit of bad news—and frankly, she had had about all the bad news she could take. She shaded her eyes even though her back was to the setting sun. The dog was probably a good sign. A man up to no good was unlikely to travel with a dog.

Just another cowboy, she decided. Probably from Texas, no doubt looking for work or a handout—maybe both. "Fix him a plate, Juanita, and send Javíer to give him the food, give the dog a bone, and take his horse to the corral while he eats."

"You can't be feeding them all, Maria," the housekeeper who had worked for their family from the day Maria's parents arrived in the territory huffed. "Word will get out and you'll—"

"You know that Papa would never turn any of them away—not as long as he had something to share." This man was hardly the first to come to the Clear Springs Ranch, and he would not be the last. Times were hard, especially for those men who had worked the herds in Texas.

"Well, your papa is not here, *mi hija*, and—you'll not like me saying it—with that no-good brother of yours taking off for the city just when he's most needed and leaving you to try to run this place on your own…"

Maria kept her eyes on the rider, all the while trying to figure out why this one seemed different. She heard Juanita's tirade, agreed with some of it, and dismissed the rest. Certainly her brother, Jess, had stunned them all when he'd left for a life in the city after their father's death just six months earlier, but so far they had managed. "I'm hardly alone, Juanita."

"Oh, forgive me. I forgot that you have your mother, who has not been right in the head since your papa died. And then there's Master Trey, who always has his nose stuck in some book and doesn't know the first thing about running a ranch. And let's not forget Miss Amanda, who from the day she turned sixteen can't seem to pass a looking glass without stopping to stare at herself for…"

Maria smiled at the housekeeper, who was like a second mother to them all. "Yes, and besides Mama and my sister and at least one brother, there's you and Eduardo and—"

Juanita threw up her hands in a gesture of surrender. "Then we are going to need more stew if you insist on feedin' every stray that comes by. Rico," she shouted to her elder son who was leaning on the corral talking to two cowhands just back from riding the herd. "Make yourself useful for once and help me in the kitchen."

Maria turned her attention back to the rider, who was close enough now for her to see his features. He was tall in spite of the fact that his shoulders slumped with weariness. He—and the horse and dog—was covered in dust. His clothing was stained with sweat. He wore a soft-crowned, wide-brimmed hat different from the stiffer Stetsons preferred by Roger and the other hands. His hair skimmed the collar of his shirt—or what would have been the collar had the shirt had one. He wore dark trousers, chaps, and boots without spurs. His horse was a mare, larger than the quarter horses most ranch hands rode. The way the dog pranced around them made Maria smile. It was as if the dog refused to be defeated no matter how hungry or tired it might be. But as the rider came closer, the thing that caught her attention above anything else was that this cowboy did not have the traditional rope and lariat so common to men who worked cattle. This cowboy had a whip—coiled like a large snake—around the horn of his saddle.

Horse and rider ambled up to the filigreed iron fence leading into the courtyard. The man kept his eyes, which were shaded by the brim of his hat, on her. He did not appear to be in a hurry—or maybe the approach was calculated to keep her from running away. Did he think she was some skittish colt in need of taming? That was certainly how Roger and probably at least half the hands still working the ranch saw her. And it was certainly the way the other ranchers at the association meeting had treated her.

"Evening, ma'am." He removed his hat and ran his fingers through his hair to push it back from his face. His hair was thick and straight and black as her father's favorite quarter horse. His face was mostly covered by stubble, and his exposed forearms were brown like leather, the same as most men who worked outdoors for long hours…but there was a difference. There was a golden cast to his tanned complexion that made her think of sunshine. He was definitely not from this part of the country, and for the first time since Juanita's son had spotted him, Maria had doubts. Perhaps he had friends waiting. Gangs were not uncommon in the territory. And if word had spread that Roger had left... There hadn't been trouble in a while, but these were desperate times.

"Evenin'," she replied as she met his gaze and offered the knuckles of one hand for the dog to sniff. She was glad to see Juanita's husband, Eduardo, coming across the yard, and she knew Juanita was probably positioned just inside the kitchen door, her hand fairly twitching to grab the Parker twin-barrel shotgun they kept nearby. "Can I help you?"

"Well, yes, ma'am. I'm hoping you and the mister can spare a bite to eat for me and my horse and ol' Cracker there." He nodded toward the dog. "I could also use directions to the Tipton Brothers Cattle and Land Company."

All Maria's senses went on instant alert. Was this a trick? Was Roger testing her? Had he sent this man?

"You work for Tipton Brothers, amigo?" Eduardo scowled up at the stranger.

"Not yet. I'm just looking for work and heard they might be hiring." He gave Eduardo his full attention, apparently trying to decide if Juanita's husband was the owner of the ranch. "Truth is, I'd just as soon work on a spread like this one."

He spoke softly with a definite drawing out of his words—from the South if she had to guess. Could be another Texan, but his accent was different from the Texas men she'd met. This man's voice lacked the roughness. There was a gentleness to him—and yet by the look of him, he could handle himself in a fight. "We aren't hiring at the moment," she said.

"Eduardo can show you where to rest your horse, and Javier will bring you out some supper and something for your dog."

"I'm most grateful, ma'am. Thank you." He replaced his hat as he turned his horse to follow Eduardo.

"Where are you from?" Maria asked, unable to contain her curiosity a minute longer.

"Florida, ma'am."

Eduardo let out a long, low whistle. "You are a long way from home, amigo."

Maria stood rooted to the spot as the two men started across the yard. Florida? Did the man know the first thing about herding and branding and such—even if she were of a mind to hire him? And what the devil was he doing so far from home?

As she headed into the kitchen, Juanita released the shotgun's dual hammers and put the weapon back in the corner before going to the stove to dish up a bowl of stew. "I suppose you want me to give him some biscuits and a slice of that apple pie as well?"

"That would be nice."

"Do you plan on letting him stay? You're short-handed now, I know, but even so…"

Maria was aware of Ricardo, now seated at the table chopping onions and listening intently to whatever she might say so he could carry the news back to the other hands. "I don't know, Nita. Like I said before, I'm not doing anything that Papa wouldn't do by feeding him."

"You are not your father, Maria."

"Have Javier take the man his food, all right?" Maria sat down in the nearest chair and rested her elbows on her knees. What would her father do? Would he give the man work? Probably. But she knew nothing about him.

*You get a sense of people, Maria*, her father had once told her. *You need to listen to that and act accordingly.*

She closed her eyes and thought about the man... and realized there had been no introductions. He had assumed she was married—that business about "you and the mister." She had liked the way he spoke—his voice deep, a little hoarse, probably from the dust of his journey, and yet soft-spoken in a way that let her know he was feeling his way and not taking anything for granted. She had also been impressed with the way he had shown respect to Eduardo. Roger would have dismissed the older man as not worth his time. This man was nothing like Roger. She was sure of that.

"Juanita?"

Juanita paused at the kitchen door, her weathered hands still cradling the bowl of stew, on top of which she'd stacked a biscuit and a saucer with a slab of pie. She looked back, one eyebrow arched.

"Now that Roger and... There's room in the bunkhouse. Have Javier tell the man he can stay the night but needs to be on his way at first light."

Juanita shooed Javier out of the way and started walking toward the bunkhouse carrying the steaming bowl. "I'll tell him," she announced. "Somebody needs to get a good, long look at this drifter." But by the way she trudged along, shaking her head the entire time, Maria had no doubt that the housekeeper had already made up her mind.

Maria glanced at Ricardo, who was watching his

mother as well. "Well, Papa *would* have let him stay," she said defensively.

"Yes, Miss Maria." Ricardo returned to chopping onions, keeping whatever he might be thinking to himself, as usual.

# About the Author

Award-winning author Anna Schmidt resides in Wisconsin. She delights in creating stories where her characters must wrestle with the challenges of their times. Critics have consistently praised Schmidt for her ability to seamlessly integrate actual events with her fictional characters to produce strong tales of hope and love in the face of seemingly insurmountable obstacles. Visit her at booksbyanna.com.

# Also by Anna Schmidt